KING'S ROAD

King's Road

Mariella Novotny

NEW ENGLISH LIBRARY
TIMES MIRROR

to
ROBERT MUSEL

All characters in this book are imaginary and bear no relation
to any person or persons living or dead.

First published in Great Britain by Leslie Frewin Publishers Ltd. in 1971
© Mariella Novotny and Leslie Frewin 1971

*

FIRST NEL PAPERBACK EDITION JANUARY 1973
New Edition March 1974

*

NEL Books are published by
New English Library Limited from Barnard's Inn, Holborn, London, E.C.1.
Made and printed in Great Britain by Hunt Barnard Printing Ltd., Aylesbury, Bucks.

45001847 4

Chapter 1

'OKAY DOLL, WHICH is it to be, a vice charge or a drugs rap?' asked the tall young man towering above Tricesta St Regis, who had just removed her clothes and was lying on the long sofa. In his left hand Jimmy held a small block of charge, in his right, a one hundred dollar bill.

'Don't be stupid,' she said, 'you're not all that stoned.' She was not in the mood for jokes.

Her fine blonde hair framed her face. She was beautiful and flushed, the effect of cannabis and anticipation.

Jimmy dropped the money on to her stomach and pulled a thin leather case from his trouser pocket.

'A police badge,' gasped Tricesta, 'you mean you're not Zac Baker's press agent?'

'Does this look like a press card?' drawled the officer. He reached for his shirt. 'Zac Baker might be Britain's answer to Bob Dylan but in my book he's just another junkie. Get dressed kid—before I move my men in.' He leaned over her and squeezed one pink nipple: 'You didn't say which charge, Miss St Regis. Anyway, you're under arrest.'

'But what for?' She jumped to her feet. 'I haven't done anything, you offered me a joint – we both had a smoke and where does bread come into it?' She was near to tears. This had to be a mistake, a bad joke.

Tricesta was in New York for a few days to sell some period costumes to a Manhattan gear shop, an aspiring copy of the one she and her brother owned in the King's Road in London's Chelsea. This was day three of her trip and being bored she had allowed herself to be talked into going to bed with this good-looking American.

'Look honey,' said Jimmy, now completely dressed, 'I'm a hard-working cop, you were about to let me lay you, you're worth a hundred dollars for one party. Agreed?'

'No – yes, of course I am, but I don't do it for money,' she quickly switched off the Stones L.P. 'Bread doesn't come into it.'

'Sure it does,' he grinned, 'you just agreed that you were worth a hundred dollars. That constitutes soliciting, unless you prefer that narcotics charge?' He laughed and pocketed the marijuana. 'And forget about telling that I had a drag. They all say the same, believe me, I would. But no one will listen.' He looked at Tricesta's flat stomach and white shapely legs. 'Pity I couldn't try out the goods,' he sighed. 'I always heard you classy English dames were cold, now I'm not so sure. You'll be booked at the Precinct. Take it from me it'll go easier for you if you take the prostitution rap. Get your mini on before I change my mind.'

That was the end of the matter. Jimmy started to search the flat.

'Just routine, baby,' he called out.

Now that she realised this was no joke Tricesta was calm. She picked up the telephone, at least she could send for a lawyer. But the line was blocked, a man's voice identified himself as a policeman. She slammed down the receiver and pulled on her clothes, cursing herself for not checking on the cop's story when he had rung saying he was Zac Baker's P.A., but he had sounded absolutely genuine and appeared to know many of her friends.

What on earth will happen when the family read about this in the papers? she wondered. Christ, she thought, I won't sound innocent anymore!

6

But Tricesta was a rare character, somehow she would come out on top – she had to. Too much was at stake.

'Miss St Regis,' the cop had returned to the elegant drawing room, 'what is this document doing in your possession?' He sounded serious and held out several closely-typed pages of foolscap paper and a long brown envelope addressed to William X the Second with an address in Harlem. William X the Second was one of the more militant of the American Black Power leaders and had recently been refused permission to land in England. Tricesta was to have delivered the package to him on the instructions of Edward X, a progressive Black Power leader in London. She had temporarily forgotten about the document and in any case had no idea of its contents.

She had been in no position to refuse Edward X, he knew too much about her private life.

'It's not mine,' she said, 'I just agreed to deliver it for a friend.'

'I found it in your bag – that makes it yours.' He walked into the hall and opened the main door. 'Okay boys, come on in.'

Within seconds the flat was filled with police, some in plain clothes others in uniform. They stared at Tricesta.

'Good work, Jim,' said one, 'this one must have been fun.'

'She looks a bit cold to me,' his colleague mumbled as they started to comb the flat.

Tricesta's King's Road friends had given her plenty of advice on how to behave if she was ever 'busted' but blackmail by a New York Police *provocateur* was something that had been omitted from her education.

'I must go to the loo,' said Tricesta. She rushed into the bathroom, locked the door and began to brush her long hair mechanically. She knew she must avoid as much publicity as possible, she would have to stall any questions.

When she had left art school Tricesta had innocently believed the fuzz were straight. She was learning the truth fast. And it's no use saying the police in England don't use the same methods, she said to herself.

A bang on the door startled her. 'Come on out,' shouted Jimmy, 'or we'll bust the door down.'

'I haven't finished,' she called out. 'Don't worry, I'm not going to do anything silly.'

They think I'm about to swallow something or slash my

wrists, she thought and sat on the loo. It might not be convenient where she was going. Tricesta was practical at times.

The law tackled the door in earnest, she unlocked it and smiled coolly at them. But she did not feel quite the way she looked.

'Get your purse,' snapped Jimmy unpleasantly. He was now the tough, professional policeman. 'Better take a coat, this might take a long time. Right boys, finish up here, I'm taking the lady in.'

The others milled about in a scene that reminded Tricesta of a third-rate television film. Jimmy grasped her arm tightly and pushed her in front of him. In the hall there were more police, who, when they saw Tricesta were hardly able to believe their eyes.

The lift dropped to the marble entrance hall of Envoy Towers, a luxury apartment block not far from the United Nations building. Tricesta had borrowed the penthouse from a friend, a successful sculptor who had rocketed to fame after being promoted by a rich female patron of the arts. This almost legendary lover of art was seventy years old, her protégé was twenty-eight and had a strong need to be mothered.

The warm June evening surrounded them. More police were standing on the pavement and a police car was beside the kerb. A couple of colourfully-dressed heads strolled past; she wanted to tell them about the betrayal. They would understand, she knew, but they were in no position to help her. No one was. For the moment she was trapped, unable to fight back. A small crowd had gathered and watched as Jimmy pushed her into the car. He had a need to exhibit his authority. Though Tricesta was shaking inwardly she managed to look completely controlled, and this irritated Jimmy. He tried hard to provoke her to tears, angry words, anything.

On the other side of town they stopped outside a grimy building. It was unmistakably a fuzz headquarters. Inside, uniformed police bustled about their business and those who saw Jimmy bringing Tricesta in passed crude comments, but her captor took no notice and pushed her into a large room. The officer in charge was chewing gum.

'Get her prints first,' he said, staring at Tricesta's thighs which were very eye-catching in fine black tights, 'then bring her back for questioning.' It was the shortest mini-skirt the sergeant had ever seen. In a skirt like that she's got to be a whore. His eyes reflected his thoughts and his jaws worked hard on the tasteless gum.

When the finger printing was over she was hustled back to the interrogation room. News of her arrival had spread. Interest in her was surprising. But why, she wondered, why?

'Her grandfather's a Lord,' one cop enlightened the rest, 'he's worth millions.'

'She looks like a film star, she must make a packet!'

'What's your name?' her inquisitor drawled. 'How old are you?' He was impatient. 'Eighteen? No use wasting time, kid, it's always harder later on.'

Tricesta did not reply but handed him her passport. He shrugged, took it and allowed his eyes to settle on her bosom. See-through shirts were virtually a novelty in New York, especially at police headquarters.

Jimmy leaned smugly against a steel filing-cabinet, with the self-satisfaction of a talent scout who has discovered a star. The man at the desk copied the details and handed back the passport.

'Tell me about William X the Second,' he said. 'He's obviously not a childhood sweetheart! What's the connection?'

Tricesta focused her eyes above his head, she wanted a glass of water and a cigarette. But she knew, to give one sign of weakness would make him more unpleasant.

What the hell was in Edward X's paper?, she wondered.

'Come with me.' The sergeant left his desk and took her arm, Jimmy at once moved to her other side and they led her away. She walked with her head in the air and did not glance either to the left or to the right. Curious coppers lurked in the dark corridors hoping to catch a glimpse of her. Tricesta was stopped before an open door and then hustled through with unnecessary roughness.

'Sit here,' she was told.

Powerful lights were trained on her pale face. They were blinding but she realised she was surrounded by reporters, photographers and police. Where had they come from? Who had arranged all this? Once she was seated at the long, plain wood table more lights were turned on her, which made it quite impossible for her to see the men who were to torment her for the next two hours.

Tricesta was acutely aware that this was more than a routine

9

preliminary. She knew special attention was being paid to her, but why? For a straight V rap this must surely be a rare procedure. She felt it was in no way due to her background or her sensational looks. The real issue must revolve somehow around her presumed connection with Black Power.

An officer sat opposite and swung his feet on to the table, directly under her nose. She remained still and silent. There was a steady stream of questions, most of them apparently coming from the reporters. Press or police, what did it matter?

'Are you on the hard stuff?'

'How long have you been on the game?'

'How many times have you been arrested?'

'How much do you make?'

'Did you expect to do better here than in England?'

She resisted the temptation to wipe her forehead. The heat and smoke were almost unbearable. She was very thirsty.

The Press was evidently annoyed at her stubbornness, they became more insistent. But Tricesta knew she must not and would not lose her cool in front of them.

'Okay baby,' said a voice from behind the smoke, 'let's have a few pictures, real swinging London crap!'

They all laughed, the photographer pushed forward with his camera.

Tricesta covered her face with both hands and leaned on the table. Her long fringe teased her finger tips.

Hoping the photographer would get bored she remained in this position for some minutes.

It worked her way.

'Leave it for now,' called a cop, 'You'll get all the shots you want later.'

'Are all the classy broads in London like you?'

The questions kept coming.

'Where do you find your customers, baby?'

A police sergeant broke in: 'Look St Regis, we're going to keep you sitting here until you give us some answers. It will be tougher on you than on us.'

The remarks from the Press became nastier. Some tried to imitate an upper-class English voice, asking vulgar questions about the Royal Family.

She knew very little about American police procedure but this public pillorying could never have happened in Britain.

10

The police made no attempt to stop the insulting insinuations. They sniggered with the others, hoping her control would break.

'Are you on the Pill?'

'What's the record number of johns you've taken care of in one night?'

And so it went on, until her silence started to tire them. Her thirst was overwhelming.

As though judging the correct moment, a cup of tea in a paper container was placed before her.

'A nice "English cuppa",' mimicked a voice.

She steeled herself and ignored the tea. She was still sitting upright on the hard chair, every sense alert, listening to fragments of conversation about her.

Suddenly a plesant, middle-aged man pulled up a chair beside her.

'Look honey,' he said in the first controlled voice she had heard, 'we only want to help you. Tell us about William X and company and we'll see you're all right.' His soft eyes strayed to her nipples pushing against the flimsy material of her shirt.

'Make it easy for yourself,' he urged gently, 'it's not you we want.' He concluded in a whisper so that she alone could hear: 'It's those damn "progressive" Black Liberals we're after.'

Now she knew why the phoney vice charge had been set up. In London she was known to be connected, in some vague way, with the Black Power leaders. New York must have been advised and had assumed her visit was tied up with the movement in America. The papers found in her possession had obviously confirmed their assumption.

Tricesta knew better than to be tricked by a soft-spoken detective. She turned from him.

'All right, get up.' Jimmy stood before her. 'I'm taking you downstairs to be booked.'

When she stood, the entire pack moved in on her. Each one wanted to be close, she felt hands touching her.

It was then two o'clock in the morning, she was weary and afraid. Jostled by ill-smelling men on the make she was shoved along the passage. Jimmy, enjoying his moment of glory, hung on to her arm, which was fortunate in the circumstances as it prevented her from being pushed headlong down the stone stairs.

In the charge room she was formally booked by a sergeant seated at a high desk and then thrust into the midst of a group of prisoners, the Precinct's evening round-up.

There were three Negroes in tattered clothes, and a young boy with blood on his cheek; it had begun to dry and he licked at the corners of his mouth. Several old men and women stood about dejectedly. Tricesta shuddered, they were all so filthy.

Her fellow prisoners stared at her, almost disbelieving; she was young, fresh, and undamaged by life.

One of the Negroes approached her and tried to stroke her clothes; there was no offence in the action but a copper aggressively knocked his hand away. Most of the other prisoners looked like junkies or pushers. At this late hour they were showing signs of wear and their need for another fix.

Tricesta stood beside a table covered with an assortment of offensive weapons removed from the prisoners: flick knives, knuckle dusters and razors, a couple of automatics and a sawn-off plumber's hammer.

'Okay boys,' shouted the sergeant, 'you can get your shots now.'

The photographers positioned themselves for their work. Some knelt on the stone floor, aiming their lenses to get the full benefit of her mini. Others preferred the suggestive hint of breasts. There was nothing Tricesta could do to avoid them. She stood motionless.

Eventually Jimmy ushered her out and towards the steps leading up to the pavement. The camera boys followed.

'Give us a smile, baby, give us a smile.' An incredible request under the circumstances.

She ignored the flashbulbs and walked up the dirty steps. Cameras worked on her from every conceivable angle. Her blonde hair swung across her face and one photographer yelled:

'Oh baby, let me bail you out!'

There was a Black Maria in front of the door.

Christ, she thought, what an exit, the meat wagon and the leading light of the King's Road in it!

The prisoners, with Tricesta in the middle, were pushed in, some of the men were given an encouraging kick.

Once inside the hot, dark interior she was uncertain what to do. The benches running along each side looked too narrow to sit on so she remained on her feet. Some of the others, however, tried to perch on the seats. The press boys kept working until the heavy rear was slammed and locked. Jimmy did not accompany Tricesta, but a uniformed officer did. He gave her the once-over with a look of curiosity; she was not the ordinary criminal of his daily experience.

Without warning the van leapt into action. Caught off balance Tricesta fell to the floor. Her companions laughed.

'There's a knack in it, babe!' said the Negro who had tried to touch her and he helped her up. Some ten minutes later, with a screech of brakes the van jerked to a halt. They had stopped at another Precinct to collect another night's takings.

A quintet of flash-looking girls were herded into the wagon. The first one glared at Tricesta and pushed her to the end of the van. 'Beginners the other end!' she snapped.

The last load were clearly street walkers, the most obvious Tricesta had ever seen. They were caricatures of the class, garishly dressed, crudely made up and spangled in cheap jewellery. One of them wore jeans and a sweater, her hair was cropped like a man's. She edged her way through the crush to speak to Tricesta:

'This your first pinch, honey?'

Tricesta nodded vaguely. Her butch admirer lit a cigarette end. 'Great kid,' she said, 'you'll just get a suspended sentence.'

'I hope you're right,' Tricesta replied, feeling her legs were about to give way.

The prostitutes were on first-name terms with the police guard and fellow prisoners. These were people often thrown together in a way of life unknown to Tricesta.

The journey continued for some time. Tricesta still had not mastered the art of remaining on both feet; the coloured boy was kind and helped steady her. Most of her companions were in need of a bath, the smell and heat had become overpowering. Her immediate problem was to remain upright and avoid fainting. Physically she was afraid but mentally her strength as always could match the toughest.

At last the vehicle swerved up to the entrance of a city prison.

'This is where we spend the rest of the night, doll,' she was informed by the butch bird.

Tricesta's heart sank: incredibly, more photographers were waiting for her. One of the tarts posed before the photographers. She hitched her skirt up to the height of Tricesta's:

'Would you like a picture of my pussy?' she drawled in a sexy voice.

'Sure baby,' laughed a press boy, 'but you'll have to pay me to take it!'

There was general laughter, the prostitute spat at his feet and was hurried into the building.

Jimmy was waiting too. He escorted her inside. He had driven over in a squad car.

The 'receiving' hall was deserted. The sergeant in charge, who was asleep behind the high counter, roused himself. A further booking-in process followed.

When Tricesta stood before him his eyes popped wide open.

'Gee, Jim,' he said, not taking his eyes off her for a moment, 'you've sure come up with a living doll this time.'

'This one,' said Jim, 'is an English LADY,' – he emphasised the word 'Lady' – 'she won't give any trouble.'

At this point the males were separated from the females.

Tricesta was passed on to an enormous black wardress. Her eyes fastened on Tricesta's antique rings.

'They look like they took a lot of working for,' she sneered. The other girls giggled. They are trying to play up to the wardress, Tricesta thought.

'Get stripped!' the wardress ordered.

Tricesta glanced around the small bare room; she did not want to undress while the other girls watched, but she had no choice. She removed her shirt, the girls followed every move. She stepped out of her white skirt and faced the wardress.

'Off with them things,' was her only verbal comment, but she did not conceal the need she felt, to look at the perfect body that she was about to handle.

Reluctantly Tricesta pulled off the sheer black tights, and let them drop to the floor. The wardress poked into every opening in her rigid body with grubby fingers, hoping to find hidden drugs. Disappointed she told her to dress but not before the back of her hand had brushed Tricesta's nipples. Tricesta forced herself not to recoil.

'Follow me,' snapped the Negress. They walked down a cold corridor, at the end of which she unlocked a heavy door. This opened directly on to a row of dark cells.

The nick, thought Tricesta, I'm really in the nick!

She was given a powerful push into the second cell. It was filthy and minute. The bed consisted of three planks of wood and was so short that it would be impossible to stretch out full length. The stone floor was covered with dirty pieces of paper, dozens of cigarette ends and a lot of dust.

In one corner was an unscreened lavatory. The flush had not been in working order for some time and the stench was revolting. Tricesta was desperate to use it but could not face the nasty object.

The wardress was locking the door.

'Can I make a telephone call, please?' asked Tricesta.

'You're a prisoner, it's against the rules.'

Tricesta glanced into the cells on either side of her, no one was watching. She took a twenty dollar bill from her handbag and held it against the metal bars. 'Please,' she smiled, 'it will only take a moment.'

The money was snatched from Tricesta, the wardress stuffed it between her huge pendulous breasts. She unlocked the door. 'Come with me,' she whispered and led the way into a tiny office.

Tricesta gave her a number to dial; she did so and left the room.

'Tarquin?' She could hear insistent rhythm and blues music coming over the line. 'It's Tricesta, I've been framed on a vice charge . . . '

'What!?' he shouted and yelled for the music to be turned down. 'What the hell do you mean, vice charge?'

'I've only got a minute, come and bail me out, I haven't got much bread on me. Yes, I told you, I'm inside now, just hurry up.' She gave him the name of the prison.

Tarquin Lloyd owned an art gallery on Madison Avenue in one of New York's smart districts. He was a super-English salesman who had made it in New York by impressing people with his aristocratic connections.

The telephone was snatched from Tricesta. 'That's enough, get back now.'

Because she had been dealt with first, the remainder of the girls had still not been locked up.

Back in the cell Tricesta could no longer deny nature. Hurriedly and furtively she used the disgusting loo. Then she spread her velvet coat over the dirty bed and thankfully sat down.

The unoccupied cells began to fill up and the girls created a racket. Some rattled objects against the bars, others sang loudly. One or two screamed insults at the wardress:

'Let me out, nigger, I'll get you if you don't!'

'Get back to the Ghetto, black bitch!'

'Drop dead you coloured . . .'

This commotion made not the slightest difference to their position but they kept it going. There was no chance of sleep, not that Tricesta wanted to lose consciousness. She sat still, surrounded by foul smells, nauseating dirt and the dregs of society.

For two hours she remained sitting and thinking.

I've got to get out of this unscathed, she thought, I'm not going to become a political patsy. This is not my scene. Damn Edward's letter! Who set this up?

She dreaded the morning's headlines. Her need for water was desperate but she wanted to avoid drawing attention to herself. She was amazed at the disgusting state of the prison. New York was by reputation an advanced modern city but this was a total and telling contradiction.

A wardress came around after a while shouting: 'Wake up!' and the girls were herded into another Black Maria for the ride to the courtroom, a short distance from the prison. Tricesta prayed Tarquin had come up with the bail money. She could not face the thought of being sent back to the cells.

Although Tricesta did not see them, dozens of bail bondsmen were touting for business both inside and outside the building. In fact, she need not have worried about Tarquin helping her. The bondsmen were only too willing to put up bail, at a price.

Surrounding the court building were small lock-ups which on first sight appeared to be British betting shops. But it was from such premises that the 'bailing business' was run.

On arrival at the court Tricesta was pushed into a large cell with the other 'criminals', but there were only enough seats for six instead of sixteen, which by this time was the total of girls.

The filth was no better than in the previous cell, with another open lavatory in an even more revolting condition than the last, and communal. The porcelain was chipped, cracked and blackened from misuse. One of the pros had just vomited haphazardly over it and the floor.

Tricesta remained as close to the door as possible. She now had difficulty in willing her burning, watering eyes to remain open. She almost fell asleep on her feet.

Suddenly a coloured wardress pulled her outside, bustled her over to a desk and told her to co-operate with the Social Worker sitting there. The Social Worker was a white, middle-aged professional, set on 'helping these pitiful creatures'.

'Why did you take up this type of life?' she asked. She waited but got no reply.

'I want to understand and help you,' she went on. Tricesta remained silent.

'My dear girl, if you don't talk to me there's nothing I can do for you.'

There was still no response from Tricesta and the Social Worker shrugged and dismissed her. Finally she was taken to another cell laughingly labelled 'Surgery'. In the centre of the room there was a long table covered with several layers of white paper.

An unsmiling Negro in his forties, wearing a white coat, stood beside it.

'This is the first one, doctor,' said the wardress.

When Tricesta entered, her heart missed a beat, fear overwhelmed her. Her body tensed.

God, she thought, if that spade examines me I'll go mad.

'On the table!' ordered a pretty coloured nurse.

Tricesta did not move.

'If you don't get up there,' said the doctor, 'I'll call a couple of wardresses.'

Tricesta walked slowly to the table, the nurse pushing her. Why are all prison workers black, she wondered. Because no one else will do the job, I suppose.

She was frightened. Since an unfortunate incident in childhood her great dread had been the hypodermic needle. She had always blamed herself for jerking her arm at the crucial moment; but over the years her fear of another broken needle remained.

'Lie flat,' said the doctor. 'Pull up your skirt, what there is of it!' His nurse tittered. 'Take off your hose and keep still.'

There was no choice for her, she would have to obey, steel herself and not make a scene. She had never had an internal examination before and these were not the ideal conditions in which to undergo one. Shaking, close to tears, Tricesta did as she was told.

Cold, steel instruments were pushed into her. The doctor

prodded and poked and caused her a good deal of unnecessary pain. He made no apology for his roughness. Physically Tricesta was a coward but on this occasion she made a supreme effort to control herself. Hot tears ran down her cheeks.

The nurse, unconcerned, continued to pass the doctor various instruments and to chew gum. Tricesta presumed the examination was expected to reveal any drugs hidden deep inside her and not detected by the previous cursory search.

The doctor pulled the final gadget out too hastily, Tricesta flinched.

'Stop fussing,' he snapped. 'A prisoner has to learn to put up with this sort of thing. Ever had V.D.?'

She shook her head and sat up feeling dizzy.

Through her partial blackout she saw him fill a hypodermic syringe. Panic shook her, he was approaching her with the object of terror. She tried to protect her arms.

The nurse held her legs and the doctor, twisting her left arm back viciously jabbed in the needle. The bruise was to remain for over a week.

They dragged her off the table.

'Tear off your sheet of paper,' said the nurse, 'throw it in the trash can.'

Tricesta resented doing a chore which should have been done by the nurse but she was in no position to argue. She tore the sheet away and flung it into the dustbin. All she wanted now was a drink.

'Could I have a glass of water please?'

Surely a nurse would not refuse? But the Negress pretended she had not heard and called for a wardress. Tricesta was locked up as another prisoner was taken out.

Tricesta's companions ignored her; she leaned against the wall wishing there was a space to sit down. Normally she had difficulty in sleeping and needed pills to knock her out, but now, completely exhausted, she fell asleep.

Minutes later she was startled into consciousness and again removed from he cell for another finger-printing session.

While she was still wondering why a second set of her prints were required she heard the F.B.I. mentioned. Had her case been raised to a national level? Surely not. But as the finger printing was followed by a further humiliating experience Tricesta felt there could be no other explanation. She was

18

photographed, full face and profile, with a numbered card hung round her neck.

When she was eventually taken back to the cells she found the remainder of the prisoners had been taken off to court. She fell asleep.

The noise of the door being unlocked awakened her and a uniformed police officer beckoned her out. She stood up stiffly, swaying unsteadily for some seconds.

'Am I going to court now?' she asked.

'No.'

'But why not?' she demanded. 'All the others have gone. Where am I going?'

'D.A.'s office,' was the curt reply. The officer led the way down endless corridors, into a lift and up several floors, then along more hollow passages until they reached an oak door marked 'District Attorney.' Her guide knocked and was told to enter.

Being taken to the D.A.'s office, Tricesta felt, was not normal procedure.

The cop ushered her into an office, that was both sunlit and spacious, then left. Tricesta blinked and shielded her eyes from the bright light; she felt dirty and dispirited to a point she had never previously experienced. She had had neither food nor drink for over fifteen hours.

The Prosecutor was young and he smiled at her.

'Please sit down,' he invited. 'Have a glass of water, you look in need of it.'

Tricesta was worried about Tarquin, he was probably trying to trace her.

'Miss St Regis,' continued the District Attorney, watching her carefully, 'co-operate with us, I mean co-operate fully, and nothing will happen to you.' He refilled her glass with iced water. 'You may not like the declaration we need from you, but,' he grinned, 'you will be free.'

Tricesta knew this was a dangerous moment; she needed to buy time.

'I want to take advice,' she replied. 'A friend of mine should be waiting in court. I must talk to him.'

The D.A.'s smile slipped: 'No one is better qualified to advise you than I am. I know the problem from all sides. Is this man your attorney?'

'No, he's just a friend, but I won't say anything unless I see him first.'

In the end he had to agree and listened to her description of Tarquin. He gave prompt orders over the telephone to have the art dealer found and brought to his office.

During the half hour it took to locate him, the young D.A. tried hard to be nice to Tricesta. He used every approach possible to soften her. She had lost her fear and was now fully in control of herself. She was in a trap, knew it and refused to speak on any subject.

Tarquin Lloyd, dressed in startling, brilliantly coloured 'gear' was shown in. At thirty-eight Tarquin was hugely successful, with a considerable reputation and business to protect and he looked as worried as he felt. His father was a famous Venetian fine art dealer who lived in one of the great seventeenth-century Venetian palaces. Tarquin, in his younger days, was insanely jealous of his father and had changed not only his name but his nationality. He used his Welsh mother's maiden name. His mother had recently been remarried to a cement tycoon but she clung to her original name and rank – The Hon. Annabel Lloyd – in preference to her newly acquired Mrs Len Cox.

'What the devil's going on?' Tarquin demanded. 'I've been chasing over half of New York, sent from one place to another. Everyone gave me a different story about Miss St Regis's whereabouts.' Although he looked Italian his manner was more British than the British. 'Wait until our Ambassador hears about this!'

Tricesta groaned inwardly, perhaps she had made a mistake in sending for him. His attitude was bound to annoy the D.A. That was why she had refrained from pulling the 'outraged English' bit herself.

This was not the time or the place for bluff.

'Mr Lloyd,' – the D.A. made his name sound almost an insult – 'can you give me the name of someone in New York who can vouch for you?'

'My gallery and reputation are internationally known,' said Tarquin. 'Give Peggy Guggenheim a ring.'

He strolled to the window.

'Miss Guggenheim happens to be in Europe at the moment,' replied the D.A. He was more than a match for Tarquin as Tricesta was beginning to realise.

'Look here, Mister District Attorney,' Tarquin said, 'Miss St Regis must be given bail. You're not entitled to block it.'

'Mr Lloyd,' the D.A. spoke slowly with a slight smile, 'you are the one who is holding up the procedure, I won't do anything until you give me the name of your guarantor.'

'I want to speak to Mr Lloyd privately, please,' said Tricesta.

'There is no reason why I should allow it, but I'll give you five minutes. You'd better make Mr Lloyd understand your position more clearly.'

When the D.A. had left and had closed the door Tricesta whirled on Tarquin.

'You bloody fool, we can't afford to antagonise him, for Christ's sake cool it; and don't suddenly come the humble underdog bit either!'

'Really! What do you mean "we", you're the one on a vice charge, you cool it . . .'

'Don't argue with me, I've got to get bail and organise myself. Telephone that man you introduced me to at your party the other night. He'll impress this "mod" version of Perry Mason.'

'You must be joking!' Tarquin explained, his Latin temperament on the boil. 'You don't know what you're saying – you don't even know who he is.'

Tricesta walked over to him, her green eyes bored into his. Self-preservation was the instinct uppermost at that moment.

'I know precisely who he is,' she said. 'I don't pump nameless bodies! It's the clamps unless I know who and what they are, if you see my point.'

'You shatter me,' gasped Tarquin. 'Did you really have it off with him?'

'Don't play the innocent, you know damn well I did, and I know you told his aide about the high-class English chick you could produce. I bet you even had the sheets changed specially, he practically thought he was having pumpage with Royalty after your little sales-talk.'

Tarquin flushed, smoothed his thick black hair and roared with laughter. 'You really are incredible.' He kissed her. 'How can you look as though butter wouldn't melt in your mouth and then act the way you do?'

'I'll explain it one day. Get the D.A. to ring him then we'll talk. I don't like being framed. It's so dishonest, isn't it?'

The Prosecutor returned.

'Can we get down to business now?' he asked.

'Telephone Massey White,' said Tarquin. 'The Governor is a friend of mine and will vouch for me.'

The D.A. showed no reaction but he must have been astonished. White was tipped to win the Presidential nomination and the D.A. had no wish to get on the wrong side of this aggressive, vital politician. But he had put himself in a position which made it impossible not to telephone.

'D.A.'s office here,' said the Prosecutor to one of White's secretaries. 'Could the Governor possibly spare a moment, it's only a small matter. I don't like disturbing him. . . . Thanks, sure I'll hold . . .'

Tricesta's confidence was apparent to the lawman, who looked keenly from one to the other of his visitors while he held on to the receiver. How is it that this young English broad can get to our probable future President? He wondered.

'Hello, good morning, Governor,' his voice rang with respect. 'Hope I'm not bothering you but I have a Mr Tarquin Lloyd in the office – says you know him. . . . ' The D.A. listened for a moment, then said: 'No, not at all, he's not in any trouble with us. A friend of his wants him to put up bail, that's all. He gave your name as a reference.'

The Governor obviously bore out Tarquin's claim of friendship.

'Thank you, Governor, you've been very helpful.'

Tarquin offered cigarettes around. 'Now can we settle bail?'

'I'll do my best for Miss St Regis,' said the D.A., 'but it won't be easy, the State have a deep interest in this case.'

'How can "The State" have an interest in such a mundane charge?' asked Tarquin, but he was not given an answer.

The Prosecutor led them back along the corridors, walking rapidly.

When they reached the entrance hall of the court a battery of journalists and photographers leapt into action. To protect Tricesta the D.A. ordered two plainclothes men to position themselves on each side of her and with Tricesta between them they elbowed their way through the crowd towards the courtroom.

The D.A. and Tarquin followed, both refusing to answer questions put by the Press, who now realised this was far from a simple vice rap.

Tricesta was astonished at the lack of decorum inside the court; members of the Press called to each other, chewed gum, smoked and propped themselves insolently against the Judge's Bench. The Judge ignored them, glanced at Tricesta and listened to the application for bail presented by the D.A. The New York Police asked for a thirty-five thousand dollar bail, a figure wildly out of proportion to the charge. Even the Press gasped. A quiet discussion at the Bench followed between the Judge and the D.A. Tricesta stood still and tried to look calm but she fell close to collapse; she knew she must have sleep soon.

Finally the Judge agreed to the D.A.'s suggestion of three thousand dollars.

'Can I go now?' she asked.

'I'm afraid not,' replied the young D.A. 'You'll be released when the bail order and money are presented to the prison authorities. Don't worry, it won't take long. Go with this officer,' he handed her over to a policeman. 'I'll tell Mr Lloyd what he should do.'

Tricesta had expected to be set free at once.

'Listen, Tarquin,' she whispered wearily, 'don't let me down and for Christ's sake get a move on.'

'It's all right, I'll soon have it under control,' he said and disappeared with the D.A.

Tricesta was driven in another Black Maria to the infamous Women's House of Detention in Greenwich Village. Before being ushered in she glanced up at its sinister bulk, the dull brickwork, the heavily barred windows, and she shuddered. What a soul-destroying prospect for a woman due to serve a life sentence, she thought. Her police escort led her into a circular reception hall, around which were barred windows and doors.

A young Negress was on duty and took Tricesta's papers from the cop, who left as quickly as he could.

'I'll be leaving in a few minutes,' Tricesta informed the coloured woman, 'I'm being bailed out.'

'Yeah, they all say that,' the wardress said. 'Your name's not on my bail list.'

'But it must be,' Tricesta insisted. 'I've just come from the court.'

'Don't try and tell me my job,' the woman said sharply. 'If

23

I get instructions to release you then I shall. But at the moment you're just another prisoner. Where do you came from?'

'England,' replied Tricesta. Another wardress grinned and said: 'She means the Bronx!'

Tricesta was led away. The atmosphere in this notorious jail enveloped her; the air of hopeless dejection was unmistakable. The prisoners looked ill cared for, scruffy and helpless. She attracted jealous attention from both the inmates and those in authority; she felt totally alone.

The now familiar routine of finger printing and photographing was gone through again, and an even more harsh medical examination, once again conducted by a coloured staff. She objected to this, not because of their colour but because of their incredible arrogance and rudeness. She was aware they would not normally behave so disagreeably; but their small measure of power had grown within their own minds. They were apeing what they considered to be the 'white' manner of authority. They need turning on to Bobby Seale, she thought.

Tricesta was locked into another cell, as noisome and filthy as the others. To her dismay she remained there until six o'clock in the evening. Twenty-four hours had passed since she had taken food or a sustaining drink.

The unsanitary squalor of her surroundings gradually receded as she concentrated on possible ways out of her predicament, a political predicament into which she had unwittingly been projected.

At 6 p.m. Tricesta was released. Tarquin greeted her in the circular hall.

'Hello, darling,' he said. 'You look ghastly, never mind, the worst is over.'

'What took you so long?'

'Believe me, love,' he took her arm, 'I did my bit. They used every delaying tactic in the book. For some curious reason they wanted you kept out of the way for a while. Come on over to my place, I've got something to jolly you up.'

'No.' she shook her head firmly. 'I'm not touching anything, they might give me a blood test. I'll have a drink but nothing else. I'll go with you for an hour and sort things out. Then I must sleep. Actually I'd rather not use my blower, it's sure to be tapped.'

Outside the sun still shone, emphasising the dinginess of the prison. From various open windows women waved and shouted through the bars. She acknowledged their hopeless gestures and vowed no one would ever force her to enter the appalling place again.

Chapter 2

TARQUIN'S MAROON ROLLS ROYCE, parked in front of the jail, seemed completely out of place.

'I'm surprised there aren't any Press boys here,' Tricesta said. 'They let them run wild in this country.'

'Oh, that's because I had a little chat with the D.A. – he was very impressed with my friend the Governor,' said Tarquin, a touch of triumph in his voice. 'But they'll be waiting for you in force at your apartment building. Perry Mason Junior nearly choked when he saw the motor!'

Tricesta was past Tarquin's predictable comments, his only use to her now was his friendship with the ambitious Governor White.

Tarquin drove uptown in a way calculated to attract attention. Tricesta had always considered him to be efficient and intelligent; but when it came to the crunch he was almost useless. He was a social ponce, an aristocratic conman. His only talent was his ability to fasten on to gifted new artists on the one hand and gullible rich snobs on the other, and fuse these opposites together with remarkably rewarding results.

Tarquin was a fairly heavy methedrine addict: this accounted for his moods, long periods of lethargy followed by spasms of enthusiasm and forceful energy.

When they arrived at the Madison Avenue apartment block Tarquin parked his Rolls among the array of flashy American cars and entered the 'Lloyd Progressive Art Gallery', gently guiding Tricesta. The impressive interior was refreshingly cool, an angular bronze staircase led into a more conservative gallery. A large door made of bronze and steel at the far end opened into Tarquin's flat.

The decoration of the flat was harsh and gaunt but there were some fine examples of eighteenth-century English furniture and Roman antiques. Surprisingly the super-modern blended intriguingly with the antique; but only exceptional taste could have made this combination an exciting success.

Charles Bodley St Regis, Tricesta's brother, nicknamed Chocolate Biscuits or C.B. for short, had been responsible for designing and furnishing Tarquin's flat. Its wide windows overlooked Parke Bernet, the great antique auction rooms, now controlled by Sothebys from London.

After Tarquin had made coffee and produced a large plate of smoked salmon for Tricesta he sat on the sofa beside her:

'So let's hear it all, what's the scene?'

'I hardly know myself,' she replied, drinking her second cup of coffee. 'The only sure thing is, someone wanted me in an awkward position. I can see that if I don't co-operate, as they call it, I'll be in a worse situation. You can be sure I'll get a visit from "them" tomorrow and they'll explain their terms.'

'Terms? Who wants to make terms?' asked Tarquin, feeling there must be an angle in this for him. He stood up and removed a tightly-cut Regency corduroy waistcoat which Tricesta had given him.

'I'm not sure yet,' she sighed. 'Why didn't you tell me you'd pulled me for the Governor?'

'Oh baby,' he laughed, 'you know your mania for never wanting to be organised. If I'd told you, he'd never have got any action from you. You're too hung up on being spontaneous. That's fine for some but a busy man like the Governor has to have it set up and at his time. It's always been the same with him, I've been pulling birds for him for five years.

27

'There's also the question of his tricky marriage to Lucy, he daren't risk a break-up. Her father has helped clear the path to the White House for him. Massey has used a lot of Lucy's money and friends. She really runs the show with that bigoted father of hers behind her. He didn't make the Presidency himself, and as he has no male heirs, Massey was the obvious choice.'

Tarquin loosened his fitted *crêpe-de-chine* shirt and went on. Tricesta was mentally filing every word.

'They've virtually lived apart for ten years,' he continued, 'but they make the happy marriage scene for every public appearance. They hate each other but both need the other; she can't become the President, he can't do it without her backing. Any sex scandal would finish them, and there's the strong religious bit, the States don't want a divorced sex maniac as President. It's not that he'll bang anything but he's got to have it every day. He gets so wound up and tense that a quick screw is the best release he can find.'

'So I noticed,' commented Tricesta. 'Hasn't he got a permanent girlfriend?'

'No, that's too dangerous, she'd have too big a hold over him. Actually I persuaded him to have a new chick each time, they hardly ever know who he is, it's much safer.'

'I knew,' she said. 'One of your discoveries told me. As far as the Governor is concerned I've never seen anyone so keen to go, but afterwards he was a different person – calm, controlled and detached. Just a ten minute bang was enough!'

The telephone rang, Tarquin snatched up the receiver, confirmed he was speaking and glanced instinctively at Tricesta. She guessed it was Governor White on the line from Tarquin's responses.

'Yes, it was that one,' he said, turning his back to her, 'an incredible coincidence. I had no idea at the time, I give you my word. What do you want me to do?'

Tarquin listened attentively then said:

'I understand, believe me there's no need to worry – I'll handle it, there's no problem. Yes, I'll ring you later, good-bye.'

'Anyway, back to the Governor,' said Tricesta. 'Let's face it, he's not popular with conservative America. The voters who will put him on top will be the young ones and the Negroes.'

'It's not that cut and dried,' replied Tarquin. 'He's got a great image, a progessive and sincere attitude. He believes in his country and knows he can help to stop the bloodshed which America is at present suffering in Asia. Sure, he has his enemies, but on the whole the people like him, he's representative of modern society, the older elements might vote for him too. After all, his family have been on the 'social register' since it was started. Both his sisters married sound European titles. His only weakness, and he admits it, is for pretty young girls. At least he doesn't allow frustration to build up and destroy. He has a lot to offer this confused country. No, I'm bloody sure the public will put White in the White House.'

'Be honest, Tarquin, you are a bit prejudiced,' smiled Tricesta. 'He may not be your bread, but he supplies all the goodies to put on it. As far as I'm concerned, his slogan "Vote White for Black Equality" is the one which might get him in. But take it from me, once he's President he'll drop his much publicised concern for the coloured community.'

'You don't know what you're talking about,' Tarquin snapped angrily, 'and don't say things like that while you're in your present position, it won't help.'

'For Christ's sake!' She jumped up. 'At least tell the truth to yourself.' His dishonesty sickened her but she concealed her feelings. 'It's not that I'm against the methods he uses to get ahead, I just hate deception. Of course he'll make grand-sounding concessions to the blacks, even go along with the Negro Vice-President idea, but that's just a pacifying technique. A clever publicity move. In his own way he'll do the blacks more harm than good in the long run. He'll destroy any belief they could have had in *themselves*. Why do you think he fraternises with Black Power leaders? He needs their support but do you really think they'll be honoured guests at the White House?'

'Don't be stupid. He doesn't mix with the Black Power boys, the papers would be on to it if he did!'

Tricesta laughed. 'When you come to London ask Edward X whose representatives it is that are busy in lower Harlem.'

'How is it you're so familiar with this scene?'

'I'm not really. An unfortunate incident got me slightly involved and then I developed a genuine interest, not that anyone knows that.'

Tarquin appeared agitated. He sat close to Tricesta.

'I need some "speed", It wouldn't do you any harm either, you look tired.'

'No thanks, you know I never do, but you go ahead.' He walked into another room and opened a concealed wall safe. After filling the hypodermic he injected himself in his left arm. Tarquin was annoyed she had refused, it made him feel an 'odd ball' but he didn't really care. Suddenly he felt fantastic, saw himself as the power behind the future President, controlling, manipulating, wielding world power.

'What you need is a first-class lawyer,' he said on his return to the drawing room. 'Massey will put us on to the best. I'll ring him.'

'No.' She sounded firm. 'A lawyer will only work through strictly legal channels. I don't want one, certainly not one of the Governor's stooges.' Tricesta flicked her hair from her eyes. 'I'm going back to my flat now. You go and see Massey White, explain to him that my presence in the States could be embarrassing to him, especially if I am pushed to answer certain questions.'

Tarquin saw her point. Normally this delicate situation would have terrified him, he felt more than able to handle everything. He always felt good after a shot.

'Before you leave,' said Tarquin embracing her, 'how about some pumpage?' He pushed into her and stared into her eyes. 'Come on, it always helps.'

'Now? Don't be silly, I'm off home to bed,' Tricesta said and kissed him. 'Unless you want to spend a hundred dollars of course!' They both laughed.

'What a shame I can't afford it!' he said. 'Still, I'll find something.'

I bet you will, she thought. As C.B. says, you're not fussy, male or female, Tarquin is everybody's friend. His good looks were undeniable but since discovering his pandering she did not want him. She was the same with cynics; once she discovered a man was cynical Tricesta found she could not make love to him.

Tarquin tidied himself, then drove her across town to the East Side block of flats.

A small knot of journalists was lying in wait.

'Damn!' she said. 'Never mind, I must go in. Ring me later, I'll be here.'

Tricesta ignored the Press and pushed through them into the

30

entrance hall. The janitor handed her some letters and a pile of newspapers.

'Are you going to see William X the Second?'

'Are you pleading guilty to the vice rap?'

'What is Lord Prestigne's reaction to all this?'

The questions were fired at her once again. Several young Press boys tried to corner her but she was too quick for them and darted into the lift. The janitor blocked two of the reporters from barging into the lift behind her.

Tricesta slammed the apartment door and locked it. What indeed would Grandfather Prestigne's reaction be to this? she wondered. Not that I really care, but I would hate to miss out on my share of the old boy's fortune when the time comes. I would make good use of it, not just surround myself with silver, servants and secretaries as he does!

The headlines and photographs in the New York papers were worse than she had thought possible:

BRITISH SOCIETY GIRL ARRESTED

BRITISH PEER'S KIN ON VICE RAP

BRITISH BLONDE HELD AS CALL GIRL

Most of the pictures were quite flattering, but her bewilderment was apparent. The articles were distorted, crude and basically untrue, especially the account of her arrest. She gave way and wept. Why had she been set up? What was behind it?

Before deciding upon any action, Tricesta ran a bath. She could do nothing until she felt right. That meant being cool, confident and in charge of the situation. She put on an L.P. of The Who and climbed into the bath. She always thought better with the hi-fi at its loudest. The music filled the enormous flat and stirred Tricesta's will to act. She wished C.B. were beside her, 'her other half': she always thought of her beautiful and artistic brother in that way. The telephone rang, it was C.B. from London.

'Tricesta?' C.B.'s voice sounded desperate. 'What the hell's happened? The papers have gone mad here. Is it true you've been arrested?'

'Yes,' she answered, 'but I was framed. I can't talk on this line, I'm certain it's tapped. My great worry is Grandfather. for heaven's sake smooth him out – tell him I have a complete answer to everything and believe me I have.'

'You'll need it,' he replied, his young voice coming clearly over the transatlantic cable. 'The bloody Press are driving us crazy. I've squared Grandpa's P.A.'s not to put any Press calls through to him: that cost a bit of bread, I can tell you! But I can hardly censor his *Times* and *Telegraph*. At least Purdy is on our side.'

Purdy was Lord Prestigne's confidential secretary, devoted to the family, a thirty-five-year-old woman fascinated by C.B.'s angelic appearance and charm. C.B. could 'handle' her.

'Shall I fly over?' he asked.

'No, we don't want to draw attention to ourselves. I'll cope. I've got an ace to play. I suppose the reporters are bombarding Grandfather in person?'

'Trying to, but Purdy can be a real deterrent! Mother wants to know if you've seen the British Consul?'

'She would,' laughed Tricesta. 'No, not at this stage. Tell her not to worry, it's all a misunderstanding. What's Father's reaction?'

'Water off the proverbial duck's back, love. He's too involved transplanting another lot of kidneys to bother with his own kid's misadventures.'

'I know. Let's face it, we really only have to worry about old Midas at Westingshire, our parents aren't any hang-up. Keep your end up. If I play this right the publicity will help the business. Just trust me, no one will step on us. Tarquin stood bail, he's almost a handicap, he nearly buggered things up . . .'

'I shouldn't let the Americans hear you use such words, her mother cut in.

'Sorry,' said Tricesta. 'I didn't know you were on the extension.'

'Don't apologise,' laughed Lady Anne. 'It's just that the Yanks are so prudish in some ways or rather pretend to be. Let them continue to think the British aristocracy use a special sort of language, let them keep their illusions.'

'You're a great mother,' said her daughter. 'Sorry about all this but it's not my fault. Anyway, I'll ring you both when I have news. Just make no comment, treat it as a joke. Give my love to Helen.'

Helen was the attractive young Rhodesian secretary who helped run the administrative side of their business.

Tricesta felt happier after being in contact with home. While relaxing in the bath she decided to ring Michael Flaxman Q.C., the Liberal M.P. for Stoneham in Westingshire. After washing her long hair she booked the call to England. It was then 9 p.m. new York time, Michael would be in bed. She had just finished drying her hair when the telephone rang. She had to wait for a few seconds before she heard Flaxman's precise voice. The M.P. had an honourable and respectable political reputation and was a friend of her grandfather's.

'That's roughly the position,' she said to him after talking for five minutes. 'I want you to ring Massey White. Tell him I don't appreciate what happened last night. And if I go before a Grand Jury I'm the type of girl who might go into all sorts of details. Details which may be considered legally irrelevant but which would still be very damaging. Have I made myself clear?'

'Up to a point, Tricesta, but on what grounds can I ring him?'

'You told me you became friends when you worked on that U.N. commission three years ago,' she reminded the eminent barrister. 'Tell him you have been a friend of my family all your life and that you felt he should know the sort of character I really am.'

'But why should he have any interest in you?'

'We got on "friendly" terms at Tarquin Lloyd's party. I don't think he knows my name has been associated with some aspects of Black Power and the police found an explosive document connected with it among my effects. I doubt if I'm the kind of person he should be linked with during a political campaign, and I'd hate to make the relationship public! Please make the call now, I've already started a similar campaign at this end. Remember, I'm innocent of the charge. You must know I am. And I'll use any method to save myself.'

Tricesta swallowed three tuinal sleeping capsules. She took the telephone off the hook and fell into bed. Exhausted as she was, her problems continued to array themselves before her.

She had replaced the magic of The Who with the aggressive driving sound of Buddy Rich. Tricesta found the most pleasant way to relieve worrying pressures was to make love. When she was alone in times of tension she resorted to self-satisfaction. This was one of those occasions. Stimulated by the frantic pace of the Rich record she soothed herself. After the emotional release her thoughts became clear and precise, and her objective positive.

At nine o'clock the next morning she awakened, dressed herself in her King's Road gear and carefully applied her make-up. She looked bright-eyed and refreshed. The moment she replaced the telephone on its hook it jangled into life. All the calls were either from American journalists or from English newspapers offering to buy her story. 'No comment' and 'Nothing doing' were her only responses.

The door bell rang while she was drinking her coffee.

Through the spy hole she saw three burly-looking men quietly dressed holding their hats.

'Who are you?' she called.

'F.B.I. M'am. Open the door please.' Tricesta had almost been expecting them.

'How can I be sure?' she said through the closed door.

One of the men removed a leather bound card from his wallet.

'Take a look at my credentials.'

She kept the door on the chain, opened it slightly and took the object. It was the real thing.

'Come in.' She stood aside, they walked in, looked at her clothes and dropped their hats on to the hall table.

'I'm afraid I've got some bad news for you,' the spokesman drawled. 'The police intend to apply for much higher bail in Women's Court this morning and ask for your passport. We'll take you over with us, but we want to ask you a few questions first. Do you mind if we sit?'

'Of course not. Why do the police want my passport?'

'They don't want you running off. Maybe it's because they don't often get a looker like you!' He smiled briefly. 'As you may be aware, Miss St Regis, the document you were sent here to deliver is of paramount interest to us.'

'I've already explained I have no idea what it contained.'

The trio sniggered.

'You were carrying a blue print for Black Power riots scheduled for August. Riots covering most of Europe and the States. Riots aimed at disrupting society, to be triggered by a signal from the movement's headquarters here in Harlem.'

'I don't believe it.'

'According to your papers, black community leaders have been trained behind the Iron Curtain, trained to organise riots and instructed in the use of arms and explosives. We've already made several arrests, and those arrested gave us a lot of information – eventually.'

'Let me see this paper,' she said.

'Playing it this cool won't help.' The F.B.I. men were getting impatient. 'From the look of you I wouldn't be surprised if you'd helped put the plans on paper.'

He handed Xerox copies to her. On the first page was a list of the major counties of England with the names of towns and cities which had a large population of coloured people. Against each town was the name of its community leader, the one alleged to be ready to ignite the fuse in his district. There were twelve such place names.

Edward X had suggested that certain cities in the U.S.A. time their 'activities' to coincide with the British riots. A list of American cities was included. He outlined several reasons for this collective act. He said it was necessary to show white society that black people were more than capable of organisation, co-ordination and discipline.

All the places chosen had ghettos or slum districts which various authorities had for years been promising to pull down and rebuild. Occasionally a new school had been built, a small playground provided; 'bones tossed to a starving dog' said the paper. But these manoeuvres no longer fooled intelligent coloured leaders; they did not help the basic problems of over-crowded houses and discrimination in employment and social life.

To her mind Edward X was clear and reasoned. It was an impressive presentation.

'We have it on record,' said the F.B.I. spokesman, 'that you know the first six names on the list, apart from Edward X and Apostrophe Brown.'

'There's no reason why it shouldn't be "on record", I've never made a secret of it. I've met them on social occasions, at parties, clubs and restaurants, that's all.'

'That's enough,' the American sounded grim. 'If you co-operate with us you'll be taken off the hook as far as we are concerned. The worst that can happen to you is to be deported.'

That would be a pleasure, she thought. Anyway, I don't believe all that you'll-be-off-the-hook crap. And if they want me to sign a confession they haven't got a hope in hell!

Tricesta folded up the document. What was the point in reading any more- She gave it back and stood up. She stretched and walked to the balcony. It was already hot, the temperature was going to soar.

When the telephone rang one of the Federal agents answered it. He waved the receiver at Tricesta.

'Your call, a Mr Lloyd.'

There was no alternative for her but to speak in front of them.

'I've just had a long meeting with a friend of ours,' Tarquin's voice sounded busy and excited. 'There's nothing to worry about, it's all plain sailing.'

'I'm due in court again this morning,' she said in a matter-of-fact voice.

'I know, it doesn't mean a thing. I'll be there with another man, we'll explain everything to you. Relax, love, there's no hang-up.'

'Got friends on the case?' asked the F.B.I. man. 'Get your bag, it's time to get over to Women's Court.'

Tricesta went into the bedroom, combed her hair and re-touched her make-up. She was sure that both Michael Flaxman and Tarquin had spoken to White, but she felt apprehensive, insecure, a target for misuse.

The three F.B.I. agents led her to the car, the reporters guessed who was escorting her. At the courthouse other reporters spotted Tricesta, took pictures and started to fire questions.

'That's enough, boys,' said one of the F.B.I. agents, 'you'll have to wait 'til the show's over. No, you can't come in this way, 'it's "off limits".'

'Since when?' demanded a journalist.

'Since I said so!'

Half a dozen uniformed cops arrived and cleared the narrow doorway. Tricesta was shown into a large office and left alone. Five minutes later a very young, well-dressed American walked in. He grinned broadly, extended a friendly hand and said: 'I'm Assistant District Attorney Simpson.' His accent was a soft Southern drawl. 'I'll be taking you into court and making certain representations to the Judge. Smile a bit more, the worst is over.'

He sat at the desk opposite her and put down a file.

'Your dossier,' he smiled and slapped the cover. 'I must say the police shots of you are terrible – I won't show them to you.'

'Mr Simpson,' she said, 'what is going on? What will happen this morning?'

'I'll explain,' he leaned towards her. 'You're a lucky girl, believe me. Before your case comes up I'll have had a talk with the Judge. This is most unusual but the charge against you will be dropped!'

'Really?' She looked at him. 'Are you sure? I thought the police wanted my bail increased?'

'Easy honey,' he held up his hands as though to stem the flow of her words. 'It's not as simple as it sounds, this is a complicated case.'

Just what was complicated? she wondered.

'Take no notice of what is said in court,' he went on cheerfully. 'Whatever is said is for a good reason. Bear in mind the world's Press will be reporting every word. It mustn't appear that the matter has been dropped. Remember, we have to consider public reaction. Is it all clear?'

'In a way,' she replied, but asked herself: What are they setting me up for now? Favours like this aren't dished out for nothing – Where's the catch?

Tricesta was sure the vice charge was being waived because of White's intervention. The judge must be bent, she decided.

'Come on,' the Assistant D.A. said, 'time for action. Remember, it's all right, before you even go in you know the outcome. But my words were strictly off the record, so forget you ever heard them!' His voice retained its cheerfulness but his warning was unmistakable.

In the courtroom all eyes turned to the aloof young girl. Tarquin appeared beside her; she barely acknowledged him but noticed his usually flamboyant clothes had been replaced with others rather more subdued.

'I'll leave you with Mr Lloyd,' whispered the Assistant D.A., 'I have to go see the boss man.' He nodded towards the Judge's Bench. 'Don't talk to anyone,' he added.

Tricesta sat in the front of the court beside Tarquin and fixed her eyes on the Stars and Stripes Flag.

'What was our friend's reaction?' whispered Tricesta.

'He screamed the fucking place down,' replied Tarquin, 'had a couple of drinks and sat in silence for half an hour. You had him by the hairs, he knew it and acted accordingly. But he doesn't control it all, there is an opposition you know. They have a very keen interest in this, particularly in the bloody

37

papers you were carrying. Some departments are sympathetic to White and his party, others support t'other lot.'

'I can imagine,' she said. 'And right now I'm trapped between the two.'

'A mere pawn, eh?' he was being facetious.

'We'll see!' she said grimly.

Twenty minutes later the court stirred into action, everyone stood, the Judge entered, sat down and the court waited. Her name was called, she was told where to stand by Simpson.

Following the formalities he approached the Judge.

'We had intended to ask for a higher bail,' he said, 'but due to the unusual circumstances surrounding the case we are willing to have the original charge set aside.'

There was a stir among the Press.

'We suggest Miss St Regis be put on probation,' continued Simpson, 'while enquiries continue. These could result in charges being filed against persons who will not be mentioned at this time. Miss St Regis may well be a material witness! We ask that she surrender her passport.'

She gasped. What a cunning move.

The newsmen scribbled away in rising excitement.

'Miss St Regis,' the Judge said, 'you are indeed fortunate that the police are not pressing the charge against you.'

Stuff it! she thought.

'I'm putting you on probation for an indefinite period. You will be released in the custody of Mr Lloyd, who I have been assured is a suitably responsible person. Obey your probation officer and talk to her if you have any problems.'

Simpson led her out with Tarquin through a side entrance.

'What's this about another charge?' she demanded.

'I told you earlier,' said Simpson, 'take no notice of what is said in court. It had to look serious, you saw the Press there. You should be laughing, it's over.'

'But what about this "indefinite probation"?' she asked. 'Can't I return to London?'

'Not for a while. The Press will watch every move. We could hardly allow the chief material witness to leave the country, could we? They're not that stupid.'

'Can I have my passport back?'

'No, that wouldn't do at all. Just relax and enjoy yourself, get a job!'

Tricesta was furious. 'So I'm expected to remain in New York with no time limit? And probably have another charge rigged against me?'

Tarquin shot her a cautioning look.

'I said before,' Simpson spoke gently, 'it's all over. You're laughing, but do remember our investigations. Now come and meet your probation officer and then you can go.'

Reluctantly she followed him to another office. Sitting at a desk was an extremely attractive black woman. Simpson handed her Tricesta's papers.

'I'm leaving now, Miss St Regis,' he said. 'When Miss Lincoln has finished with you, you can leave with Mr Lloyd. Good luck!'

The pretty P.O. glanced through the papers. 'Now my dear, tell me about your background first.'

I'll settle this one, thought Tricesta feeling suddenly amused.

'Well I was born in Bath . . .'

'You don't mean IN a bath?'

'No, the historic city of Bath, Miss Lincoln.' Tricesta adopted a very superior English attitude. 'Father is a famous surgeon – he transplants various human bits into other humans, I expect you've read about him. Mother is the only child of the Earl of Prestigne, Lord Lieutenant of Westinghire. The title is rare in that it can pass through the female line . . .'

'Really, how fascinating,' said the P.O. already lost.

'Yes, most unusual. My brother Chocolate Biscuits and myself will inherit the bulk of the estate on the death of our grandparent, then when Mother dies C.B. will become the seventh Earl. Father was recently knighted for his services to medicine. Mother is a successful 'movement" painter, sells a lot of her work over here.'

'Where were you educated?'

'My brother and I went to Dartington Hall because of our artistic talent. As you know this advanced co-ed school was founded by a progressive American woman, Mrs Elmhirst.'

Miss Lincoln had not known but nodded uncertainly.

'The freedom there is remarkable: no locks on the doors, communal bathrooms, no compulsory lectures or entrance exams, no competitive games. The result is that everyone really wants to study, the standard of education is very high. We both won scholarships to The Royal College of Art, did well and again both won Rome scholarships.

'I remained in Italy for a year, my brother too. On returning

39

to London we decided to open the finest antique showrooms in the King's Road. C.B. combines ultra-modern interiors with period furniture and other objects of art. The result is really sensational. I started a department dealing in period clothes, this is a big hit too. After nine months in business people have taken to our ideas and it's swinging. Now this has happened.'

'Oh dear,' murmured the P.O., 'I suppose you fell into bad company. Is a man responsible for all this?' Her eyes gleamed with curiosity.

'You could say that.' Tricesta nodded, smiling slightly.

'How did it happen? Who was he?'

'I can't tell you how it happened but he is a Negro leader!'

'Black! And he brought you down to this?'

'Down to what?' Tricesta asked quietly.

'Well I mean this charge you were on, a life of vice!'

'Do you really think I'm a call girl?'

'I don't know, we've had them from all shades of society. But a girl from your illustrious background . . . '

'Forget the background bit!' said Tricesta angrily. 'I'm on the threshold of a fabulous business career. Do you think I'd be likely to endanger it? All I care about is succeeding and standing on my own two feet. I'll make it without the background of family. I'll make it by my own efforts. And I'm not likely to let my brother down.'

'I'm sure you're not, not intentionally.' The P.O. was making rapid notes and went on: 'But perhaps you fell in love with this man? Perhaps he supplied you with drugs? Perhaps he was blackmailing you?'

'As you say, Miss Lincoln – perhaps. Which of the three do you go for?'

'I'm waiting for you to tell me,' replied the P.O. 'Which "perhaps" is it?'

'How about all three?' laughed Tricesta. 'There's a thought or two for you. Are you a supporter of the Black Panthers?'

The switch of subject threw Miss Lincoln. 'Certainly not,' she snapped, 'I never support violence for any reason.'

'But they're trying to help your people.'

'President Kennedy and Dr King were the men who really tried to help.' she said.

'Christ! You really think they were on your side. You'd better vote for Governor White . . . '

'I intend to,' she replied smugly, as though such a move put her in a special position of power. 'You appear to have a very close relationship with your brother.' Miss Lincoln preferred to change the subject too.

'I have. We work well together and have the same views on life. We complement each other in our work.'

'How fortunate,' she replied, now rather cool. 'This is your probation card, come and see me next week at the address on it. Don't break any of the rules, it's in your interest not to.'

The ninth rule amused Tricesta: 'Abstain from having sexual relations without the benefit of marriage.' She wisely decided not to have the word 'benefit' clarified. The other rules were just as infantile and not likely to be taken seriously by any miscreant.

Miss Lincoln and Tricesta parted; with a mutual dislike.

Tarquin was hovering in the corridor, he escorted Tricesta to his Rolls.

'We'll talk at my pad,' he said, speeding through the garbage-strewn streets of the Lower East side. New Yorkers dump everything on to the pavements: beds, refrigerators, everything they no longer need. There is apparently nothing to prevent them doing this but the law does demand that the doors be removed from fridges and safes, ensuring that children playing in the dirty streets do not trap themselves inside.

A cross-section of 'art lovers' were strolling around Tarquin's gallery. One greeted him elaborately, but he hurried Tricesta through to his own apartment.

'The public are only tolerable when they're signing cheques,' he observed. 'Sit yourself down and I'll make a cuppa.'

Apart from making tea he surreptitiously had a shot of 'speed'. He had a tricky situation to go through – or so he imagined. His orders from Governor White were to broach the subject to Tricesta of getting her out of New York, fast.

But Tricesta was a step ahead. 'I want you to sit down,' she said firmly when he returned with the tray of tea and cakes. 'Don't try arguing with me. I mean every word of what I'm going to say, so listen carefully.'

Tarquin looked puzzled.

'All right, shoot.'

'It was made clear to me this morning that they intend to keep me here for as long as it suits them. That doesn't suit me. They may keep me here for months, just to satisfy the Press and public. I can't afford to be away from London, the business needs me. Besides I've been framed and I'm furious about it.'

Tricesta stood up and prodded Tarquin with a finger. 'I intend to leave New York! I need a false passport, an air ticket and dark wig. If I don't get them I may tell the Grand Jury about my little encounter with the Governor. Morally and politically I know how to make it hot for him. He can't afford for me to remain in New York. I want to fly out tomorrow.'

There was a heavy silence. Tarquin pretended astonishment but he was relieved he had been spared the necessity of spelling it out and suggesting she put herself in contempt of court by jumping the country.

'I'll tell White what you've said, but he's bound to ask what will prevent you from telling the Press the story when you're in England.'

'He knows damn well what will prevent me,' said Tricesta sharply. 'Anyway, I doubt very much whether any newspaper or magazine, even a German one, would print the story I could give them. Who would listen to a girl that's been on a vice charge?' She inhaled deeply on her cigarette. 'Oh, no, he knows that it's stalemate. And in any case I want to be able to revisit the States. Slandering the Head of a State is not the way to be welcomed back. No, Tarquin, the Governor is sitting pretty and he knows it.'

He smiled and shrugged. 'Very clearly stated, love.' He blew on to a suspended mobile. 'I'll go and see him. Be careful who you telephone and I advise you not to leave the flat. I'll come over in the morning, I won't ring.'

Tricesta made her way back to Envoy Towers by taxi. Only two Press boys were hanging about. She hoped this meant interest in her was diminishing; she pushed by them and hurried up to the penthouse flat.

She got through to C.B. at their flat in London without much delay. When she had outlined the morning's events she said:

'I am still bothered about Grandfather. Have you been to see him?'

'Yes,' replied her brother, 'I drove down last night. I explained about the frame-up, he hardly said a word. We've got to straighten him out somehow. One stupid act could cost us his estate.'

'Don't worry, angel,' replied Tricesta. 'Take it from me we'll both get our share. I've always been told we're his pride and

42

joy, not that he's ever shown it!'

'But the papers said you knew Edward X. You know how he feels about bloody niggers, he's no Albert Schweitzer. Anyway, the shop's busier than ever, I've got a couple of fabulous *carte blanche* commissions.'

'Keep it up and I'll ring when I have more news. Do you miss me?'

'Can't you guess, it's terrible. You've got to get back quickly.'

Tricesta spent the remaining part of the day resting and thinking. At nine o'clock, determined to have a sound sleep, she took three sleeping pills. She was sure she would be leaving, she was certain Massey White wanted her out of New York as much as she wanted to leave.

Chapter 3

AT EIGHT O'CLOCK the next morning she had breakfast: black coffee and toast. She rang down to the porter to bring up the post and papers.

The newspapers were having a last fling. One article read:

A VICEREGAL MATTER – MISS ST REGIS IS PRESENTED AT COURT

Had she been a visiting royal princess and not an alleged hundred-dollar call girl, twenty-two year-old Tricesta St Regis could have received no more preferential treatment than she was accorded yesterday when her V charge was waived in Women's Court.

Not once during her visit to the sedate court building, where justice is traditionally meted out impartially to all, did she have to mingle with the ordinary, run-of-the-mill wayward women who daily traipse before the court.

Instead, the beautiful blonde Tricesta, daughter of Sir John and Lady Anne St Regis, was spirited into court by devious means, protected by an 'off limits' rule which ensured her privacy. All this apparently to protect her from the glaring eye of publicity.

The Judge placed Tricesta on indefinite probation while police make further investigations. She was accompanied in court by Mr Tarquin Lloyd, British Director of the Lloyd Progressive Art Gallery. He was said to be a friend of the family.

During the whole of her period at the Courthouse, Miss St Regis was surrounded by four policemen to protect her from the Press and public. Accused persons normally enter and leave the building without such elaborate escort service.

Who ordered it could not be learned.

Tricesta, a leader of the 'King's Road élite,' was a symphony of style for her court appearance. She wore a polonecked white shirt, black suede hot pants with matching cap and shoulder bag. These trimmings did nothing to downgrade what they were wrapped around. But her behaviour from now on must be suitable for the drawing room rather than the bedroom.

Other accounts were similar, but one was a little more outspoken:

WHY IS UNCLE SAM RUNNING ERRANDS?

You would have thought the lovely Limey was a royal princess, she could not have been more graciously received. The dolly with the Vogue look was wrapped in cotton wool.

While the mob milled around hungrily trying to get a peep at the ravishing Tricesta, government officials sneaked her up back stairs and put almost everywhere she went 'Off Limits'.

When the Judge dismissed the charge, onlookers decided something fishy must be going on. But court officials weren't talking; this was clearly only the beginning. She was treated with exceptional consideration. Everybody was unusually kind to her – the cops and the F.B.I. (who had suddenly developed a mysterious interest in the case).

Why was the charge dropped? Why was she given the red carpet treatment? Why do Scotland Yard profess no interest in a girl for whom the F.B.I. have such a great liking?

Massey White doesn't control those papers, thought Tricesta. In a fury she flung them all down the incinerator chute.

She killed time in different ways, bathing, re-varnishing her long nails and repeating on the telephone that she would not write the 'inside' story. She listened to a Soul L.P. and wished she had some grass.

Tarquin did not turn up until three in the afternoon.

'Sorry, love, but it was better to get the errands over with,' he said cheerfully. 'I've got the lot. Don't ever contemplate telling the story will you?'

'Don't be a drag,' she said softly. 'What guarantee have I got that I'll not be arrested at the airport?'

'None, my sweet, but provided you play it carefully you'll get out. Just take a few precautions. I'll go through them with you. Try the wig on.'

In the bedroom Tricesta pulled on the titian coloured, short curly wig. It was a perfect fit and suited her.

'Makes you look sexy,' observed Tarquin, 'but it destroys your icy innocent look. Still, you can whip it off at Heathrow. By the way, this block is being watched twenty-four hours a day by F. B. I. men. They want the Press to know they're doing their job; we can't do anything about them.'

Tricesta nodded and Tarquin continued:

'I've bought some boring clothes for you and you must change your make-up. You'll have to leave in a couple of hours. I'll stay on here and stall any callers. Take a couple of taxis around town – just in case. Of course you don't take any luggage.'

'Are you sure the passport's a good fake? Let me see it.'

The psuedo British document looked perfectly genuine, the photograph resembled her in disguise and the entry stamp into the U.S.A. was dated three weeks previously.

'Do you want a smoke?'

'I did,' she said, 'but not now, it would make me more nervous. I'll start to get ready.'

An hour and a half later she looked another person. Different hair, different make-up, and clothes that had gone out in the 'fifties. 'Angela Howard' was provincial and dowdy, and Tricesta felt just that.

'I'll forget I ever saw you like this,' laughed Tarquin. 'Once the plane has taken off get rid of that passport, that's bloody important. No one will recognise you, take my word for it.

Lots of luck, love. Give me a ring when you've made it.'

He gave her the first-class Pan Am air ticket and she left the flat, frightened and vulnerable. She walked two flights down the stairs and then rang for the lift.

The porter was inside when it arrived, glanced at her but certainly did not recognise her.

Outside, she soon found a taxi and asked to be driven to Grand Central Station. At the sprawling terminus Tricesta alarmed herself by imagining the uniformed police there would recognise her and guess her plan to leave the country. She knew this to be absurd but carrying a forged passport worried her.

After mingling with the crowd for some time she decided to hesitate no longer; it was now or never. If they were planning to pick her up it would make no difference how many detours she took.

'Kennedy Airport,' she told the taxi driver.

A sense of separateness enveloped her as the cab sped through Manhattan. She had been given no chance to become familiar with this vast, vital city. It had not been her fault, and one day she would return.

The driver did not stop talking but fortunately expected no reply. His chief subject concerned the graft and corruption which he said were rife in the city. All New Yorkers, he told her, knew the situation but did nothing about it and did not expect anything to be done.

After paying him off she went into the terminal and made for the loo, which was clean, bright and busy. Her reflection in the glass was thankfully unfamiliar to her.

At the Pan Am desk she showed her ticket and asked where she should wait. In the first-class lounge she forced herself to sit down and keep still. She buried her head in *Time* magazine and made a great effort not to look nervous, although she drank four cups of 'coffee with cream'. It was not done to ask for black or white coffee. The same rule applied to grapes – they were light or dark!

When her flight number was called she mingled with her fellow passengers and went through passport control. Once through she felt elated and light-headed but managed to settle into a comfortable first-class seat without showing any outward emotion. Tricesta hated flying and had never found a way to control her unreasonable fear. She was sweating, the wig was hot and uncomfortable, her hands were tense and damp. Had she walked into a trap? But the Governor had not double-crossed her. Take-off was on schedule. The jet roared into the air.

I've done it, she thought, and tears of relief ran down her cheeks. She kept her face to the window, her eyes shut, but the stewardess noticed and leaned over her.

'Can I get you something?' she asked sympathetically.

'No, thank you,' whispered Tricesta, 'I'm just afraid. I'll go and wash my face.'

The stewardess unfastened her seat belt and guided her to the loo.

Inside Tricesta pulled the lavatory seat down and sat on it. Impatiently she tore off the wig and shook out her hair with a sigh of relief. I'll put on my usual make-up, then I'll feel better, she thought. Her image was of great importance to her: if she knew she looked good then she felt good.

Fifteen minutes later the stewardess knocked on the door.
'Is anything the matter?' she called.

'No,' replied Tricesta, 'I'm re-doing my make-up, I won't be much longer.' She stuffed the wig into the used towel container. It occurred to her that other passengers might want to use the loo, but she was not leaving until she was satisfied with her face.

She tore up the passport as much as was possible and stuffed it down the lavatory, flushing away every piece of paper.
When she emerged she looked fresh and calm.

'I couldn't stand that new wig any longer,' explained Tricesta to the startled stewardess. 'Could I have some coffee please?'

The remainder of the flight was uneventful. The only diversion offered was the colour film which Tricesta watched without listening into the sound. She ate everything put before her. Her seating companion was an American businessman who spent the entire time reading documents and writing reports.

On landing, Tricesta was weak but overjoyed. When she reached an officer in charge of passport control she said.

'I don't know how it happened but I've lost my passport!'

'I see, Miss,' he replied coldly and beckoned to one of his colleagues. 'This young woman says she's lost her passport. Take her to the office and confirm her identity etcetera.'

The people behind her in the queue stared curiously after her as she followed the official to a large office.

'Sit down,' said the middle-aged, bespectacled man. 'Are you a British subject?'

'Yes I am. In order to help speed this up, can I ring a member of my family?'

'Yes, if he can help prove your identity.'

Scarcely able to control her delight she dialled C.B.'s number and he answered.

'It's me!' she said, rather unnecesssarily. 'I'm in a spot of bother.'

'Oh Christ,' he moaned, 'what now? Have they brought a new charge against you?'

'Not yet,' she laughed. 'I'm at London Airport, I've lost my passport and can't prove who I am. Will you come over at once with Benson?'

'You're in London! I don't . . . Okay, say no more, I'm on my way.'

'One more thing, bring me a decent skirt and shirt, I'm dressed in Mary Poppin's leftovers!'

C.B. rang off and immediately telephoned their solicitor, Benson.

Tricesta gave the immigration officer her name and other details. He wrote them down steadily, asked a few elementary questions and ordered a cup of tea for her. Then he disappeared for half an hour. She flipped through an out-of-date *Playboy* and *The Field*. Eventually he returned with a plump cheerful man who declared himself to be a Home Office official.

'We've spoken to your mother and father,' he said, 'There's no problem there. I understand someone is coming over with your birth certificate.'

'Yes,' replied Tricesta. 'I'm sorry about all the trouble I'm causing. My brother and solicitor will be here soon. Are there any other problems?'

The door opened and the Home Office man was joined by a thin, dry-looking man.

'Not really,' smiled the first man, 'but your unexpected arrival here has leaked out. I'm afraid the Press are turning up in force, it's rather like a Jagger arrival.' He seemed quite amused by the situation but his companion, who scowled at Tricesta, was another matter.

'How did you manage to leave the States?' he asked.

'I just flew away, man!' she joked, imitating Edward X. This did not go down well. She refused to answer his questions,

49

which she knew were being asked on behalf of the now furious F.B.I.

The telephone rang and was answered by the immigration man. 'Good, bring them to my office please.' He replaced the handpiece. 'Your brother is here, Miss St Regis.'

Charles Bodley St Regis, looking younger than his twenty-four years, was shown in, followed by Benson.

Like his sister he was tall and slim with blonde hair. His face was almost too perfect, with small neat features; his lips were full. He would have made a beautiful girl but Tricesta could vouch he was all-male.

'Fantastic! fantastic!' he repeated between kisses and embraces. 'I've brought you some gear. Most of Fleet Steet is waiting outside, how about a see-through?'

'No!' she laughed, nearly crying with joy. 'I'll be daring but demure, Grandfather will see these photographs. Mr Benson,' she said to the lawyer, 'will you please prove that I'm me?'

The lawyer and C.B. went over to the desk with the officials, C.B.'s clothes were, to put it mildly, astonishing: *eau de nil* silk shirt, tight white pants and sandals, the tops of which were finely interwoven pieces of soft gold leather. The effect was most unusual.

Around his neck he wore an antique pectoral gold and jewelled cross. It was made in the Italian High Renaissance period and C.B. had acquired it in Rome. He was the target for bitter criticism from Roman Catholics for wearing it, but as he said to them: 'It's not my fault if you're hung up on symbolic paraphernalia. It's just a beautiful object of decoration to me. My conscience doesn't tell me I'm committing a sin by wearing it, and believe me, I've got quite a conscience.'

Tricesta took off the dreary-looking dress she was wearing; suddenly the Home Office man noticed.

'Miss St Regis!' exclaimed the little man. 'You can't strip in this office, it's most improper!'

They all turned to look at her, her upper half was bare.

'I'm not setting foot outside unless I'm wearing my own gear. Don't look if it upsets you.'

'Really, have you no sense of occasion?' the pompous little man said.

'Oh, leave her,' said his more human colleague. 'Just tell yourself it's your daughter!'

'If my daughter did that I'd – I'd kick her out of my house!'

C.B. was smiling and winked at Tricesta who was getting into a black mini.

'Her brother is here!' said the dry man accusingly.

'Don't worry,' called Tricesta, 'we often have a bath together, we don't mind seeing each other!'

'It's unbelievable,' he muttered, glaring at the others for support, but they were too busy with the documents to worry about his indignation.

When she was satisfied with her appearance she called C.B. to her.

'I'm not going to talk to the Press,' she said, 'They'll only twist what I say. Do I look all right?'

'You look groovy,' he said, 'I can't believe you're really back. You're a witch!'

'That's all in order,' said Benson. 'We've established your identity. Now we can leave. I wouldn't say anything to those reporters,' he warned Tricesta.

She shook hands with the officials, again apologised for any inconvenience and left the office feeling on top of the world.

'I'll bet the officials here leaked the news about my arrival,' said Tricesta.

'That's for sure,' replied C.B. 'Look out, here they come!'

The full force of Fleet Street rushed towards them, sweeping other member of the public out of the way. Cameras clicked and bulbs flashed.

'How did you escape from America?'

'How were you able to fool the F.B.I.?'

'Will you return to the States?'

'I can't comment on any of your questions, I'm sorry,' Tricesta said as the trio pushed ahead, but the barrage continued, they did not give up.

C.B.'s beige Aston Martin was parked outside the building. Tricesta climbed provocatively into the back seat, the photographers made the most of her bending backside. The silent solicitor sat in front with C.B. who drove quickly through the tunnel and on to the M4.

'Thank God that's over,' sighed Tricesta. 'I will tell you everything when we get home, I don't feel like talking now.' Actually she did not want Benson to know the full truth of how she had contrived her escape.

The drive to the King's Road was without incident, C.B. pulled up in front of the shop with its vast expanse of glass window which went from the first floor to the pavement. Above, on a black marble background, was their name in gold letters, 'ST REGIS.' Through the window could be seen fine examples of English period furniture and modern sculpture. C.B. was becoming well known for his use of unorthodox materials.

'I'll pick up my own car,' said Benson. 'Congratulations on getting back, however you did it!' he went on. 'Ring me if there are any problems. I suggest you go and see your grandfather, he'll need careful handling.'

Benson said goodbye and walked over to his white Rover 2000.

'Just the car for him,' commented C.B. 'Come on, you must feel a wreck.'

They entered through the side door and went up to their flat above the showrooms.

'I just feel numb,' Tricesta said, 'it hasn't hit me yet. I was terrified. Make some coffee and I'll tell you about it, switch the blower on to "automatic answer" otherwise we'll be driven mad by the Press.'

He made breakfast, she switched on their powerful sound system. Music by the late Jim Hendrix throbbed through the room.

'We're getting back to normal,' he laughed, putting the tray on the low malachite-topped table. 'After your arrest music was my only comfort. I played the records you would have played. Now tell me all about it. Did you really have pumpage with a State Governor?'

'That's the only reason I'm here now!' she laughed.

Two hours and two pots of coffee later, she flung herself into his arms.

'So there it is, it wasn't Edward X's fault, it's messed up all his plans. It was so bloody unfair. If I'd been up to some villainy I wouldn't have minded so much.' C.B. kissed her mouth tenderly for a long time. Then the tenderness turned to urgent passion. She gasped for breath and pushed him gently from her.

'Not now, not now,' she repeated. 'As Mick sings – "Time is on our side". I shall not feel relaxed until I have placated Grandfather.'

He held her closely, words between them were unnecessary.

'I'm going to have a bath and change,' she said. 'Then I'll drive down to Westingshire, might as well face him now as later. Put the telephone on again. You stay here, it will be better for me to go alone. How is Helen shaping up?'

'Quite well, she almost tries too hard, you know the type, anyway we'll see. The two "boyfriends" are great, they open at nine-thirty without fail and really get it all put together. Let's hope they never have a row! Here take one of these,' he gave her a white capsule, 'I nicked a few from Father's cabinet. They're new and really incredible. I heard him telling old Doctor Dawe about them and they don't give you the shakes.'

They both took one of the capsules, not having a clue what was in them. The effect was all that mattered. C.B. went down to the shop while Tricesta dressed herself. She put on a simple white cotton dress, only three inches above her knees. She added knee-length white socks and brushed her hair to look like Alice in Wonderland. She looked totally innocent and about sixteen. The right image for old Midas, she decided.

On her way out she greeted the others in the shop. 'Is my car in the usual place?' she asked. Her brother said it was and that he would walk round the corner with her.

The King's Road action was in full swing. It reflected the best and the worst of young taste. An intriguing mixture of vivid beauty and vulgar exhibitionism. The regular crowd was interspersed with tourists and thrill seekers. They feasted their starved senses on the goods freely displayed. Dreamed of touching but knew they never could. If old age was not the bar then a conformist unbringing was. They had to be satisfied with sensual fantasies and wishful thinking. People like C.B. and Tricesta had no need to fantasise, they had no hang-ups with their bodies. Sexual self expression was a part of their life, automatically accepted. They needed no titillation, no pseudo stimulation. But the onlookers went home nursing their erections, hurried for cover and masturbated, feeling guilty.

'Help me put the hood down,' said Tricesta, climbing into her bronze E-type.

'Good luck with Grandpa,' C.B. said. 'I would like to come with you but, as you say, it wouldn't help. It's a pity he's so intolerant. Drive carefully, angel,' He kissed his sister on the forehead. She roared spectacularly up the King's Road, acutely aware of the sensation she caused in her favourite toy. Rock music blared from her stereo cassette speakers, she began to feel better. The sun shone and Tricesta felt she was coming out of the darkness.

Two and a half hours later she turned into the long drive of Castle Mordaunt. Dating from the thirteenth century and elaborately added to throughout the centuries it was architecturally the most important house in Westingshire. She drove through the wrought-iron gates which swung on pillars upon which a pair of huge stone griffons.

After parking in the outer court Tricesta walked through the open doorway into the colonnaded forecourt. As she went up the wide, shallow steps of the west entrance, she could detect no sign of life through the windows which were heavily draped with white scalloped curtains.

Tricesta opened the door and walked quickly through into the great hall where she bumped into Purdy.

'Hello,' smiled Tricesta at the thin virginal woman, 'is Grandfather about?'

'Yes, he's up in the library. I'm glad you're back, Miss Tricesta. Come with me.' Her taut face showed no expression. She had worked for Lord Prestigne since leaving commercial college and showed no signs of ever leaving, not that anyone wanted her to do so. She kept herself to herself and never made mistakes. She was an enigma to everyone, secretive and shy.

Tricesta followed her up the famous walnut staircase which was probably by Wren. Purdy opened the double doors of the library and said loudly: 'Miss Tricesta is here,' and closed the library doors behind Tricesta.

The Lord Lieutenant stood erect in front of one of the bookcases, a gold-rimmed eyeglass in his left eye.

'Well!' he said, closing a volume of Hume's *History of England.* 'So you've managed to find time to come and see me.'

Christ, this is going to give me the horrors, she thought, walking towards the old boy. Why must he be so difficult, so inhuman?

'I'm sorry about the fuss, Grandpa'. She kissed him on both dry cheeks. 'There really is a good explanation . . . '

He looked as fit as usual, he still reminded her of a slim Charles Laughton. He let his eyeglass fall from his eye, lit a cigar and sat heavily in a high-backed walnut chair.

'You think I'm a fool, a mean old tyrant, don't you?' he said. She sat down quickly.

'Of course not, we all love you.' She nearly choked on her words thinking how insincere they must sound. He reached for a newspaper and threw it at her, she groaned and opened it. The *Express* had used one of the New York pictures of her leaving the Precinct, her clothes left little to the imagination. She automatically glanced down at her demure dress. So it's a blasting about my gear first, she thought.

'Why am I never allowed to see you in a mini-skirt?' he demanded. Tricesta was thrown off balance, for a second she thought she had detected a hurt note in his voice, but no, she must have been mistaken. He went on:

'Why do you wear skirts down to you ankles when you come down here? Do you think I'm an insensitive old fossil? Do you think I don't like youth and beauty? Why do you hide yourself from me?'

She was astonished, he had never spoken like this before. She was lost for a reply. He said:

'I know exactly what happened in New York, oh yes, I don't live in the dark ages, you know. The moment I heard there was something wrong I rang a contact over there and had three top private detectives find out what was going on. I was kept informed of developments every three hours. So you don't have to dream up a carefully censored version for me! I know you were framed. I'm delighted you had the guts to do something off your own bat and get out. I'm bloody proud of you!'

She stared at him in disbelief, was this really the old autocrat speaking? And was he smiling?

'Thank God you've got some spirit, now I know you've got my blood in you. I'm more proud of you now than I've ever been!' He spoke with sincerity. She was still unable to understand his unusual behaviour, he seemed almost human!

'I never thought you could make me feel like this,' he said, his leathery cheeks beginning to gain colour. 'Tricesta, I've never shown you a picture of your grandmother, now I'm going to. You are the living image of her. She was the only woman I ever loved.'

He stood up and walked slowly to his bureau. Tricesta sensed she was about to see a side of him no one else had ever seen before; she was bewildered. She looked at the exquisite little picture when he handed it to her; it was of a beautiful girl of about twenty, her neat breasts were naked, her blonde hair framed her lovely face.

'Why it's . . . ' gasped Tricesta. 'It could be me! it's incredible!'

She looked at the old man as she handed the picture back and felt a pang of sadness. Tears were filling his eyes, tears she thought he could never cry. He sat down again, holding the miniature.

'Your grandmother Henrietta was an American heiress. We married when we were very young because we fell deeply in love. We were to have had a belated honeymoon after she had visited her family in Philadelphia. My father agreed to accompany her there as she wanted to see her parents and show off your mother, who was three months old. They went on the Titanic, its maiden voyage. I couldn't go, I was just setting up the property company. I was working very hard. As you probably know the Titanic hit an iceberg and was sunk. I not only lost my father but my wife of twelve months. But your mother was miraculously saved by the nanny.' Tears wet his cheeks.

'I inherited his title and her fortune. I vowed to honour her memory and maintain the estate the way she would have wanted it. Every bit of strength I possessed went into making the business what it is. I have never since touched another woman, the only one I wanted was taken from me.'

He made no attempt to conceal his grief.

'I've never told anyone this before,' he said, looking at her. 'You would have loved her as I did. You look so like her, I couldn't help telling you . . . .' he buried his face in a hand-kerchief.

Tricesta, nearly in tears herself pulled off her dress. She posed herself in a chair, simulating the position of her grandmother.

'Look at me, Grandpa,' she said gently. 'Do I look like her?'

Lord Prestigne, his eyes damp, looked up at his grand-daughter and he saw his wife Henrietta.

'You are her, it's true, nothing is different.'

He stared at her slender body. He looked from the picture of his wife to the girl and saw the same image. Tricesta left her chair and knelt on a stool in front of him. She clasped his hands which still held the miniature.

'Thank God my daughter Anne was spared to give birth to you,' he murmured. 'I hope you live life the way Henrietta lived it, with honesty and without hypocrisy.'

They remained holding each other for a long time.

Tricesta knew she had helped him, from now on they could communicate with one another.

She put on her dress and went to help him to his feet.

'I haven't felt so happy for more years than I care to re-member,' he said. 'Please don't ever speak of this to anyone. Let them keep thinking my feelings were lost in making millions.'

'This is our secret, Grandpa.' She kissed his forehead. 'Thank you for telling me about Grandma, I always wondered. I'm sorry I behaved so stupidly with you, it will never happen again, you'll see me in the very latest gear!'

She felt close to him, suddenly his money was not important any more, she had made a real friend, a most unexpected friend and she felt great.

For as long as she could remember Tricesta had thought and schemed of what she would do when she and C.B. eventually inherited their grandfather's considerable fortune. The only reason she had pandered to what she thought were his Victorian standards was the fear that he might revoke his will.

Only death could prevent C.B. from eventually becoming the Earl of Prestigne but that had counted for little compared with the millions, the millions Lord Prestigne had made because his great love had died so tragically. But for this personal catastrophe he would never have made so dramatic an impact upon the business world. All his thoughts and strength had been poured into his work. Now Tricesta wiped the fortune from her mind, it no longer bothered her.

It is true, she thought, still hugging the old man, one behaves towards one's fellow men in the way they deserve. Their atti-tude brings the reaction which befits them.

Originally when she and C.B. planned their venture they had discussed the possibility of asking their grandfather to finance them. But they felt, wrongly she now suspected, that he would not lift a finger to help them. He had virtually made it alone, he would expect them to do the same.

They had needed at least £100,000 to get them off the ground, at the level they wanted. Their parents did not possess that sort of money, but their father's twin brother Eric did. Unfortu-nately he was just about the meanest man in England. His meanness was legendary. He was a most successful antique dealer, specialising in English and French period furniture, a well-known personality in Sothebys and Christies and other London salerooms.

Tricesta knew the only chance they stood was to prise the capital out of Uncle Eric. C.B. had laughed with scorn when she had suggested it.

'Do you know, a man once committed suicide because of his meanness?' he had said. 'Father told me about it. It happened when Father was a penniless medical student and Uncle Eric was a successful young antique dealer. A fellow student, a friend of Father's, was desperate to put his hands on ten pounds, something to do with his girlfriend but neither Father nor any of the other students could help. Father suggested Eric would lend him the tenner, he could afford it. The boy broached Eric but Eric's reply was: "If I kept dispensing charity I'd never be in the position to be able to do so. Go and earn the money, I've had to!"

'The poor chap was desperate, at breaking point and our dear uncle pushed him over the top. An hour later the student had blown his brains out with a shot gun.

'Uncle Eric would never admit he could have saved him. Father has never stopped blaming himself, that's why he's such an easy touch today. He's never forgotten.'

Tricesta was not put off, she was in a most powerful position, she could force Uncle Eric to put up the money if he became difficult.

Not many months later Tricesta herself was to be on the receiving end of similar pressure.

Chapter 4

ON THE RETURN drive to London the following day Tricesta reflected on how she had come to be in her present position of power with her mean uncle. The beginning had been so innocent, she had been fourteen at the time. The St Regis's home was a charming period house in Bath's famous Royal Crescent.

Uncle Eric was spending the weekend with the family and on this particular Saturday her parents and brother had gone to the Bath races. Tricesta had little interest in racehorses and Eric was too stingy to risk losing a couple of pounds on the tote! As they were left alone in the house except for the servants, Tricesta took the opportunity to ask him about Angelica Kauffman's work with the Brothers Adam. Eric was always willing to get on his hobby horse and display his vast knowledge of antiques.

The twin brothers, Eric and John, were born into an upper middle class home and had to make their mark in the world by their own efforts. John put himself through medical school and

Eric when he left public school became personal assistant to a well-known London antique dealer. Emotionally and artistically the twins were opposites. Lord Prestigne was not sold on either of them, he mistrusted the medical profession and referred to Eric as 'that furniture dealer fellow'.

On certain occasions they were grudgingly invited to Castle Mordaunt; for Christmas, Easter and the like. Uncle Eric invariably tried to buy some pieces from the Earl, which always resulted in an argument. John spent the entire playing croquet or backgammon with the local GP. His wife Anne took her painting gear with her and continued in her recluse-like way. Family communication with Lord Prestigne was nil. Tricesta and C.B. kept their secret supply of grass and other soft drugs at the castle; the Lord Lieutenant of the County was hardly likely to be busted!

They would wander off into the formal garden, conceal themselves among the topiary, roll a joint, and plot how when they inherited the estate they would run it.

Returning to the St Regis day at the races, the fourteen year old Tricesta discussed various aspects of art with her uncle.

It struck her that he looked rather like a younger version of Harold Macmillan, not that she mentioned it to him.

'I must say the young people of today have an easy time,' he said after a long discourse on how hard he had worked to acquire his knowledge. 'Look at the freedom you have, even at school.'

'I know, it's an exceptional school,' she replied stretching her long legs, 'but just because you once saw us all in the nude at the pool doesn't mean we have it off left, right and centre!'

'I didn't suggest that it did,' he smiled, 'but the opportunities are certainly there . . . . '

'Frankly uncle, I'm too busy studying to try anything. There's so much of interest going on. Although we're never pushed, we work, we want to learn. Some try it out, I know, and to be honest I often wonder what it's all about but I leave it there.'

She was unaware of her fully-developed body and vaguely thought she was above such trivial pleasures!

Tricesta pulled at her fringe: 'I suppose there must be something in it,' she said, 'but I doubt whether it merits all the fuss made of it.'

'You sound like your pompous grandfather,' he laughed,

'you're in for a surprise one day, take it from me – it merits the fuss.'

'Perhaps so,' she sighed in confusion. 'What really puts me off is the thought of getting pregnant.'

'Ah, now you're being more honest,' he said lighting a cigarette, 'but of course there are plenty of precautions one can take, that's no problem these days.'

'But I understand it's painful,' she said, unconsciously lowering her mental defences. 'I couldn't stand any pain, I'd rather never do it than be hurt!'

'Again that's not necessarily true, it depends with whom you do it. If you choose a crude roughneck for your first lover, one who just wants to satisfy himself, then you will get hurt. If you start with someone with understanding and patience, then you'll want more and more.'

'Maybe,' she nodded, 'but none of my friends have that sort of patience or experience. I'll forget it and keep studying. I'm not likely to meet a man with those high qualifications . . . '

'Except the one you're talking to now.' The words slipped out before he could prevent them. Startled they both stared at each other. Suddenly their conversation had assumed a new meaning. A negative chat had become a positive proposition.

'I never thought of you like that,' Tricesta gasped in surprise. 'I'm shattered, but' – she hesitated – 'I might try it if you promised me I would not feel any pain or get pregnant. I must admit I'd like to know what I'm missing, what it's really all about.'

Eric saw her freshness with new eyes, a shock of fear and excitement ran through him. 'Why not?' he argued with himself. 'It's better than her experimenting with some yob. I'll be helping her, she's obviously ready to find out, whatever she says. No one will ever know. God, she's beautiful, why shouldn't I have her?'

The battle with himself fought and won, he moved close to her, took her small white hand and said: 'I give you my word you'll only feel pleasure, I would never hurt you or do anything you don't like. This will be our secret.' He did not point out it was against the law. Tricesta was naïve in many respects but was eager to explore the unknown in a safe and easy way.

'But I haven't a clue what to do,' she said blushing, feeling the warmth of his body. Uncle Eric put his left arm around her and held her tightly, gently he put his right hand on her breast.

'I know, but you'll soon learn. Just relax.'

Her first reaction had been to stiffen, no one had ever touched her before.

Gradually she lost her tenseness and squirmed from the new sensation as Eric transferred his hand to her thigh.

'Actually,' she said breathlessly, 'I think I might get to like this! Let's go up to my room, we'd be safer there.'

She bounded up the stairs and flung herself on to the bed.

Uncle Eric locked the door, loosened his tie, and pulled up her skirt. She wore no panties, she never did.

Eric gasped. Tricesta was embarrassed and covered her face with a pillow but eventually allowed him to kiss her.

He coaxed her to a height of bliss she had not dreamed possible.

Almost unconsciously she pulled off her dress, leaving her soft body naked.

Eric touched each small pink nipple, they became hard and more pink. Tricesta still felt shy and a little embarrassed about enjoying everything so much, but she made no attempt to pull away.

How can such a mean, middle-aged man make these beautiful feelings in me? she wondered. He's not even attractive.

But Uncle Eric knew exactly what he was doing.

Her lithe body writhed and twisted uncontrollably, until suddenly in a frenzy of delight she cried out and squirmed away, she could bear no more. She rolled on to her stomach and clutched the pillow.

'Uncle Eric,' she whispered, 'no one ever told me it was like that. It was wonderful but was I awful?'

Eric laughed softly.

'You were perfect, just perfect. Don't ever listen to anyone who tells you sex is wrong. If anyone does, you will find that they are either a hypocrite or a pervert. You are very beautiful, I'm sure you know that.'

Tricesta blushed and bit her lip.

'I wish I could do something nice to you,' she said with sincerity.

Her schoolgirl blasé manner had disappeared, she felt no need now to put up a barrier of false confidence, based on fear of the unknown.

'The trouble is I still don't know what to do . . .' she finished apologetically.

'Just use your imagination,' Eric said.

Ten minutes later she lay back relaxed, she felt proud of herself. As Eric's passion subsided she kissed his neat moustache, which until then she had loathed.

'I hope that was all right,' she smiled, 'I really do want to learn. You must teach me everything but please be patient with me, and you mustn't ever cause me any pain, that might finish things.'

'As I said before, I'll never do that, and I will teach you everything, sweetie,' he said breathing heavily. 'You will never regret it. Tomorrow I'll buy you a month's supply of birth pills. Follow the instructions carefully, I think you have to wait until the end of the curse before taking them, nothing can go wrong then.'

'But that means at least two weeks,' she said with disappointment, 'what a drag!'

He laughed and stroked her narrow hips. 'Of course starting your sexual life with a man of my understanding and experience may spoil things for you in some ways.'

'I don't follow you.'

'What I mean is,' explained Eric, 'a man of my age usually thinks of pleasing the girl and he has learned countless ways to do this. A younger man would not take the trouble, he would only want self-gratification. I will do everything possible to give you pleasure, that in itself will give me great satisfaction.'

'I see,' she nodded. 'Anyway get the pills quickly. Are they expensive?' she asked remembering his incredible meanness.

'No', he replied. 'When you start them give them a few days to take effect then see what you feel like doing.'

'Oh, I'll want to do it? As long as there's no pain.'

'Why is it so firmly in your mind that it is painful?'

'Because I heard a girl at school talking about it.' Tricesta had lost all her shyness. 'She said the man was so big he nearly killed her. She said it was agonising and she was covered in blood and it hurt for days. She said the pain was brutal. I felt put off and quite sick at the thought of it.'

'Forget all that,' said Eric, 'she must have chosen an animal.'

'He was a Nigerian student,' she said.

'Oh well,' scoffed Eric, 'there's your answer. A nigger, a native brute! Probably the first white girl he'd ever had. I hope you'll never let a black touch you. I couldn't take that, it's not right. Don't try experimenting with anyone at school either,' he said, a note of jealousy creeping into his voice, 'keep your aloofness, it usually pays off.'

Uncle Eric was terrified that others might discover his prize. He wanted the sole rights to this virginal property.

When they left the bedroom they unconsciously assumed their usual uncle and niece relationship.

Tricesta was thrilled with her new experience, she felt she was getting the edge on the other girls of her age. She was gaining first-hand knowledge, which she felt would be of enormous value to her.

On the spur of the moment she decided to test his meanness. There were numerous stories of his selfishness, both calculated and instant.

Tricesta dashed back to the bedroom, went to her purse and hurried down to the drawing room.

'Here is a pound for the birth pills,' she said, holding out the money. Not for a second did she think he would accept it. But to her astonishment he pocketed the pound note.

'Ah! Good girl,' said Eric. 'I like to see a sense of independence. Always pay your way in life, the way I've done.'

My God, Tricesta fell into a chair, he really took it! That must surely rank as the height of meanness. One day he'll pay for doing that.

Uncle Eric did – to the tune of £100,000.

When Tricesta had been on the pill for a week she took a bus to Salisbury where her uncle had a delightful house on the Southampton Road.

'I'm still afraid,' she said sipping a bitter lemon. He lifted her legs on to the sofa and sat down stroking her thighs.

'Then we'll leave it,' he said watching her with interest.

She was amused that he had put an up-to-date selection of pop L.P.'s on the record player. He had borrowed them from one of his young apprentices when she had rung to say she would like to spend the Sunday with him.

The insistent, vibrant sounds made her move her body rhythmically. Eric began to pay small attentions to her. She closed her eyes and did not restrain him.

Having gone this far Triesta's attitude was one of determination, and she did feel very nice. Uncle Eric was indeed out to please. He took her to the edge of bliss.

'Don't stop – don't, don't, don't,' she moaned.

'You're beautiful, sweetie,' he said. 'Hold me tightly.'

Tricesta scarcely heard his words, the aggressive music and her desire were almost too much for her. She felt him pressing gently against her. She stiffened, knowing that this was the moment; the moment that had filled her mind for two weeks. She had almost reached the point of no return.

'I'll never make it,' she moaned nearly in tears, her face flushed with effort, 'I knew I'd be too tense, and too small.'

'Sweetie,' he whispered, 'what do you think we're doing now?'

'What? You mean you've done it? But it didn't hurt!' She was surprised.

'I told you it wouldn't,' he replied. 'You're no longer a virgin.' Tricesta lost her last reserves of nervousness.

'Do it properly,' she insisted. 'I'm really a woman now. Do everything.'

As the months went by they did indeed 'do everything'. Things that even her uncle had not previously attempted.

By the time Tricesta was fifteen she had learnt two things: firstly that one man would never be sufficient for her, and secondly that through sex she would be able to get what she wanted.

Throughout their association Eric's meanness persisted. Tricesta often wondered whether he was conscious of it. In a sense he gave her a great deal, a knowledge of men and how to please them. This, she knew, would be a great asset when she was let loose upon the world, after leaving school.

From her formative age she had been taught by her mother that sex was both beautiful and beneficial. Tricesta had now learned the truth of this. To her there was no such bogey as 'good or evil', except within herself. 'A man's misdeeds should affect his conscience.' Tolstoy's words were, in short, her total moral belief.

At school Tricesta could have had numerous sexual experiences but she refused. She disliked the gossip which followed these affairs. She chose to remain aloof. Her reputation inevitably became that of a 'goody goody'. This was unfair but it was no worry to Tricesta.

Uncle Eric did not know of her abstaining behaviour at school, he lived in torment. His jealous imagination tortured him; he was quite convinced she slept with all the masters and every boy over the age of twelve.

During these fits of jealousy he wrote to Tricesta. These letters were extremely erotic and highly compromising to himself.

At the time Tricesta did not realise how foolishly he had committed himself. She kept the letters because they amused her. It was unusual to have an uncle madly in love with one.

Throughout her years at school she was in constant contact with her brother C.B. But they did not develop that deep relationship that each was aware could grow. Whenever they met they communicated a feeling of mutual fascination and respect. They were both exceptionally beautiful and talented, it was inevitable that one day they would meet head on. They both knew it and perversely tried to delay the moment. Together yet separately, they went through school, The Royal College of Art and The School of Art in Rome.

When they left Italy they were well qualified and eager to make their mark in the world, but not quite sure how to set about it.

Confused and worried the pair went to stay for a weekend with their grandparent, Lord Prestigne. He received them in his usual gruff manner and demanded to know what they intended to make of their lives, now that they had finished their education. They both affirmed their desire to work hard and make money, as he had done. When he asked how they proposed doing this they retired moodily to the garden.

Dejectedly they strolled in the sunlight, down the delightful pleached alley and cradle walk till they reached the garden house.

'We might as well smoke a joint,' sighed C.B., his profile was like that of 'The Head of David'.

'That's not going to solve our problems,' said Tricesta sitting down in the cool, dark summerhouse. 'We've got to settle our future, if we don't do it now we never will.'

'I know, angel, but I'll still roll one,' he started sticking the skins together. 'All I want to do is design and furnish exciting interiors. I know I can do it really differently but I can't cope with business hang-ups. We need a large lump of bread for capital, then we can get going.'

'I agree, it's no good starting in a small way. One's got to make a big splash and carry on from there. If we put our minds to it we can be the greatest.'

Chocolate Biscuits' aesthetic appearance often made him appear effeminate but he had no homosexual tendencies. He had affairs with many beautiful girls but in all other respects he was totally reliant upon Tricesta. He possessed no business acumen and was inclined to panic when faced with making a decision by himself. C.B. did not want responsibility other than in his creative work. He depreciated his materialistic grandfather and deplored his lack of taste, although he had a sneaking respect for the old man's ability to make money. He could not see himself handling finance, yet he was hip enough to realise that without large capital he would never get his ambitious schemes off the ground.

C.B. could not visualise life without Tricesta, he knew he could not survive without her support. Like his sister he had always admired his parents but he did not love them. They had kept their distance and given over the upbringing of their children to nannies, governesses, boarding schools and Art Institutions. Neither the parents nor the children had any desire to close the gap; they were all good friends and demanded nothing deeper. But C.B. had come to idolise his sister. His fantasies of her had increased over the years until he had become obsessed with the thought of a close relationship with her. He found himself becoming insanely jealous towards any man who captured Tricesta's attention. A purely sexual encounter did not disturb him, but he knew if Tricesta was ever to turn her affection elsewhere, his emotional security would be threatened and his normally creative nature could then reverse itself into a destructive force.

C.B. passed the joint to his sister, she lit it thoughtfully and passed it back to him. They smoked quietly, each thinking of the future. She watched his hand movements. She considered C.B.'s hands were the most elegant ever: slender, with long white fingers which he posed and stretched to emphasise his words. The effect of the pot caused Tricesta to focus on them. They fascinated her.

'You're staring at me,' he said softly.

'It's because I've been smoking,' she replied quickly, 'I always get mesmerised by just one thing, don't you?'

'If I allow myself to,' he said. 'Get up for a minute, I want to have a look at your eyes.'

Puzzled she stood and faced the light, he put his hands on her shoulders. He looked into her clear green eyes, the awareness of them grew. C.B. pouted in exaggeration and shook his long hair.

'Must you imitate Mick Jagger?' she asked, trying to distract him but he continued to stare at her. Finally she smiled and said: 'So it's come at last.' He nodded and she went on: 'We both knew it would. All our lives we have been building up to this. We've both played around, experimented with this and that but we've never stopped moving towards one another.'

Slowly, anxious to appreciate the birth of their love they kissed and held each other tightly. It was all there, they both felt it. They parted and sat on the floor holding hands.

'We weren't ready before,' said Tricesta, 'we couldn't have handled it.'

'I know,' happiness reduced C.B.'s voice to a whisper, 'but we've got to be clever and careful, then we'll make it all the way.'

They rolled on to their stomachs, still holding hands.

'The point is,' said Tricesta, 'we must live and work together. The qualities I lack you have and vice versa. Together we can be a formidable combination, we could achieve almost anything. I don't believe in marriage any more than you, and as that is impossible between us, that makes it just fine. I have never met anyone with whom I would rather share my life. Have you?'

'No,' he replied, 'we're both grown up enough to know what we want. Neither of us is jealous, if we dig someone else then we'll have them but I don't see myself doing much of that. I must work but how do we start and where do we get the capital?'

'Not from Grandpa, that's for sure!' she said aggressively. 'The mean old so-and-so doesn't realise how hard it is to get started today. I will have to think of something. Let's face it, you'll never be a schemer or an organiser you're always either up in the clouds or down in the dirt. You'll never handle that scene.'

'I know I won't,' he laughed, 'but if you can set it up, my talent will make it grow. I mustn't be distracted from creating or I'll never keep at it. I've got some great ideas but I must be given the right environment. Of course, you're a pretty good designer yourself.'

'I'm not in your genius class,' she said. 'I have taste and knowledge but I'm not particularly creative. It's up to me to put it all together, then train someone to run the business side, that part would bore me to tears. We've got to promote a progressive and modern image, not only in our work but in ourselves as well. We will have to project our mood into our work.' She stopped for breath and gave the matter thought.

'The King's Road is the right setting for us,' she continued, 'an expensive, super-attractive place. A combination of the antique and the new.'

They became wildly enthusiastic about the plan; they could see it all, they had the taste, the knowledge and the ability but not the money. Their ideas grew, they talked for two hours and what emerged was an immovable determination to make it.

'But who's going to back us?' asked C.B., half way down on earth. 'I can't create from a stall in a market. What are we going to do?'

'Get the bread,' she replied with assurance. 'Within the week I'll have a hundred thousand pounds!'

'Oh angel,' laughed her brother. 'I know you're fantastic but I think you're still stoned, or you've tripped out! What do you propose we do? Rob the old boy?'

'Stop talking rubbish!' she said. 'I'm serious. Uncle Eric has the money and I'll get it.'

'Now you've definitely flipped! Uncle Eric wouldn't give a starving man a crust, you know that.'

'But he'll give it to me, not willingly I admit, but the result will be the same.'

'Why the hell should he? Give me one good reason.'

'Because he won't want to spend the next five years in the nick.'

'The nick?' he repeated. 'But he's never broken the law in his life, he'd never do anything that's forbidden. But I admit he'd never do anything right either. What are you going on about?'

'Uncle Eric has been pumping me since I was fourteen!'

'That old misery? I don't believe it!' C.B. was for once truly astonished.

'It's true and I've got letters to prove it. He de-virginised me, our relationship was pretty interesting. It continued until I went to Rome, he's mad about me. I'll get a real kick out of making him pay up. Imagine, I used to give him a pound **every** month for the pill.'

'That's as mean as anyone can get.' C.B. laughed. 'Anyway it'll be an investment for him, he'll get his money back gradually, and we will pay him a good rate of interest. I know we'll be a big success but the first two years will be tough.'

He leant over and kissed her.

'You clever bitch, everyone at school thought you were square! I'm really proud of you, we're lucky to have found each other, it could easily have gone wrong. It needed courage to face the truth. I always knew I loved you, unconsciously I always compared you with other chicks. None of them ever came near you, you are way out on your own. Don't ever let anything mess us up.'

'Never!' she said emphatically. 'If we have any hang-ups we must talk about them honestly, we must never allow ourselves to be diverted from what we know to be right. Physically I haven't much strength but mentally I'm nearly unbreakable. You are a romantic and artistic, don't try to change that. I can cope with the practical side.'

This then was the basis for their unique relationship.

That night nothing could part them. Behind Tricesta's locked door they found happiness beyond description. They had come to terms with what they wanted, each other.

At breakfast the next morning they were particularly polite to their grandfather.

'I hope you two have now given careful thought to your future,' he said, filleting his fried kipper meticulously.

'We've made our plans, Grandpa,' said Tricesta sweetly, 'we'll not disappoint you. We're going to open a fabulous shop in the King's Road. It is going to be outstanding. We will de-sign interiors and sell expensive antiques to put in them.'

'And who will finance this ambitious project?' he demanded. 'Have you given that any thought?'

'Oh yes,' she replied with gentle confidence, 'we have found someone who recognises and believes in our talent. And he is only too delighted to back us, and there will be plenty of others if we want them.'

'Well, I'm not one of those,' said Lord Prestigne, convinced they were working up to the 'grand touch'. He called to Corbett to serve him with his kidneys on toast.

'We know that, Grandpa,' she said with a smile, 'we would not dream of asking you. We want to make it without your money and influence. We've virtually raised the £100,000 which we need to get started!'

Lord Prestigne was taken aback and felt a pang of guilt, perhaps he had misjudged them. But his nature would not allow him to relent, he merely said: 'Let's hope you don't let anyone down, a hundred thousand isn't peanuts. Don't make rash decisions. Justify the confidence this man has put in you. Haven't you got anything to say, Charles?' He always used C.B.'s correct name.

C.B. fluttered his hands expressively towards his sister:

'Tricesta has said it all, sir,' he replied. 'I just want to be allowed to work in my own way. I can't take anyone telling me what to do. I must be free to create. If I'm allowed a free hand we'll succeed.'

'Never did understand your wishy-washy attitude,' grumbled his grandfather, 'you get it from my dotty daughter I suppose. So your sister's the business brain and you're the creative genius? Well, as I said, don't get carried away by your so-called "artistic temperament", it's no excuse for inefficiency.'

On that note they took their leave. Lord Prestigne trudged off to his study-cum-office, he still kept up an active interest in his property companies. His two grandchildren collected another packet of grass from their secret hiding place and returned to Bath.

Their father had recently been knighted for his services to medicine and was at a medical conference in the north. Their mother had gone to Venice to help set up The British Pavilion at the Biennale. Although she was fifty-nine she looked only forty. This she attributed to leading a happy and active sexual life. She had implanted in her daughter the importance of sex, and her belief in the superiority of the female. Equal rights for women were not for her! Lady Anne knew which sex really held the power. She could not understand why so many women failed to control and influence their husbands and force them to achieve great things. Had she not encouraged and guided her husband, he would have remained a mediocre surgeon. She had believed in his talent and had forced him to exploit it.

Tricesta collected all the incriminating letters Uncle Eric had written. The most damning were the ones he had sent her when

71

she was in Rome. The twelve-month separation had almost un-balanced him. His infatuation for her had grown over the years and she could now do virtually anything she wished with him; with one exception, she could not change his mean nature. She would have to use pressure to do that.

On the day she went to see him she dressed more pro-vocatively than usual. She painted her nipples red and the surrounding area dark brown. The effect through the near transparent pale blue micro-dress was intriguing and tantalis-ing. Over flesh-coloured tights she wore knee-length white socks and nothing else.

'You look really cool,' said C.B. approvingly. 'Good thing I'm not jealous, you certainly turn me on! Tell me all the details when you get back.'

'I hope to do more than that,' she said. 'I have every intention of bringing back that large slice of bread we need.' He kissed her.

'You know, angel, metaphorically speaking, all my life I've been a wanker, now I'm going in there to have a bloody good fuck! I have to make a move now or I'll be left in the starting stalls; you know what I mean, don't you?' She did.

Tricesta took her mother's 1100 and drove rapidly to Salis-bury. Although nervous she was confident she was doing the right thing.

Uncle Eric had not seen her for a long time; when she was shown into his drawing room at teatime he was shaken.

'Tricesta!' he grabbed her clumsily, 'why didn't you let me know you were coming? I've missed you, let me see you.'

He held her away and stared at her, his eyes seemed riveted upon her.

'You look different,' he said.

'I'm a year older,' she replied, her nervousness gone now that she was face to face with him.

'Have a drink,' he said.

'No, I still don't drink. I've come to see you on business.'

The vodka and tonic in his hand did not reach his lips.

'Business? Oh, I see, you're getting a job – you need a refer-ence.'

'Not quite,' she said, switching the old-fashioned radio-gramophone on but quickly turning it off again, Strauss waltzes were not her speed. Tricesta twiddled the knobs and tuned

72

into a pop music radio station. She hoisted herself on to a Chippendale commode and watched him finish his drink. The drawing room contained some fine antiques but the overall atmosphere was dreary and dark brown. Although he possessed great knowledge of furniture he had no sense of presentation or decoration.

Eric St Regis was not a showman. He was strictly a dealer in antique furniture with a vast knowledge of his subject. His incredible meanness prevented him from living in a style which he could well afford. Although he was a sad, introverted character his pompous manner warded off any sympathy one might feel towards him. His self-sufficiency and avaricious nature were totally opposite to his twin brother, John, who always showed considerable consideration and tolerance of others. Eric was automatically opposed to anything in which he was not involved. He would resentfully find fault with any new or fresh ideas. Knocking the younger generation, especially those in the world of art, was his speciality, particularly those with a nonconformist approach.

'How can I advise you, Tricesta sweetie?' he asked, sitting on the sofa and looking at her thighs.

'C.B. and I are going to open the most super showrooms in the King's Road,' she said slowly, still holding her handbag which contained the letters, 'the theme will be progressive and expensive . . . ' She explained their ideas to him. His mind was still on her thighs. He had another drink and said:

'Sounds quite good, you couldn't go into a better business. I've just opened a new shop in Cheltenham, I've got eight showrooms in England now and one in Paris. Good luck to you both but you'll find the King's Road a bit expensive I'm afraid.' His moustache twitched, he was fed up with small talk. They all get so full of themselves when they've been to art school, he thought. That year in Rome has spoilt her, she's too ambitious now. A year ago we'd have been at it within minutes, without all this chat.

'Oh, we won't . . . ,' she said.

'Won't what?' he was frowning.

'Find the King's Road expensive.' She brushed her hair aside. 'You will, uncle!'

'I will! What the devil does that mean?'

'I want you to back us, we need a hundred thousand pounds,

73

you can easily afford it . . . . '

'Don't be ridiculous, child!' he snorted, 'I wouldn't dish out that sort of money to a financial genius let alone to a pair of "arty" kids. You can rely on me for advice but that's all.'

Eric lit a cigar. Tricesta went on: 'It will be a good investment in the long run, you'll get a good return on your capital.'

'I've no intention of pursuing this stupid conversation, let's have tea and talk about something more sensible.'

'Like making love to me I suppose?' She smiled, he reddened, scratched his moustache and grinned.

'Well, why not?' he replied.

'Why not, indeed, but first we settle this "stupid conversation" as you call it. Uncle Eric, it is in your best interest to back us.'

'I can only conclude you're on dope,' he snapped, 'and must we have the bloody Beatles blasting at us?'

'It's the Stones and I enjoy their sound.'

'You can't seriously like that racket? Now listen to me, I get propositions like this every week, often from highly qualified dealers who want to expand. So give me one good reason why I should finance a pair of amateurs.'

He stood up, supposing that this would add authority to his words.

'The best reason from your point of view is that you won't have to go to prison. Is that good enough for you?'

Eric turned white.

'What nonsense are you talking now? I've done nothing wrong, I'm trying hard not to lose my temper with you!'

'Having your fourteen year old niece is breaking the law, had you forgotten? And it's illegal at any age!'

He thrust a hand into his trouser pocket and tried to look stern.

'Tricesta, you've gone too far, you'd better go home. Come and see me when you're more rational.'

'Uncle, if you don't pay up I'll have you arrested and don't think I'm fooling.' Her voice was slightly mocking but very serious. A little of his confidence slipped, small beads of sweat glistened on his forehead.

'What are you saying?' he whispered. 'Have you gone mad?'

'No, I just kept all your loving letters!'

'You bloody fool! I told you to burn them.' He watched her closely. 'Stop bluffing, I don't believe you have them.'

She pulled the wad of letters from her bag and waved them at him.

'I kept them all. I used to get a kick out of reading them. Especially when I made love to myself at the same time! You've got a rather corny turn of phrase but to the point. "Your maidenhead is the pinnacle of my pleasure." "Please I implore you, never deny me," and so on.'

Furious and confused he made a move for the letters, he lunged at her. She kicked him in the stomach, he doubled up gasping with pain.

'You bitch, how could you stoop to blackmail .... why don't you ask your precious grandfather for the money?' He fell back on to the sofa.

'Because I haven't made it with him and because it's time you signed a cheque to do someone some good. You're the meanest, most selfish man I've ever met. Everyone knows it, it's a nasty family joke. A man once took his life because you refused him help. You've been pumping me for years, you've never even bought me a dress and I've even had to buy my own pills. I'll never get over that! It'll do you good to pay out, but you'll get the bread back with interest when we can manage it. And I'm willing to bet you'll ask us to keep it because you'll be doing so well out of us. You like to be in on a good thing, don't you?' She teased him with the truth.

Eric opened his shirt, he looked terrified and broken.

'How could you do this to me?' he whined. 'Your own flesh and blood. It's not only illegal, it's immoral!'

'That's a great line coming from you. Who are you to pronounce on morality? Don't do it again, the price might go up.'

'Even if it did, it would make no difference, I haven't got £100,000 in my account,' Eric hedged.

'Uncle, please, you may not have that amount in your personal account, but you've certainly got it in your company account. I've seen you write larger cheques than that after a successful day at Sothebys. And I get their list of buyers and prices each week. Only a fortnight ago you paid more than fifty thousand pounds for one piece of French furniture alone. I know what sort of liquid capital you need to deal in your type of goods. Antique dealers don't often buy on credit.'

'Will you destroy the letters if I give you a cheque?' he asked, choking on the words.

'No,' she smiled, 'you could stop the cheque. Don't worry, I'll not double-cross you, I only want the money for the business, there is no other quick way of getting it. Calm down, you're not really in a bad position, you could be in the nick! Let me give you some advice: if you want us to do well and if you want our special "association" to continue, then help us. Give us the money and the practical advice we need. Apart from our purely artistic training, both C.B. and myself have taken courses in antiques but naturally we lack experience. It's in your interest to put your knowledge at our disposal. Apart from not wishing to waste money I'm sure you'll still enjoy making love to me.'

'I don't have a choice, do I? Ruination or co-operation. God, you're just like your grandfather, ruthless – ruthless – ruthless to the point of being unscrupulous.'

'Uncle,' she said, 'be careful what you say. Anyway I take it as a compliment being compared to Grandpa. After all he made millions before he was forty. I'll ask Doris to make tea while you make out the cheque.'

Tricesta flushed with triumph left the room, asked for tea and tidied herself.

When she returned to the gloomy drawing room Eric was sitting at the bureau. His Coutts cheque book was open in front of him. He attempted to pull himself together but his hands were shaking and his face was grey. With an effort he made out the cheque, signed his name and handed it to her.

'Thank you,' she said sweetly. 'I can't say it was given in the spirit I had hoped but thank you anyway. Your hair is sticking up, smooth it down before Doris sees you. Now don't forget, we shall need practical help from you as well.'

'You can't get more practical than that,' he snapped, pointing at the cheque. 'I suppose you've told that pretty boy brother of yours about us?'

'Yes, we don't have any secrets, but don't worry, you can trust him. And don't insinuate that he's a fag, either say it straight out or shut up. You shouldn't judge people by their appearance, his girlfriends never seem to complain! Now cheer up, as soon as this is cashed I'll come and visit you, the way I used to.'

'Do me a favour – don't.'

His pseudo bravado did not fool Tricesta. She knew he still

wanted her desperately. He'll adjust in a week, she told herself. It's the shock of not being in the position to dictate any more. At his age it must be hard to lose control. But within a few months he'll hardly notice, I'll see to that!

Chapter 5

TRICESTA DROVE BACK to Bath in a happy state of mind and gave C.B. the news.

He kissed the cheque childishly. 'Well done,' he grinned, 'pity you didn't do the same with Grandpa! That would have been worth £500,000!'

'I don't think he could have turned me on, anyway the strain might have killed him off. Now, we're ready to go. We'll see Benson tomorrow, he can set up the company. We'll get Tony's company to find us premises.'

They sat together talking for a long time, their dream was now tangible.

'At the beginning most of the stock should be bought by Uncle Eric,' said Tricesta. 'We'll tell him the type of goods we want, it's up to him to get the best, but no "old-fashioned" or "brown" antiques. One of our first problems will be staff, we must employ only the grooviest, the cleverest people. We'll need a sort of super shareable secretary, got any fantastic ideas?'

C.B. gazed thoughtfully at his long, beautifully manicured fingernails.

'All my ideas are fantastic,' he laughed.

'I know,' she kissed his fair hair, 'but they must also be practical. We want a great-looking bird who is capable of running things smoothly when we are not about. Someone who thinks we're the be all and end all!'

'It's funny you should put it like that,' said C.B. putting an L.P. of the late Janis Joplin on the deck. 'Do you remember that Rhodesian chick we met in Rome?'

'How could I forget her? We picked her up in Dave's Dive. She never took her eyes off you, said you looked like David Hemmings and Mick Jagger rolled into one. Why?'

'Well, she arrived in England two days ago, staying at some crummy hotel in Kensington, wants to know if I'll meet her.'

'Hmm, yes, Helen Williams, I think she said she was twenty-three, and been through commercial college and had a good job with a film director. But you'd never stand her hanging around you all day, she obviously fell for you. Mind you,' said Tricesta thoughtfully, 'she could be useful if we played it right, she's very attractive but what a drag, she's so colonial. I'll never forget when we first met her, she wore skirts down to her knees. Then she began to copy me and they crept up to her . . . well you remember!'

'She was fascinated with you,' said C.B., 'she not only copied your minis and hot pants, she copied your make-up, hair style, even the kind of food you ate. Anyway, I'll leave it to you, let's see her but you decide if she's for us. Just keep her off my back, make it clear you will be running the show and making the decisions.'

'Fine. She must never learn how close we are,' she took his hand, 'don't forget our relationship is illegal. There is no such thing as "Consenting Brother and Sister" in law.'

'There jolly well should be,' said her brother. 'If some dirty old bugger with a hobnail fetish can have it off with an avaricious guardsman, why can't we? Damn it all, we do do it in private.'

'Yes, usually!' said Tricesta.

'I hope we can get a shop with a flat above,' said C.B. changing the subject. 'I'd loathe the drag of commuting across London. I'm afraid officially we'll have to kip in separate bedrooms and we'll need at least one spare bedroom.'

'Fancy a joint?' asked Tricesta.

'Yes, but we'd better not. Father rang while you were out and said he'd made his speech and was splitting from the conference.'

'I'm sure he never said "splitting",' she laughed.

Half an hour later Sir John arrived home. He resembled the film-maker's concept of a famous surgeon: smooth manner, immaculate clothes and always sporting a clove carnation buttonhole. Most men liked him and he was extremely popular with mature women. Sexually he was unadventurous but tolerant about his wife Anne's escapades, the most notable of which had been her affair with her three cousins while John had been on a year's lecturing tour in the States.

Lady Anne had kept the three affairs going for six months; no one, not even she, could say which of her cousins was the father of Tricesta. There was one sure fact, her husband was not.

When she had told him about it on his return, his only reaction was to hope there would be no hereditary weakness. His concern was purely clinical.

The affair had ended abruptly when the three Prestigne boys were all killed in a plane crash. The eldest had been flying the others to Paris for a party. When the aircraft ran out of fuel they died in the English Channel, too drunk even to cling to the wreckage.

'Enjoy the conference?' asked Tricesta when the great surgeon greeted his family.

'I never enjoy conferences,' he replied, pouring himself a whisky and soda. 'I've eaten, what about you two?'

'We'll have something before kipping. We've got some great news for you,' said Tricesta.

She recounted a suitably edited version of their plans. When she had finished John said: 'I'll never understand how you got Eric to agree to back you! It's incredible – he's the last man in the world I would have expected to cough up. Well, good luck to you both, you deserve it, I never appreciated how persuasive my daughter could be.' He smiled at Tricesta. 'But then you are your mother's child, that may explain it!'

After C.B. had gone to bed Sir John said to Tricesta: 'I'm only sorry I couldn't give you the capital you needed to start you off.'

'Don't be silly, Father,' she smiled, 'but there is one favour you could do me. A repeating prescription for the pill, I can't face going to some dreary Family Planning Centre. Would you mind?'

'Of course not,' he laughed. 'Thank God you've got the sense to take proper precautions, I only wish more girls would. How did you manage in Italy?'

'There were a couple of fellows who flogged them to the students. We paid over the odds but it was worth it.'

'Did these men sell any other kind of pills?' he asked in a matter-of-fact way.

'Yes, they were regular pushers. They offered an assortment of pep pills and grass, occasionally acid and now and again coke for the more way-out freaks.'

'Hmm.' He looked at her but knew he had no reason to worry or to demand an assurance that she would never hit the hard junk. 'Thank you for telling me. I'm afraid it will always be available, where there's a demand there's always a supply. It often starts in school among the thirteen and fourteen year olds. They usually "fix" because they don't want to be rejected by their group or it's the old story of curiosity killing the cat. The school pushers are a vicious menace and no punishment can be too severe for them. I feel very upset when I think of these teenage junkies. I'm sorry to bore you, it can be of no interest to you.'

'You're not boring me and it is of interest, it's part of my scene. I do have a social conscience, you know.'

She kissed him goodnight but before going to bed rang Helen and arranged to meet her at the Sun Tavern in Belgravia.

Early the next morning she and C.B. drove up to London. Their first call was on the family solicitor – Alexander Benson of Benson and Benson. They gave him the cheque, instructed him to arrange bankers and accountants and to set up the company, to be called 'St Regis Limited.'

The next call was on the estate agents in Mayfair. They promised to act quickly and find suitable premises for them in the King's Road.

Feeling exhausted they hurried on to the renowned Sun Tavern run by Sandy O'Donnell, a larger than life Irish character who attracts the famous and the infamous, from foreign royalty to conmen, from film stars to columnists. But his customers all have one thing in common – they adore the proprietor. Sandy has a heart of gold and will help anyone in trouble but he does everything possible to pretend he is a 'toughie'. The walls of his bar are covered with bounced cheques and photographs of himself with world famous personalities.

His colourful language is made the more startling by the muted expensive district that he inhabits. But controversial behaviour is expected from him; no one is ever disappointed.

Tricesta parked the 1100 at a meter and walked with C.B. into the pub. The downstairs bar, run by Sandy's sister, was crowded, they dashed upstairs to the 'élite' department.

A slender girl with long legs was standing beside the bar.

'Helen!' called Tricesta and kissed the auburn-haired girl. 'Sorry we're late, it's great to see you!'

'It's great to be in "swinging" London,' said Helen. C.B. groaned inwardly, her voice was very loud. 'You two look fabulous, you really belong here. Have a drink with me, I insist!'

'What do you kiddies want?' shouted Sandy handling Helen's buttocks. 'Have this one with me, it's a pleasure to see some pretty people here instead of the usual poxy crowd! You poxy ponces!' He bellowed to the other customers in general, they either ignored his comment or laughed.

'Is he drunk?' whispered Helen, looking confused.

'Of course he isn't,' smiled Tricesta. 'Why should you think he was?' Helen shrugged and felt foolish. 'Let's grab a table, we can talk more easily and I'm starving.'

Polly, the cockney cook-cum-waitress mothered them and sat them in the far corner beside an open window.

Warm summer air drifted in. 'Now, dears,' said the tiny woman, 'there's roast lamb, steak and kidney pud or chicken salad – that's a bit off so have the lamb! Isn't the weather lovely, makes such a difference, anyway, that's three lambs, any soup first?'

They all shook their heads, Polly hurried to the kitchen patting her permed hair into place.

Tricesta told Helen about their proposed business. She listened intently glancing occasionally at C.B. who sat smoking and watching the curious mixture of customers. Helen enthused at every opportunity and when Tricesta had finished she said:

'Wow! That's just the sort of set-up I'd like to work with. Have you chosen anyone yet?'

'Not definitely,' replied Tricesta, unable to stomach any more of Sandy's food. 'It must be a girl who will be happy to take orders from me and she must always look good. I couldn't take a jealous bird and above all she must be capable. If we can get a place with enough rooms she must live with us.' C.B. kicked her ankle but she went on: 'It may be necessary to work at all sorts of odd hours, I wouldn't want to feel tied to a nine to fiver. Whoever I choose must also be a friend and be on my wavelength. The money will be good and expenses nil. She'll meet a lot of groovy people and be in at the start of something exciting. Hey, Polly, any chance of a cuppa?'

'I'll put the kettle on for you, dear,' winked Polly. 'Don't any of you fancy a bit of apple pie?' Again they shook their heads. Helen repainted her lips and fluffed up her already over-back-combed hair.

'I think I'm what you are looking for,' she said, 'my references are good.'

'References don't mean a thing,' said Tricesta, 'I will make up my own mind. Why did you leave Rome?'

'I got bored with the scene,' she drawled, 'everyone tried to get into bed with me, I got fed up with it. If I love a guy I'll do it, but I've got to feel something for him, don't you agree?'

'Oh yes,' smiled Tricesta, 'I'm a great believer in feeling something!' What a provincial prude she is, she thought, this could be a laugh.

'How long do you want to stay in England?' asked C.B.

'Oh, forever,' declared Helen, 'I really identify with it. But I suppose Rhodesians are not very popular over here.'

'Depends on how they behave,' said Tricesta. 'Colour prejudice doesn't have the approval of the government, nor of us as a matter of fact.'

'I've got nothing against black people,' said Helen, 'as long as they conduct themselves properly, and provided they don't bother me I don't mind what they do. Of course I can't understand how a white girl can go to bed with one. I'd have hysterics if a Negro touched me!'

Tricesta nudged C.B. in amusement, she got a kick out of exposing hypocrisy. Helen, she decided was for them.

'I'll give you a ring tonight,' said Tricesta, 'and see if you still feel the same way about the job.'

'Oh I will, darling,' she gasped. 'By the way, I want to have my hair done by the best hairdresser, who should I go to?'

It's already begun, thought C.B., she'll copy Tricesta's hair-do for sure.

'More tea, dears?' Polly bustled over to them wiping her hands on her apron.

'Yes, thank you,' nodded Tricesta. Helen had wanted coffee but did not like to say so.

'I've always been dying to ask you,' Helen smiled provocatively at C.B., 'how did you come to be called Chocolate Biscuits?'

'Because when he first made it with a girl he got carried away and shouted "It's the best thing since chocolate biscuits!" and it stuck, he was fifteen at the time,' explained Tricesta, 'his initials are C.B. anyway.'

'That's crazy,' giggled the Rhodesian girl. 'Well, thanks for lunch and please call me later.' She kissed them both, much to their irritation and rushed off to the hairdresser. Male heads turned to watch her exit, she certainly looked good in an obvious way.

On the drive back to Bath Tricesta, who was driving, said: 'I think Helen will suit us, I know she'll bore you but just treat her as a joke.'

'She's a real drag doll,' moaned C.B., his feet stuck up on the dashboard, 'I don't even find her pretty, she's bloody vulgar, but you go ahead, she might improve under your influence. If she's efficient that's marvellous, but just let me work in peace.' He closed his eyes and imagined beautiful scenes.

'The more I see of life and people,' said Tricesta, 'the more I realise everyone basically falls into one of two groups. They are either hustlers or ponces, but in the widest possible sense of the words. Take us for instance: I'm a hustler, I know where it's at and can get it together. You're a ponce . . .'

'Hey, steady on,' he said mildly, 'I also know where it's at but as I told you I can't work from a garret, I need the right environment otherwise I'll fold. It's just the way I am, put me with beauty and I'll make more beauty. Put me in dreary surroundings and I'll become morbid and do nothing.'

'I know,' she agreed, 'That's why it's so important for me to give you what you need, but however hard you work you'll still retain your basic ponce-like character, it has nothing to do with background, it's nature. Father is a ponce, Mother is a hustler, so is Grandfather. I'm sure you see what I mean.'

'Of course I do,' he squeezed the back of her neck. 'Thank

God you've been able to set the scene for me, I would never have attempted to make it alone, I admit it.' He laughed.

C.B. was more than aware of his limitations and knew he was fortunate to have a partner like his sister. He was confident that he would not disappoint her, once he was launched.

They soon obtained excellent premises on a corner half way down the King's Road almost opposite the 'Drugstore'. The flat above the showrooms had one very large living room and four bedrooms. Using marble and gold coloured metal with great effect in the decoration C.B. achieved stunning results, both in the showrooms and in their own apartments.

Helen was engaged and allocated one of the bedrooms. She worked well, did as she was told and did not commit any serious blunders. A working permit had been obtained for her through the influence of Michael Flaxman, the Q.C. Tricesta later used to put pressure on Governor White.

Tim and Jim were both twenty-seven, they were artistic, good-looking and lovers. Their hair was bleached a delicate shade of blonde and during the day they wore discreet make-up. Their clothes were expensive and of the minute. This curious pair of boys were engaged to work under C.B., whom they soon came to idolise. They shared a flat in the World's End and an equal dislike of Helen.

The highly publicised opening of the St Regis showrooms was a tremendous success. The Press party was covered enthusiastically by every National newspaper and magazine. Uncle Eric was outwardly full of criticism, he considered the overall atmosphere was hard and unfriendly. But he knew they had captured in the décor something new and exciting; something so compelling that success must follow. He almost felt he might see a return on his investment.

Tricesta had opened a small shop within the showrooms. This intriguing department sold fine period clothes, the antique 'gear' much sought after by pop stars and artistic eccentrics. The clothes were expensive but were not likely to lose their value provided they were not mishandled.

After the sensational opening C.B. received so many commissions he was forced to use subcontractors and delegate much of the work to Tim and Jim. Chocolate Biscuits was in his element and worked hard. He was approached to write a monthly article in an expensive magazine but he declined, pointing out it was not his line but suggested that Tricesta do it. She agreed, provided she was not expected to follow any set formula. The editorial management willingly gave her a free hand to express and explain the combination of the 'way out' and the 'antique' in decoration which was the aim of C.B. and herself.

She also set out to dispel many myths surrounding the antique trade and encourage young people to take an interest in the old and classical.

Helen's precise position was never clearly defined. At the beginning of their association when she was not working, she spent much time in her own room, leaving C.B. and Tricesta to talk and plan alone. But as the weeks passed and tensions relaxed, Helen joined the others in their discussions at night in the long drawing room. She wanted so much to be a part of their scene, she wanted to be accepted. But even she knew it took more than a few conversations to be 'in'.

Since arriving in London she had neither smoked, tripped nor pumped, and she made the foolish mistake of continually informing C.B. and Tricesta of her abstinence from these activities. This did nothing to endear her to them.

One weekend Tricesta visited her grandfather at Castle Mordaunt and brought back a block of hash.

The brother and sister sat on the sofa and expertly cut off small chunks, using the long marble table as a chopping block.

'What's going on?' asked Helen as she burst in wearing a short towel dressing gown, 'it all looks very mysterious.'

'Come and get turned-on,' invited C.B. sticking three Rizzla papers together.

'No, I don't go for that scene,' she said, 'there's no telling where it might lead.'

'Put that new Hendrix L.P. on,' said Tricesta, ignoring her reply.

Helen fiddled with the deck and managed to drop the head on the record. C.B. shuddered but warmed a lump of hash and crumbled it between his gloved fingers. He rolled a huge cigarette and passed it to his sister who started it off.

The throbbing music vibrated through the flat. After smoking for a few moments Tricesta passed the joint casually to Helen who pretended to be reading Tricesta's latest article. She stared at the cigarette, gave them a look which said: 'I don't approve but I'll do it to prove I'm not a drag,' and started to smoke.

They had not eaten for some hours and they soon became high. C.B. told Helen to finish the cigarette, he prepared another for himself and Tricesta.

The effect on Helen was extraordinary, she seemed unable to take her eyes off C.B. After the first few drags she made no attempt to put the joint down; she enjoyed it.

By ten o'clock they were stoned. Helen still gazed at Chocolate Biscuits who wanted Tricesta. They had spent very little time intimately together due to hard work and the fact that Helen was around. 'Why the hell can't she pull a fellow?' grumbled C.B. in a whisper to his sister.

'Do you often play with yourself, Helen?' asked Tricesta. Helen replied naturally, unable under the drug's influence to summon her usual defences.

'Yes, quite a lot,' she said and smiled at C.B., 'otherwise I'd get frustrated, but I couldn't fall into bed with any Tom, Dick or Harry.' Her glazed eyes begged C.B. who stood up and said:

'I'm starving, I must eat, let's go over the road to The Spot. Give them a ring, Helen.' She jumped up obediently swaying slightly.

C.B. signalled Tricesta into the hall. 'She's getting on my nerves,' he hissed, 'What can I do?'

'Just keep playing it cool,' said Tricesta, 'leave it to me.'

'I can't take much more, she's like a school kid with a crush on the Games Mistress!'

Tricesta grinned and went into her bedroom, then returned to the drawing room. Helen had flopped on to the sofa, her dressing gown open, revealing all.

'C.B. and I have just had our delayed action sleeping pills. They take a couple of hours to work but hash gets you so smashed you'd never kip without them.' She walked towards Helen with a bottle of barbiturate capsules and a glass of water. 'They'd never work after food, take them now.'

'Oh! I never take sleeping pills,' she murmured, 'but if you've had some I suppose I'd better.'

She swallowed them and made no attempt to get up and dress.

Tricesta hurried into her brother's room, smiled and said: 'I've just given her three knock-out sleeping pills, on that empty stomach she'll be out in ten minutes. We can eat and talk in peace!'

C.B. hugged her and quickly changed his gear.

'Hey, you two,' Helen called, slurring her words, 'I don't feel like eating, I just want to sleep, do you mind going without me?'

'Do we mind?' C.B. smiled. 'Of course not, we'll help you to bed, what a drag you can't make it!' he said convincingly. To Helen's delight he carried her into her room and laid her on the bed. Tricesta pushed Helen's supple body under the clothes and looked down at her attractive face.

'Have a good kip,' she said, 'We'll see you tomorrow.'

They put the lights out and closed the door.

Feeling pleased with themselves they hurried across the road and went down the stairs into the tiny crowded restaurant.

'That was really cool,' C.B. enthused, 'she'll be out for hours – are you thinking what I'm thinking?'

'Don't I always?'

She grinned as they were shown to a table.

'Hello Janie,' said Tricesta to the girl sitting at the next table with her boyfriend, 'this is great, how are you?'

'Fine, let's pull the tables together.'

Janie Craig was a pretty twenty-three year old English girl, the daughter of a High Court judge but she had left home after a violent family quarrel. She had taken a degree in Sociology at Oxford. She looked like a young Liz Taylor, her hair was long and thick, dyed blue black which emphasised her pale skin and blue eyes.

Her nonconformist beliefs had forced her to disassociate herself from her family. Fortunately she was financially independent and was making a big impact with her outspoken articles in *Our Times*, an underground newspaper of which she was features editor. She had already atrracted the attention of the serious National Press.

Her reputation was that of a violent young rebel fighting against tradition and hypocrisy and an active campaigner for the legalisation of cannabis, but a fanatic opponent to the use of hard drugs. Government enquiry committees on drug addiction among the young found her help invaluable, as did the Medical Colleges investigating the side effects of hard drugs. On her own initiative she had had many startling case reports printed, and not only sent copies to every Member of Parliament and Local Government Committees, but also distributed them among teenagers associated with the underground movement.

Janie's latest project was setting up of 'Protection', a legal advice department for her underground news-sheet. This helped her to raise funds to bail out busted kids and procure the best legal representation for them, ensuring that those on drugs charges, unable to pay for their own defence, were dealt with fairly by the courts.

Janie's boyfriend was a West Indian musician, they had lived together for two years.

'How's that Rhodesian chick making out?' she asked, smiling at her two friends.

'Not bad,' laughed Tricesta, 'but she's hung up on C.B., it's getting to be a bore.'

'I'll get a cat to cool her down,' joked Les, the musician.

'That's a good idea,' said Janie, 'Shall we set it up?'

'What do you think we've been trying to do?' asked Tricesta. 'But there's not a chance, it's C.B. or nothing!'

'I'll have a bet with you on that,' said Les. 'Have you ever turned her on to a black cat?' he grinned cheekily.

'You're crazy,' said C.B., 'she's Rhodesian, she'd never speak to anyone darker than an Italian. She won't even drink black coffee!'

'Don't give me that crap,' said Les, 'bring her down to the pub on Sunday morning and cool it.'

The quartet finished the spicy food and drank the last of their orange juice and Perrier water. The majority of customers were on soft drinks or watered down wine. 'Smokers' rarely drink alcohol.

'Edward X wrote a great article for our sheet,' said Janie, 'he's a very hip cat, it's a pity his image is so bad.'

'I think he makes a mistake in advocating the use of violence,' said Tricesta. 'I've never met him but I'm told he's quite intelligent.'

'He is,' agreed Janie, 'he's a beautiful talker and really believes in the movement, but he's too fanatical.'

'He's the coolest hustler around,' said Les, focusing on the conversation again, 'but he's not my speed, I don't go along with violence. He turns me on but not to that scene. Anyway, bring the chick down on Sunday, it'll be a gas!'

'We're splitting,' said C..B and stood up, he tossed a fiver on to the table and smiled a farewell to Janie whom he liked and respected.

'Come back to my pad,' she said, 'I've got some wild stuff.'

'Another time, love,' he kissed her, 'we've got a heavy morning. See you both on Sunday.'

Tricesta and C.B. walked slowly back to the shop. The King's Road was bustling with attractive life but they ignored it and went home.

'She's flat out,' whispered Tricesta, closing Helen's door quietly.

Her brother grabbed her hand, pulling her into his bedroom.

'At last . . . ,' he sighed, pushing her on to the bed, 'I couldn't have taken much more – it's like being spied on, I never feel private.'

'Don't be silly,' she kissed his fluttering hands, 'she's just out of her element, she's not watching us, she's just infatuated with you. Why don't you give her a bang and cool her off?'

'You're kidding,' he laughed, 'she'd never leave me alone after experiencing one of my pumps! No thanks, I'll keep my distance. Do me a favour and hint that I'm queer. Tell her I've got a strong scene with Tim or Jim.'

'Forget her,' said Tricesta. 'Let's have a bit!' she joked and took off her clothes. C.B. adored his sister and looked at her for a long time.

'Neither of us plays around as much as we did,' he said at last.

'Perhaps we just don't have the time,' she replied and pulled him on to the bed.

When she left his room she tiptoed to her own pad, where she fell happily into bed. Before she went to sleep she wondered if Helen could be 'humanised'. Les's idea appealed to her rather off-beat sense of humour. The mentality of a copycat was new to Tricesta and the idea of experimenting with such a girl, particularly one with a built-in colour prejudice, was intriguing. how far, she wondered, could she induce a conformist personality to follow her, or even endeavour to outstrip her?

Helen was totally unoriginal, a secondhand personality, she desperately wanted to be the planet and not the satellite, but in her subconscious she knew she would never make it. Sexually she was inhibited, because for years she had lived in the shadow of her lively extrovert sister, Debbie. She had tried to emulate and outpace her, forcing herself to keep up with Debbie in an endeavour to draw attention to herself, but everything she did was without inspiration.

When Helen was projected into the King's Road scene she did everything to excess, hoping to be thought hip. She had a desperate need to be popular and loved but the way she sought this provoked the opposite reaction in those on whom she focused her attention.

Added to this she was slightly ashamed of her middle-class colonial background. A feeling which had become exaggerated in England. She had taken to telling lies in order to boost her self-importance. She weaved elaborate fantasies concerning her life and work; then the wishful thinking became reality to her. She found it difficult to distinguish between fact and fiction.

Helen had tremendous determination, but a determination channelled towards useless objectives. She had a huge ambition with no talent to back it up, and her selfish motives made her behave with a strictly calculated kindness.

The next morning after their Spanish daily woman had made breakfast, and they had both glanced through the morning papers, Tricesta and C.B. went down the marble staircase to the showrooms. Tim dressed in white and Jim in black had their backs defiantly to each other. They were both arranging flowers and Tricesta sensed a chilly atmosphere between them.

'Good morning,' she said sweetly. 'Those chrysanthemums look fabulous cut down in that shallow dish,' she said to Tim, 'rather like large yellow sweets in a box.'

'Thanks, that's not what Lady Muck over there said,' snapped Tim. Jim was creating an enormous classical arrangement in a huge bronze Warwick Vase and ignored the remark. 'He thinks he's doing it for Buck House!' said Tim sarcastically, decapitating the last chrysanthemum and aggressively sticking it into the glorious blaze of colour.

'They look great, Tim,' said C.B. looking down at the table. 'Come up to the flat for a cup of coffee,' he said, hoping to ease the tension.

Tricesta turned away, guessing this would cause even greater friction between the lovers. She went into the office and dictated several letters on the tape machine.

Upstairs Tim, in his high-pitched voice, complained about Jim's callous behaviour and let it slip that his friend had stayed out all night and what was worse had offered no explanation or apology.

C.B. uttered sympathetic noises and made a pretence of admiring Tim's Moroccan gold necklace which he wore over his black high-necked shirt. As C.B. was fingering the necklace Helen entered the room and saw the innocent act. But she automatically misinterpreted the scene and became flustered. 'Oh, I'm terribly sorry, I didn't know you were in here . . . I slept late, I'll just get some coffee . . . ' Her voice tailed away. C.B. instantly pulled Tim on to the sofa and called to Helen.

'Don't worry, there is no need to go, we were just having a chat.' The word 'chat' sounded open to doubt, which was C.B.'s intention.

Ten minutes later Helen appeared in the gallery.

'I'm sorry I'm late,' she said to Tricesta, 'it must have been those pills, they were fantastic.'

Jim stepped back from the urn to admire his flowers and Tim reappeared looking pleased with himself.

'Sucking up to the boss are we?' said Jim. 'Private chats upstairs now, eh? You're getting like this one,' he nodded nastily towards Helen, 'getting well in are we? You'll be copy-ing his gear next like madam here models hers on Tricesta's, of course it's a vulgar joke on her!'

Tim and Jim made up their differences as they tittered over Helen's embarrassment.

Chapter 6

THE FOLLOWING SUNDAY at twelve o'clock Tricesta and Helen drove the 'wrong' end of Fulham Road to The Fulham Star Inn.

'I never knew you were sold on jazz,' said Helen, combing her thick hair as they got out of the open E-type.

'There's a lot about me you don't know,' smiled Tricesta. 'I love unrehearsed jazz sessions especially in a place where everyone is relaxed and being pleasant.'

'What a drag C.B. wouldn't come,' said Helen.

'I think Tim was going to check some designs with him . . .'

She left the sentence open. Helen desperately wanted to ask whether C.B. had any homosexual tendencies, but she did not have the courage to do so.

They walked slowly towards the notorious pub, Tricesta felt a surge of excitement as she saw the crowd of odd characters gathered round the entrance, they were from all parts of the world.

As the two girls approached, the men in the crowd focused their surprised attention on them.

'Hi there! Where you chicks goin'?'

'That's what I call class!'

'Are you film stars?'

'I'm goin' to a groovy party later, I'll take you both.'

'I dig your crazy shades!'

Tricesta removed her dark spectacles, ignored the comments and took Helen's hand. Together they pushed their way into the hot, crowded Public Bar. The bar was filled to capacity with similar types to those on the pavement outside, but these were willing to buy drinks. The two girls were 'accidentally' touched in the most sensitive places as they slowly edged towards the musicians' corner.

'Take a look at the local bird life,' said Helen who had never been in such close proximity with Negroes before, 'no wonder they've flipped over us!' The other girls were a scruffy and untidy lot and looked as if they had knocked up too much 'pump' milage.

Tricesta and Helen made no attempt to reach the bar, they stood quietly in the corner opposite the impromptu group. This combination of West Indian and European musicians almost immediately started their first set; a mixture of rock and reggae. This was clearly popular with the customers, many of whom waved and swayed rhythmically.

Helen had been determined not to enjoy the scene but after some minutes she could not conceal the curiosity she felt. Unconsciously her body followed the music and she stared with interest at everyone. Some of the sights were worth a glance. The gear was bright and unusual but the concentration of bodies and the bright lights sent the temperature soaring.

'Hi,' Janie's boyfriend Les pushed towards them, 'where's Chocolate Biscuits?'

'He couldn't make it, how about Janie?'

'Half a dozen kids got busted in Chelsea last night, she's helping on the case,' replied Les easing towards Helen. 'And how's the groovy Rhodesian today?' he asked, chewing a piece of gum.

'I'm here to listen to the music,' she replied coldly, 'aren't you playing?'

'No thanks,' he grinned, 'today's my day of rest, like the good Lord says, cool it for one day out of seven! I want to catch

Apostrophe Brown, he's going to blow sax in a minute, he's a great cat. Ever met him?' he asked Helen.

'With a name like Apostrophe I don't think I want to. Is that really his name?'

'Yeah, lucky his old man could write apostrophe, it could have been "exclamation mark" or "full stop". He's a real cool number. There he is, picking up his instrument.'

The girls looked across to the corner where the twenty-six year old Jamaican stood. Tricesta had heard of him, he was the right-hand man of Edward X, but unlike his leader he did not advocate the use of violence in their movement. He preferred to emulate the technique of the late Martin Luther King. Apostrophe was devoted to Edward X and hustled for him. He did not hesitate to push drugs to earn money for the 'cause', or run a number of 'professional' girls, giving all the profit to the party funds.

Suddenly a new group burst into sound. Conversation was impossible, you went with the music, very few wanted to cut out.

Tricesta watched Apostrophe, he was tall and well built with medium dark skin and closely cropped wiry hair. His musical talent was undeniable. Helen, despite her inhibitions could not take her eyes off him.

Finally, at the conclusion of the exciting set Les called Apostrophe over. He carefully placed his saxophone on the piano and eased his way towards them.

'Hi Les man,' laughed the Jamaican staring at the girls, 'are you going to introduce me?'

The introductions completed, Les went off to get them drinks.

'Everyone calls me Apos,' grinned the sax player. 'I'm dry after that blow. Did you dig the music?' he asked Helen.

Tricesta noticed a tall, slim, good-looking West Indian standing next to her.

'Would you like a drink?' he asked.

'No thank you,' she replied rather distantly, 'there's one coming.'

'This your first visit?' She nodded in assent. 'And your last I suppose,' he said, glancing at the rough crowd. 'By the way,' he added, putting his drink down, 'your dress is open down the back.'

'It doesn't matter,' she said quickly, convinced it wasn't.

'I'm not putting you on,' he said in a hurt voice, 'would you like me to do it up?'

Instinctively she checked the buttons, they were open half way down her back. She felt ashamed and smiled at him. 'Yes, 'if you wouldn't mind.'

He fastened them carefully, smoothed the silk and said:

'There, quite decent again and unmolested!' His brown eyes were laughing. 'That was the most pleasurable incident I could have wished for,' he said softly and walked away.

'Your South African friend is real crazy,' giggled Apos to Tricesta who was looking at the tall, aloof man's back.

'Rhodesian!' Helen said sharply, and took the drink Les held out to her.

'I'm sorry,' apologised Apos in a mock humble voice, 'I should have known better after my good colonial college education!'

'Are you playing again?' asked Tricesta.

'Yeah, it'll get rid of my tensions for the week,' he smiled brilliantly. 'Some of the boys are going over to Michael's pad for a party afterwards. I want you both to come along.'

His eyes were fixed on Helen who looked confused and flattered. Most of the crowd kept well back now that Apos had joined the group. They still stared at the girls but made no attempt to push their attentions.

'We'd love to,' Tricesta answered for them both, 'where is it?'

'The Grove, don't worry, you're safe with us. The black men won't eat you!' He gave a high-pitched giggle and went to talk to another group of friends. Les excused himself. Tricesta and Helen went off to the loo for a 'conference'.

'Do you think it's wise to go?' asked Helen, secretly wanting Tricesta to insist.

'Why not?' she laughed, 'I've known Les for some time, he wouldn't try to pull one on us. It should be a gas! Surely you want to see where it's all at – I do.'

'I suppose it's always interesting to see how the other half live,' said Helen, tugging the comb through her wiry hair. 'My family would disown me if they could see me now.'

Tricesta smiled inwardly.

At two o'clock the landlord made frantic signals to the musicians, time was up. The customers grumbled but began to disperse, reluctantly. Various cliques formed, ready to move off to a club or a party. The serious living of the day was about to begin.

96

Apos, Les, Helen and Tricesta made their way to a West Indian restaurant off Portobello Road. It was crowded and the food smelt tantalising.

Tricesta thought about the work she had planned to do but decided to go with the scene. She was determined to watch Helen's behaviour with the coloured boys and because she herself had never mixed with them before she was intrigued.

'You ever eaten soul food?' asked Apos of Helen.

'No,' she drank her coke, 'I don't even know what it is.'

'You soon will,' he replied, 'it feeds the soul.' He giggled, enjoying a private joke.

They ate spiced beef served on a bed of rice.

'It's great nosh,' said Tricesta, enjoying the food.

'That's real soul food,' said Apos, clearing every bit off his plate, 'but the avocado wasn't ripe enough. You should taste the fruit on our islands, it's crazy, nothing like you get here. It's stale and dead when it arrives in England. I think you'd love our part of the world, it's so natural, nothing false . . . '

'So why do you prefer to be in London?' asked Helen coldly. Apos gave a high-pitched shriek and slapped his thigh.

'This chick is too much! Baby, does a miner "prefer" to live in the grime of a mining town?' His voice no longer had a laugh in it. 'He could sit on a beautiful mountain top and starve with his family, but he would rather give himself silicosis and feed his children. There's no question of "preferences", the choice is one of survival. You educated me, you showed me what progress meant, you told me it was the right of every human being to have an equal chance. But you suppressed and exploited me . . . '

'Of course I didn't,' snapped Helen, Apos shouted her down.

'Your bloody white society did and you want to propagate it. Our people are useful to you, that's your angle. But not any more, we don't want revenge, just justice, a fair deal for our people. If we don't get it there'll be real trouble soon, not because we want violence but because we are being pushed into fighting back.'

'All that you black people have ever done is fight,' said Helen, 'usually yourselves, tribe against tribe.'

'Cool it, cool it kids,' laughed Les, people in the restaurant were watching and listening to them. The atmosphere had become very strained.

97

'Let's get over to Michael's pad, We'll probably get turned on there.'

Somewhat sullenly the quartet split, Tricesta drove Apos as Les wanted to give Helen a gentle hint, but it was doubtful if she had sufficient sensitivity to respond to anything subtle.

They parked outside a crumbling terraced house off Ladbroke Grove. The paint was peeling and faded curtains hung haphazardly at the grimy windows, many of which were cracked or broken. Tricesta feared the worst.

Apos used his key and led the way into the cluttered hall. The broken furniture and torn wallpaper did nothing to allay her fears. The stale smell of cooking nauseated her.

Energetically Apos dashed up the linoeleum-covered stairs and Tricesta followed.

The door of the first-floor flat was open, music from a Jimmy Smith record filled the air. Helen and Les were already dancing, so were most of the other couples. Attractive white girls partnered black men. To Tricesta's surprise the flat was clean and pleasantly decorated. There was a large collection of books and a good selection of records. Black Panther party posters were stuck on some of the walls and red velvet curtains were drawn across the windows to keep out the sunlight and one presumed, the sordid view.

Apos danced with Tricesta without touching her, they each moved to the music in their own individual way. His body bent and twisted lithely, Tricesta swayed gently but provocatively. When the record finished Apos went to get her a drink, she sat on the sofa and watched the others.

'I didn't expect to see you here.' Tricesta looked up and saw the tall, good-looking West Indian who had fastened her dress in the pub.

'Why not?' she smiled.

'I can hardly think this is your speed.' He sat down beside her. 'Your first visit to the pub and all that. Who are you here with?'

'My girlfriend, the one over there,' she nodded towards Helen who was shaking her body with vigour. 'She doesn't look your speed either,' he said, 'she's not your class. How long have you known her?'

'Not long,' laughed Tricesta, amused at his perception. 'Actually she works for my brother and myself, she's our joint secretary but I usually tell people she's my girlfriend, it seems to make her feel better.'

'I dig, I dig,' he nodded. 'Will you allow me to get you a drink now?'

Before she could reply Apos handed her a bitter lemon.

'I think I'll groove with your girlfriend.' he winked at the pair and gave an appropriately wicked giggle.

'He's a nut,' said the man. 'Oh man, he's not true. I'm Bradford Kingston, but I'm always called Brad.'

Tricesta introduced herself and in spite of his rather arrogant manner she liked him.

'Everyone's freaking out,' said Brad, 'Shall we join them?'

They stood and joined the dancing bodies. The reggae rhythm did not irritate her as much as usual. She danced fairly close to Brad who moved beautifully. He neither pushed nor forced her to move with him. But somehow he coaxed her movements to co-relate to his.

'Who taught you how to move?' he asked in his deep voice.

'No one,' she whispered, 'I'm just following you.'

'I'd like to think you'll never stop,' he said unexpectedly.

The monotonous reggae music continued but they returned to the sofa. Helen danced with anyone who asked her, she out-shook and outwiggled all the other girls, coloured or white.

'Your friend really gets turned-on,' said Brad rather dis-approvingly. 'If she was my girl she'd never get away with that, You can see she's not from a stable of thoroughbreds.'

Tricesta smiled and wondered how much he knew about thoroughbreds, but he was interesting. His features were not at all African.

'My family have an agricultural estate in Tobago,' said Brad. 'We're a large family and my father is in the government there, he hopes I'll follow him one day. It's a lovely island although you'd consider it unsophisticated, but we're rapidly developing.'

'What do you do here?' Tricesta asked.

'I've got my own minicab business,' he replied proudly. 'It was a drag getting started but now I'm keeping my head above water. I can see you don't dig the music. Come into the other room, we can cool it there.'

He took her hand and pushed through the throng of dancing couples.

The combination study-bedroom was already occupied by

four men and two girls. Heavy, sweet smelling smoke hit them. Inside, another record player was at full volume with an Aretha Franklin L.P. on the turntable.

'This is a freaky spliff,' said Les, holding the joint out to Tricesta. She shook her head. 'No thanks, I don't smoke,' she lied and passed the thick cigarette on to Brad who squeezed her hand approvingly.

'Hey baby,' said Les, 'come and get turned-on to black poetry, listen to those lyrics!'

Tricesta sat with them and listened to Aretha. She did not like to say she had been a fan of Franklin's for years. Les was delighted to think he was 'educating' her.

Slowly the others became stoned. 'Anyone got another piece of shit?' asked Les; one of the men produced a small lump triumphantly.

Tricesta felt it was time to leave and returned to the larger room where Apos was dancing with Helen. His hands were holding her buttocks, her arms were firmly clasped around his neck, her lips on his. I don't believe it, thought Tricesta, I just don't believe it.

Watching her with the Jamaican, Tricesta decided C.B. had been overcritical of her. Helen was extremely attractive, but she did use many mannerisms copied from herself. Tricesta was not sure whether Helen was aware of her secondhand personality. She was bright, even cunning, but without a constructive brain in her head. Original thinking was unknown to Helen. Tricesta's ideas of one day were Helen's theories the next.

Tricesta pulled Helen into the old-fashioned bathroom.

'I'm going home to finish some work, are you having a ball?'

'It's quite groovy,' laughed Helen, somewhat flushed. 'Where did you sneak off to?'

'I was "communicating" with that tall coloured cat,' she smoothed a slight wrinkle from her tights. 'To be honest I dig him. He's the first negro I've ever wanted. I think I'll put that together.'

Helen pretended surprise.

'You stay around and have a good loon,' Tricesta said, 'The party's just beginning.'

'I'll stick it out for a while,' said Helen endeavouring to appear bored, 'but I'll be back within the hour.'

Brad seeing Tricesta about to leave asked: 'Can I drive you home?'

'No thanks,' she smiled, 'I've got my car here, my girlfriend is staying.'

'She would.' He seemed disappointed Tricesta was going. 'Will you have dinner with me one night?'

His almond-shaped eyes were fascinating. Tricesta was attracted.

'Yes, I'd love to, give me a ring,' she handed him her card and for no reason blushed.

'Your girlfriend's in with a fast crowd. Has she ever been out with them before?'

'No, she's Rhodesian, never spoken to a black cat until to-day.'

'She acts like a real crazy swinger,' he said, 'she's not my speed. I'll phone you, cool it in this car.'

Tricesta accelerated rapidly down the road and glanced in the driving mirror. Brad was watching her.

C.B. broke off his work and listened with amusement to his sister's tale.

'What a gas, I wonder if she'll have it. She's not had a man since she came to London – waiting for Mr Right!' They laughed. Tricesta said: 'I don't think she had any in Rome either, she's almost a virgin. She told me she had a boyfriend at home but that's her only experience. Her kicks are in the mind! But not after tonight I suspect!'

'Do you really dig this spade, Brad?' asked her brother.

'I don't know, he seems intelligent, I enjoyed talking to him, he's pretty cool. We'll see.'

C.B. returned to his drawing board, a slight frown on his brow that Tricesta did not notice.

At 11 p.m. that night, the brother and sister were exhausted from work. Helen had not appeared, nor had she telephoned.

'She's never been on the missing list before,' remarked Tricesta. 'I'll guarantee Apostrophe put it together. I knew she would try to beat me. I gave her the opening she needed. Let's eat and get to kip.'

Too tired to carry the cold food into the living room they sat in the bright, gadget-filled kitchen. They were even past talking; when they worked they gave it all they had. Nevertheless Tricesta needed sleeping pills to knock her out. At night her mind was always over-active. C.B. kissed her when she was in bed, looked lovingly at her and put out the lights. Their relationship was very natural and successful. They often joked about it being rather like a marital set-up.

The following morning C.B. and Tricesta re-arranged the shop windows before Tim and Jim arrived to disagree with them. Helen had not returned to the flat, an unheard-of omission. Suddenly like an excited child she burst into the cool showrooms.

'I had the grooviest night ever!' she exclaimed, her eyes sparkling, and almost danced around the shop. C.B. went off into the office.

'I wish you had been with me,' she said to Tricesta who was astonished at her exuberance so early in the day. Normally she was deadly until lunchtime.

'So let's hear about it.'

'We stayed at the party for a while, then we . . .'

'Who is "we"?'

'Apos and I, of course. We went with a crowd of others to eat at The Mangrove where they serve soul food. Your boyfriend Brad, was there. I don't think he likes me. Apos says he's a lone scout, never gets involved in anything . . .'

Helen had clearly transferred her preoccupation from C.B. to Apostrophe Brown.

'Then we split and went to see a cat called Edward, a real cookie, dressed in long black robes. They left me alone while they talked in another room.'

Tricesta guessed the other man was Edward X, the Black Power spokesman. Helen started to re-make-up her face and went on: 'This Edward is the most beautiful talker I have ever heard. He's not tall but fabulous looking, in the face he resembles Cassius Clay a little.'

'Did he make a pass at you?'

'No, I wish he had.' Tricesta could hardly believe her ears. What had happened to Helen's apartheid?

'A great-looking spade bird joined us, we had a few drinks, a couple of joints and split . . . I felt uncomfortable when Edward looked at me, his eyes seemed to burn into one. He's a bit frightening. Apos and I went to a couple of clubs, he's the most fantastic dancer, every part of his body is alive . . .'

Tricesta did not look at Helen but continued to arrange lilies in a pair of Sheffield Wine Coolers.

'I take it you two made a great connection last night?'

Helen threw her arms wide. 'It all happened, it was the greatest. I've never told you this before, but I've never been able to have an orgasm. Apos was the first one to make me, I just went on and on – it seemed suddenly I couldn't stop. I used to think I was abnormal, thanks to him I know I'm not.'

Helen had come alive, she shone with happiness. Through a defiant gesture she had accidentally discovered real pleasure. Helen was hooked, but what on exactly? wondered Tricesta, sexual fulfilment alone could hardly cause such a dramatic reversal of attitude.

'I was terrified of getting pregnant,' admitted Helen, 'but the curse has just come on. It's a drag in a way, I'm meeting Apos again tonight.'

'Don't worry,' said Tricesta, 'I'll turn you on to the pill.'

'Thanks. I suppose having a father in the medical game is a great advantage.'

'Hmm,' grunted Tricesta, still puzzled over Helen's behaviour.

Tim and Jim arrived, glanced at Helen and smiled at Tricesta and bowed a 'Good Morning'.

'We had the wildest freak-out last night,' said Tim.

'So did I,' interrupted Helen, dancing her version of the dated boogaloo.

'We can see that, dear,' said Tim. 'Where was your scene?'

'Bayswater,' she replied, still practising her boogaloo.

'North of the park!' gasped Tim in a horrified voice. 'Did you hear that, Jim, she goes slumming NORTH OF THE PARK!!!'

'What else can you expect from a provincial,' replied Jim. 'I've never visited any one on the OTHER side of the park, I just couldn't. Still, peasants have to go somewhere I suppose.'

Tricesta turned away laughing, Helen told them to 'get stuffed' and shot up the stairs and slammed the door.

Brad telephoned Tricesta, they arranged to meet that evening.

C.B. and Tricesta lunched in The Sun Tavern. The pub was filled with its usual quota of off-beat customers.

Sandy introduced a thin, dark-haired young man to them. 'I want you to meet Bobbie Peters, commonly known as "Peters the Pipe"!' Sandy laughed and slapped the young man on the shoulder. Bobbie's deep blue eyes looked questioningly at Tricesta.

'I've seen you around quite a bit,' he said, his voice neither educated nor uneducated, product of an English grammar school. Tricesta liked him. 'I don't remember seeing you.'

'Ah, well you wouldn't,' he replied, emptying his glass, 'I like to see and not be seen, it's better for business.'

'So what is your business?'

'You're great, even a copper wouldn't ask that. I've been away for four years and I'm ready to have a ball. What do you two beautiful people want to drink?'

C.B. and Tricesta explained they were in a hurry and were about to eat. Bobbie invited himself to their table, his conversation was so amusing they were not displeased.

'Don't you know why I'm called "Peters the Pipe"?' He grinned, they shook their heads. 'I make my bread going up pipes,' he said seriously. 'It's a bit dangerous but the money can be good.'

'Surely if you're in that line of business you don't want people to know?' said Tricesta. 'If you really were a villain you'd never talk about it.'

'You could be right,' he laughed.

'I've got a great admiration for you two,' he said. 'What you pulled off took guts and a lot of bread.'

'The important thing now is to keep it expanding,' said Tricesta.

'You'll do it, kid,' he said, forking up a large portion of his shepherd's pie. 'But what is it you really want from life? What is your ultimate goal?'

'Power,' she replied simply and truthfully.

'Don't we all,' he agreed, 'but power is so relative. I'm not boasting when I say I could place in your hands more power than you've ever had or dreamed of having. You think I'm putting you on, I'm not. Think about it – I'll be around.'

Tricesta and C.B. returned to the King's Road, both puzzled by the cat burglar's last words. His individuality appealed to Tricesta, he was obviously a ruthless man who lived by his own rules.

She learnt later that he was a successful international thief who was sick of the life he led and the crowd with which he had to mix. Four years behind bars had made him very cynical.

There was a reverse side to this tough villain; while serving his prison sentence he began to read and appreciate poetry. He started to write verse, which was published in the prison magazine. This interest continued and grew. Whenever he wanted to cut out from his way of life he wrote poetry. Bobbie found this relaxing and it bridged him over until he was forced to plan his next job.

His dreams for the future were of solitude in the sun, as far away as possible from his old life. But to achieve this he needed a lot of bread . . .

Helen's extraordinary change astonished Tricesta. When she had left the flat to meet Apostrophe, Tricesta said to C.B.:

'It's incredible how easily one can influence Helen. The moment I said I dug Brad she was determined to get into bed with Apos. Have you noticed how she tries to copy our expressions?'

'How could I miss it?' he said, smoothing cream on to his hands, 'but it just doesn't suit her. I'm delighted she is off my back. It's funny how some chicks get hung up on spades once they've tried it. I hope you don't go the same way – have a ball but don't get involved.' Tricesta was surprised to detect a hint of disapproval in his voice, he had no colour prejudice, or so she had always believed . . .

Bradford S. Kingston was already drinking in the upper bar of The Sun Tavern when Tricesta arrived. He was dressed in over-immaculate casual clothes; beige polo-necked sweater, crisp well-fitting fawn trousers and highly polished leather shoes. He suggested they dine at an expensive restaurant but quickly realised Tricesta wanted to extend her experience of his scene. They settled for soul food at The Mangrove. The small restaurant was busy, other West Indians walked in, checked who was there and left at once.

'They're just sussing it out,' Brad informed her. He appeared to know everyone there, especially the more attractive girls.

Tricesta enjoyed the meal in spite of the garlic.

'Tell me about the Black Power movement,' she said.

'That's not my speed,' he replied, signalling for the bill. 'I think they've got their good points but I don't go along with violence. I don't want to be a part of any group. I suppose I'm too idealistic but I'm not going to fight anyone. I've come up against discrimination, but once you talk honestly to people you find they're pretty cool. I refuse to get involved in Black Power although I respect their aims.'

Tricesta got the impression that Brad was conservative and a humanist. His own people would consider him to be a 'super spade'.

'Do you feel like going to a club?' he asked.

'I couldn't face dancing tonight,' she said. 'Why don't you come over to my flat?'

He opened the car door for her. 'I'm easy,' he shrugged, 'but why don't you come up to my pad, I've got some great sounds, do you dig Jazz?'

'I don't know much about Jazz,' she started the engine, 'but I'm willing to learn. I grew up with Classical and then went on to R and B and Pop.'

Brad lived in a pleasant block of flats in Maida Vale. The living room contained modern furniture and an elaborate sound system.

'I'll turn you on to Zoot Sims.' He put on an L.P. and joined her on the low divan.

They sat in silence listening to the music for some minutes then he took her hand.

Tricesta was conscious of an excitement within herself, she felt she was on the verge of a new experience. Brad impulsively pulled her on to him and kissed her. Her response was passionate and impatient.

Tricesta moved her body with his and held his face with her hands.

His eyes were turned up, only the whites showed. She pressed herself against him. His powerful body beneath her coaxed and excited her.

'Christ,' he muttered, 'I never expected anything like this.' He kissed her for a long time.

'Let's take our clothes off,' he whispered, 'I must be close to you.' Gently he undressed her and stood up to remove his own things. With fascination she watched him, his wide back narrowed down into his waist and slim hips. His legs were very long and perfectly proportioned, she had not seen a more perfect body. His dark skin enhanced his shape she thought. He bent over the deck and put on a King Curtis record. The daylight was fading, he walked over to the bed and Tricesta turned away, pretending she had not been watching him.

Words were unnecessary, she wanted him, he wanted her. They were both accustomed to getting what they wanted.

'I don't want to hurt you,' he whispered, 'but I can't help the way I'm made or the way you make me react . . . ' He squeezed and bruised her breasts; she made no attempt to stop him.

His sexual movements involved every muscle of his body. This was an act directed against all her senses. He was determined to give her the greatest possible pleasure.

Tricesta had never before experienced such fulfilment. When he was sure she was totally spent he clasped both her hands, held them down on the bed and pumped his life into her.

'Oh God – oh God!' he moaned as he fell limply across her body.

It was some minutes before he spoke again; then he said: 'I'm afraid I was over-excited.' He eased his weight off her. 'Next time I'll try and be less impatient.' She laid her head on his chest, relaxed. Usually after making love she would leap up and dismiss her lover with a curt 'Thank you, that was nice,' but this was different.

'Lots of chicks try and make it with me,' Brad said, 'but usually I don't want to know, I can take it or leave it. But something forced me to ring you. I'm confused about it myself. It's not just your looks or class, I cannot define it, but after I'd buttoned up your dress in the pub I knew I had to touch you again. I'm talking too much. I know,' he said and jumped up, 'I'll make you a cup of tea!'

To Chocolate Biscuits, Tricesta made little of her exciting evening, but Brad telephoned her twice the following morning and C.B. was present when the calls came. As she put down the receiver on the second occasion he said:

'That's going it a bit strong, isn't it? Even Helen doesn't have to talk to hers all day long.'

'Why shouldn't we say "hello" on the blower?' she asked, rather upset by his attitude.

'Of course you can, but it was over twenty minutes each time. Like a couple of school kids after their first date!'

Uncle Eric called at the gallery that afternoon on one of his regular visits. Tricesta offered him a drink in the flat. He accepted eagerly. C.B., Tim and Jim were all out, visiting various clients. Helen who had met Apos for lunch and had returned full of sparkle, handled the shop alone. She never considered it strange that the financial backer and his niece should go upstairs for an hour or two on each of his visits. They had to talk business! Anyway she enjoyed being left in charge.

'Apos invited you to come for a drink with us tonight,' said Helen to Tricesta, when Uncle Eric had been disposed of. 'He said you would have a surprise – I haven't a clue what it is. Will you come?'

Tricesta was reluctant but her curiosity was aroused, so she agreed to join them for a short time. Brad rang again and asked her out, she wanted to accept but she had already committed herself.

The two girls, dressed in startling gear, drove to meet Apos in Notting Hill Gate.

'Hi-Hi,' he grinned at them. 'How are the Chelsea chicks?'

'Fine thank you,' said Tricesta.

'Good. Follow me, baby.'

He drove like a lunatic to The Grove and screeched to a halt outside a gloomy looking house. Apos leapt from his car and leaned over to Tricesta, the hood of her E-type was down.

'Come inside with me,' he said, 'someone special wants to meet you – he's my great friend. He saw you in The Mangrove and flipped.'

'Why should I meet a stranger?' she said, a little crossly. Helen was smoking a cigarette. 'Go on – be a devil,' she said, 'Apos wouldn't put you on.'

'Oh all right, just for a minute then,' said Tricesta, 'but I think you should have been straight with me about it. Aren't you coming Helen?'

'I'll call her if it's all right,' said Apos, 'he doesn't like a lot of chicks around. Come on – he's real cool.'

Somewhat nervously she followed Apos into the house, unsure why she had agreed to go with him. The interior was brightly lit and filled with political posters, banners and press clippings.

She was led towards a back room, Apos stopped outside the closed door and told her to wait a second. He slipped inside and closed the door again. Tricesta was mystified, she looked up the stairs but she could see nothing unusual. Suddenly without warning a tall Negro appeared beside her dressed in a long black robe. She supposed he was a priest and smiled at him.

'Peace and love to you,' he said and waited beside her.

A heavy silence hung over the hall. At last Apos came out

of the room and said 'Hi, man' to the robed Negro and, turning to Tricesta: 'You can go in now, don't be shy or afraid.'

He stood aside, opened the door and shut it quickly behind her.

Chapter 7

TRICESTA GASPED AS she entered the room, it was full of black men, all wearing long robes. They eyed her coldly, most of them were smoking. She panicked and turned to leave the room. The door was locked.

'Apos,' she called, 'Stop playing the fool, open the door.'

'Apos ain't here,' shouted the man on the other side of the heavy door, 'he split with his chick.'

She turned and faced the robed figures who made no comment. Tricesta was physically afraid, what was she supposed to do, she wondered.

A second door that she had not noticed, opened and a handsome West Indian entered the room, pushed through the others and walked over to Tricesta.

'I'm Edward,' he smiled, 'there are a few of our workers. You look terrified,' he spoke perfect English, 'don't be, they won't hurt you – unless I give the word.'

'But why did Apos trick me – why do you want to see me?'

'Sit down, Tricesta,' he said, pulling up a chair. 'He didn't really trick you, I said I very much wanted to meet you, he doesn't know anything about this scene. He doesn't have much aggression in him. Do all these black cats scare you?'

'Not really,' she lied. 'But why are they here?'

'They want to know whether you're happy about giving us bread. We need a lot of money to keep our paper *The Black Press* going. They like to meet new contributors to the cause!'

'If you're hoping I'll give money to Black Power you're wrong,' she said. 'I don't support any organisation that advocates violence.'

'We're not an organisation,' he said sharply, his eyes glittered, his 'boys' moved closer. 'We're an organ,' he shouted, 'a repressed organ of the human race. What does colonisation mean to you?' he demanded.

Tricesta was frightened but was determined not to show it. 'This is an educated society now,' she said, 'Surely you should use educated means.'

'You're fucking mad!' he yelled at her. 'I'm more "educated" than most white cats, my Cambridge Economics Degree says so. Don't talk to me about educated society, it's a load of shit. That's what white society means . . . ' he pointed aggressively to a huge poster pasted on one of the walls. It had a red swastika on a white background, bordered by a thick black outline and printed diagonally across it were the words 'WHITE PIGS'.

'That's what your society stands for – complete Fascism,' he said, mixing Nazism and Fascism indiscriminately. 'We're not going to take it any more, it doesn't matter how much blood flows, black or white, we'll get our rights. Now Miss St Regis, we want a large amount of bread from you. If you don't pay up you'll bloody soon wish you had!'

The robed Negroes watched her, she managed to appear calm.

'Otherwise your people will wreck our place and destroy everything!' she said. 'A very educated act, I must say!'

Edward X started to laugh and stood up. Tricesta sat still, waiting for the next move.

'Okay cats, you can split. Ambrose, check me out later. Cool it – the fuzz are concentrating on The Grove for a couple of weeks.' He unlocked the door, the men sauntered out without glancing at Tricesta. Edward re-locked the door and sat down again. She was relieved the others had gone, yet she sensed the real pay-off was to come.

'You're cool,' he said, studying her. 'Relax, baby, I wouldn't touch a white chick. I believe in racial pride. I'm engaged to a groovy Sociology teacher from my own island of Tobago. I'm proud of my own race, I don't want my kids watered down with your blood. Our people have to be re-educated. They have to learn their own history. Years of white brainwashing has got to be eradicated. It's beautiful to be black. And I can tell you, the only hope for the white race is for a white chick to hitch up with a black cat!'

Tricesta laughed. 'That's the stupidest remark I've ever heard . . . '

'Oh no, look around, everywhere you'll see white birds with black men, they know it's the smart thing.'

'I think you've got it back to front,' she said. 'A Negro feels the only hope for him to become integrated is to have a white girl. It makes him feel good, you know that's the scene.'

'White Fascist!' he screamed at her. 'You'll see, there's going to be trouble! Violence! Bloodshed! When we're put together we'll smash this society, then see who struggles up from the wreckage. Take it from me it won't be Whitey!'

He was immediately calm again.

'Anyway,' he twirled the beads that hung around his neck, 'I want a lot of bread from you or certain other forms of payment . . . '

'Forget it,' she said ,'payment for what?'

'So you don't get locked up in Holloway, so you aren't disowned by your family and so your business doesn't fold!'

'You're talking rubbish,' she said. 'How could you do anything to me?'

'The fuzz would be delighted to hear you make it with your brother! But your family and your financial backer wouldn't. It's that simple, baby.'

'That's a lie, I could take you to court for slander.'

Edward laughed in great amusement, all his white teeth showed.

'Cool it,' he giggled, "I can prove you have it with your brother.'

'Don't be stupid, you're mad. I want to go now, open the door.'

'Oh no, we have to settle terms first. Your secretary gave

Apostrophe the scene, she's our star witness.'

Tricesta felt a sickening shock, even though she knew Helen could not possibly know the truth.

'I don't believe you,' she said, 'Helen would never tell such vicious lies about me.'

He smiled arrogantly, walked to his desk, sat down and switched on a tiny tape recorder.

'Yeah, she's been really cunning about keeping the truth from me,' it was Helen's voice, 'she even tried to pretend he was queer, just to cover up their affair . . .'

'You mean she has sexual intercourse with her brother?' said Apostrophe Brown's voice.

'Yes, I've seen them making it, but they don't know that. She's a real bitch, won't let him near me. He always makes a pass at me but she steps in and breaks it up, she's bloody jealous of me!' Helen's excited voice continued to elaborate upon the subject.

'I've heard enough,' said Tricesta clearly. 'I don't know why she's said those things. I suppose she wanted to impress Apos, make herself look more important than she really is.'

Edward lit a cigarette. 'I don't want to do this,' he said, 'but it's the only way we can get a lot of bread. You either pay us cash or agree to do anything I tell you, I won't make foolish demands, just things I can't do myself. Which is it to be?'

'What are the "anythings"?'

'Basically, having it off with a certain Member of Parliament and a stockbroker.'

'I see. Well, I'd rather go to bed with a few men than give up any bread. But this tape means nothing anyway, no one would accept its authenticity. Anyone can buy a recorder and turn out that sort of stuff.' She sat stiffly, wishing she felt more in command of the situation. Had Uncle Eric suffered like this? she wondered.

Edward X lost none of his cool, he said: 'You have missed the point, Helen is a living witness. Think it over for a few days and see how you feel then, or would I do better to call on Chocolate Biscuits?'

'My brother must never be told about this,' she replied quickly without thinking, 'the strain would be too much for him. He'd never be able to work and our business would be ruined.'

'Well,' he said, 'We certainly don't want the business to break down, do we? As I said, Apos knows nothing about this, he

113

would never agree to such a civilised trick! He just gave me the tape for a laugh, he thinks it's a gas!'

'Now I would like to leave,' said Tricesta.

'Of course, but before you go, I would like to tell you what I have in mind.' He smiled and continued:

'It is necessary that we have a private member's bill presented to Parliament. The only way to get that done is to apply pressure to an M.P. The M.P. we have selected is Michael Flaxman and he is the one you are going to screw.'

Tricesta fell back on to the sofa laughing.

'You'll have to forget him,' she said, 'there isn't a bird alive who could get him into bed. He's a strict Plymouth Brother. It can't be done. He's also a friend of my grandfather, I know him and his family.'

'He would not resist you,' said Edward confidently. 'I can give you something which will guarantee he'll bang you! Something which can give you power over any man, or woman for that matter.'

Tricesta stood up again smiling.

'You're too ambitious,' she said walking towards the door. 'Take it from me, you can forget Michael Flaxman. He's a good politician and a brilliant barrister, but as a sucker for sex he's a nonstarter. I don't want to hear from you again. Please open the door.'

'Certainly,' he unlocked the door, 'but I still think you'll feel differently in a couple of days. Goodbye, Miss Fascism!'

Edward roared with laughter as she hurried down the steps and jumped into her car.

Heart pounding she drove fast out of The Grove. That tape is meaningless, she told herself again, but I can't risk challenging Helen about her remarks, my position is too precarious. She accelerated over an amber traffic light.

The bitch, saying I was jealous of her! The drag is, on the sex scene she has told the truth, although she doesn't know it! I'm certain she's never seen us together, but just suppose she came to on the night I gave her those sleeping pills, went to the loo, overheard us and peeped through the keyhole . . .

Tricesta, a little calmed by the drive, arrived home just as C.B. was opening the flat door.

'Hello,' he smiled, 'I've just had a freak-out with Janie and Les.' They went into the drawing room. 'She's just had a delivery of some great gear. I'm glad they picked me up, I came back by taxi!'

'Why didn't you stay with them?'

'Darling,' he hugged her, 'what a question, the other birds there were a drag. I just wanted to be with you. Thank Christ Miss Rhodesia is out, I feel bloody sexy. Come on, let's get a good scene going.'

After her evening's experience Tricesta was not mad for C.B. to make love to her, but she knew she must, he had obviously had her on his mind while getting stoned, and that would have exaggerated his need for her. She could not say she had the curse, he knew that had been last week. C.B. pushed her gently into her bedroom.

'Don't bring me down, darling,' he said' 'I'm high and happy, let's groove for hours.'

'But Helen might come in,' said Tricesta.

'Never,' declared C.B., 'I happen to know she's looning around at The Revolution. Lock the door if the thought bothers you. I haven't touched you since the week before last, I'm not being put off any more. You're the only chick that really turns me on . . .'

She bolted the door, aware that she must keep C.B. at an 'up' level. She understood his delicate temperament, he was just like their mother. One jolt and he would withdraw for days, he would not be able to eat, work or sleep.

'Even when I pump other chicks you are the one I think about,' he confessed, kissing her. 'I always picture you while I'm having them. Our decision to live together was adult. We tried it all, we knew the score, now we've got it made. Christ, that joint is making me talk.'

C.B. caressed her and despite the distractions of the night she reponded quickly. 'We're lucky to have this groovy set-up,' she said. 'I suppose eventually we'll take over Castle Mordaunt, think of what we can do in that place! Have you ever had a coloured bird?'

'Never!' he said vehemently. 'I couldn't, they just don't appeal to me. I suppose some of the Eurasians are passable but I don't dig them. Hey – lie on me, I want to feel helpless and I can see you if you're above me. I want to see everything.'

Tricesta did as he asked, she enjoyed the position, it emphasised her control and domination. She responded eagerly until they reached a simultaneous climax.

'Of course you are really my half-sister,' C.B. brushed the hair off his damp forehead. 'On paper of course we're full brother and sister, but we know the truth, don't we?'

'I'm afraid our relationship is still illegal, half-sister or full-sister. So don't lose your cool. If Helen ever found out she could blackmail us.'

'You're kidding!' he laughed. 'She'll never find out, even if she did she wouldn't know how to put it together. Anyway the law, preventing brother and sister enjoying their natural instincts should be changed.''

'In early times,' Tricesta said, 'the daughter of a noble house always married her eldest brother. They believed it kept the line pure, provided of course, the brother was groovy. If not, another brother took over. Anyway you're safe,' she joked, 'you don't have any brothers!'

Tricesta left C.B. after giving him his cup of hot milk. A family ritual before sleeping which he had never abandoned. She took three sleeping pills and tried to force the memory of Edward X from her mind. Helen was now her problem.

Tricesta lunched with Brad at an Indian restaurant.

'Have you any brothers or sisters?' she asked him.

'Dozens!' he laughed. 'Some are only half ones, I don't see many of them. I've got a younger brother in London, we were very close once but I've had nothing to do with him for two years.'

'Why, what's the trouble?'

'He changed a while back,' said Brad, spooning up his curry, 'got involved with Black Power, really bought the Fitzpatrick ticket. At first it was just a new scene to run around in, then he got serious – too serious. He flipped. I won't have anything to do with him or his movement, both are destructive and vicious. He tried to pull me in, we had some bitter conversations over it. I can see how dangerous it is, especially the way it's run at the moment.'

'Talking of Black Power,' said Tricesta, 'Helen said she'd met a wild cat called Edward X.'

Brad poured a glass of iced water and shook his head.

'That's my baby brother!'

'What?' she gasped. 'Edward X is your . . . I'm shattered! You don't support his party in any way?'

'NO man,' he said. 'As I told you, that'll never be my scene. It can't work their way, it'll blow up with them in the middle but one thing is for sure I won't be in there with them. Promise me something . . . ' he held her hand and looked earnestly at her, 'please don't ever go near Edward. That has nothing to do with jealousy, he's a crazy cat, he does stupid things and he doesn't care a damn who he drags down. Don't let Helen ever talk you into going out with her and Apos. I know I've got no right to make these demands but they're entirely for your own protection. I can't tell you everything or what I suspect, he's still my brother, however bad he is. He honestly believes he's helping our people, he's very clever but he got messed up two or three years ago.' Brad communicated a real sense of danger to Tricesta who said:

'I've no reason to meet him, I hardly ever go out with Helen. Is Apos dangerous?'

'They're all dangerous, but Apos is basically a hustler, he raises bread for the paper, organises demonstrations and so on. There's one point in his favour, he won't tolerate violence. He relates more to Luther King, Edward to Matt. I know most of their grievances are genuine but I don't go along with their methods for reform, I'll tell you about mine one day. But' – he kissed her hand – 'don't go within a mile of Edward, he's a great talker, he'd convince a Bishop there is no God, but he's a killer, for the cause,' he added. 'You would never be able to handle the cat. I can, but only because I'm bigger and I know where he's at. He can't fool me, we grew up together. I've given him too many beatings for him to try anything with me. Edward hates my guts, he says I've chickened out to white society. He's very jealous of me, I was always Mother's favourite. All my talk must have been a real drag for you – come by the pad for an hour, and forget it.'

'I was fascinated,' she said truthfully. 'I'm glad you've been so frank.'

'That's the only way our relationship can survive,' he said.

On her return to the King's Road, pad, Tricesta found C.B. dictating an estimate into the tape machine. She blew him a kiss and went to her bedroom, and gazed at her reflection in the glass. Lost in a world of delightful fantasy she combed her hair. The telephone rang, she answered it quickly, resenting the interruption of her daydreams.

'Miss Fascism?' Edward X's voice said over the line, she stiffened and automatically glanced at the closed bedroom door.

'What do you want?' she asked quietly, terrified in case C.B. overheard.

'Just wondering if you'd changed your mind, baby.'

'You must be joking,' she replied. 'I gave you my answer. Please don't ring me again, there's no point.'

'I guessed you'd say that,' he continued gently. 'You'd better get over to me now. I've got a real incentive for you to change your mind. I'm not playing games, I'm too busy, get round here – like now!'

There was no mistaking the positive sureness with which he spoke. Again that nausea hit her. 'I'm fed up with this,' she said. He laughed so loudly that she had to hold the receiver from her ear. 'Are you alone?'

'Yeah, don't worry about those black cats, they're cool. I just want to have a further private chat with you, there's another record you must hear! It's the greatest. I'm not fooling, get over here now.' And he replaced the receiver.

Tricesta quickly put on more make-up, and changed her dress.

'Where's Helen?' she asked her brother as she walked through the living room where he was working.

'Running the business!' he laughed. 'Will you be out for long?'

'I don't think so,' she said, 'I'll ring if I get involved.'

Tricesta remembered the house only too well. Her sparkling bronze E-type looked out of place parked between the battered wrecks in the street.

She ran up the steps and rang the bell. Edward X, wearing his multi-coloured robes opened the door.

'Hi, that was fast,' he said, not even glancing at her long, exposed legs. 'Do you dig my traditional dress? Very "native" isn't it?' Again his hysterical laugh. She followed him into the back room and sat on the edge of the sofa.

'My requirements are still the same,' he said. 'I want Michael Flaxman compromised or a big pile of bread.'

'No deal,' she said, 'now surprise me.' Tricesta sat back, simulating cool boredom.

'I'm afraid our relationship is still illegal, half-sister, or full-sister. So don't lose your cool. If Helen ever found out she could blackmail us.' Tricesta's voice on tape was clear, she froze from shock. This was no trick recording.

'Shall I rewind and go back to the start?' asked Edward softly.

'Switch off,' she said, lighting a cigarette.

'I've got it from the beginning,' he said, 'and we all know why you were so reluctant last night. Are you convinced?'

'Yes.' She nodded, still in a state of shock. She wished Brad could help her; but no one could.

'How did you manage it?'

'Cool isn't it?' he smiled. 'Of course having shown my hand I can't repeat the scene, there's no need. There's a bug behind your bedhead, remove it later and return it to me. I can't afford to lose it, they're hard to come by and cost a lot of bread. Okay, now we both know where we're at, let's settle our business.'

'Who put it there?' she asked, already knowing the answer.

'Little Miss Apartheid,' he giggled. 'She didn't object, she's got her own angle.'

'She hasn't heard the tape, has she?'

'Of course not,' he said, 'neither has Apos, he's too busy hustling. I'm the only one to have heard it. I want a straight deal with you, nothing more.'

Her mind adjusted quickly to the facts. Again a serious crisis and she was cool, in a minor upset she lost all sense of proportion. Small incidents meant nothing to C.B., a major disaster unbalanced him.

'I agree you have the upper hand,' Tricesta said, 'but I'm not having Helen on my back as well as you. If you are reasonable with me, then I'll co-operate. Apos must have tricked her in some way to get that scene on tape. I know she's jealous, but there must be another factor, I know this chick too well.'

Edward X got up and left the room. He returned a few minutes later and locked the door.

'I told you last time we met that I could give you power. This is it.'

Casually he dropped four tiny white pills on to her palm. She began to understand.

'What are they?'

'Speed, baby,' he returned to his desk, 'medically labelled methedrine. Apos gave it to Helen in her drink that first night. Under the influence of this drug one is incapable of mental or physical resistance. And it's not generally known that it's also a strong aphrodisiac. If you start on a sex scene after giving it, you've got it made, it doesn't matter how much of a resister you've got on the bed, you'll get it!' He lit a cigarette. 'It is

119

what you could call a "one track" drug, so you mustn't start talking politics or religion, otherwise you'll have them talking about Enoch Powell or the Pope all night. Start on the subject you mean to continue with.'

'I've heard it's a highly addictive drug,' said Tricesta. 'What happens when the effects wear off?'

'It all depends on the amount of addiction, if well hooked they'll go crazy for more, then that's another sort of power. It's rather like a fertiliser, a dose now and again is a great booster but given too much the plant will die.'

Tricesta looked at the pills, fully aware of their potential. 'Is Helen still under its effect, she's very energetic?'

'Yes, but Apos has had his kicks and I've had what I want from her. There's no point in giving her any more. It's very expensive and like gold-dust to get. All the heroin and cocaine addicts went on to it when the new drugs act became law. God knows why it was left off the list.'

'I can see there's no point in you giving her any more, but look at it from my angle,' Tricesta leaned forward, her brain active. 'She's a terrible threat to C.B. and myself. Like you she could blackmail us, I'm not taking that from her. There's only one way out of that . . . '

'Sure, baby,' he laughed, 'no one listens to a junkie. You'll have to get the chick hooked. If you do it correctly she'll never get cured, it eventually destroys certain very useful cells in the brain.'

'All right Edward, I'll buy the methedrine from you, it's the only way I can protect C.B. and myself. You must see Apos gives it to her, I can't handle that. Is it a deal?'

'Okay, but it costs a lot of bread and the risk of handling it is pretty big. But if you pay me I'll guarantee Apos feeds it to her.'

'And there must be no hang-up.'

'Baby, we're not fools, we know the scene, if I say I'll do it, I'll do it. Within a few weeks Miss Rhodesia will be a junkie.'

Mentally Tricesta sighed with relief.

'I've got to have Michael Flaxman in my pocket,' said Edward. 'You'll have to get him in the sack and bug the affair. I don't want to hear about the hang-ups, just tell me when and where it's to be done.'

Tricesta frowned and put the pills on the arm of the sofa.

'You couldn't have picked a trickier victim,' she said. 'I don't think you know the meaning of "Plymouth Brother".'

'The cat's still human, baby,' he said. 'He's a great barrister and a straight politician. Any private member's bill he puts before the House will receive consideration. He used to be a Tory but changed parties. Being a Liberal doesn't lessen his standing, he's known as a man of integrity and I want him. So what's all this religious shit?'

She ignored his last word and replied: 'Admittedly he's not a member of the Closed Brethren, they are the bottom, you can't even eat or sleep with your wife if she doesn't embrace the faith. With the Open Brethren their rules vary from one Gospel Hall to another. But none of them believe in having a priest, anyone can ad-lib during their Sunday sessions, when the spirit moves them that is. Well, that's the theory, in practice there's great rivalry between the aged Elders to get up and have a go. Hard seats are arranged in a square and there's no set communion service, they just wait for the "spirit" to get things going. Bread and wine are only taken by those that have been totally immersed in baptism. Two Elders swathed in old bedsheets are responsible for the ducking!'

'What a gas!' Edward laughed. 'And people really go for this shit? I thought voodoo was primitive but this is plain nutty. So what are the rules of this crazy scene?'

'Well, firstly, no smoking. They saw that if God had intended man to smoke He would have provided a chimney in his head. Secondly, no alcohol, but there is always a hang-up over this because of the Biblical command – 'take a little wine for thy belly's sake,'' and ''medicinal purposes'' can cover a hell of a lot of brandy.

'Then sex – that disgusting performance is right out before marriage, even petting, as they call it, is out. After marriage they can have one bang a month and no more. If the girl becomes pregnant then the poor chap's had it for the next nine months.

'So what do they do?'

'They're taught that masturbation results in blindness or imbecility. Do you want me to go on?'

'Don't! But I just can't see how an intelligent cat like Flaxman could fall for that stuff.'

'When you're a child and you are told something long enough

121

and loud enough you eventually believe it and it stays with you. I suppose that's what happened. But of course most of them are just out and out hypocrites.'

'Are you?'

'Don't be stupid, everyone knows I can't stand hypocrisy or cynicism.'

'Are you going to tell your family and friends that you've got a spade lover?'

She blushed. 'What do you mean?'

'Cool it baby,' he said, 'you know bloody well I'm talking about my integrated know-it-all brother. I know you're looning about with him. Your friends would call you a nigger lover, yeah, it's true – a nigger lover!' He laughed with delight. 'Still, you'll soon get over it. At the moment it's a novelty to have a black man pump you, good luck to you but what would your set say?' He laughed again. 'What price hypocrisy now, or are you going to present brother Brad to the Earl at the ancestral seat?' His mocking tone infuriated Tricesta.

'Brad doesn't know I've ever spoken to you,' she said quickly.

'Keep it like that,' snapped Edward. 'That cat might be my brother but I don't want him near my scene, he sold out to Whitey. He's just a super spade, he's sick, always has been.' The long standing jealousy was evident.

'I want quick results,' said Edward. 'Set the action up where I can operate the receiver and tape in safety. When you're ready I'll give you the speed and tell you how to handle it. Don't lose your cool over Helen, I'll see that Apos gets her well hooked. How much bread you got with you?'

'About fifteen pounds. '

'Okay, let's have it, just as a starter for Apos.' She gave him the money and stood up. 'I forgot to mention that I have to go to New York briefly.'

'When?'

'Within the next few days, I can't slide out of it. I'm taking some period clothes over for a very good customer. I will only be away for a day or two. It will be impossible to set Flaxman up before leaving.

'Don't start hanging me up,' he said. 'If it's straight business I dig, but you can still suss out the Flaxman scene. I hope you see where I'm at, no one will have problems if I get what I want. Get some more bread for Apostrophe.'

Edward let her out of the house, she assured him she would

not let him down – he knew damn well she wouldn't!'

'You look worried,' said C.B. on her return to the flat. Helen was telephoning Apos. 'Cool it, have a smoke.'

'I can't be bothered,' she flopped beside him on the sofa, 'I'm just tired. Is everything all right?'

'Yes,' he smiled, 'and your trip to New York is set for the day after tomorrow. I had a telegram from Bezel, he's waiting for the costumes and he'll pay your price, provided they are delivered within the next three days in perfect condition.'

'Oh, I can't face putting myself together for the trip, I hate flying.'

'Helen will handle the details, just cool it and be glad you pulled the order.'

'Tell me what to do,' said Helen brightly, slamming the receiver down, 'and it'll be done. I'm going out in half an hour, is there anything I can do now?' Since Apostrophe had put her on speed she seemed more solicitous.

'All I want is a mug of tea,' said Tricesta, 'and a long kip.'

Helen immediately made tea for Tricesta and coffee for C.B. Her skirts were if anything shorter, her flamboyance even more exaggerated.

'I'll see you tomorrow,' she called gaily to them. 'I'll probably be late back, don't leave any lights on. Bye-bye!'

'Is she still grooving with that nigger?' asked C.B.

'Yes, she's really keen.'

'I think it's priceless, a Rhodesian of all people, and how's your nig-nog?'

Tricesta shrugged and ignored the slight petulance in his voice.

'For heaven's sake let's have a smoke,' he said, 'you're in a terrible mood, get stoned.'

'No, I'm fed up with smoking,' she replied. 'I think a completely false glamour has been built up around grass. To be frank I think it's mainly used by addictive types who are cool enough to know that the hard stuff will destroy them, and yet don't want to be out of the drug scene. Cannabis is in my opinion a safety valve. Am I making sense?'

'Yes, I'm with you,' he replied thoughtfully.

'I enjoy a joint now and again and so do you,' she said, 'but I could never become addicted, not to anything, simply because I like to be in complete control of myself and if possible the situation. You're not an addictive type either, you have a joint in the way Father has a "sociable" drink, in order to put other people at ease. I don't think it means much to you, it's little more than a friendly gesture to make other cats feel relaxed if they're getting stoned. Don't you agree?'

'In a way I do,' he smiled. 'You've hit the big smoking scene on the head – it's a safe halfway house for the kookier cats. I dig your perception, now I'll roll a joint!'

The day before her departure Edward X sent for Tricesta.

'Here's your little toy,' she said, handing him the minute German bugging device. She had removed it from the drapes behind her bed. 'Is that the type I'll be using with Flaxman?'

'Yes,' he nodded, 'cool isn't it? So you'll be in New York for a few days, great, but don't make it longer or I'll get restless.' He lit a joint and put a Blue Beat L.P. on the hi-fi deck. 'Must support my soul brothers,' he said jerking with the beat. Suddenly he sat down behind his desk and removed a long envelope from a drawer.

'Deliver this letter to William X the Second,' he said without a smile. 'Don't allow anyone else to see it and don't even consider opening it yourself. I've sealed it very carefully.'

'Why don't you post it?' she asked.

'Oh baby,' he sighed, 'our people get very little of their mail delivered and what they do get is censored. Deliver this to him at the address on the envelope, it's just before entering Harlem proper. If he's out, wait for him. You've seen photographs of him, you'll recognise him, he'll be expecting you. Apostrophe needs more bread for the chick's speed.'

'Already?' she said. 'Aren't you piling it on a bit?'

'No!' he snapped, then grinned. 'The fuzz are making things tough at the moment, they are concentrating on The Grove, right now they're very busy. Supplies are scarce and expensive, even shit is a hang-up. Have you seen the latest edition of *The Black Press?*' He tapped a thin newspaper.

'No, I haven't seen any of them.'

'Take this,' he passed it to her, 'it tells you where it's all at, no whitewashing as you call it. You might just find it interesting. How's Brother Brad?'

'Fine.' She folded the news-sheet. 'Let me have the letter, I must get home.'

'Remember, don't let anyone see it – for both our sakes. Check me out when you get back.'

Edward X showed her out as a group of his robed 'boys'

strolled up to the house. They looked at her briefly and turned into the Black Power Headquarters.

She drove off and was unable to avoid noticing the huge slogans painted on the brick walls.

'BURN, BABY, BURN' and 'ALL YOU NEED IS DYNA-MITE.'

'Dynamite' was written in brilliant red paint. Tricesta did her best to forget about the letter, it was just part of the payment she had to make. It was better than handing over her hard-hustled capital.

Chapter 8

THE DISASTER WHICH overtook Tricesta in New York was a shock to everyone, especially the militant Black Power leaders. The capture of their programme for the proposed international summer riots was a bitter blow to them. Much of their finance had gone into their terrifying projects. They possessed sufficient explosives and arms to seriously disrupt the peace of a number of countries for many weeks.

This was the first time the organisers of black violence had been able to put themselves together to constitute a positive threat. In the end the law would have coped but the damage to life, property and trade could have been considerable.

After Tricesta's return to England and she had managed to cool off her family, friends and Press, she rang Edward X.

'I'm in a public box,' she said, 'I'm coming round now.'

Still worried that she was being watched she drove to the unfortunately familiar house. A tall robed Negro admitted her without speaking and indicated she should go into the room at the rear.

'That was a great mess you dropped me into,' she said at once to Edward, who was sitting on his steel desk.

'Cool it, you got out. How do you think we feel? Months of research and hustling gone to waste. Are you sure you didn't fall apart?'

'You must be joking!' she said. Then she noticed Apostrophe standing in one corner holding his saxophone. 'I didn't see you, Apos,' she said. 'How's our problem child?'

'It's for real,' he grinned and hooked his index finger illustratively. 'But,' he shrugged, 'the bread has run out!'

'I'll give you some more before I go,' she said, having anticipated this predictable situation.

'Cool it for ten minutes, man,' said Edward to Apos, who walked from the room with his sax.

'How did you get out?' asked Edward when they were alone.

'That doesn't matter now,' she replied, 'I just did.'

'Little Miss Innocence is pretty cool.' He smiled, stretching his body. 'I must say I began to think I'd have to go and see your beautiful brother!'

'Don't ever do that,' she said sharply, 'if you do you'll destroy everything. You gave me your word you would not go to him. Are you sure Apos has done his stuff with Helen, you're not both putting me on?'

'It wouldn't pay me to put you on, if you're worried, put it to the test. I'll tell Apos not to see her tonight.'

'What will that prove?'

'Just observe the chick, that's all. I'd better give you the stuff though, you'll probably have to give it to her. I don't know how hard it'll hit her. Anyway, go to it and set Flaxman up. After the exposure of those plans we've got to go to work on new ground. I'll check you out tomorrow and I'm glad to see you made it back!'

For the first time they smiled at each other. Although he stood for all she hated Tricesta was aware he had brains and courage.

What a pity he went off on the wrong lines, she thought, he could have done great things.

'I'll give you eight methedrine tablets for Helen,' he said. 'You can give them to her without her knowing if you'd rather.'

'How does Apos give them?'

'Just as they are. She's at the mainlining stage but the needle scares her. However she takes them the results are the same, except that a shot in the arm or bottom will act within seconds. In pill form it takes twenty minutes or more depending on the amount of food in the stomach. Now get hustling with Flaxman.'

Tricesta kept the pills in her gloved hand, just in case the fuzz stopped her, in which case she would have to swallow them. That amount would blow my mind, she said to herself, I doubt whether I could handle them.

Her surprising encounter with her grandfather had lessened her worries considerably. For the first time in her life she felt close to him, he was now her friend and no longer an acid old man whose money she wanted. She could not imagine herself scheming for it any more, but he would be useful in helping her to set up Michael Flaxman, unwittingly of course!

Tricesta was far from convinced that Flaxman would go into reverse after a lifetime of near celibacy. His wife being over fifty, I don't suppose he's had his monthly rights for years, she thought.

When she returned to the pad at six o'clock C.B. was drinking a cup of coffee with Helen, who was sitting beside the telephone. She'll be out of luck, smiled Tricesta to herself holding the pills.

'That nig-nog Brad has been on the blower three times,' said her brother moodily.

'Thanks,' she said casually, 'I'll ring him. Are you going out for dinner, or having it with us?' she asked Helen.

'I'll be eating out,' she replied. 'I'm waiting to hear what time we're meeting.'

Since going on junk Helen had become secretive; previously she would have said who was taking her out but not now. C.B. buried his head in a new book on French interior decoration.

Helen painted her nails.

Tricesta rang Brad, she had not spoken to him since her escape from America.

'Darling,' his voice sounded thick, 'I've been so worried about you – you'll never know how much . . . I've got to see you.'

'I've missed you,' she said truthfully. 'I've been on a bad scene, I'll explain when we meet.'

'Can we meet now?'

'I wish I could, but I'm in bed, the doctor has given me a

128

sedative and my parents are here,' she lied. 'I'm sorry, we'll meet tomorrow, I just wouldn't be allowed up now. You know what families are like.'

'Darling, kiss me.'

They exchanged kisses over the telephone. Brad sounded close to tears, his emotion affected her.

Tricesta's naturally romantic nature responded. When she finally put the receiver down she was also in tears. She dried her eyes carefully and repaired her eye make-up. I wish it was completely waterproof, she thought, then I could cry uncontrollable buckets and still look beautiful.

Half an hour later Tricesta returned to the drawing room. C.B. did not lift his head. Helen stared at her nails, her hair was untidy and she sat sloppily.

'It's freezing in here,' said Helen, pulling a cardigan around her shoulders, 'and I'm starving. That bugger still hasn't rung.' She looked angry and fidgety.

'Come and eat with us,' said Tricesta, 'he may not ring now.'

'Oh yes he will,' she replied, wandering about the room restlessly. 'He'd better, or I'll give him an earful, you two go ahead.'

'Not yet,' said Tricesta sitting down with a king-sized novel.

'I'd better do my face and hair,' said Helen, 'then I'll be ready to go when he calls.' She darted from the room and tripped over a footstool.

'What's the matter with her?' asked C.B., disturbed by the commotion. 'She's like a bitch on heat, it's that bloody nig-nog I suppose.' Then he smiled. 'Let's have some orange juice, we'll eat later.'

Tricesta opened a can of cold juice and settled down to read, C.B. continued to look at his book and made occasional notes. For once the record player was not on full blast, Tricesta wanted to hear whether Helen used one of the extension telephones.

A further hour passed without a telephone call for Helen who had continued to get ready. Finally she joined the brother and sister, wearing spectacular gear and looking stunning.

'Have a drink,' said C.B., putting his book aside. Helen's face was set, like a mask. She walked to the drinks' table to pour herself a vodka. Tricesta watched every move she made. Suddenly Helen dropped the bottle of vodka on to the marble table, it shattered loudly and she screamed. C.B. jumped up to collect the pieces of glass and noticed Helen's hands were shaking.

'Don't worry,' he said, 'it was an accident, there's no harm done. Do you want some codeine?'

'No – no,' she said and burst into tears. Tricesta was ready for this and watched her crack. 'I must have some time off,' babbled Helen, black tears coursing down her matt cheeks, 'I'm going to have a nervous breakdown. It's the reporters – they got me down when Tricesta was in trouble – they pestered me, I must be by myself for a while – I must be alone . . . ' Her sobs became more violent, her whole body shook, her immaculate white skirt was stained with eye-make-up, soaked into the linen with hot tears. Her carefully lacquered hair stood out in all directions in pointed clumps, she moaned and clutched at her stomach. Tricesta guided her to the sofa where she collapsed.

'I'll call the doctor,' she said to test Helen's reaction.

'No, I won't see the doctor,' she gasped vehemently, 'he'll just say I'm anaemic. He'll say I've got weak blood and give me vitamin pills and he'll tell me to rest more – I'm not seeing the doctor, I just need to be alone, I've got to be alone . . . . ' Her body trembled, she was clearly suffering, her hours of patient preparation for Apos were wasted, she looked dreadful. A broken doll. So this is withdrawal, Tricesta said to herself, I'd better give her the stuff, I know damn well Apostrophe won't be around!

'Listen – listen to me.' She held the girl's shoulders, Helen raised her head a little. 'I've got some great gear I pinched from Father's poisons' cabinet. I've often taken it myself when I've felt bad,' she lied and glanced at C.B. who looked out of his depth. 'They're pills and they are fantastic, take them and in fifteen minutes you'll feel on top of the world. I promise you they're the greatest. I'll let you into a secret' – again she looked at C.B. who gave a puzzled shrug – 'I've been taking them since I got back, I needed them. Come into my bedroom, I'll let you have my supply.'

Helen was clearly past caring what she had, provided it pulled her together. With the help of C.B. she managed to stumble into the bedroom and fall on the bed. She covered her red blotchy face with her hands and continued to cry.

'Get a glass of water,' Tricesta told her brother and produced the eight tiny white pills.

'Is this the right thing to do?' he asked nervously on his return. He had seen addicts suffering from lack of junk before and realised what was happening. Tricesta gave him a silencing look and indicated he should help Helen into a sitting position, but she flopped back again on to the padded headboard and seemed unable to focus accurately. Tricesta placed four tablets on her tongue, held the glass to her lips and told her to swallow them. She obeyed and then repeated the dose making no attempt to look at the pills.

'I'll be back in a minute,' said Tricesta and left the bedroom with C.B.

'She's a bloody junkie,' he said when they were out of earshot, 'we can't keep her here, she's dangerous, she's a liability, she's . . . .'

'Cool it, angel, I've got it under control,' said Tricesta calmly. 'I was expecting this, that's why I had the stuff.'

'But where did you get it, you haven't been home.'

'Don't worry,' she smoothed his frown, 'the cat she was meeting tonight ran into me, he gave it to me and said to let her have it if things got rough. He's cooling her off now but she's desperate about either him, the stuff or both. That should give you a lot of amusement.'

He smiled at her and nodded. 'All right, bring her down but keep out of any trouble, remember junkies can be a responsibility.'

They returned to the bedroom, C.B. put on a Hendrix L.P. Tricesta lay beside Helen who had stopped shaking. She opened her swollen, smudged eyes and looked at Tricesta, who moved her arms rhythmically to the music. 'Well, do you feel like eating now?' asked Tricesta. 'What would you like?'

'Make love to you!' replied Helen seriously. C.B. looked up from where he was sitting, Tricesta pretended she had misheard. 'What did you say?'

'I'd like to make love to you,' replied Helen, blushing and burying her head in the lace bedcover. 'I've always wanted to,' she mumbled, 'but I didn't think you'd . . . '

Tricesta was taken aback but put her hand on Helen's wiry hair and re-thought this unexpected twist, quickly. If I have a scene with her, especially after giving her the gear she'll always associate the junk with a sex kick. She'll replace me with Apos if I want that. She could come to rely on me, but it's not really my scene or is it? She looked at Helen's attractive body,

I'm sure she could give me pleasure, she's very pretty and as long as there's no suggestion of her imitating the male I'm for it.

Tricesta had always spurned the attentions of other girls, the 'butch' lesbians always depressed her. She supposed Helen would not want to act in that way so why not try it out?

C.B. sat attentively watching the two girls stirring into awareness. As he had often remarked: 'I always have been more of a watcher.' He refrained from making any move in case it put either of them off.

They held each other tenderly and tightly, gradually they became accustomed to one another's delicate scents.

Tricesta's body automatically followed the insistent beat of the sound, Helen raised herself and kissed Tricesta nervously, then more passionately when the response was encouraging.

'Take my clothes off,' said Tricesta knowing she must remain in control, 'and I don't want to be naked alone, you must undress too.'

She ignored C.B. who she knew would be enjoying the scene.

When they were both lying together, their perfect young bodies locking tightly, Tricesta had to admit to herself the sensation was delightful. It was not what she had expected at all. It had always upset her to see an ugly old dyke walking in the King's Road with a pretty young les, who was probably doing it for the bread. This was different.

'Your hair is so silky,' said Helen running her hands over Tricesta's head. 'I love you, I know you can't feel that way about me, but I really do love you.' Tricesta became a little suspicious; like her grandfather she never trusted anyone fully. She's only saying that to keep me happy, she thought, but sighed with pleasure as Helen kissed her breasts and slowly moved towards the more sensitive parts.

Tricesta jerked with surprise as she felt Helen's lips on her.

'Please tell me if this is no good,' said Helen, raising her head. 'But it is, it's beautiful,' gasped Tricesta, 'perfect, yes don't stop.'

C.B. unable to control himself, walked over to the bed. He had often fantasised such a scene.

Helen knew exactly how to stimulate Tricesta. With obvious enjoyment she brought her to the edge of satisfaction, and when Tricesta realised C.B. was beside her she went over the top. C.B. doubled over and rushed from the room. Tricesta felt wonderful and pulled Helen up beside her.

'It was great, really great, now I want to do the same for you.' To her own surprise she meant it and immediately proved her sincerity.

Helen responded, her breathing was deep and rhythmic. Tricesta looked at Helen's flat stomach and firm breasts, her figure was as faultless as her own.

Helen clasped Tricesta's hands and moved her head from left to right in a staccato movement. She almost squeezed the life from Tricesta's wrists, then went limp. 'God that was wild,' she gasped. 'We should have done it before. Is your heart beating quickly?'

'A bit,' laughed Tricesta and sat up unsteadily, then fell exhausted beside Helen.

'I never thought I could dig that,' admitted Tricesta. 'I don't go for copying the male with that invitation scene, it's sick. We both remained feminine.'

'You're right,' agreed Helen, 'I dig a manly man or a girl type bird, but each in their own way. Then it's beautiful, then it's not an unnatural scene. I've wanted you for ages but I did not have the nerve to say anything. That stuff you gave me was great, I feel groovy, fuck that bugger!'

Tricesta took it she referred to Apostrophe and said: 'If you really want to get that jealous cat hooked, there's only one sure way to do it.'

'Oh?' Helen was at once interested. 'He is madly jealous, although I've promised never to have anyone else I don't think he really believes me. What can I do to convince him?'

'Do something that proves no other man can possibly have you.'

'How the hell can I do that!'

Tricesta stroked her blonde hair, sensing one of her great moments of humour was at hand.

'In this day and age you can't wear a chastity belt, it's too bulky and too dirty,' she said, 'but you can go one better. I've been toying with the idea for myself for some time, but it takes a bit of courage. I'll make it, in the end, you see I also want to give myself completely to a man,' she lied.

'If there really is a way, please tell me and I'll do it. I want this bloody cat.'

They moved their position, holding each other face to face.

133

'Instead of giving Apos a mental lock and key by promising fidelity, give him a real one that he can use physically, so that he alone can control you.' Helen listened intently to every word Tricesta said.

'A real lock?' she asked, puzzled and curious.

'Yes, a strong metal lock, it just needs guts and determination to fix it.'

Helen gazed at her. 'What must I do?'

'You must be pierced and have gold rings inserted into each side of your inner lips!'

'You mean in my. . . . ?'

Astonishment showed in her face. 'But how can I get that done? And then what happens?'

'You must be pierced in the same way your ears have been pierced, gold rings inserted and then held together by a tiny padlock having only one key. You must not cheat, give the key to Apos then no one else can make love to you unless he wants to loan or hire out the key for the night.'

'That's fantastic,' said Helen. 'I've never heard of anything more exciting.'

'Apparently some women have rings put through their nipples, but I think that's more for decoration than use. I'd have it done but physically I'm a coward.'

'I'll do it!' said Helen. 'I want to give myself completely to Apos. I want to belong to that man.' She flushed. 'I wish you could see his body – it's perfect. Every muscle and vein like a piece of sculpture. They are different, it's their bodies, the way they move. I must get it done quickly, tomorrow, will you help me?'

'Of course,' smiled Tricesta triumphantly, 'we'll go to a piercer and see if we can get it done professionally. I wonder what his reaction will be?'

Tricesta had guessed that a chance to get a step ahead would be enough to make Helen interested but even Tricesta was a little surprised that such a bright girl would seriously agree to go to such bizarre lengths. Tricesta had thought the whole thing up as she lay on the bed with Helen, never dreaming she would be taken seriously.

Helen closed her eyes. 'Imagine Apos's reaction when I give the key to him! Oh – what about going to the loo?' she said, and opened her eyes again.

'It won't get in the way,' replied Tricesta, now entering the game seriously, 'but I suppose when you have the curse he'll have to let you have the key, just for those few days.'

The two girls joined C.B. in the kitchen and fried eggs and bacon. Tricesta said nothing to her brother who did not refer to the scene.

Helen went to bed happily imagining herself being owned by a black man, quite oblivious of the fact that she had become stupidly masochistic.

Tricesta felt elated. Planting such an unorthodox idea into such an unlikely subject was a gas.

In the morning Tricesta told C.B. she would be out with Helen for a while. 'All right,' he said, 'but what are you two up to? You might let me in on the action.'

'I will, give me time.'

Tricesta telephoned her grandfather to say she would be down for a few days and asked him to invite Michael Flaxman to the Castle for the weekend.

'Don't tell him I want to talk to him,' she said. 'I can't explain, but I need to ask his advice. Please, Grandpa.'

'I'll ask him,' he boomed over the wire. 'In any case I want to see him on a county matter. He's sure to stay, he won't drive forty miles to get home. His wife has gone to the Bahamas for a couple of months so he's quite free.'

Excellent, thought Tricesta, delighted that she could now communicate so easily with the old boy. Then without delay, she looked up the telephone number of an ear-piercer and made an appointment.

Helen looked slightly depressed. Tricesta said: 'I've got something to cheer you up, Father gave them to me.' She was finding her father useful!'

Tricesta went to her secret hiding place and removed three powerful amphetamine tablets. Occasionally she had been offered drugs by amateur pushers in need of bread. Although neither she nor C.B. took them Tricesta thought it wise to buy them when they were offered. One never knew when they would be useful.

Half an hour later, driving towards Mr West's consulting rooms in Wimpole Street Helen was in high spirits.

'There's just one thing,' she said as they flashed down Baker Street, 'would you mind seeing him for me? I feel a bit awkward.'

135

'All right,' agreed Tricesta, not overkeen, but she could not back out now. 'Of course he might refuse, it is an unusual request! But I'll do my best.'

'Good morning, Miss Wells,' greeted the white-coated man – she had made the appointment in a false name – 'sit down and relax!'

He was old, small, and spoke with a mid-European accent.

The consulting room was tiny, full of dusty objects, piles of papers and yellowing photographs of out-of-date personalities. Both the men and women in the photographs were wearing earrings.

'I've done them all,' he said proudly, 'royalty, filmstars, they've all passed through my hands.'

'How interesting,' said Tricesta, mentally deciding that he would not get at her, anyway she loathed earrings. Prostitutes, barmaids and maiden aunts seemed to be the ones addicted to them.

'Have a look at some sleepers,' he said, pointing to a glass-covered tray.

'I want them small but strong,' she said.

Mr West picked out what he considered a suitable pair and sat down opposite her.

'Don't be nervous,' he said reassuringly, 'you won't feel a thing.'

'Actually,' she said, sitting further back in the chair, 'I came to see you on behalf of a girlfriend. I don't want to be pierced.'

'Oh, I see.' He looked annoyed. 'Where is she?'

'At home, she is very nervous.'

'That's a little childish of her,' he said sharply, 'but even children have their ears pierced.'

'It's not her ears she wants done. . . .'

'Hmm,' he looked at her, 'well, where is it to be? Nose or breasts?'

Tricesta was startled and felt herself becoming scarlet. 'Neither,' she replied. 'I didn't realise other parts were so popular.'

He chuckled sarcastically. 'You'd be surprised what I get asked to do. Let me show you some pictures.'

He almost jumped to his feet, fumbled in a Victorian bureau and produced a fat, battered album.

Even Tricesta was astonished when she looked at the extraordinary photographs. Women presented themselves proudly to the camera, rings were everywhere, or so it seemed. Not one ring but rows of them, almost wherever it was possible to be pierced. The women were not particularly young and the effect was vulgar but fascinating. Gold chains had been threaded through some, others had jewelled pendants hanging from them.

'You see,' said Mr West, 'it's all been done before.'

'Almost,' Tricesta said, smiling.

'Then where does your friend want them?' he asked looking confused.

'In her lips!'

Mr West was not completely put together, he wrinkled his forehead and touched his lips.

'Impossible,' he declared, 'it can't be done. How could she eat? They're too fleshy.'

'No, not those lips. . . . '

'What! You mean – ' For one moment he looked shaken.

'Exactly,' Tricesta said losing her embarrassment on seeing his, 'the inner lips. Will you do it?'

'Is she some sort of stage artist?' he asked, staring at her.

'No, her fiancé suspects her fidelity. This is his version of a chastity belt.'

Outwardly Mr West recovered his compsoure and detachment; he nodded understandingly.

'To be frank,' he said in his most professional manner, 'I've never had such a request before.' He glanced at the floor. 'I'm afraid I must refuse.'

'But why?' Tricesta showed her disappointment. 'You've shown me pictures of women with rings almost everywhere. You didn't refuse to pierce them.'

Mr West sought for words. 'That was different,' he said feebly. 'In this case the risk of infection would be much greater. Suppose she was taken ill – rushed into hospital, imagine the reaction of the doctors and medical staff. If she revealed my name I would receive ruinous publicity.'

'I assure you she would never give your name to anyone.'

'My dear young lady,' he thrust his hands into his overall pockets, 'I can't possibly be sure of that. I have a reputation to protect.'

'She would pay a very good fee,' said Tricesta, irritated by his petty concern.

137

'I'm sorry but I can't take the risk. You may find someone less prominent in the profession who will.'

'Is it difficult to do?'

'Not really,' he replied grudgingly, 'Provided you're not nervous and have the correct equipment.'

'Would you agree to be present provided someone else did it?' she asked hopefully.

His eyes gleamed at the thought. 'Much as I would like to help you and your friend, I can't. But I respect her motives.' He smiled at her, convinced Tricesta was the girl with the kink.

'Will you tell me what is needed?'

'Yes,' he agreed, his attention on her exposed thighs. 'You can buy a chemical which freezes the skin.' He had become helpful, she wrote down the details. Finally she paid him his normal piercing fee, thanked him and hurried down the stairs with the gold sleepers.

When Tricesta recounted her experience Helen was upset and asked: 'What do I do now?' Her determination to see the job through was obvious, she was not going to chicken out.

'Let's buy the lock and key and the gear from the chemist,' said Tricesta, 'then we'll decide what to do.'

They combed stores, hardware shops and jewellers. None could show them the non-rust type of padlock they sought. The last jeweller suggested a large department store.

Exhausted and dispirited they left the car and went to the store. To their delight they found exactly what was wanted: a minute light aluminium padlock with a tiny key, both beautifully made and gilded.

'Come on,' said Helen happily, 'let's get home and get on with it!'

C.B. was out, they hurried upstairs and into Helen's bedroom. She spread the gadgets on her bed, rolled a strong joint and said:

'I'll do it myself! I can freeze the spot and use a looking-glass.'

Tricesta squirmed at the thought. 'I'm sorry I can't help,' she said, 'but there might be blood, I can't bear the sight of it. You're damn brave to try. Apos will flip when you give him the key.'

'That's what I want,' she said gazing at the thick blue rising smoke. 'Can I have the sleepers?'

Tricesta gave her the gold rings and tried not to think of the needle pushing through Helen's flesh. She left the bed and went down to the showrooms.

After working for an hour she began to feel nervous, perhaps she should check that Helen was all right.

Cautiously she tapped on her bedroom door. There was no reply.

Quietly Tricesta opened the door and crept inside.

Helen sat naked on the bed, her long legs wide apart with a looking glass propped before her. Various pieces of equipment were spread around. She looked about to faint, sweat glisted on her body, her hair was damp and disorderly. She was moaning softly and did not look up. Tricesta felt sick and began to back out.

'Are you okay?' she asked.

'I'm in agony,' gasped Helen, 'that fucking freezer is useless. I've managed one side – but the skin on the other side keeps slipping, I can't get it aligned . . . .'

'Why don't you give it up?' Tricesta said, unable to look.

'What! Don't be bloody stupid,' Helen said breathlessly, 'I must give Apos the key tonight.' She jabbed the long steel needle into herself once again and gasped with pain. 'Christ! This has to pull him for sure. Pass me another joint, there's one in my bag . . . .'

Tricesta lit the cannabis cigarette and put it between Helen's trembling lips, not daring to glance down at the needle sticking through her flesh.

'Call me if you want me,' she said and rushed from the room wishing she had never begun such madness. She worked frantically on her monthly magazine column in an attempt to distract her vivid imagination.

Three quarters of an hour later Tricesta plucked up courage and gingerly returned to the bedroom. Her physical cowardice at the sight of blood seemed odd in such a mentally sadistic person. But Tricesta was aware that brave people were usually masochists, they did not fear pain.

The air was smoky and sweet. Helen was lying on her back, smoking and groaning softly. 'I've done it! It was torture but worth it. Would you like to see it?'

'Mmm,' murmured Tricesta reluctantly. 'Is there any blood?'

'No, I thought there would be but there's not a drop. Look.'

Helen opened her legs, exposing herself. She carefully pulled the outer lips apart so that Tricesta could see the tiny gold rings

139

           the delicate inner lips.

        admit to herself it looked more attractive ␣ected.

    you put the lock on?'

    Give me a chance, I'm bloody sore,' said Helen leaving legs open. 'I'll put it on before I meet him tonight. Do ␣ike it?' Helen sounded very satisfied with herself.

'Very much,' lied Tricesta beginning to recover. 'You have certainly set a new London fashion. You must be excited by the thought of handing over the key.'

'I can hardly wait,' she said. 'Wouldn't it be the end if he refused it?' She looked worried.

'Of course he won't,' replied Tricesta adamantly. 'What man would refuse such a unique gift?'

'You're right,' she agreed, sitting up slowly feeling reassured; tears of strain and relief trickled from her red eyes.

'I'm in agony,' she said. 'Pass me my bag, there's another spliff in it,' she said, unconsciously using a word from Apostrophe's vocabulary. 'I suppose I shall have to keep twisting the sleepers around, to prevent any adhesion, that'll be hell,' Her speech was slurred as she lit the joint.

'Does charge help?'

'I've got to have something,' she said, 'wouldn't you?'

Tricesta saw her point, opened the windows, covered her with a blanket and left the room.

C.B. had returned and suggested a late lunch at The Sun Tavern.

Sandy was in fine form when they walked into the bar.

'Hello my pretty things,' he shouted to them, 'glad to be back among English ponces once again are you?' Tricesta laughed and nodded.

'Come on, poxy Peter,' he shouted to Bobbie, 'buy the children a drink, you're bloody lucky to be able to booze with the aristocracy! Should make a change from the bums at the Scrubs!'

'As I'm buying,' Bobbie said to Tricesta, 'I insist on taking you out tonight.'

'I would have liked that,' she smiled, 'but I'm busy tonight, make it tomorrow.'

'Fine,' he said watching C.B., 'I'll pick you up at eight. Wear some decent gear, I might be able to nick it when you're not looking!'

The brother and sister sat alone in a corner and gave their unexciting order to Polly. Tricesta told C.B. all about Helen's extraordinary manifestation of masochism, and one-up-manship.

'You're having me on,' he laughed, 'no one could be conned into doing that!'

When she had convinced him he collapsed with laughter.

'Doesn't she realise that a cat like that will just sell the key or hire it out to any punter?' He was still laughing. 'He's just a spade ponce, he could make quite a bit of bread out of her. She must be blocked-like permanently!'

They forgot about Helen and discussed other business. He agreed to spend the weekend at Castle Mordaunt with her.

'Not that I'm thrilled with the idea, three days with the old boy will send me goofy,' grumbled C.B.

'He's not so bad,' said Tricesta, 'he's just a lonely old man.'

'You've changed your tune,' he said quickly, 'you have always been anti-Grandfather. You puzzle me sometimes and now you've arranged to go out with a cat-burglar. If it's not a spade it's a villain,' he sounded piqued. 'I'm not prejudiced or anything like that but what would you think if I went out with a prostitute or an African chick?'

She laughed at this and they dropped the controversial subject. Tricesta had found difficulty in explaining to him why she had been in possession of Black Power documents. But he soon lost interest in her explanation when he saw the matter was no longer a problem.

Tricesta telephoned Edward X and confirmed she would be going to Castle Mordaunt for the weekend. He told her to call at his house before she left.

Helen arranged to meet Apostrophe Brown that evening and Tricesta went off on her date with Edward X's integrated brother, Bradford S. Kingston.

He opened the door to her and seemed lost for words, then he pulled her inside and embraced her passionately.

'I've been going mad – you don't know what I've been through,' he said at last, 'don't ever give me another scare like that.'

He had cooked a special soul food dinner and fussed over her.

After they had eaten the spicy West Indian food he looked seriously at her.

'Darling, I know you've been through a bad scene but I must

know. Are you in any way involved with Edward? Please tell me the truth. Has he threatened you?'

Tricesta realised she had to give Brad an acceptable version of the American episode even if it were not the truth.

'Of course not,' she said calmly, 'and I'm not involved with him. An English friend of mine asked me to deliver an envelope to William X the Second. I didn't even know what was in it.'

'Oh Jesus,' he screwed up his handsome face, 'that bastard, that cunning brother of mine. I'll see him about this, I'll settle him once and for all, the way I should have done years ago. . . .'

'No,' she was alarmed, 'promise you won't, I couldn't bear it. Promise! He was not to blame!'

Brad was not convinced, he believed totally in her innocence, thinking she had been viciously misused, which was true.

'But darling,' he led her to the divan, 'unless I stamp on him now he'll use other tricks. You don't know how cunning the cat is. He'll stoop to anything, especially if he gets to know you're my girlfriend.'

'Girlfriend' – he already thought of her as 'his'. God!

'You must give me your word you will say nothing to him. Believe me, Brad, it's for the best. So don't mention it again.' She lit a cigarette and changed the subject. 'Have you been thinking about me? Have you missed me?' she asked.

'Oh honey,' his pent-up passion was obvious, 'I haven't stopped.' He smothered her with his body and kissed her. 'I've never been through a trip like this before. No other chick has ever turned me so completely upside down. When I met you I was just playing the game, so were you, but suddenly it got serious, for me. I always thought I was a high liver – but this is something else!'

The telephone rang at an inappropriate moment, it seemed to ring at ten minute intervals. Usually with a hopeful girl-friend wanting to come over for a 'chat'. Birds went for Brad like men went for Tricesta.

'No Judy,' he said quickly, 'there's a hang up, I'm just rush-ing out, I'll call you, bye love.' Brad slammed the receiver down, then took it off the hook.

'They only want me for one thing,' he said disdainfully, 'they're a real drag, these chicks never give up. Darling,' he lifted her on to him, 'I don't need anyone but you, you're too much! I don't want anyone else, can you understand?'

'Of course,' she said softly, 'I know how you feel but we've

142

both got it all so why spoil it?'

'It won't be spoilt if you don't go with anyone else.'

'I don't need to any more,' she replied, lying for the sake of peace. Agreement saved an argument and his pride. He could never appreciate her attitude towards sex. Puritanical Victorian hypocrisy had been well pumped into him on the once British island of Tobago. In a sense Edward was right, Brad was a 'super spade', moulded by white society. To her surprise Tricesta was still interested in him. Of course he was a fabulous lover but even when her passion had been satisfied she did not rush away from him.

'I know now that I'm in love with you,' he said seriously. 'I've never said that to a chick before,' she knew he was not lying, he was not the type, 'they usually say that to me. You're the only person who has the power to hurt me, please don't.' His sincerity startled her.

Chapter 9

C.B. WAS DRINKING a cup of hot milk and filing his immaculate nails when Tricesta returned.

'Nice evening?' he asked with a hint of sarcasm.

'Very,' she replied noncommittally, trying to suppress her high spirits, 'very quiet though. I'm just going to make a telephone call.' Tricesta began to walk from the room.

'Can't you make a call in front of me now?'

'Don't be silly,' she laughed and dialled Brad's number.

'Yes – no, no trouble,' she said, he said goodnight and blew kisses. She blushed feeling C.B's eyes on her, 'I'll talk to you tomorrow.' But he insisted she 'send' him a kiss.

Annoyed with herself for feeling guilty she quickly blew a kiss, said a tender goodnight and replaced the receiver.

'Well, well,' said her brother, 'you've just left his hot little bed and within ten minutes you are ringing him.'

'He asked me to let him know that I got home safely.' She sat beside him. 'I'm beginning to think you're jealous!'

'Oh cool it,' he snapped, pushing too hard at his fine cuticles, 'but you've lost all sense of proportion. And now Miss Copy-Cat has followed your lead – I'm surrounded by niggers!'

Normally they would have laughed at his ridiculous statement but he was not joking. Tricesta had never seen her brother in this mood before and said so.

'I'm no different,' he replied coldly, 'it's you that has become a nigger-lover! Before you can say "nig-nog" you'll be expecting his baby – a half caste, neither fish nor fowl! As I've said before, have a good loon around with the cat but don't get involved. These people lose their cool on that kick, especially over a bird like you, think of the boost to their ego. He'll be proposing marriage next!'

Tricesta felt hot with worry and put an arm around his shoulders.

'Please don't go funny on me, we've never had hang-ups before.' He was almost in tears. 'You know I adore you and no one else, I'll never change. I just dig him and feel something for him, he's different. Don't resent his colour. I haven't surrounded myself with blacks, he's the only one I'm friendly with.'

'And do you know why?' he looked at her. 'Because he's near European in his behaviour, that's why you tolerate him, if he behaved as most of them do you'd never put up with it.'

Deep inside she suspected he was right.

'By and large they're a pretty unpleasant race,' C.B. went on, 'they demand self-rule and look what happens when they get it. In Africa it's chaos, bloodshed and starvation. They have always been warriors, they'll never change, they'll always fight among themselves. Just because you've met one decent, English educated cat you imagine they are all like him. Forget it!' C.B. was really wound up. 'Matt Fitzpatrick hasn't a chance of getting them to ignore the traditional white system, they know it offers a damn sight more than a black society ever could. That's why Black Power will never win, the majority know where advancement lies. Of course they'll make a stink now and again but that's all it will be, a militant minority flare-up. Agreed it can cause trouble, but not insurmountable trouble. Look how they all pour over here, they know fucking well where it's really at. I don't hate them but I believe they should stay in their own country. I don't dig interbreeding.' C.B. was astonishingly articulate. 'Look, you don't cross a poodle with a terrier, not if you want to be proud of your pet.'

'You can't liken humans to animals,' said Tricesta feebly.

'Why not? I know many mongrels can be delightful creatures but the individuality of each breed is lost. There are many races on the earth, each has its own unique qualities, peculiar to them, it's wrong to wipe them out. I just can't go for an impure breed, the way I can't dig a piece of antique furniture that's been "married up" as we call it. Often they're useful pieces but they offend me.' He looked at his sister with genuine concern. 'I give you my word I'm not a nigger-hater but I'll never dig interbreeding. Surely you see my point? We should communicate with them, trust them, they have talents which we could never possess, enjoy them, but don't water them down. This is Fitzpatrick's theory, he stands for a pure black race, he doesn't go for the blacks losing their individuality. You know he is right, you know I'm right.'

'But you said Black Power could never work.'

'What I meant was, their leaders will never stop them apeing our society. But they may, and I hope they do, instil into them that black is better than "coloured". Fitzpatrick wants to encourage them to mate with a partner of their own race, and I go along with that.'

'I never realised how strongly you felt,' said Tricesta quietly. 'I see your point but I still dig Brad!'

'Fine,' he laughed holding her hand, 'but don't lose your cool. Have a ball but bear the facts in mind. And please keep away from Black Power, even if a glittering cat like Leary O'Leary did give them five thousand quid, he happens to be a mummer in the gold. They still stand for violence so don't get innocently caught up in one of their outbursts.'

'Of course not, and in any case Brad has completely disassociated himself from the movement. He won't have anything to do with it, even though Edward X is his brother.'

'You see,' he smiled, 'he really is an "integrated super spade", that's why you go for him.'

'Okay,' she said, 'I'll smoke to that!'

They both laughed, the rift repaired.

But Tricesta was left with a bitter-sweet aftertaste. Could she ever lose it?

Helen did not return to the flat until 10 a.m. the following morning. C.B. was cross with her for offering no apology, but he appeared as charming as ever towards her.

'Are you very busy?' she asked Tricesta. 'I'd like to talk to you.'

'Let's go upstairs,' said Tricesta, curious to hear her tale.

When Helen had fixed herself a black coffee they went into her bedroom. She sat on the bed and said: 'Apos and I went to a couple of clubs, got stoned and ended up at his pad. I felt very excited even though I was in terrible pain, but whenever I felt the key around my neck I forgot how sore I was.'

Helen talked without animation, her eyes were lifeless.

'After we'd been in bed for a while he tried to make me, of course I had to stop him. I said to him: "I've done something which proves my love for you and will prevent any other man pumping me." He just said: "Yeah?", obviously not believing me. Then I threw the bedclothes off, knelt up and took the chain and key from my neck. I handed the key to him and said: "There, now you control me! Take me!" Apos stared at the padlock between my legs and held the key, he collapsed laughing. "This is something else, man!" was all he said. I told him I hadn't cheated, that he had the only key there was. After he had examine it carefully and worked the lock he said: "You're too much, just too much!" He didn't say anything else, he took the padlock off and practically raped me. I made such a stink that he gave me something to kill the pain, I don't know what it was.'

Tricesta had a fair suspicion and noticed Helen now glowed as she went on: 'Anyway it worked because he really did rape me . . . ' Helen was excited by the memory. 'I refused to have it but he overpowered me, believe me, I'm on fire now!' Helen began to undress, the chain and key hung around her neck, she fingered them and said: 'Yes, he actually refused it! It hasn't really hit me yet.'

'But why didn't he want it?' asked Tricesta.

'I don't know,' tears filled Helen's eyes, 'I just don't know. He said it wasn't his scene and gave it back to me this morning – after he'd had me again. I dreaded him not wanting me – I only did it for him, he knew that but it made no difference. He locked me up and said I was a gas!'

She dropped on to the bed, naked and exhausted, tears flowed, her beautiful body shook.

Tricesta walked to the bed and saw a large bruise just above the inner bend of her left arm. Helen had had her first main-line 'fix'. There were two tiny needle marks. The first injection must have been clumsy and caused the bruise. Tricesta left her alone and related the story to C.B. in the office. He was greatly amused at Helen's rebuff.

'But why would a ponce like Apos reject such a fantastic opportunity?' he asked.

'I think I can work that one out,' replied Tricesta. 'Consciously or unconsciously the black races feel inferior to the white. Here is a pretty young girl who comes from a racialist society, just about the worst of the lot, and this girl, who could pull most white cats begs a black cat to take her, in a unique way. Imagine the kick it gave him to refuse! Imagine the boost to his black ego to turn down a Rhodesian chick. He can live on that story for the rest of his life. I'm sure that's why he refused, not because he wanted to lose control but because rejection was an enormous aid to stifling his inferiority complex. A complex which Fitzpatrick and his supporters want to wipe out.'

'That's not bad thinking,' agreed C.B., 'I go along with that, what a shock for her ego though!' He answered the telephone.

Janie Craig invited them to her flat for dinner that evening. 'I'd love to come,' said C.B., 'but Tricesta can't make it, she's got a date. Okay, I'll see you about eight o'clock.'

'Any exciting new commissions in?' Tricesta asked C.B.

'A couple,' he nodded. 'This playboy Arab, Prince Ahmed, wants us to furnish and decorate his huge flat off Eaton Place. Money no object he said, he's young and went to Oxford of course. He keeps asking to meet you, seems to be a thing with him. Perhaps we'd better dine with him one evening. It won't kill you to be a "traditionally English" upper-class bird for once. Prince Ahmed digs the British bit. I'll arrange it for next week, provided our black brothers can spare you!' His undertone of sarcasm was lost in his laughter.

Their business had grown steadily, Uncle Eric almost felt he had made a good 'investment'. He nearly fooled himself that he had been very shrewd.

Tricesta arranged to see Edward X at five o'clock. She worked until it was time to go, Helen remained in bed, suffering from reaction.

Tricesta parked her car some distance from Edward's house and walked along the litter-filled streets. The stench from rotting garbage was appalling, young children played and fought

148

among the filth and their parents made no effort to prevent them or to protect them from traffic. The council's promises of play areas were never fulfilled, apathy spread through the slum area, and bad conditions became worse.

'And that's what we're going to end,' declared Edward X, 'we'll make them abolish the slums, we'll make them look after our children. We won't allow them to be repressed any more. Our hope lies with the kids, we'll make sure they start out with the right education. We'll see that African culture and traditions are taught in the schools. They have the right to know their history, European history is instilled into white kids, so African history should be taught to black kids. They must learn to be proud of their background . . . .'

'But what background?' asked Tricesta. 'Voodoo and inter-tribal squabbles, the building of mud huts and eating each other?'

'There speaks Miss White Fascist,' he screamed at her. 'Do you see how you've been brainwashed?'

'But what I've said is a matter of history,' she said. 'Don't go for me, I sympathise with your position.'

'I sympathise with your position,' he mimicked, 'like Hell you do. Your type is more dangerous to us than an out-and-out Powellist. You profess to help us but in fact keep the brakes on even more cleverly. That tolerant bit doesn't fool us any more, we're not tolerant, we've been that for two hundred years, it's finished.' His eyes became bright. 'Black Power is growing and your people are scared, you know it means the end of white supremacy. I can smell the fear. Take a normal white party and a black cat comes into the room. Everyone senses his presence, they are aware that a spade is among them and they are afraid!'

'You're kidding yourself,' snapped Tricesta, forgetting her precarious position. 'What they show for the spade is distaste, not fear. He is an interloper in their midst, they don't want a Negro among them. Fear my foot!'

'So now we have the truth, at last we know where we stand,' he shouted and walked over to her. 'So you admit we're fighting prejudice. But you're a nigger-lover, aren't you?'

Showing his fury he pulled Tricesta to her feet and held her viciously.

'You don't pull away when a nigger touches you! You dig brother Brad turning you on, don't you? That's why white cats

149

fear us, baby, because we know what to talk with!' he pushed his hard body against her. 'White chicks know where it's at, don't they?' he taunted her, 'but then my brother would pass for a Whitey if you shut your eyes, wouldn't he? Don't get worried, I won't touch you. If I wanted to I could but you're too kinky for me. You like to keep it in the family unless it's a nice integrated spade like Brad. You're not my speed, baby . . .'

But she knew he was lying, he wanted her, in the way Apos had wanted Helen.

He hated Tricesta, he hated not being able to fool her about the magic power of black men. 'Interloper' was a dirty word to him, it rang in his ears. Edward released her aggressively, she fell on to the sofa.

'Has Flaxman been set up?' he asked, returning to his steel desk.

'Almost,' she said, 'he'll be staying at the Castle tomorrow night. Show me how to work the bug.'

Edward explained the device to her and then said: 'You'll have to hide me near the house and give me some sort of signal. I'll have to keep tuned in, it's a drag but that's the scene. Where can I set up my equipment?'

She gave it thought.

'There are several pavilions and summer houses but I think the best place would be in the main stable block. You can't miss it, there's a clock tower above it.'

'Is anyone likely to use it?'

'No,' said Tricesta, 'not at that time. I'll come down to the stables when the time is getting near. If you come in by one of the big gates remember to close it after you. I'll draw you a map of the estate and outbuildings. There's no point in arriving before nine o'clock, even that's too early. Will you be alone?'

'Yes, in a scene like this I trust no one. I'll give you six pills to give him, that should shake his P.B. principles.'

'Not necessarily,' said Tricesta, 'if he is an unconscious resister I still think he won't give in. It's impossible to predict how he'll react, especially after a lifetime of sexual repression. Whatever happens you must believe I shall have done my best,' she looked concerned. 'What about Helen? Can I still rely on Apos to keep her hooked?'

'That kooky chick is too much!' giggled Edward. 'Apos told me about the chastity scene! Did you see it?'

'Yes,' said Tricesta, 'she asked me to help her. Why did he refuse the key?'

'Just not his speed, he's got a dozen chicks like her, she could become a drag. That key was valuable but what a hang-up. He'll still freak out with her,' said Edward, 'but on his terms.'

'Give me a good supply of speed,' said Tricesta, 'in case he lets her down, I can't afford to let the hook slip out.'

'Okay,' he agreed, 'That's cool but I need bread for the stuff – I told you it's like gold-dust.'

Edward collected the things she needed while Tricesta sketched a rough map of Castle Mordaunt's grounds. She went through it carefully with him. Finally, the speed and bug in her possession she was ready to leave.

'I'll expect you to show in the stables around ten tomorrow,' said Edward, folding the map. Tricesta took it from him, smiling.

'I'm sure you can remember everything, I'll take the map.'

'You're too much!' he laughed, appreciating her common-sense and to her surprise made no attempt to keep it. They now understood each other too well.

Tricesta drove carefully from the 'Viet Grove' district, so labelled by the militants. She felt nervous and guilty carrying two highly illegal items, but she arrived home without incident at seven o'clock. Quickly she hid the drugs and bugging device and joined C.B. in the flat. Brad telephoned, pleading to see her, she wanted to meet him but explained she had to see her grandfather for the weekend.

Helen had arranged to meet Apostrophe and was busily gilding the lily. C.B. was preparing to go over to Janie's flat.

'Chocolate Biscuits and I have to spend the weekend at Mordaunt Castle,' said Tricesta to Helen, who was automatically impressed, 'we wondered if you would care to come with us. The house is fabulous, I think the scene will amuse you. Would you like to come? We leave at ten in the morning.'

'Gosh, I'd love to,' her Rhodesian accent very pronounced, she sounded as though she had received a royal invitation to Windsor Castle. 'What do I wear? I don't suppose his Lordship digs gear?'

'Don't you believe it,' laughed Tricesta, 'wear your mini-est skirt and you'll be well in. Just be your usual gay self. Are you still very sore?'

'Yes, I keep smearing boracic ointment on myself but I can

151

only sit in certain positions and when I walk it gives me hell.'

'Why not take it off now that Apos has refused the key?' Helen joined Tricesta at the dressing table, her voice was humble.

'Because I want someone else to have the key. I realise now Apos would have misused it,' she said. 'Tricesta, please will you accept the key?'

Christ, she's flipped! thought Tricesta, taken once again by surprise. 'But why me?' she asked, watching the flushed Helen.

'You're the only one who knows how to handle it,' she said softly, still with a note of humility in her voice, 'you'll know who to lend it to. I trust your judgement and I can always ask you if there's someone special.'

'And I can always say no!' said Tricesta, responding to the surprising situation.

'I know that,' agreed Helen, 'but I still want you to have it.' She lifted the chain and key from her neck and hung it around Tricesta's shoulders. Impulsively Helen kissed and embraced her.

Within seconds they were both on the bed. Helen was particularly responsive and gave the impression she wished to be totally dominated by Tricesta with whom she was fascinated.

Half an hour later there was a frantic rush to wash, make-up and dress. Helen hurried away to meet Apos.

C.B. listened to Tricesta's description of her encounter with Helen, she showed him the key. He became amorous.

'No,' Tricesta pushed him away, 'Peters the Pipe will be here soon. Save yourself for Janie.'

'You're kidding,' he said. 'I haven't got a chance with her spade hanging around. I'm beginning to believe those jokes about their superior sexual prowess. Is it true?' he asked, hoping to be reassured.

'I don't know,' she hedged, 'I suppose that some of them groove better, I only know one spade.'

'Don't evade my question,' he persisted. 'Is he better at it than any other cat you've had?'

'If you mean does he pump better, yes he does. But is that the be all and end all?'

'To a lot of people it is,' said C.B., 'but what is it that's so much better? Is he just bigger?'

Tricesta laughed. 'It's nothing to do with size,' she said, 'but his whole body makes it. All his nerves and senses are in action.

152

Do you follow me? Most men imagine the only way to groove is to put it in, of course that's important, but there is a bit more to it than that. Put it down to having soul. I can't define it for you.'

'Do you feel that that is all it is with me?' he asked quietly.

'No,' she said positively. 'I belong with you. Sex with you is great but we could survive without it.'

He nodded and held her closely before leaving the flat.

Bobbie Peters, looking, as usual, very like Steve McQueen, arrived half an hour late.

'Sorry, luv,' he breezed into the drawing room, 'got held up on business. This isn't a bad pad – not bad!'

He continued to admire the decoration, Tricesta put on a new Black Sabbath L.P. and poured Bobbie a large whisky. She sat down and noted his precise clothes.

'So this is how the other half lives,' he joked, sitting beside her. 'Where's big brother?'

'Out grooving,' she smiled. 'Don't worry, we're quite alone.'

'A crowd doesn't bother me, I often go for a gang bang but I just like to know the scene first. Mustn't be caught out with dirty knickers! Where do you want to go?'

'I don't know,' she sighed, 'I'm pretty tired and I've got to be up early tomorrow. We're going to Westingshire for the weekend.'

'Oh yes, summoned to the family seat are we?' he said, taking a large gulp at his whisky.

'Do you know what I really fancy?' he asked. She groaned inwardly, surely he wasn't going to be corny. She wanted him to be a law unto himself, not follow the usual pattern.

'No,' she said, 'what do you fancy?'

'Well, apart from you,' he looked hopefully at her, 'I fancy getting blocked. Got any grass?'

Although Bobbie Peters was a villain he was in his own way completely trustworthy. He was not a gossip. Tricesta was safer smoking with him than with the majority of their fast clique.

'I would never have thought that was your scene,' she replied, 'especially as you drink.'

'Anything is my scene, baby,' he smiled cheekily, 'anything that might give me a kick – I'll try it all. I often get turned-on. Where is it?'

'I'll get some,' she said, 'it's not kept in the flat.'

She left the apartment and hurried up to the top floor. In an unused cupboard in the attic she fumbled for the small brown block.

'I haven't got any skins,' she told him on her return, 'We'll have to empty a few cigarettes.'

'Did you bolt the door?' he asked.

'Of course, you'll just have time to swallow the lump!'

Bobbie kept up a flow of dirty stories which he imagined would titillate Tricesta, he was wrong. She wished he would behave naturally, and drop his 'front'.

Half an hour later, with six cigarettes refilled with crumbled cannabis and tobacco laid neatly on the marble table before them, they sat back on the sofa and lit up.

Both were silent, listening to the Indian inspired sounds of Alla Rakha.

'It's a great scene,' said Bobbie looking at his joint, 'and it's getting better every moment!'

She thought this remark, in its present context funny and laughed, and lit her second cigarette.

'But you fast young people turn on every day,' said Bobbie, 'this is the regular scene in Chelsea.' She allowed him to remain under the false impression that she was a heavy smoker. That was the image he wanted to believe.

'You're not exactly old,' she said. He smiled and reached for her hand. 'Thirty two,' he replied, 'but in my game that's getting on. I can't go up pipes all my life. Have you any idea what a shitty life I lead? It probably sounds exciting to you,' he was not smiling, 'it's dirty, degrading and if you have to "go away" for a spell it's hell. I want to make a packet and get out of England – live with a clean girl like you. Live a new life, maybe in Canada or Australia, the beaches there are a dream. I'd write a book – several books. I'm sick of this filthy farce called life. London is the most destructive city in the world, take it from me – I've been to a few places, for one reason or another! But London is the most vicious, you've been lucky to have the backing of your family and the protection of people who have power. Without those you can't survive. I can hardly make it and I'm no tenderfoot. I've got no principles or morals. I was raised in a tough, poor but highly religious household. When I asked my father certain obvious questions about the faith he beat the living daylights out of me. I was ten at the time. I kept my doubts quiet after that until I was fourteen. My father wanted me to become apprenticed to a plumber, I refused and he

154

kicked me out of the house. I haven't been home since but I often telephone my sisters. My mother died two months after I was thrown out. The old man committed all his crimes in the name of God. I commit mine alone, with my conscience. Wow – what a joint, sorry about that history bit.'

'Thanks for telling me,' sighed Tricesta, 'your father sounds a bastard.'

'He is,' agreed Bobbie, 'in all senses of the word! The chip on his shoulder will kill him. I must say I like your set-up. Got a boyfriend?'

'No, not really,' she said, thinking of Brad, 'and I'll never get married, I don't believe in the bit of paper.'

'Another independent female,' he said with sarcasm, 'what with the pill and equal pay the birds are flying too high.'

'Oh I don't believe in the equality of the sexes,' she smiled, 'I believe the female is superior, and that the male was designed to work for and be controlled by birds . . . '

'You're totally stoned,' he laughed, 'but imagine what a team we'd make. Think of all the loaded people you know, I could nip up the pipe on your advice – ' Tricesta also laughed, treating his underlying seriousness as a joke. But he was not fooling. Men in his business however much they enjoyed themselves always looked for the perks. Pleasure alone was not enough, they wanted a pay-off. Bobbie dropped the subject and looked into her eyes. 'So how do you get your kicks? How do I get you to freak out, as I believe you people call it. How do I make you happy?'

'I'm happy,' she sighed, fantasising his sadistic character, wishing he would not treat her like a piece of porcelain. All men made that mistake she thought.

'I know you are,' he said, lighting both their last cigarettes, 'but not ecstatically, wildly happy, are you? You know, Tricesta, although we've only just got together I've watched you for a long time. You're like a butterfly and it's impossible to tame a butterfly, even if you catch one. They flutter and flap for freedom, then die if they don't make it out. You are a butterfly, a beautiful butterfly. He put the final joint between her lips, admired her face and swallowed the last of his whisky.

A tiny sense of frustration was born inside her, she turned to look at him. He was great but . . .

'So what sort of man are you looking for?' he asked.

She focused her eyes on to his and said:

'A man who thinks he can tame a butterfly.'

He blew thick, sweet smoke straight ahead. 'Don't ever let anyone tame you,' he said, 'you're unique, stay like that.' He finished his joint and asked for a Jimmy Smith record.

Tricesta was high and she wanted him, not in a tender loving way, she wanted him to live up to his ruthless reputation. As she turned from the deck he caught her, pulled her on to the floor and ripped off her skirt. Her excitement rose, he tore off her tights.

'Christ!' he exclaimed. 'You do want it, are you always as desperate?'

She ignored his question and sought his mouth, she had never experienced a more passionate sexual need. He held her hands above her head, his unruly black hair fell forward. Tricesta urged him with her body, she infected his desire. He responded viciously and slapped her face hard. The shock stilled her briefly. 'No one's ever hit me before,' she gasped and was immediately swept by an orgasm.

'I'll do it again unless you tell me what you want.' His body pressed her on to the floor. Do it again, she thought. Why doesn't he do it again? Why ask when he must know I want him to dominate me? Christ! Why doesn't he hit me?

'Tell me what it is you want,' he repeated, 'tell me. I'll do anything to satisfy you. I can do anything and enjoy it. Just tell me what I have to do.' Those few words lost her to him forever. He had killed her fantasy. He should have felt what I wanted, she thought. If I have to ask it becomes a charade.

'Tell me baby,' he murmured, 'I'll do anything to please you.' But the magic had died, the last sentence had sealed his coffin.

Utterly disappointed Tricesta simulated sexual excitement but she didn't want to be near him any more. And he could have been very close. Bobbie had no idea what he had almost won and now lost. He shuddered and collapsed over her body. Tricesta wanted him to leave.

'I've got to have a drink,' he said. 'Christ what a girl!' She pushed him off and stood rather unsteadily, she was still high. He drank half a pint of cold milk and kissed her.

'You're great, don't ever get tamed, I suppose this is chucking out time? Big brother is watching . . .'

'He will be soon I'm afraid,' she pretended to be sad, 'I'd love to go out and groove but I'd never get up in the morning. Will you ring me soon?'

'You can depend on that,' he said, stepping into his trousers. 'By the way, I could do with borrowing your car in a week or so. You wouldn't mind would you?'

'You're joking,' she said, full of alarm, 'that's my favourite toy. I'm certainly not lending it to a madman like you. Forget it!'

'No harm in asking is there. I've got this job coming up. I need a really fast auto. Never mind, you're still beautiful.'

Tricesta was glad to be alone, she was depressed and disappointed. She swallowed two sleeping pills, reflected on this barbiturate soaked society, told herself not to feel sad and fell asleep.

C.B., Tricesta and a tired-eyed Helen breakfasted at nine o'clock.

'Was Les about last night?' Tricesta asked her brother.

'No, he was playing in a session,' he smiled. 'I had a long talk with Janie, it was a good scene.'

Helen disappeared into the bathroom. 'Did you groove?' she asked.

'We did,' he smiled again, 'twice for me. I was beginning to think I'd have to black my skin with boot polish! Oh, I didn't mean that, forgive me, that was sick.'

'I'm glad to hear you agree,' she said and followed Helen. She called her into the bedroom and held out three pills.

'Father's specials,' said Tricesta, 'you'll feel the greatest in half an hour.'

Helen swallowed them eagerly and asked Tricesta what she should wear. Tricesta suggested the most outrageous gear in Helen's wardrobe.

'I'll take my car,' said Tricesta, 'you know I like to feel independent. Helen, you drive with Chocolate Biscuits.'

C.B. liked to drive in silence while he daydreamed of exciting new creations; the effect of the methedrine on Helen made this impossible, she would not stop chattering.

After C.B. and Helen had roared off down the gaudy King's Road, Tricesta returned to the building to collect the bugging equipment and drugs. The pills were wrapped in cellophane and hidden in her body. She was not prepared to swallow ten tablets if stopped. The black bug looked like a leather covered cigarette lighter, this she left in her handbag.

As she drove she unconsciously chewed on a quill toothpick. C.B. hated this habit she had picked up at Art School in

Rome. 'It's healthier than smoking,' she would reply to his criticism.

C.B. waited for her to arrive outside the main gates of the Castle.

'Here we go,' said C.B. as Tricesta pulled up alongside his car, 'feathering our future nest!'

'There's no need to think of it like that,' she smiled, 'I shouldn't worry about it.'

'As I said before, 'replied her brother, 'You've changed your tune. You used to be worried in case Mother copped a few bob!'

'Get stuffed!' she laughed and swished through the gates, up the drive and into the outer court.

Purdy was arranging a bowl of peonies in the hall, she looked at Helen and stiffened.

'Lord Prestigne is in the Saloon,' she said with another frosty glance at Helen's gear. Tricesta's aloof manner enabled her to get away with outrageous clothes and behaviour, even Purdy was acquiescent.

'By the way,' Purdy called after the trio, 'your uncle Eric is here for lunch.'

'Thanks,' said Tricesta, 'that's a surprise, I suppose he's still trying to buy Grandfather's candle stands.'

She led the way into what was often called the Fish Room because of its fine plasterwork ceiling. Thirty-two square panels decorated in low relief with dolphins, mermaids and other sea monsters were framed in strapwork borders with deep hanging pendants at the corners. Rather like a stalactite cave formation.

C.B. loved this early seventeenth-century room but always criticised the quatrefoils above the cornice which he said 'were obviously added at a later date because they show no continuity with the Jacobean ceiling'. This criticism, although correct, did nothing to endear him to his grandfather. The old man belonged to the school who thought if something was over a hundred years old it must have artistic merit!

'Grandpa, this is Helen Williams,' Tricesta said after kissing her grandparent, 'she's a great help to us in our business. You know Uncle Eric, Helen.' Eric gave a weak smile to Helen who was overawed by the vastness of the Saloon. 'I hope we're not late for lunch,' said Tricesta, sitting on a Gainsborough chair, 'We had to do some work before leaving.'

C.B. hid himself in one corner of the grand room and looked across the south elevation to the fish pond.

'Well, Charles,' boomed Lord Prestigne, determined not to let him escape notice, 'your uncle tells me the business is holding it's own.' That was his way of saying 'doing bloody well'. I hope you keep it up, you're damned lucky to have had the capital to start things.'

'Yes sir,' said C.B. strolling back to his grandfather, 'but we can always do with more money, for expansion.'

'I dare say,' replied the old man, not prepared to go any further. 'Eric here is still trying to persuade me to sell him the pair of gilt stands.'

Tricesta seized her opportunity. 'Oh uncle, you're fabulous,' she said, 'you knew they were exactly what C.B. wanted for Prince Ahmed's entrance hall.' She looked at her grandfather. 'Are you going to let Uncle Eric buy them for us? Why didn't you tell Grandpa why you wanted them?' she asked her furious uncle, who looked uncomfortable. 'It was to have been a surprise,' he said weakly.

'That's different then,' said Lord Prestigne. 'I'm prepared to sell them to Eric provided they go into your showrooms.' He smiled at Tricesta. 'It's my way of encouraging you both. I won't give you money but these two things, whatever you call them, will be a feather in your cap. Raise your last offer by another thousand,' he said to Eric, 'and they're yours, for the St Regis Shop, King's Road branch!'

Eric was neatly trapped, unable to back down. That will teach him to try and take bites out of our inheritance, thought Tricesta.

'What a glorious room,' said Helen to Lord Prestigne. He looked at her and adjusted his eyeglass. 'Thank you, Miss Williams, but Michelangelo here,' he nodded towards C.B. who was doing some hand exercises, 'isn't satisfied with the bits above the frieze.'

'Cornice,' mumbled C.B. 'I merely said they were painted in much later on, they spoil the purity of the original design.'

'Rubbish,' declared Lord Prestigne, 'any minute you will be telling me all my furniture is faked stuff.'

'Money can buy fine articles,' said C.B., 'and knowledge can be acquired, but taste is a gift that can never be bought.' He fluttered his elegant hands drawing attention to the paintings and furniture. 'The majority of people buying works of art

159

today do so as an investment. They have no fundamental feeling for the objects. They enjoy quoting the prices they have paid, and watching the value increase year by year.'

'Well, we can't all live up to your high-falutin' artistic ideals, if we did you would be out of business,' said Lord Prestigne and let his eyeglass fall, 'and what sort of a fancy price will you charge for those Chippendale garden things Eric just bought?'

'Chippendale Rustic Candle Stands,' muttered C.B. unable to stifle his love for correct descriptions. Although Lord Prestigne had no taste he had a knowledge of basic design and periods. He purposely needled C.B. with the wrong words, he knew perfectly well the candle stands were not meant for the outdoors!

'In my book rustic means rural,' said the old boy with a large wink at Tricesta, 'whether they're for indoors or out they're bloody fine. I hope this wog prince fellow will think so too. I'm hungry,' he stood and tugged down his waistcoat, 'let's have some rural lunch.'

He led the way along the hall to the dining room. Helen was bewildered and for once remained silent. Uncle Eric was no longer hungry, the thought of writing a cheque for £6,000 just left him thirsty.

'I can't understand how Grandpa, brought up surrounded by the finest antiques, still hasn't a clue,' said C.B. to Tricesta when Lord Prestigne was out of earshot. 'What a waste of environment. Doesn't he realise there were untalented artists and craftsmen in the past? That only a handful were great and made the top.' He became flushed, his fine fair hair became more untidy. 'Think of all the crudely-drawn antique furniture we come across. We don't want it as a gift, it offends the eye, because it's two or three hundred years old it does not necessarily have artistic merit or value. It makes me sick!'

'Cool it,' whispered his practical sister, 'don't get involved in an argument. Remember, we got the candle stands, thanks to Uncle Eric.'

Lunch was served by an ageing but efficient footman dressed in immaculate green livery. He had been in Lord Prestigne's service for thirty-three years. Helen was confused by the Georgian silver. She did not eat until she had seen which 'tools' Tricesta used. The dining room was a typical Chippendale affair, even the wallpaper was Chinese of the Chippendale period. Conversation was dominated by Lord Prestigne until Eric suffered one of his frequent sneezing fits. The hideous noise caused everyone to cringe. Tricesta and Lord Prestigne particularly hated these unfortunate attacks.

'I can't help having hay fever,' Eric said, between noisy blows and snorts into his handkerchief.

'I know,' replied Tricesta, 'but the noise is terrible, and each sneeze has a horribly long build-up! Can't you stifle it more?'

'No I can't,' he snapped, 'it would burst my ear-drums! I wish you could experience it, anyone would imagine I enjoyed it. Now I've got a tight chest . . . ' The wheezing and blowing got worse. 'I'll have' – wheeze – 'to get' – wheeze – 'my puffer' – wheeze – Eric said, leaving the table.

'He makes more damned disgusting noises than all my pigs put together,' said Lord Prestigne, 'he can't even breathe quietly! Still, it must be bad luck to be asthmatic.'

Eric returned with his neo-epinine filled atomiser and gave four quick puffs down his throat. 'I'm not going to apologise for having asthma,' he said, 'it's better than having chronic migraine like my cousin. I don't complain when others sneeze or cough.'

'But yours are always so much louder,' said Tricesta, 'and the heavy breathing build-up sounds as though you're preparing for a blast off. What time is Michael Flaxman arriving?' she asked her grandfather.

'In time for a drink before dinner – if you can call sherry a drink,' he replied.

The remainder of the day was spent in the garden. Uncle Eric left after tea without the superb giltwood candle stands, and minus a cheque for £6,000.

Tricesta took Helen for a long walk around the estate and checked the stables were unlocked. Six horses were kept for the benefit of Lord Prestigne's guests. 'Gee, I'd love to have a gallop now,' said Helen.

'Another time,' replied Tricesta, 'I want to show you the organgery and the ice house.'

'Why do you keep chewing a tooth pick?' asked Helen as they strolled past a classical lead figure, which Tricesta, when she was somewhat younger, considered rather vulgar.

'It's just a habit, it makes me feel casual.' She refrained from asking Helen why she constantly combed and back brushed her hair.

'Good evening, sir,' Michael Flaxman greeted Lord Prestigne respectfully.

'Haven't seen you for a long time, Michael,' he replied. 'Heard from Enid yet?'

'Yes, she's just arrived in Tobago.' Tricesta entered the drawing room and was startled to hear the word 'Tobago' but quickly realised the context. She had just set up the bug behind her bed, hoping she would be able to get Flaxman into her room. It would be more incriminating, but if she failed she would go to his room by walking along the balcony. There was no need to use the corridor. Tricesta smiled at Michael as she greeted him, his severe good looks were well preserved, but the half-moon spectacles were rather off-putting.

'Just a small, dry sherry, thank you,' he said to the butler, looking at Lord Prestigne's very large whisky.

'Well m'boy,' said the Lord Lieutenant, 'how's the Liberal front coming on? Still pleased you renounced Toryism?'

'Of course,' nodded Flaxman.

'I never did understand why you made the change,' Tricesta said.

'To put it briefly, I had a serious disagreement with the 1927 Committee. Rather than betray certain life-long principles, I decided to change parties,' he replied rather curtly and sipped his sherry. It was obvious Michael did not wish to go further into the question.

Dinner was in the traditional English county manner: fresh grilled trout, crown of lamb followed by cook's special apple and loganberry pie. Talk covered a wide range of topics. Helen succeeded in remaining one subject behind in discussion and would occasionally break in with a totally irrelevant question, this would bring the flow of conversation to an abrupt halt. She was oblivious of her irritating habit. Lord Presigne lost patience and remarked it was a pity the colonies seemed to lag behind in everything.

Before arriving at the castle Helen had planned to seduce the old boy. During her masturbatory fantasies she had visualised the possiblity of becoming Lady Prestigne! But when she saw the imposing house and met the dignified owner she lost her nerve. She was overwhelmed by the scene and felt like a duck in the desert. So her fanciful scheme to become mistress of Castle Mordaunt never got off the ground. Nevertheless she felt there was a vague hope if . . . if she could marry C.B. who would eventually inherit the title, but Chocolate Biscuits was not going to propose marriage voluntarily!

After dinner they had coffee in the drawing room, Michael Flaxman poured himself a glass of 'medicinal' brandy and the servants were dismissed.

Tricesta excused herself and in the fading light hurried to the stable block.

'I'm over here,' Edward X's voice called softly to her, 'what's happening?'

'Nothing yet,' she replied squatting beside him in an empty horse box. He held a powerful torch and showed her a neat, shiny radio receiver and the tape recorder.

'It's set to the right frequency,' he said, 'how's the patient shaping up?'

'He's very tough,' she said, 'if that stuff doesn't mess his mind up nothing will happen.'

'It never fails,' he replied, 'given the right circumstances. Remember it's in your own interest not to fail. This is a wild pad, is any of the mansion let off?'

'Of course not,' she smiled, 'Grandfather wouldn't share his house with strangers. It will all belong to C.B. and me one day.'

'Unless the revolution comes first,' he said quietly.

'What "revolution"?' she asked crossly.

'The black one, baby, the black one. Open your eyes, can't you see the preparations going on? You can only survive by joining us. Just wait, when Africa is ready no one but no one will be able to save Whitey in Rhodesia or South Africa. Believe me, they're already terrified, that's why apartheid is being stepped up. Go, get hustling, Miss Fascism, we're all waiting!'

Tricesta refrained from replying and hurried from the stables.

Chapter 10

ON HER RETURN to the drawing room her grandfather was yawning.

'Shall I get you some hot milk?' she asked.

'Yes,' he nodded, 'I'm ready for bed. Will you have hot milk, Michael?'

'No thanks,' he replied, Tricesta's heart sank. 'What about Ovaltine or Horlicks?' she asked.

'Very well,' he smiled, still sitting upright in his wing chair. 'I'll have Ovaltine as you're making it.' C.B. indicated his wish for hot milk and Tricesta set off for the pantry. She disliked the English habit of drinking milk before retiring, she felt it was something of a dated joke.

Tricesta melted six tablets of methedrine and stirred the dangerous liquid into the Ovaltine.

Michael Flaxman added two spoons of sugar and thanked her warmly. Conversation lagged, Helen said goodnight and disappeared to her room. She appeared taken aback when the three men stood as she left the room. C.B. normally never bothered in London, certainly not with her.

Tricesta glanced into Flaxman's half empty cup and said: 'Drink it while it's hot, then I'd like to have a word with you. Would you mind?'

'Good heavens no,' he said and picked up his cup. She kissed her brother and grandfather goodnight and collected the empty cups and saucers. Back in the pantry she meticulously rinsed Flaxman's cup and spoon. Apart from Mrs Halfpenny, the housekeeper, Tricesta was the only person allowed into the butler's hallowed sanctum.

'I'm very hot,' she said returning to the drawing room, 'do you mind if we walk in the rose garden while we talk?'

'Not at all,' replied Flaxman, 'personally I never retire without taking a little fresh air. Goodnight, sir, goodnight, Charles.' He nodded to Lord Prestigne and his grandson.

After elaborately sniffing the warm rose-scented air for some minutes, Tricesta said: 'I want to ask your advice on writing a novel.'

'A book you plan to write yourself?' he asked, peering at her over his half-moon spectacles. 'How can I help you?'

'It concerns the trouble I had in New York,' she said. 'If I wanted to fictionalise it. Would there be any legal hang-ups?'

'By hang-ups I take it you mean problems. It would depend largely in which countries you would want to publish it. There should be little trouble here, the only ones in London that had any connection with it were the Black Power group and I can't see them bringing any legal action. If you wanted to publish it in the States then that would be a different story. Their laws of libel are very broad, but I can't see Governor White letting it pass, however well you disguised his part in the matter. It's not the sort of thing that would endear you to him, and even though it might not reach the courts, you could find that when the time comes for you to renew your visa, you would get a polite refusal.'

'I had thought of that,' she nodded, 'but suppose I said that he had been given a mind-bending drug and was quite incapable of resisting pressure, would that make any difference?'

Tricesta linked her arm with his, to her surprise he did not pull away.

'I'm not convinced that a completely honourable man

165

couldn't resist,' he said, 'but why should you want to write about it?'

'It wasn't that in particular, but in one chapter I wanted to illustrate how a respectable politician could be got at,' she snuggled closer to him, still he did not rebuff her, 'that incident would only be a small part of the book.'

'But what about your antiques business?'

'Oh, that's great, but there will come a time when it won't need all my attention. Provided the business side is efficiently handled by experts, C.B. can cope. We're doing very well. It was a great challenge for me to put it together, but I get a real kick out of writing my monthly column. A couple of weeks ago a publisher suggested that I might be able to write a novel.'

Suddenly she kissed him, he flinched but did not resist. His spectacles fell off. 'You look groovy without them,' she whispered as he bent to pick them up. 'I just couldn't help doing that. I've had a crush on you since I was at school. Did you know that?'

'No – of course not.' He adjusted his spectacles but she could sense his mounting excitement. Tricesta held his hand and went on: 'Yes, I've been approached several times to write about the New York scene and I dig the idea of doing a novel. Of course everyone I meet is writing a bloody book, it's a drag, it sounds so corny. Like calling yourself a company director, no one believes it, unless they are interested enough to check the Register of Companies. Would you do me a great favour?' She felt that the drug should have had a considerable effect on him by this time.

'When we go in, will you come to my bedroom and talk to me? I need someone with your experience, Chocolate Biscuits lives in the clouds. Please help me, I'm terribly confused. There would be no need to go into the corridor, just walk along the balcony to the right, I'll leave my window open. Will you do that for me, Michael?'

'I don't know, Tricesta,' he hesitated, 'you're not a schoolgirl now, people could misunderstand.'

'No one will ever know,' she slipped her arm around his waist, 'that's why I suggested you use the balcony. I really am going through a difficult phase, I need mature help and you are a great friend of Grandpa's. I know he respects you. I can't sleep until I've talked my problem over with someone.'

Tricesta pulled him to a stone seat and put her head on his chest and sighed: 'Please help me, I'm so confused.' She could hear his heartbeats, she pretended innocence, like a child seeking wise counsel. 'Of course I want to help you, my dear,' he said, beginning to sweat, 'I'm flattered you think enough of me to ask my advice.' Flaxman saw himself as teacher-guide to the muddled youth of today. His ego took command. He put a fatherly arm around her limp shoulders. She leaned trustingly on him, smelling and disliking her scent.

'I can see you're very concerned about things,' he said soothingly, 'if my experience can help you in any way I shall be delighted. You've always distinguished yourself and now you and C.B. are the leading lights in the *avant-garde* interior decoration world. That unfortunate affair in New York must have been terribly distressing. But you survived and you must continue to do so. In my youth I went through difficult, confusing phases but I never lost sight of my objective, nor must you, my dear.' He gave a reassuring squeeze to her slender shoulders. Tricesta nuzzled closer and sighed.

'It's marvellous to be able to talk to a sympathetic person like you.' C.B. would choke if he could hear this, she thought and went on: 'Grandpa is just that bit too much out of the scene. Uncle Eric is only concerned with profit, he doesn't understand my problems and C.B. can't be burdened with them. Father's too busy swopping bits of people from one to the other and Mother can't see past her easel.'

'And it's often easier to talk more freely with someone outside your immediate family circle,' Michael finished for her, and put a hand to his forehead. 'Have you got a headache?' she asked, full of mock concern.

'No – no, perhaps I've had too much rose-scented air! And I haven't taken a medicinal brandy for some weeks. I'd better go indoors . . . '

Tricesta held his shoulders firmly and kissed his thin lips. They remained set but slowly she coaxed them apart, his hands hung uncertainly beside his body.

'You've got to help me,' she murmured against his chin, 'you're the only capable and trustworthy friend I have. I'm trying not to cry . . . ' she hid her face.

'I'll be waiting for you, turn to the right on the balcony, all the windows open to the floor.' She kissed him on the cheek, turned quickly and ran down the topiary-flanked path into the house.

Everyone had gone to their rooms, Tricesta melted another two tablets as a precaution and went upstairs to her own bedroom.

Would this unbending Plymouth Brother weaken and overcome the habits of a lifetime? she wondered. How much easier things would be if I didn't have a power complex, she said to herself as she removed all her clothes. It's a big hang-up, I've got to make it on my own. I've got to prove myself to myself. She combed her hair and went over her make-up. I sometimes think I should live an ordinary mundane life, marry and be faithful to one man, but I know I would be fooling myself. I funk Women's Lib but I love power, the way Grandfather did. There are thousands of great-looking birds but they don't count for a thing, they could but they've been brainwashed into being dominated and they like it. I happen to be in the minority. I loathe doing some of the things necessary to achieve influence and I hate some of the people I have to tolerate, they really turn me off. She saw herself reflected in the looking glass and sighed. I love C.B. because he understands the scene. I feel safe with him, I can hide behind him if people get too close. He is my shell and I need him as much as he needs me.

To others I appear self-sufficient. That is true, I am, provided my escape route is always open. I adore Brad but not the way he wants. I feel uncomplicated with him and I don't have to assert my superiority.

I'm totally 'me' with Brad and he knows that. I do like him, she sighed again with a tinge of sadness, but I'll never go to Tobago and marry him. If I didn't feel something for him everything would be easier. He should never have fallen in love with me, he was better off with a new chick each day. Eventually I'll hurt him but God knows I don't want to.

Her naked reflection in the looking glass brought her back to the urgent present. If it's the last thing I do I'll show Flaxman that he's fooled himself all his life. Religion can be a terrible thing.

She hid the drug in her bathroom and paced around the Adam decorated bedroom. The beauty and elegance of the room always made her feel happy, even time had not damaged it.

Twenty minutes passed, the net curtains moved gently in the

varm night air. Tricesta wanted to play a record but knew t could interfere with the recording.

She remained unclothed, deciding a good shock might throw Michael off balance.

Five minutes later, the bespectacled barrister parted the cur-ains and stepped into her bedroom. He still wore his dinner acket and carried a Bible from which he intended to quote apt assages.

'I'll be out in a second,' called Tricesta from the adjoining ressing room.

'I felt quite absurd creeping along the balcony and climb-ng through your bedroom window,' he sounded a little em-arrassed, 'that's the sort of innocent action that can sound hastly in court. Do you feel any easier now?' He stood beside he marble chimney piece holding his Bible.

'Right now there's only one way I could feel easier,' Tricesta trolled into the room, 'and I hope you know what to do about ¸'

Flaxman's reaction surprised even Tricesta, he appeared to e mesmerised, he dropped the Bible and swayed.

'I've . . . I've never ever seen Enid undressed,' he stuttered, ollowing her with his eyes as she walked towards the bed. He elt his brain was floating in infinity. No longer were there any arriers. The drug had worked, Flaxman felt free, no sense f guilt, just serenity.

Conscious of the bugging device Tricesta beckoned Michael join her. His legs were very shaky but he obeyed without esitation and sat beside her. She took his damp hand and laced it on her breast.

'Tricesta, what am I doing? I feel unbelievable, I've never en a girl with nothing on before, and now I'm touching ne. What's happening to me? I want to touch you – I want . . ' He squeezed her nipples. She removed his spectacles and arted to undress him. Flaxman fell back groaning, not from onfusion but from years of repression. At that moment he ould see no reason for those unnatural repressions of the past, e had been fooled, he had fooled himself.

'I'm very hot, would you mind getting me a glass of water, lease?' he murmured. Tricesta ran into the bathroom and pped the remainder of the drug into the glass and filled it ith cold water. He drank the lot in one draught.

'Do you dig me?' she teased, leaping on to the bed.

'You're fantastic, perfect. I'll tell you something I've not tol[d] anyone else,' he allowed himself to be pulled down besid[e] her, 'I haven't slept with Enid for six years!'

'You mean you haven't made love to your wife in all tha[t] time?' He blushed and swallowed loudly. 'That's right, si[x] years. To be frank, after twenty years of marriage I couldn['t] face another quick incident in the dark, especially knowin[g] Enid felt she was doing me a favour. It had become sordi[d] and degrading. Have you ever been intimate with a man'[?] Tricesta laughed.

'Lots and lots, and I've never found it sordid or degradin[g] Are you shocked?'

'An hour ago I would have been, but not now,' he replie[d] solemnly. Tricesta kissed him gently. 'Have you ever kisse[d] Enid?' she asked.

'Of course but only when she's taken that infernal red pai[r] off. I'm glad you don't use lipstick.'

'I didn't mean her mouth,' she said, 'I meant . . . '

'That's right,' she said, 'Don't be afraid, it's perfectly natura[l] it was meant to be. Oh! That's beautiful, Michael, beautifu[l] don't stop. Don't ever stop!'

He fought for breath but continued without flagging. Su[d] denly she pushed him away, sat up and looked down at hi[m] His face was scarlet, his thick brown hair was in disarray.

'Michael,' she said, 'you are a great lover, that was groovy[.]' After a long pause he said:

'I always understood that that was unnatural.'

'How can pleasure be unnatural?' Tricesta asked. 'You en[-] joyed it and I enjoyed it. How can it be wrong?'

'It can't of course,' he smiled, 'now everything makes sens[e] I have been a fool and because I've been a fool I have denie[d] myself the greatest of God's gifts to man.'

'Then don't deny yourself any more,' she said, still amaze[d] at his behaviour. Edward X had been right about the drug, i[ts] effect had been dramatic.

Tricesta looked at Michael. He was extremely well endowe[d] she had expected meagre insignificance. Impulsively she kisse[d] him, he flung himself on to her. 'God, why was I taugh[t] this was wrong? Why did I believe those lies?' He snatched [at] Tricesta's hair, he shook from head to foot but Tricest[a]

170

would not allow him to pull away until he was drained of all resistance.

When she eventually stood up she realised Michael Flaxman was different. He had lost ten years, his eyes sparkled, he was alive, he was free.

She left him to recover from his shattering experience; for him it was just that. Tricesta tidied herself, drank a glass of water and rejoined him on the bed.

'Tricesta,' he murmured, 'you can have no idea of my feelings. You have just shown me that throughout my life I have been misled by wicked misinterpretations of the Bible.' He wanted to talk, to clear away all confusion. He sat up unsteadily not attempting to cover himself, he had lost his sense of shame.

'I have never consciously betrayed the faith into which I was born,' he said, rubbing his eyes, 'however, one member of my family did manage to break away.'

'Really?' she said with surprise. 'Who was that?'

'My younger brother Jonathan, he was the traditional black sheep. When he was up at Cambridge he got mixed up with a fast crowd, he totally rejected the P.B. teachings on the grounds that they were primitive, steeped in prejudice and had only a narrow and bigoted outlook. He had illegitimate children at a rate which would have astonished Robert Burns!' They laughed and she rested her head in his lap and encouraged him to continue. 'He went to work for a company in Texas, bought land and made a fortune out of oil. Jonathan never married – didn't believe in such a contract. He was ostracised by the family but he often wrote to me, with honesty about his life and his work. Though he was considered beyond salvation by Mother and Father, I always had a sneaking regard for him. Three years ago he had a heart attack and died. To my embarrassment he left his fortune to me!' Michael still seemed stunned by the memory. 'I have never told anyone about this, not even Enid. Only my solicitor and Jonathan's attorney in the States are aware of the position. I have never touched the money, I felt it would have been wrong for me to do so. Yet at the same time I knew I was being unfair to Jonathan and I suffered terribly from false pride, of which I was ashamed! I still can't bring myself to use the money but I now know what to do with it. I am giving it to you.'

'What!?' she almost shouted, staring at him fearing the

drug had damaged his brain.

'Yes, you've proved yourself to be competent and serious in your work. You could have lived a life of idleness and pleasure but you chose to work hard. Both you and C.B. believed in self-achievement, the way Jonathan did. Please accept the money and use it wisely, as he hoped I would. Will you?'

'I don't know what to say,' she replied in confusion. 'I'm flattered, but you may feel differently tomorrow. Of course I could use the bread but – Oh, I don't know . . . '

'I do,' he said firmly, 'just take it. I'm not being generous, it doesn't affect me, I'm a rich man without it. It is a burden to me, and the waste offends me. God knows why he did it.' He kissed her tenderly, as though a weight had been lifted from him. He felt real, human, for the first time in his life.

'You can't begin to realise what it feels like to know you've been blind for years, or pretended to be,' he said with a nagging doubt. 'I've been a fool, a stupid fool! Jonathan tried hard to tell me but I ignored him. Then you came along and forced me to see the truth.'

'Can you remain a Plymouth Brother?' Tricesta asked.

'No,' he said solemnly, 'I can't live what I now believe to be a lie. Of course my faith in Christ remains unchanged but as far as the hocus-pocus goes, well, that's all it is. I hope Enid will understand, her father is an Elder of the faith. You must have laughed at me for years.'

'No, I just felt sorry for you. Sorry that you allowed yourself to be persuaded to lead an unnatural life.'

'But I still have to face the fact that I committed adultery,' he said.

Tricesta was not in the mood for a religious discussion. 'Anyway I'm glad you feel happy about making love. One's conscience always tells one when something is wrong. And yours has not done that, has it?'

'No,' he shook his head and stroked her well-shaped thighs. 'I agree that one's conscience is the real judge of one's actions. I know this sounds silly, but I have always known that to be so but I have never been allowed to believe it.'

'I understand what you mean,' said Tricesta.

'Now,' Michael said, changing the subject, 'you will agree to take over Jonathan's estate, won't you?'

'What does it amount to?'

'That's better!' he laughed. 'I'm not quite sure, but not less than three million dollars – something over a million pounds.'

Tricesta thought she had taken the drug herself by mistake. This can't be true, she said to herself, but he never lies or jokes. It's ridiculous, and I'm helping to blackmail him – but against my will. Why was I forced to do such an awful thing? Edward X must have flipped when he heard that in the stables!

'Michael,' she was distressed, 'I'd love to use the money, but can we leave it for a few days? There is a reason, please leave it for the moment.'

'If you prefer to,' he said, 'but I'll not change my mind. We'll discuss it next week. I always thought you were beautiful but I never realised how sympathetic you were.' He hugged Tricesta and rocked her to and fro. Tears stung her eyes as she stared over his shoulder.

I shouldn't have to feel so dirty, she thought, desperately trying to fight back the tears, so degraded – I never wanted to hurt him. He trusts me and I'm betraying him. He'd never upset anyone, he's so sincere. The only straightforward relationship I have is with Brad and I feel that's doomed. I've never wanted to be nasty to people, even if I've loathed them. Yet I have to assist in blackmailing an honourable person. I'm trapped in my own scene.

An overwhelming distaste for her actions swept her. Unreasonable guilt and remorse filled her. She thought of the scene with her grandfather. How wonderful it had been to discover true affection. To be freed from the desire to deceive, to react with honesty to an old man who loved her. A love she had almost thrown away through selfishness.

Tricesta broke down and sobbed in Michael's arms. He could not understand but he knew she was deeply unhappy. She collapsed completely. Hot, salty tears flowed down her cheeks and on to his arm.

'What's the matter?' he asked softly, trying to soothe her.

'You'd never understand,' she whispered. 'I can't explain, not now. I'm sorry, I feel awful. Ignore me. I've just hit the bottom, I'm sorry.'

'Don't keep apologising,' he said, confused and worried, 'you've been wonderful to me. It's me who should apologise to you, I've been boring and clumsy. I'll never stop being grateful to you.'

Those words brought on another storm of tears. Michael

continued to hold Tricesta knowing he could say nothing to help. Eventually she exhausted her grief and stumbled into the bathroom.

Fifteen minutes later, her make-up repaired she returned to the bedroom.

'You must think I'm mad,' she said. 'One day I'll explain 'You're not at all what I expected you to be,' she kissed him gently, 'this could be so beautiful . . . '

'It will be,' he replied. 'I'm not going back to that half-life I'm going forward, with your help – I hope. You have a special magic.'

Sadness swept her again, she held him and kissed his shoulder

That should be enough for Edward X's needs! she thought aggressively, feeling angry at the helplessness of her situation.

Michael returned to his bedroom via the balcony, he sensed Tricesta wished to be alone.

Tricesta could not sleep even after a heavy dose of barbiturate, finally she gave up trying, dressed and crept along the gallery to C.B.'s bedroom. She looked at him, soft and vulnerable and knew she had done the right thing in protecting him from the blackmail of Edward X.

'Wake up,' she shook him, 'wake up . . .'

'What's up?' he asked, not opening his eyes, 'What's the matter?'

'I can't sleep,' she said, 'I'm going back to London, now. I'll leave a note for Grandpa.'

'Going back in the middle of the night?' he opened one eye 'Why?'

'Don't ask now. I feel hung up, it's pretty bad,' she went on 'The drive will help me to think.'

C.B. was wide awake. 'Shall I come with you?'

'No, I'll be better on my own. Just appease Grandpa and say I had to get back suddenly. Come up after breakfast. Be nice to Flaxman, he looked a bit down this evening.'

'Okay, but I wish you'd tell me what the scene was. Is it Brad?'

'No, it's just me, I'll be all right tomorrow. Go back to sleep, I'll see you at the pad.'

Tricesta kissed him and hurried downstairs. She left a noncommittal letter of apology for Lord Prestigne and ran out to the stables.

There was no trace of Edward X or his equipment. She drove

up to London very fast and tried to find a solution to the situation.

But there was no easy answer. If Edward X was a criminal, doing this for self-gain I could cope more easily, she reflected. But he believes his actions are justified. He wants to help his people, he thinks the accepted channels of reform are useless. Perhaps he's right. Basically he's a 'good' man, but he should reject violence, then people would listen more sympathetically to his views. He could have forced me to give him a lot of money but he kept to our agreement, vile though it was.

The King's Road at 6 a.m. was not the jumping, freaky scene of a sunny afternoon. In fact at that moment it saddened Tricesta. It was like a beautiful girl caught in hair rollers and face cream.

Tricesta found distraction in work. Amid mugs of tea and three chewed toothpicks she strived hard on her column. Whenever she thought of Michael Flaxman she felt sick. She tried to counter this by switching and applying her full concentration on a rough outline for the novel.

For three days she would not accept telephone calls and remained in bed. Michael Flaxman rang every day. She worked without a break on the story outline and realised the legendary 'inspiration' for writing was just that, a legend, a myth which guaranteed no work would get done if one waited for the magic urge. Her sound system was turned to a deafening volume. But Tricesta insisted the pace helped her to think. She telephoned Brad and said she was ill. He desperately wanted to see her but refrained from suggesting that he visit her flat. Brad sensed he would be tactfully put off. He refused to dwell too deeply on this aspect of their relationship.

Tricesta could not face talking to Flaxman and to her surprise Edward X did not try to contact her. He had in fact made an appointment to see Flaxman on the pretext of being one of his constituents.

Edward arrived at his house in Stoneham two days after Flaxman's encounter with Tricesta. The M.P.'s private secretary, a staunch Plymouth Sister in her forties, ushered the West Indian into the library. He was dressed in the English tradition, with a sober suit and a subtly coloured tie. Only his brown and white suede shoes were in dubious taste.

'Good morning Mr . . . ' Flaxman tried to read the false name in the diary but could not decipher the first letter. His secretary closed the door and the Black Power advocate said:

'Edward X, sir.' The 'sir' was not a sneer.

Flaxman stared at him over his half-moon spectacles for a couple of seconds.

'Of course,' he said, indicating a chair for the West Indian, 'You often get yourself into the newspapers, I've read a few of your speeches.'

'I have also read some of yours,' replied Edward.

'Why have you come to see me? You're not a member of my constituency. What can I do for you?' asked Flaxman, a little puzzled.

'I believe you could do a great deal for our people,' replied Edward, refraining from his usual slang. He felt absolutely sure of himself and the method of pressure he was about to use. 'I know you're a busy man, Mr Flaxman, but I want you to listen to a part of this tape.'

He opened his briefcase and took out the neat tape recorder. Part of the most compromising dialogue between Tricesta and Flaxman filled the room. Michael turned pale, he was confused, and shocked. 'Switch it off,' he said quietly. Edward was not smiling, he put the machine away and said: 'I wanted you to have a fair idea of my strength before we talked business. But first I want to explain something. I don't have to, but I want to be fair to you and the girl.'

'So Tricesta was in on this – this trap.' Flaxman was very distressed, not quite sure how to cope.

'Yes,' nodded Edward, 'but only because she had no choice in the matter. I'm telling you this because I have nothing personal against either of you. When I heard her break down on that tape I was sorry for her. She had to do as I said or be ruined professionally and socially. It's not that I care either way but I like the facts to be understood.' He lit a cigarette and went on: 'When I told her what I wanted from you she said it was impossible. She explained how straight and religious you were, she told me to forget it. But I still insisted, she was unhappy about it but there was nothing she could do.'

Flaxman looked at him oddly though not in any great anger. 'Was I drugged?' he asked.

'Yes, I believed the chick when she said you would resist. I couldn't afford failure, I have to use any methods that work.

176

Again I say she had no choice. You must admit the results were not unpleasant.' He smiled but not too cheekily. His mind was set on business.

'I don't necessarily hate white people but we're being repressed and exploited by them. And it's often pretty subtle, you can give us some help. I don't want money from you, although that's always useful . . .'

The M.P. sat back in his chair trying to think clearly. But his chief thought was: Thank God she didn't really want to do this. How she must have suffered, no wonder she broke down. He controlled his mind and concentrated on the immediate problem.

'Blackmail is an ugly business,' said Flaxman. 'If you don't want money what do you want?'

'With this tape I can destroy your political career,' said Edward in a most polite manner, 'but I have no such intention. All I want you to do is present a private member's bill to Parliament, and persuade your colleagues to support it.'

Flaxman felt a little happier, his political career meant a lot to him. But he was still suspicious of Edward.

'What sort of a bill?'

'Firstly it must deal with education,' said Edward. 'Black people want separate schools for black children, equal in every respect to white standards. In these schools Black African history and culture must be taught and I mean the true facts, our children must be given a pride in their history and achieve an identity of their own. We don't want them to be carbon copies of white kids, apeing your mannerisms. Not only must the teachers be black but also the principal. It's useless having black teachers controlled by a white head. That would destroy the entire image. Our kids must be taught how to relate to today's society. The bill should also deal with special housing estates and other matters of importance to our people. That's all I want from you.'

'But private member's bills are a slow business, it can take years. I sympathise with your aims but I'm not the Prime Minister, or even a member of the Government.'

'No, but you are a highly thought of politician, others will listen to you. And bearing in mind the tape I have I'm sure you'll try very hard to press the matter in the House.'

Flaxman spoke to his secretary on the intercom. He asked for tea for himself, Edward X preferred coffee.

'You're a fool, Edward X,' said Flaxman.

'I don't think so. I'm acting in the best way I can. We've tried all the usual channels of reform but nothing ever gets done. The establishment blocks us almost without appearing to. As an M.P. you know the civil service scene.'

'You're still a fool,' said Flaxman. 'If you'd come to me in the normal manner and aired your point of view with sincerity I would have agreed to help you. There was no need to pressurise the girl or me. I would have helped you in any case.

Edward X grinned for the first time. 'You're great! I don't doubt your integrity, but the system would have stopped you all along the line. It still will but with my recording of your little indiscretion you'll really push. Maybe you'll become the big champion of the blacks. No, I like to have bullets in my gun, I don't have to fire it. But you know I'm not fooling.'

Their tea and coffee were served. Flaxman's secretary gave a cold glance at the West Indian.

'See what we have to fight,' said Edward, referring to her almost imperceptible prejudiced attitude, 'it's always there, even if it's well concealed.'

'Where will you keep the tape?'

'Don't worry about that,' he replied, pouring cream into his coffee, 'no one will get near it. I'm the only one in the movement involved in this. Just remember the girl didn't want any part of it.'

'You clearly believe the end justifies the means, but you're still a fool, a misguided fool.'

'I'll be seeing you in London,' said the Negro, 'I'll map out the points I want in the bill. Naturally you must knock it into proper shape, I trust your integrity.' He grinned at his own words.

'Do I get the tape back afterwards?'

'We'll see,' he smiled. 'Don't get uptight about it, I'll not make impossible demands. I'm not the fool you insist I am. Would you please write down your private telephone numbers, both here and in London.'

On this note they parted. Surprisingly the encounter had not become too unpleasant. The ingredients had been there for a vicious incident, but Michael Flaxman, with his intuitive sense for sincerity, felt that Edward X was not out for personal gain. Somehow this took the sting out of his demands, Flaxman understood dedication to a cause, however misguided the dedication. Had he not been guilty of stupid, blind loyalty to the Plymouth Brethren? Of course I would have helped the fellow without being blackmailed, he repeated to himself. But he had to admit the incentive would not have been so strong.

That evening Michael tried again to telephone Tricesta, he wanted to assure her he bore no animosity towards her, but most of all he wanted to see her; he needed to. But she still evaded him.

He wrote a letter of resignation to the Elder Brethren. His reasons for leaving the faith were diplomatically veiled, he referred only to his 'conscience' and 'a more enlightened appraisal of his beliefs'.

He also wrote to his wife, Enid, but felt she would not understand or be in sympathy with him. Narrow confines of behaviour suited her way of life. She had no desire to seek answers to any doubts she had about the faith. Like many who follow rigid man-made rules, she was lazy. It was too much trouble to question the accepted pattern.

On the fourth day after the weekend at Castle Mordaunt, Michael Flaxman was not to be stalled any more. He arrived determinedly at the St Regis showrooms and asked Tim to send for Tricesta.

'So sorry, sir,' smiled Tim, 'Miss Tricesta is not too well, I can't possibly disturb the poor girl. She's in bed,' he said, fluttering his eyelashes at Flaxman.

'Ring her on the internal telephone and tell her I'm not going until I've seen her.'

'I can't do that, sir,' he simpered, 'She'd be absolutely furious with me! Really sir, furious!' Flaxman was not to be put off. 'Where's her secretary?'

'The Rhodesian? She's doing her nails in the office. Do you want her?' He cheekily emphasised the last question which Flaxman ignored. 'Yes, tell her Michael Flaxman is here.'

'Oh, of course, sir. So terribly sorry I didn't recognise you.' He became more humble. 'My friend and I might vote Liberal next time.'

'Really,' said Flaxman dryly, 'I wouldn't like you to become over-liberal! Restraint can be admirable.'

'I'll get Miss Tricesta's secretary,' Tim said, not wishing to continue the conversation.

'Hello,' Helen greeted him gaily, holding her freshly varnished nails in the air, 'wasn't that a groovy weekend with Lord

179

Prestigne?' She spoke loudly, making sure Tim overheard.

'Most pleasant,' he said. 'I want to have a word with Tricesta. Would you please take me upstairs. I've got some good news for her.

'Great,' said Helen, anxious to do as he asked, 'she could do with glad tidings. She seems a bit gloomy. I think it's this new writing bug.' Helen blew on to her nails.

'I shouldn't disturb Miss Tricesta,' said Tim, determined to assert his authority, 'she'll be furious!'

'I know when Tricesta wants to be disturbed,' Helen replied tersely. 'Come with me, Mr Flaxman, she'll be pleased to see you. Answer the blower for me, Tim!'

He turned away and ignored her remark. Michael followed Helen from the shop and watched her backside peeping below her skirt as she went up the stairs.

'Come in,' called Tricesta from her draped bed when Helen gave their 'signal' knock.

'Surprise, surprise,' said Helen, flinging the door open and pushing Flaxman into the bedroom.

'Oh, hello,' said Tricesta feebly, annoyed that Helen had taken advantage of her position to allow Flaxman to catch her off her guard. She smiled warmly at Michael.

'Come and sit down, have some tea.' She asked Helen to make the tea.

'How can you concentrate with this din?' he asked, pulling a pained face at the blasting sound of a pop group.

'It helps me to think clearly and quickly,' she said. 'Turn the volume down a bit, the knob on the left. I haven't been feeling well,' she offered tentatively, pulling her fringe around her eyes. The hair made her feel a little protected. 'I had a temperature, nothing much.' He still did not help her out, she felt obliged to keep talking. 'I'm sorry I rushed off the other night. I had a problem, I thought the drive would help. And then I felt ill . . . ' She hated feeling cornered. Helen appeared with two tall green mugs of Indian tea.

'Shall I change the record?' she asked Tricesta, wanting to wait around.

'No thanks,' replied Tricesta, 'just keep an eagle-eye on the shop, Prince Ahmed may come in. Say I'm out if he asks for me.'

Helen withdrew sulkily, she loathed being told what to do by her beautiful young boss. She was worried too about the gold rings dangling in her flesh. They were turning an unpleasant shade of green.

'How's the constituency?' asked Tricesta, hoping to divert attention from herself.

'Perfectly normal,' Michael replied, sipping the foul tea. He pulled the armchair closer to her bed. Tricesta fiddled with her manuscript and made rapid, meaningless notes.

'You needn't worry, my dear,' he said quietly, 'I know you didn't want to do it.'

'Do what?' she asked, her heart pounding. Edward X had not told her anything. She felt exposed but tried to pretend innocence.

'Tricesta, for goodness' sake look at me, stop playing the idiot. Edward X came to see me. He explained how he forced you to compromise me. I don't blame you in any way.'

Relief swept her and a grudging gratitude towards Edward X for his sense of honesty. 'I've been worried sick,' she admitted. 'I hated myself for having to do it, but I had no alternative. I'm so depressed, what can we do?'

'Nothing at the moment,' he said. 'In fact the man's not unintelligent. I had a pretty straight talk with him and I'm convinced his motive is purely to help his community. If he followed the rules of our society he'd make a good leader, at least he cares. Of course, if he was ever in trouble he'd pile the pressure mercilessly on to us. Let's hope he doesn't get cornered until we can sort something out. For the moment I'll do what he wants, it's nothing that offends my conscience. I'll be honest with you. What worried me was your position in all this. I couldn't bear to think you were voluntarily mixed up in it. Do you understand what I'm saying?'

'Of course,' she nodded, her fair hair veiled her pale face, 'That's why it hit me so badly. What must you be thinking of me? I wanted you to like me, I never wanted to hurt you.'

'Forget Edward for the moment,' he said and sat on the bed, 'I want to talk about us. I've already left the Plymouth Brethren and I've written to Enid and tried to explain things but I don't think she'll understand. She may even divorce me, that wouldn't upset me too much, although I'll never cause her any embarrassment if I can avoid it. I still want you to have Jonathan's money. Will you take it?'

'Thank you, Michael,' she said. 'Now that you know the truth about that night I will take it. But I won't tell anyone about it.'

'Good, I'll tell my solicitor to make the arrangements with yours. I wish you'd trusted me enough at the time to tell me. But your behaviour was touchingly honest, I see that now when I look back. I'm sure you've realised that I'm becoming very fond of you.' Timidly he reached for her hand. 'A whole new life has opened up for me. I can't turn my back on it a second time. I don't want to hurt Enid but I'm not going to deny my feelings any more. I'm fifty-one, it's time I faced reality. Could you get to like me a lot?'

'I already like you a lot,' she hedged, again not wishing to be committed, 'otherwise I wouldn't have been so upset.'

Tricesta pulled him to her and kissed him. He reacted instantly.

Michael was an inexperienced lover but tried hard to please; even so, as she made love to him her thoughts were of Brad and the manner of their society which restrained their relationship. If she dwelt too deeply on their hopeless future she saddened herself. She forced away her tears and desperately tried to re-channel her emotions. The result of their second love-making was a triumph from Michael's point of view.

'It's dangerous to fall in love at my time of life,' he said, holding protectively on to her, 'but that's what is happening to me. If I become a bore to you, please tell me. I don't want to get in your way but I'll do anything I can to make you happy.'

Tricesta sighed with satisfaction, she had emerged on top once again. And he can be very useful to me, she thought, he can give me lots of privileged information for my book and Jonathan's bread is going to be most useful. I can pay off Uncle Eric for a start. And set C.B. up in Paris and New York. So her daydreams went. But they were more than idle dreams. She would make them come true. Her nature would compel her to do so.

Chapter 11

AFTER SETTLING MATTERS with Michael Flaxman, Tricesta made an instant recovery. She returned to the shop and spurred everyone on. Helen asked to have a 'private' talk with her. They went upstairs and Tricesta gave her a further four tablets.

'I've never felt so fabulous,' Helen began, sitting on the long sofa, 'but I'm worried sick about these rings. Do you think I'm getting a disease?'

'Of course not,' laughed Tricesta, 'I'm only sorry I haven't been able to handle things better. I should have given specific men permission to have you and then locked you up again. But I felt so depressed that I dropped everything. Are you still sore?'

'Yes,' she frowned, 'and I don't think I could do anything. Pumpage is out of the question, well I mean, with a man anyway . . . ' She looked questioningly at Tricesta, but Tricesta had lost interest in her. Helen was no longer a challenge in any sense.

For a short time Tricesta had been curious about being intimate with another girl. But since she had gone through that scene with Helen the novelty had worn off. She was sick of her. Helen's clumsiness and insensitivity irritated Tricesta but more than that the girl was a threat to C.B. and herself. They both wanted to be rid of her.

As for the rings, Tricesta had never been a lover of perversion, not when she had to be involved. Her little bit of fun at Helen's expense was now a bore to her.

'Have you kept the skin clean with disinfectant?' she asked, putting the conversation on an unromantic level.

'Yes, I've been very careful,' replied Helen, 'but the gold has turned a funny colour and I'm still in pain. Let me show you.'

Without hesitation she raised her dress above her waist and parted the flesh. The metal did look unpleasant.

'Hmm,' Tricesta frowned, 'I think you'd better take them out. You could get an infection, in any case you have proved your point. Where's the fun if you can't have pumpage?'

'Exactly,' Helen agreed, 'I'm glad you said that. You're quite right, I have proved my point. I'll take them out. Can I have the key, please?'

Tricesta removed the minute key and chain from her neck and handed it to Helen. 'There, the end of an episode,' she grinned. 'Excuse me if I don't hang around, I'm a bit squeamish.'

Helen smiled and departed with the key to her bedroom.

I never really believed she'd do it, reflected Tricesta. I suppose it made her feel a jump ahead of me. What a nut! She turned the Cream's L.P. over.

Tricesta dined with Brad, instinctively she was at ease with him, she felt natural and responded to his adoring attention.

After their usual soul food she said on an impulse:

'Drive me around The Grove. I want to see just how bad conditions are.' He smiled and said nothing. 'so far I've only read about the black slums. Let me see them.'

'It's not your speed,' he said, 'but I'll take you. We'll drive in my car, it's not so flashy!'

Brad drove well, as he seemed to do most things. He was still something of a mystery to her. He always had something good to say about everybody. He would never take sides in a dispute. He feared no one and was not the type who could be pressurised. He was unusual in that he had no inferiority complex about his colour, and he believed in the equality of all people and declared that no race was superior to another. Some, he agreed, had progressed technically and artistically faster than others. He was a dependable person and honourable to himself. Mentally and physically he was strong, immovable to the point of stubbornness. He was slow to make a decision but once having made it nothing would make him change his mind. His enemies were often astonished at the vigorous way he would help them, if he felt they had had a raw deal. But in some ways he appeared to be dull and bourgeois, particularly when compared with his extrovert brother.

'I'll never dig Black Power,' he said, 'they're trying to tell black people how to behave. I don't go for that. That way they're in danger of becoming as dictatorial as some of the systems they want to smash.'

Tricesta nodded and looked down the long undulating Ladbroke Grove. At the Notting Hill end the houses were delightful, some even grand but one did not have to go far before dingy, faded buildings began to appear. The freshness of the South end faded rapidly.

'There's a lot to be done,' said Brad, 'but not the way those cats are planning things. They have approached me to join them. They spend hours trying to convince me they are right, but they never will, they're cooling it now. *The Black Press* does a good job for local community information, but's it's too limited. And I think they're stirring up too much anti-white feeling.'

They parked in Talbot Grove South, W.11. Tiny, three-storied dilapidated houses comprised the depressing terrace. They left the car and were at once surrounded by coloured children playing in the dirty road.

'Who do you want, mister?'

'Is she a film star?'

'You doing a survey?'

Continuous questions came from the poorly-dressed children. Brad was kind to them but Tricesta was embarrassed.

'Is your mummy in?' Brad asked an African boy of about ten. He nodded, looking nervously around.

'We'd like to see her please,' explained Brad, 'this lady is doing some research.'

The boy ran ahead and they followed. The stench of the unhealthy, stinking garbage in the gutter filled their lungs.

Tricesta was upset by the squalor.

They were led down into a dark basement area, filled with over-flowing dustbins, then into an ill-smelling hall.

Brad went ahead, Tricesta held back, rather confused. She heard Brad tell the boy's mother the position. She left the room and greeted Tricesta. Three small black children, half naked, followed their tired-looking mother into the dimly lit hall.

'Go ahead,' she said, 'but I don't expect anything to change. It's been the same for years. We've had it all before.'

'Thank you,' said Tricesta, 'I'm sorry to disturb you.' They walked through to the back, the wallpaper was hanging away from the damp walls. Some of the broken windows were blocked up with rusted corrugated iron, others were just left broken. In the tiny yard there was the only lavatory for the whole house. It had been kept as clean as possible but the plumbing was hopelessly inadequate. The drains stank. Dingy lines of washing hung from one end of the yard to the other. The sun could never penetrate this unhealthy pit.

'It's unbelievable,' said Tricesta, genuinely shocked, 'I don't know how they put up with it.'

'They have to,' he replied, 'there's no alternative. Come and see the kitchen. That lavatory should be condemned.'

The kitchen was not recognisable as a kitchen. But there was a cracked sink with one cold tap. The interior was crumbling, the plaster was falling on to the stone floor. Curious children peered at them from the hall and stairs.

The remainder of the tour was equally squalid, poky rooms, broken banisters and overcrowding everywhere.

'Buy some ice-cream for your brothers and sisters,' said Tricesta, giving a pound note to the young boy. He looked astonished and hurried to his mother with the money.

Tricesta was anxious to leave, it was unbearably depressing. England should never have places like this, she thought. It's so uncivilised, and she smiled at the word.

'I can show you many more like this,' said Brad, 'but it'll upset you.'

'I've seen enough,' she said, stumbling over a pile of rotting refuse, 'I can't take any more of this. Make me some tea at your place.'

'Only an English person could have said that!' He laughed, teasing her.

'Don't be stupid,' she snapped, feeling angry and ashamed of what she had seen, 'you know what I mean.'

'Forget it,' he said, 'I was joking. I should never have brought you here.'

They drove back to Maida Vale in silence. He made tea, put on a new Ben Webster L.P. and sat beside her.

'After seeing that,' she said, 'I don't think I blame Black Power for the way they behave. If I were black I'd join them!'

'No you wouldn't,' he replied firmly, 'their attitude is wrong. As I've told you before, they're tackling things the wrong way. But people like you can help, just by being aware, by not denying its existence.'

They left the disturbing subject. But she would never forget what she had seen.

Brad made some strong tea and sat on the sofa while Tricesta poured it into brightly coloured cups. 'I know this will come as a shock to you,' he said, 'but don't say anything now, I just want you to know how I feel. I want to marry you.'

Tricesta nearly dropped the teapot, so great was her surprise. She could think of nothing to say.

'First you must visit the island, get to know the people, meet my family. You'll love the place, it's so natural. But I won't say too much, you'll see for yourself. Let's go for Christmas!'

'That would be nice,' was all she could manage to whisper.

Making love to Brad was one thing but marriage was quite another matter. He certainly understood her moods and knew how to treat her when she became difficult. Although he was proud he never gave the impression, like so many of his race, of thinking himself the greatest. She was not surprised his telephone was constantly ringing, usually with a hopeful bird on the other end.

Tricesta felt no jealousy towards them. Even if he made love to them it was of no importance. He was desperately in love with her, he idolised her.

'They're just platonic girlfriends,' he said, 'I don't need them now that I have you.' Tricesta knew he was telling the truth but she wished he had not given up his girlfriends. He was becoming much too possessive.

'It wouldn't worry me if you had them,' she said, 'I don't suppose it would affect your feelings towards me. I can't be jealous.'

'But I can,' he admitted with fervour, 'I don't have sexual

intercourse with other chicks now. And I'd hate you to go with another cat.'

That was the crux of the matter. Brad was unable to under-stand a relationship without jealousy. Tricesta did not argue with him. She would continue to behave as she always had.

Soon after the estate of the late Jonathan P. Flaxman had passed into Tricesta's hands, there was a minor disaster within their circle. Janie Craig's boyfriend, Les, was arrested for being in possession.

'They planted it,' said Janie positively when she went to see the brother and sister. 'Not only the fuzz, but everyone knew he smokes so what can we do?' she asked. 'In this case Les was innocent, but being a West Indian . . . '

'It's sickening,' agreed Tricesta, 'there but for the grace of God and all that. I was about to ask, is it his first offence? Of course what I mean is – has he been busted before?'

'Yes, once. He was given a conditional discharge last time,' she said, 'he'll do time on this one. There's no point in him telling the Magistrate he was clean when they picked him up. No beak will ever believe the fuzz are planting the stuff. I've told him to plead guilty. Are you going to The Notting Hill Gate Carnival on Sunday?' she asked Tricesta, C.B. remained con-veniently deaf.

'I might,' replied Tricesta, not wishing to show too much enthusiasm in front of her brother, 'is there likely to be any trouble?'

'No, it's a very jolly affair,' smiled Janie, who was dressed in her idea of gipsy gear. 'I've been to the last two. The West Indians try to reproduce one of their island carnivals. It gives them a chance to let off steam and the kids love dressing up. The standard isn't high but the steel bands are very good. I'll be covering it for *Our Times*. Edward X has written a decent leader for the next edition. He's outlined his ideas on educa-tional reform but unfortunately he still refers to the "grow-ing need for violent protests". He's too unstable to be a good leader. The movement needed cats like him at the start, but they should never have been allowed to take the reins. Wow! Sorry about the Black Power speech,' she laughed, 'I'm afraid the Press are inclined to overplay the scene. We're just as guilty. I don't think Chocolate Biscuits was listening anyway.'

'Sorry Janie,' he looked up from a sketch he was doing, 'what were you saying about the Press?'

'Forget it.' She stood up, looking quite exotic in the old Liz Taylor style of the early 'fifties.

'Anyway,' she went on, 'the so-called "underground" have organised a protest march against the police for their recent manhandling of coloured people. We're doing our stuff in the King's Road on Saturday.' She smiled at C.B. 'Don't worry, I'll keep the action off your doorstep! What a gas if the fuzz bust me! But that won't happen, even if smoke is pouring out of my ears! They know it's the kind of thing I'd want them to do, they can't tell the difference between pot and herbal cigarettes, so they dare not take the risk! I'm doing another "Youth in Revolt" interview on the box tomorrow night. I suppose it's useful publicity but I'm only allowed to say so much. It's claimed to be unedited but – forget it!'

Janie Craig left them and went on her individualistic, rather flamboyant way. Tricesta admired her, she appeared so alone, so out in front. Janie was committed to total involvement. Whether she was wisely involved was not the point; she believed in direct action.

Eric St Regis attended an important sale of French period furniture at Sothebys on the Friday morning. Before returning to Salisbury he called at the King's Road shop, delighted that he had been able to spend £15,000 on goods well worth the money, but it had been a good morning for Eric.

Tricesta was alone in the office when Eric arrived. Tim and Jim were busily re-arranging the furniture in the showrooms. They both uttered elaborate greetings, they could detect a provider of bread a mile away! He resembled Mr Macmillan even more startlingly that morning. Tricesta had eventually commented on the similarity and he had carefully cultivated the image.

'Well?' he greeted his niece, 'how's business?'

'Excellent, uncle,' she said, smiling, 'in fact it's so good I'm going to repay your investment!'

'What!' he gasped, 'the whole lot? Now?'

'Yes, why not, we can afford it,' she indicated he should follow her up to the flat. 'We were terribly grateful for your financial help, I told you we would pay it back when it was possible. 'Uncle . . . ?' she asked coyly, 'didn't you believe me?'

'Why yes, naturally I did,' he lied appallingly. 'I just didn't expect it so soon.'

Tricesta felt great being in the position to pay off Uncle Eric, it was a marvellous feeling. 'Mind you,' she joked, 'it might be two hundred thousand the next time!'

'This must be my lucky day,' he laughed, still a little suspicious. But he watched her make out a cheque for £106,000 and another for £7,500.

'That's interest at $7\frac{1}{2}$ per cent,' she said indicating the smaller cheque, 'and the six thousand covers the Chippendale candle stands you nicked from Grandpa!' she went on and signed the cheques with a flourish. 'There, and thank you again for the loan.'

'Can I have my letters back too?' Tricesta sat on the sofa and appeared to give his question consideration. 'I don't see why not,' she said, enjoying the situation. She really felt in command, 'but I've kept them for all these years – I think I'd like to keep them a little longer. After all, they remind me of a very tender, enjoyable period in my life.'

His face fell, he knew the pressure would never be removed. But the cheques did a lot to soothe him.

'Let's have half an hour's revival scene,' she suggested uncrossing her legs.

'No,' he said quickly, 'I don't think it's wise. Someone might come in.' But Uncle Eric could not tear his gaze from her legs. She led him to her bedroom and locked the door. His understanding of her needs was as astute as on the first occasion.

Uncle Eric returned to Salisbury elated. Not a bad day's work, he told himself and dismissed the possibility of future demands. Most unlikely, he decided, she likes her independence too much! It annoys her to be under an obligation to any man!

Edward X, Apostrophe Brown and six other top Black Power advocates met on Saturday night to finalise the first large scale destructive plot to be staged in London by them. Originally they had planned to blow up part of the Stock Exchange. Edward X believed that the financial heart of England really controlled the politics of the country. He said: 'If we disrupt the centre of their financial system the city will insist Whitehall cool the pressure on the coloured community! I don't think the Stock Exchange has ever been attacked before, it'll be a real shaker for them. But we need proper equipment and precise information. Before we bomb any part of the city we'll sabotage a less important objective. We must test our organisation and timing.'

Most of his colleagues agreed with his reasoning but some were anxious to disrupt the bastion of white supremacy at once.

As usual Edward X had his way and persuaded them to concentrate on a secondary project in Notting Hill. After the discovery by the New York Police of the document, carried unwittingly by Tricesta, their plans had to be changed. Edward X was bent on militant action but on this he was strongly opposed, mainly by Apostrophe Brown who would not tolerate violence of any kind, or so he maintained.

After hours of hysterical argument Edward X agreed that on this first occasion there would be no violence. This was entirely due to the insistence of Apos, who was anxious to soften the image of their movement.

'Yeah, boys,' Edward addressed the robed Black Power men when they had been called in, 'we blow the south side of Ladbroke Street East on Sunday during carnival. You are to make sure every house, every room is empty by half past three, that is your responsibility. I'm praying for a hot afternoon. Fortunately the street is small and one of the worst slums in The Grove.' They all paid careful attention, at last they felt they were in on the action. So often they had been accused of doing nothing but talk. Now they would show their critics.

'As you know,' continued Edward, savouring his leadership, 'I have repeatedly, asked the syndicate that owns Ladbroke Street East to re-house the tenants. The syndicate own blocks of flats, a lot untenanted, all over London, but because of the enormous profit they get from this slum they have refused. We will force them!'

'Yeah man!'

'That's cool, that's cool!'

'It's time we forced them!'

'But there's no law that can make them put those who are about to become homeless into new flats,' said Apos, 'suppose they end up without anywhere to go.'

'Forget it man,' said Edward aggressively, 'the power of the Press will force them to do the decent British thing! I've got friends in Parliament and in the Press. We've got photographs and sworn statements concerning the condition of this terrible area. No big business syndicate will want the bad publicity I intend to dish out if they do not re-house everyone.'

There was no doubt he meant what he said.

'We'll start the fires at three forty exactly,' continued Edward. 'Sammy, you'll be responsible for filling and re-sealing the coke bottles with petrol. Even if the fuzz notice the bottles they'll not dig. Raving at carnival is thirsty work! I want all twelve of those stinking houses burned to the ground. They should go up within seconds. The fire brigade will be hampered by the carnival crowds. When you've got the blaze going you can help to block the street. Work out all the details with Apos. After this test we'll really let Whitey have it! Right where it hurts most. In the money bags!'

Most of the boys were carried away by Edward's talk but Apostrophe foresaw tougher recriminations against the coloured community, for what the Press would surely label on 'outrage'.

Brad asked Tricesta to go to the carnival with him, he had no knowledge of the plot instigated by his brother. C.B. pulled a face when his sister said:

'I don't suppose you feel like coming to a native do?'

'You suppose correctly,' he replied, 'And watch it – you know how fanatical some of these cats are getting. Just don't get involved in anything. Give my love to Janie.'

A group of Black Power boys stood together at the corner of Portobello Road. They were thankful the weather was unusually hot, 80 degrees the thermometer on the newsagent's shop read. 'Before you chuck the petrol in,' Edward X said, 'make sure all the windows and doors are wide open. At three forty precisely throw in your lighted cigarettes. Don't muck it up, see that they land on the petrol.' As they talked they could hear, in the distance, the steel bands warming up. 'For tonight, all those that are burned out will be put up at the Notting Hill Centre,' continued Edward, noticing a Black Maria drawing up nearby. 'I'll hold a meeting and dish out compensation to those that have lost their furniture and clothes. We don't want any of them going to the fuzz. Are you sure none of the tenants have rumbled the plan?'

'No man.'

'They're cool. There won't be any trouble. Provided you get them re-housed in that new block of flats,' said Apos, carrying three petrol-filled coke bottles. 'I will,' replied Edward impatiently, 'we'll split now, go suss out the houses and keep any curious cats well away.'

The group dispersed to their allotted tasks.

Tricesta parked her car in a quiet side street, Brad jumped out and opened her door.

'Does it get this hot in Tobago?" she asked him, pulling her wide brimmed hat lower. 'It's a different heat,' he said, 'there's a continual breeze, it never gets this uncomfortable.' He greeted several people, they all seemed pleased to see him.

Brad and Tricesta strolled towards the floats. These consisted of three beaten up old trucks which had been tarted up for the occasion. West Indian musicians sat or stood wherever they could find a space on them, some tried to tune their instruments, others exchanged jokes with the crowd on the pavement. Following the band trucks were five open carriages, these were vividly decorated with plastic flowers and paper streamers.

The girls occupying the carriages wore a haphazard improvisation of West Indian dress. The horses were hung with bells and garlands of fake flowers. Everywhere there was an atmosphere of – 'We're going to get high, for sure.' Black faces grinned and groups gossiped, all were determined to outdo their friends and neighbours in joviality. One large, smiling Negress had left huge rollers in her hair, she had covered them with a bright pink hair net but had forgotten to take off the price tag. An African danced past Tricesta, he wore minute blue shorts and a red shirt, he carried a green child's umbrella above his head, he was taking no chances with the English sun!

The steel bands were ready to go, encouraged by impatient shouts from their fellow countrymen. There were a few 'white folk' and an assortment of hangover hippies smoking herbal cigarettes and pretending to be stoned.

'Let's go up front with the lead band,' said Brad, pushing through the crowds. Tricesta saw Edward X standing on the steps of an Edwardian terraced house. He was talking with one of his boys and did not notice her. Between his lips was an unlighted cigarette.

The ice-cream and cold drink vendors were already doing a brisk trade. The parade was headed by six professional musicians, carrying half pans, supported from around their necks by leather straps.

Tricesta remained on the fringe of the crowd and looked for Janie. Brad went over to the musicians and talked with them, there was a great deal of laughter. Beads, bells and bright clothes were everywhere. Parked at the corner of the street Tricesta saw another Black Maria, just in case . . . The uniformed police on duty seemed to take the unusual scene in good humour. They tried to keep people off the road and on the pavements but it was an impossibility. The fuzz went through the handbook actions but did not press their authority. There was an unspoken truce between them and the coloured community on this carnival day.

Brad left the boys and rejoined Tricesta, she saw why. Edward X had a couple of his boys with him and they were walking towards the band.

'My brother's playing a set with them,' he said.

'Do you want to move back?' she asked. He laughed. 'Don't be silly, I go where I want to go. I just don't want to be involved.' The unlit cigarette still hung from Edward's lips and he carried a long sausage shaped drum. She avoided catching his eye, nervous in case Brad became suspicious.

Edward X glanced at his watch, it was 3 p.m. He consulted the others and then turned to the crowd behind him.

'Okay, carnival's started!' Amid an approving roar the band crashed into life. The beat throbbed and infected everyone. They walked, danced and skipped forward. Laughing children surrounded the leaders, the pace was unhurried but full of movement.

Professional and amateur photographers ran ahead and clicked a variety of cameras at the oncoming crowd and at one corner there was a mounted television camera. As the mass of colourful people pressed ahead, Tricesta and Brad were pushed closer to the leaders. She began to enjoy the rhythmic motion and saw Brad had been handed a motor starting handle, he struck this with a spanner and contributed to the beat. Suddenly Tricesta found herself beside Edward, his unlit cigarette was still in his mouth. He glanced coolly at her.

'Hi, you dig our carnival?' She blushed and fell back forcing her way to Brad's side.

'What did he say to you?' Brad demanded.

'I couldn't hear,' she shouted over the noise, this reply satisfied him. The police remained beside them and did a good job holding up the Sunday traffic. No one seemed to object.

'Hello, fancy finding you up front.' It was Janie. She kissed Brad happily and attracted a lot of attention. Tricesta was unaware Janie knew Brad. Her gear was more flamboyant than ever, she pushed her way towards Edward and kissed him. It was almost impossible to talk, the noise was building

194

up and so was the temperature. Squibs were thrown at the feet of the prettiest girls. They screamed predictably and the guilty youths yelled with delight. Tricesta came in for her share of minor explosions.

'It's a great way for them to let off steam,' shouted Brad to Tricesta, 'this is what we do at home, we miss it.'

'Smokey,' Brad called to one of the players, 'Why we going down Ladbroke Street East?'

'Don't know man,' he shrugged, 'makes a change for the cats there.'

The parade had swollen to a record size. Tricesta was a little alarmed, if one was to fall it would be virtually impossible to get up again, there were too many excited people squashed in the narrow street. She did not relish being trampled to death, and anyway she had had enough and wanted to get out. Starting to panic she looked around for an exit route. She could see no possible way, every inch of road and pavement was jammed with the singing, dancing multi-racial crowd.

Tricesta noticed Edward X pass his drum to a friend, and at last after forty minutes he lit his cigarette. She saw him fight his way towards the row of rotting houses.

'What's the hang-up?' shouted Brad to the lead pan player.

'I guess the next street is jammed up,' he called back. 'Wave them to cool it.'

'Hold it man, stop the floats, there's a traffic hang-up!' Brad yelled, waving his arms vigorously.

Gradually the heterogeneous column of men, women and children stopped surging forward but they continued to move their bodies rhythmically. Tricesta realised the music had increased in volume. I suppose it's because we're not moving, she told herself.

'Any chance of splitting?' she shouted to Brad hopefully. He laughed and shrugged: 'I'll get you out as soon as I can.'

I've never seen the sun reflected so brightly before, thought Tricesta looking at the windows of the houses opposite, Christ! That's not sun – it's fire!

'Fire – fire!' suddenly everyone was screaming the dreaded word and endeavouring to back away. Flames surged powerfully through the open windows and doors. Tricesta was terrified and looked around for Brad. She lost a shoe and her hat was knocked off.

'That's my house!' one old woman shouted. 'My house is

on fire! Oh! My God! Everything I own is in there!'

The flames spread through the tinder dry buildings with startling speed. Through the open doors Tricesta could see the flames funnelling up the stairs, roaring towards the roofs. The draught encouraged by the open windows caused the fire to travel in a spiral, all the time moving upwards.

'They're all on fire,' a man shouted, 'the whole bloody lot are burning!' Those unfortunate enough to be jammed near the burning houses screamed and fought to get clear. Tricesta could feel the heat on the far side of the road.

'Burn, baby, burn! Burn, baby burn!' she heard a voice chant behind her. Turning, she saw one of Edward X's men watching the blaze. Then she understood. He met her eyes with a smile which said:

'It's started baby! No one really believed we'd do it, but this is just the beginning.'

She turned back to the fire with a horrified new interest. She was scared but she heard the noise of distant fire engines. How the hell can they get through this lot? she wondered, then realised the hold-up was a part of the plan.

Edward X reappeared and shouted through an electric megaphone: 'Cool it, cool it. There's nothing to worry about. Those of you that have lost your houses make your way to The Notting Hill Centre, I want to talk to you.' He turned to the lead float.

'Let's keep the carnival moving!' No one disputed Edward's leadership, there was no one else.

As the noise of the fire engines came closer the lead musicians quickened the beat. Police forced their way along the pavement in an endeavour to keep the children away from any danger but apart from this they were helpless. The flames were already flicking through the flimsy roofs. In a few minutes the squalid houses would be gutted.

Brad fought his way back to Tricesta: 'You poor thing,' he shouted putting a protective arm around her. 'We'll try and get out through one of these north side houses, I think there is an alley at the back. Hold on to me.'

At the end of the alley they found themselves in the 'T' road at the end of the blazing street. Squad cars, unable to drive any further had been abandoned and their crews were trying frantically to clear a way for the fire engines. In the distance Tricesta saw Edward X leap on to the bonnet of a police car retrieving his megaphone from a fellow West Indian as he did so.

'Don't anyone panic,' he shouted, 'those who lived in Labroke Street East keep cool. Those rat-traps are better destroyed . . . ' He went on: 'The Movement will compensate tenants for the loss of their belongings and we'll force the slum landlords to rehouse everybody, and I mean everybody!' A colossal roar of support went up as Edward finished: 'There will be a general meeting at the Centre at six o'clock. I want to see you all there!'

Tricesta and Brad slipped down another dirty alley and into a less crowded street. They doubled back to her car and managed to drive out of the chaotic Grove and made for Brad's flat.

'The bloody nut!' said Brad. 'He's flipped!'

'Who has?' she asked, knowing perfectly well.

'Edward, my baby brother, he's gone crazy, I never thought he'd go this far.'

Neither of them voiced their thoughts but both were aware that this was just the start of a wave of ambitious violence. After this initial success it was not likely that anyone would be able to hold Edward back. Not even Apostrophe Brown.

Tricesa went home early. C.B. was watching the television news when she entered the flat, he blew her a kiss.

Her attention was drawn to the screen. They were showing scenes from the carnival and fire. The narrative was impartial and gave extracts from Edward's speech made that evening at the Centre. He had apparently stated the case for the black community remarkably well and had insisted that the fire was a blessing in disguise. The newsreader continued: 'Edward X has sent a letter by hand to the owners of the destroyed slum houses. He is confident everyone will be given new tenancies in a recently completed block of flats owned by the landlords. The Black Power movement have guaranteed financial compensation to everyone who lost their possessions as a result of the blaze.'

'Switch it off,' said C.B. 'I warned you not to get involved in trouble. They're just a bunch of rabble rousers and you're mixed up with them. It's too much!'

'I'm not mixed up with them,' she snapped, 'It's not my fault if a row of houses burns down. I've lost a shoe and my hat,' she added irrelevantly.

'The whole thing sounds like an inside job,' he declared.

'You sound like an amateur detective,' she laughed. 'They'd

never want to make themselves homeless. Let's forget it.'

'You know what I mean,' he replied, dismissing the subject. 'You might be amused to hear Helen has taken up the pen!'

'What?' Tricesta grinned, 'You mean she's started writing?'

'Just that,' he smiled, 'but she's very furtive about it, won't let anyone see any of it. I asked her what she was doing and she said – "just making notes". Is it my imagination or has her work become slipshod?'

'Yes, you are right, it has,' she replied, 'And her moods are getting more frequent and worse. She's never been the same since she fell for Apos. The fact that he couldn't care less doesn't seem to deter her. He'd never bother unless she made the dates. She doesn't know how to play a game. She takes everything too seriously.'

'I can remember her saying she would never chase a man,' said C.B. 'It's a different story now she's involved. Any kid can see this spade doesn't want to know. He only pumps her because it's so eagerly offered, what man wouldn't? Doesn't she realise she's making a fool of herself, can't she see she's losing her dignity?'

'No, she can't,' said Tricesta, 'her ego won't accept rejection. The girl is hooked on him and he isn't interested.'

Tricesta went to the kitchen to make C.B. his hot milk, when she returned to the drawing room she said: 'I must say her moods are getting me down, but I think I can do something about it.'

'Then do, or get rid of her,' he replied. 'When things get messed up it interrupts my flow of work. You know how easily I'm affected. I can't take the temperamental bit from her.'

'I'm sorry,' Tricesta said kissing her brother, 'I'll see you're not bothered any more. It was my fault for letting things get out of hand.'

The next morning Tricesta gave Helen six tablets of methedrine.

'Your father certainly knows the good stuff,' said Helen an hour later, 'I feel wonderful, nothing worries me now.' She tackled her work enthusiastically and was particularly pleasant to everyone.

Chapter 12

EDWARD X TELEPHONED Tricesta, he insisted she meet him at his H.Q. at 7 p.m. She did not care for his tone at all. That evening she drove apprehensively into The Groves and parked some distance from Edward's house. He admitted her jubilantly, success written on his face.

'Hi – hi – come on in.' He was dressed in vivid African robes and almost danced down the hall into his office. She felt unnerved and sensed she had an unpleasant time ahead of her.

'Did you enjoy the carnival?' he asked. 'We did, it was a fantastic triumph for Black Power.' He giggled with confidence. 'So now we've begun the fight and what a fight it's going to be! You'll be pleased to know the slum syndicate have agreed, under pressure from us and the Press, to re-house the homeless. Now try and tell me my methods don't work. Come on – tell me – I don't hear you . . . ' He shouted at Tricesta who remained silent. She appreciated Brad's antagonistic attitude towards his brother and why Apos had trouble discouraging his violence.

And now that Edward had tested its potential he would strike again and lose no time about it.

'Now,' he said, 'you know where it's at and so do I. It's all in that one word "force", that's where it's at.'

'Why did you ask to see me?'

'Baby, I didn't ask, I told you.' He enjoyed the sound of those words and continued: 'I want to open an African Cultural Centre. A gallery that sells old and modern art, books and clothes made by and for black people. There's never been a shop in London, which deals solely in work by black people.'

'It's a great idea,' she said cautiously, fingering her jet beads.

'And it'll pull in plenty of bread and attract a lot of publicity,' Edward went on. 'I want to begin with Benin River Art and progress up to the present day. And I want the gallery in a good position. You're the perfect one to put the project together!'

'But I couldn't,' she protested, 'I don't know anything about African art, old or new. I've got my own business to look after. You need an expert.'

'Don't give me that,' he snapped, 'I want you. I watched you put that King's Road scene together, you are an expert; an expert hustler, now you can do the same for us. I know you'll do well!'

Once again nausea swept her, she had been here before, the pattern was becoming familiar. And she sensed the full picture had not yet emerged. She was correct.

'With your talents it shouldn't cost more than a hundred thousand quid!' he looked at her, as if to say, 'it could be worse!'

'Has the movement got that kind of capital?' she asked, hoping for a contradiction of her fears.

'The movement, as you call it, doesn't need to have; not when you've got a cool million, which came your greedy way through me. One tenth of that on a Cultural Centre for our people is not much to ask.' He watched her, knowing how she must feel. 'I am in a position to insist on the lot, but I don't operate that way. Organise this and spend one hundred thousands of your pounds and that's it.'

But she knew that would not be 'it'. She knew only too well one did not relinquish power if it was not necessary to do so. When she had repaid Uncle Eric she had kept the letters and left the way open for another demand, should she ever need it. I've got to refuse now, she thought, or his demands will become more and more outrageous.

'I'm not doing it,' she said.

Edward grinned. 'I don't see it that way,' he replied softly.

'It's got to end now, I'm not taking any more pressure from you or your movement. I did what you wanted with Flaxman, be satisfied. I'm not going to Africa to mug up on Black Art and I'm not dishing out a hundred thousand quid.'

'You rotten whore!' he shouted. 'You bloody well are! Or else . . . ' The door opened and Apostrophe Brown walked in. 'I heard part of that, man,' he said softly, 'What's been going on with the chick?' He ignored Tricesta and stood firmly in front of his leader.

'Cool it man,' said Edward, 'She's high – I just want her to help with our new art scheme, it's in her line.' His change of attitude was remarkable. He knew that Apos was willing to break the law of the land but never the law of his conscience.

'I heard you threaten her,' he accused Edward, 'that's not the way to ask for help.'

'Oh man,' Edward lost patience, 'it's time you faced up to facts. With Fascist cats like this – ' he pointed angrily towards Tricesta, 'you don't ASK. You fucking well tell them, that's the only language they understand! They only recognise force, that's how they got where they are, through violence. Do me a favour, Apos, and take a look at the truth.'

Tricesta felt they had forgotten her, she sank back on the sofa and listened to Apos. 'No man, it's not force that finally counts,' he spoke slowly, as if to a child, 'what will count in the end is compromise, on both sides. Peaceful compromise will win new laws. Burning down houses, blowing up the Stock Exchange and killing a few cops can only lead to disaster. We can only make it by playing the game Whitey's way – we live in his society, let's play it his way but better. Man, you might be our spokesman, but unless you back down on violence I'm splitting and so will many of the others.' Then he buttoned his jacket carefully and spoke very quietly:

'To make you see how serious I am I'm going to tell you something. I had the riot plans intercepted in New York!'

Edward was stunned into silence and fell back in his chair, his mouth open. Apos continued: 'I'm not putting you on, man, I was sorry they gave Tricesta a hard time but I didn't go for your ideas. You put me down every time I tried to stop you here, so I had to kill it over there. You know in your heart violence is wrong. So we kill a few people, destroy a few buildings, that's not going to make white society respect us. It could give them an excuse for using stricter repressive measures. That's why I decided to have the papers intercepted, believe me, I did us a favour.'

'A favour . . .' Edward was speechless with fury, his trusted right-hand man had sabotaged months of dangerous, careful planning both here and in the U.S.A. 'I told you before, man, you're chicken, you've been brainwashed! I should kick you out – I should . . .'

'Do that man,' Apos stood quietly, tempting Edward. But Edward X believed in others handling the violence, at a personal level he didn't want to know!

Tricesta pushed back further into the sofa, this was not her fight. She saw the apparently casual Apostrophe Brown in a new role. He was positive, immovable, he made Edward X appear impotent and cowardly.

'This time we settle the fight,' said Apos, 'once and for all we decide where we're going and how we're getting there. You'd better leave,' he seemed suddenly to notice Tricesta, 'and forget what you've heard tonight.' She stood up and walked to the door. 'The Arts Centre,' shouted Edward, 'that remains – start putting it together now!'

Knowing this marked the beginning of the end for one of them Tricesta drove away from 'Viet Grove' deep in thought. She wondered who could help her. Brad was out of the question; he would half kill his brother. That would only lead to more aggravation. All she wanted was the tapes. With those destroyed Edward would be powerless. Only one course of action was possible. Steal the evidence.

'Peters the Pipe' was the obvious answer. She could afford to buy his talents. That evening she was lucky. The Sun Tavern was crowded but she spotted him at once.

'I thought you'd dropped me out,' he greeted her, 'I've phoned a few times but you're never there. Have a drink – what brings you to this wicked den?'

'You do,' she smiled, his blue eyes registered suspicion, 'it's true, I want to talk to you, it's important.'

Bobbie Peters smiled wryly. 'The only thing of importance to me is money, kid, and somehow I don't see you keeping me in the manner to which I want to be accustomed!'

'Maybe not forever,' she said, 'but for a month or two, yes. It depends on your rate of spending.' Her voice had dropped to a promising whisper, she noticed several of the regulars watching them. 'Let's talk somewhere more private,' she said, 'right now, we're making news.'

He flicked some money on to the bar and took her arm.

'Where do you want to go?' he asked outside.

'My car,' she replied, preferring to be on her own familiar territory.

Bobbie's hand crept up her thigh, 'So where are you taking me for a couple of months?'

'You can go where you like,' she said, replacing his hand on his own thigh, 'I want you to do a job for me, that's the right expression I believe.' He quickly wound the open window shut. 'It depends what you want done, luv, I thought you wanted me for my body, etcetera,' he laughed to himself, 'tell me about it.'

'Don't ask too many questions, only the relevant ones,' she said fidgeting with her tooth pick. 'I insist on coming with you when you do it.'

'No,' he shook his head, 'I never take a bird on a job, they're too excitable in an emegency. Besides I don't see you climbing a pipe!'

She was equally determined. Tricesta had no intention of allowing the tapes to slip into another hustler's hands.

'You won't have to go up a pipe and unless I come with you it's no go. I want you to open a safe and let me remove some tape recordings, that's all. You'll be well paid but I handle the gear, otherwise I get someone else.'

Bobbie was frowning. 'I'm the best you can get, luv, but what is "well paid"?'

'A thousand before and a thousand when it's done.'

'You are anxious,' he said, betraying his surprise at the amount of bread offered, 'where is the stuff?'

Tricesta told him only what was necessary. He was bursting with curiosity but decided to play it cool. 'It doesn't sound as though the place is loaded with alarms,' he said, 'but I'm not anxious to run into a bunch of spade heavies.'

'Nor am I,' she agreed, 'leave it to me, I'll find out when the place will be empty, it often is. Will you do it on my terms?'

Apart from being the best in his dubious profession, Bobbie was also a businessman. 'Yes, but on my financial terms. I'll break the rule of a lifetime and take you. But a grand first and another two on completion of the contract.'

'That's robbery!' she laughed.

'No, business, luv. It's just my bloody luck to be out with the sexiest bird in Belgravia and have to talk business. Do you agree the terms?'

'I have to,' she sighed, but felt satisfied.

'What the hell are you mixed up in?' he asked.

'It's not me,' she replied sharply 'I'm doing this for someone else.'

'That's what we all say.'

'You're a cynic,' she accused him. 'No,' he said, 'just a bit more honest. Don't worry I'll not dig any deeper. When do we go?'

'I'll have to ring you.'

'You can't,' he smiled, 'I'm not on the telephone, I'll phone you every day at one o'clock.'

'Suppose something goes wrong? Can you fight?'

'Only with you in front of me and a weapon in my hand!' He was not joking. 'Make sure nothing can go wrong. Remember, I'm no gallant gentleman, I'm the first to get out if there's trouble. Let's go and have a drink.'

'No,' she shook her head, 'not until our work is over, I can't relax just now.'

Bobbie shrugged and put a hand on the door handle. 'It's up to you, it's a pity to waste a good body like mine! I'll ring you tomorrow. Let me know what type of lock the main door has. 'Bye luv!'

He strolled down the mews to his own car. He was puzzled but he did not lose sight of the bread. Light summer evenings were bad for trade.

Tricesta returned home and found Janie smoking a joint with C.B.

'You look depressed,' said Janie, immediately passing the powerful cigarette to her. 'I am a bit,' replied Tricesta drawing on the joint. She had not been high for some days but now felt in the mood to relax. Janie put on one of Otis Redding's records, they sat quietly, thinking, smoking and 'free wheeling' as they called mental drifting.

'This spade debate should be a gas,' Janie said at last, 'the joke is I'm chairing the establishment opposition panel!' She giggled.

'What debate?' asked Tricesta pulling herself into the present.

'On the box tomorrow,' drawled Janie, reaching for her glass of orange juice, 'it's called 'Why Smash The System?'' It's a live studio programme. Basically young black militants versus young white people from our set. They are trying to establish they have a valid case for rebelling. They've never been able or allowed to state their views so clearly before.'

'No,' said C.B., 'when they've tried their spokesmen have been either stoned or stupid. I can't wait to see it, but I don't think you should be leading our side, Janie. You're colour prejudiced – in reverse!'

'Balls!' she said. 'You don't know where I stand. Just because I live with a spade doesn't mean I dig the whole race. I like peaches but I don't eat fruit salad. I have a selective prejudice. Wait and see. This is the first realistic unedited confrontation we've had with the violent majority.'

'Who are the speakers for Black Power?' asked Tricesta, floating high and fast.

'Edward X, Apostrophe Brown and their crowd, the lot my pet, it should make tele-history, if the studios aren't burnt down!' All at once Tricesta had put herself together. 'What time is the debate?'

'Half past nine, it goes on for a whole hour. Would you like me to get you into the audience?'

'No – no thanks, I'll watch the box,' her heart was racing, 'Will there be a jury vote on the issue afterwards?'

'Yes,' replied Janie, 'for what it's worth! And we all know who picked the twelve men and true. The six spades on the jury work for the television company!'

'So they'll be allowed so much rope and no more,' smiled Tricesta.

'Just as it should be,' interrupted C.B. 'If a white militant went to a country with a black establishment and advocated violence he'd be put away for life and have his hands cut off or worse. It's only in a democracy like ours that these hothead anarchists can have their say. They certainly couldn't in a communist country, and they know it. Why do they all come to this country? Simply because they wouldn't be tolerated anywhere else. I hope you'll remind these rabble-rousers of that, Janie.'

'It's not that simple . . . ' she said. 'Of course it is,' he snapped, and the usual argument began in earnest.

Tricesta left them. What luck! she thought. Black head-quarters will be deserted tomorrow night. All those that matter will have converged on the studio.

She counted on the tapes being in Edward's office. Tricesta hoped to recover Michael Flaxman's tape as well as her own. If that villain doesn't ring tomorrow I'll – I'll cut off his pipe! Such an ideal opportunity was unlikely to occur again in the near future.

Bobbie Peters kept his word and rang the following day at lunchtime. 'Hello, luv,' he said, 'when would you like us to meet?'

'Let's have a late lunch in our usual pub, I'll leave now.' He agreed and Tricesta picked up her handbag and left the show-rooms. She felt nervous but excited. Since formulating her plan she had been unable to eat; this was her big chance to free herself from Edward X's blackmail. A pressure that she knew was bound to increase with each success he had. She drove too fast into Belgravia and forgot to put money into the parking meter.

'Good morning, my pretty,' Sandy kissed her loudly, 'is it your usual Perrier water?'

Tricesta nodded and smiled at the regulars whom she knew.

Although the pub was a cosmopolitan place she felt safe there. Sandy and Polly would never allow anyone to pester her. 'You can have that corner table now,' said Polly, 'and I suggest you have the chicken salad,' she laughed, 'and you needn't ask – the kettle is on!'

Tricesta enjoyed being fussed over and given small privileges not normally granted to other customers. She waited impatiently for Bobbie to arrive. Being a business appointment he did not keep her waiting long. After she had explained the situation to him she said:

'I think the door has an Ingersoll lock.'

'O.K. I can handle it,' he said, sending Polly for another large whisky. 'I want the first grand now, we can just make the bank.'

'But you might not turn up when I've given you the bread,' she protested.

'When there's the chance of more cash I always turn up,' he squeezed her hand. 'I'll meet you at nine o'clock at Sloane Square underground station, just drive up and I'll jump in.'

She had some doubts but she forced them out of her mind.

He insisted she get the cash from the bank. This done Bobbie pocketed the money and switched on the car radio.

'Will you carry a weapon?' asked Tricesta.

'If I do you won't know about it,' he replied. 'Are you sure you've told me everything I should know?'

'Yes,' she nodded thoughtfully. 'The important thing is they will not be expecting burglars at their H.Q. They're not exactly loaded. Only one of them is concerned with the tapes I want and he won't have drawn any attention to them inside the party. You won't let me down, will you?'

'Not me, luv,' he said, 'as long as our luck's in we'll be okay. I'm off to get what I need for the job. See you at nine.' He slipped nimbly out of the low sportscar and strolled away whisling. I hope he's as cool as he looks, thought Tricesta, returning to the King's Road.

To her surprise her parents were there, talking to C.B. After kissing them both she asked Lady Anne: 'Why didn't you let us know you were coming up?'

'But I did, darling,' she replied, 'I spoke to your secretary a couple of days ago, she must have forgotten.'

Helen had forgotten, these days her thoughts were focused solely on Apos and starting a career of her own. C.B. showed them around, their mother made constructive comments but their father merely muttered: 'Charming,' or 'very interesting.' He soon rushed off to a medical conference and their mother shook her fair head indulgently.

'He's very impressed,' she said, 'but he would prefer to do a tour of a patient's intestines!' Lady Anne glanced at the masculine-looking watch on her wrist.

'Now I'm afraid I must go too,' she sighed. 'I've got to varnish one or two of my canvases at the gallery.'

'The exhibition opens to the public tomorrow. I want you both to come to the preview tonight, then we'll take you out to dinner.'

'Oh, I'm sorry, Mother,' Tricesta felt guilty, 'there's something vital I have to do tonight. I'd do anything to get out of it but I just can't. Please forgive me.'

C.B. frowned and Tricesta turned away.

'Oh I understand,' smiled their mother, 'it can't be helped. Goodness knows I was usually too busy to attend open days at your school, so I've no right to complain when my children can't drop everything just because I appear.'

'It's nothing to do with not seeing much of you when we were kids,' Tricesta protested, 'we both knew medicine and art couldn't be regulated to meet our timetable. Don't be cross with me, tonight's hang-up has nothing to do with a man, it's work that must be completed tonight. I'd do anything to be with you,' she kissed her mother affectionately. 'Lots of luck, make sure they don't hang any upside down this year!'

All Tricesta's thoughts were concentrated on recovering the tapes. She went up to the flat and made coffee. Lying on the low malachite table was a student's exercise book. Absent-mindedly she opened it and saw the title, written in scrawling longhand – 'WHY RHODESIA MUST REJECT APARTHEID by Helen Williams.'

Tricesta collapsed with laughter and refrained from reading any more. So that's her big scene, she thought, she's writing a progressive book on integration! I can't believe it. She'll be flying home to get it published next! Christ! That's not a bad thought, she'd be off our backs if she was sitting in a Rhodesian prison! Helen burst in and pounced on to her manuscript but avoided making any reference to it. 'Are you going to the studios tonight?' she asked Tricesta, hugging the book to her bosom.

'I may,' she replied, 'what about you?'

'Oh definitely, I'm going with Apos, he's asked me to make some notes,' she said importantly.

Good, thought Tricesta, that's you out of the way. I bet you pestered Apos to get you in. He wouldn't want you hanging around from choice!

'How's it going with Apos now?' she asked, watching Helen's blank face.

'Groovy – better than ever,' she lied, 'We understand each other now. He respects me more and I dig his work. I see clearly that we Rhodesians must integrate, or be wiped out by civil war. There's more of them than there are of us.'

'That doesn't prove much,' said Tricesta, 'numbers don't signify capability. Anyway, whenever African countries get self-rule they make a mess of it.'

'But that's because they're still fighting Western Imperialism.'

'Really, Helen, even you can't be that confused. They'll always be what they are, a continent of warring tribes. I'm more sympathetic towards them than the majority of people but even I have to admit that. And when one of your Black Africans comes to this country he is either bone-idle or a trouble-maker. Only occasionally do you find one with commonsense and keen to work.'

'Like Brad?' she asked, with a taunting smile, as though she shared a terrible secret with Tricesta.

'Brad is a West Indian,' Tricesta said, 'and just because he doesn't dig violence and doesn't dig our government it doesn't meant that he has the secret for peace, in fact, in his own way he's pretty keen to assert his own impractical opinions. He likes to be considered a humanist, he wants the world to abolish money! The way Cuba tried. He says a barter system would be much better. I suppose to the impractical all things appear practical!'

Helen was confused and dropped out of the conversation.

For the remainder of the day Tricesta carefully avoided being alone with C.B. He clearly wanted to know why she had refused to attend their mother's preview party. She guessed he thought she was seeing Brad. He did – I'm sure it's that bloody nig-nog, he told himself angrily.

Tricesta apologised to her father on the telephone when he rang. As usual he was unworried and merely said it was a pity. He was just as likely to be absent himself.

By half past eight in the evening Tricesta was shaking so much that she had to take two tranquillisers. She forced herself to eat several slices of bread and honey, followed by half a pint of ice cold milk. The stodgy food and pills helped to calm her down a little. Wearing unspectacular clothes she drove up the bustling King's Road to collect Bobbie.

True to his word he was lurking in the shadows of the station entrance. He immediately saw her car and jumped in. Not wishing to attract attention she had not put the hood down.

'I'm not bothered about the law,' he said, as they drove north up Sloane Street, 'it's those dusky gentlemen I'm worried about.'

The idea of failure did not occur to Tricesta. Bobbie, in spite of his flippant attitude was a ruthless professional. He had no intention of going 'inside' again. On reasoning the position out she knew they were bound to succeed; security at the house was nil and all the top men would be elsewhere, pleading their doubtful cause.

At twenty-five minutes past nine they parked a short distance from Edward's H.Q.

'What about your gear?' she asked, climbing out of the car.

'This is my scene now,' he said. 'In case you're worried, techniques have advanced since the gelignite days! Just keep an efficient lookout for trouble.'

They remained silent and strolled towards the house. The street was quiet, most of the kids had gone indoors. There was practically no daylight, dusk was an excellent time for such a job. Bobbie followed her up the steps, no one appeared to notice them.

'Ring the bell first,' he said, positioning himself.

There was no response to their ringing, as Tricessa had anticipated.

'Stand in front of me,' he said, 'look as if you're waiting for someone. Keep your back to me.' She obeyed and leaned against the stone pillar picking her teeth delicately. Behind her she could hear Bobbie manipulatinng his skeleton keys. She wanted to watch but forced herself not to do so. He worked quickly and she was infected by his sense of urgency, this made her heart beat fast. Two or three spades looked her up and down but she was sure they had no connection with the movement. In fact they seemed in a hurry to pass the entrance, they obviously preferred a less important but more peaceful existence. Even so, her stomach heaved when anyone passed the doorway.

She heard the door open, Bobbie pulled her sleeeve and they hurried inside. He closed the door and bolted it.

'Lead the way,' was all he said in a whisper. She was scared. After all, she said to herself, this is my first burglary. She tapped on Edward's office door. After a second or two she turned the handle and walked into the dark room.

Bobbie hurried over to the window and drew the curtains, 'Put on the lights,' he said. She did so, he glanced briefly at the posters and press cuttings, he shook his head at her. 'You nut,' he muttered, 'where's the safe, luv?'

They found it together. An old fashioned contraption wedged back in the kneehole of Edward's desk.

No wonder he keeps sticking his feet on the desk, she reflected.

'This should be child's play,' said Bobbie, giving the ancient safe a kick.

And it was, within seconds he had opened it. In fact even

he seemed a little surprised at the lack of effort needed.

'I'll bet they buy the most elaborate combination affair after this,' he grinned. 'Okay, it's all yours, get to it!'

Excited beyond words Tricesta fell to her knees and pulled out carefully filed packets of papers. These she ignored and liften out eight spools of tape recordings. One was labelled 'Flaxman', another 'Brennock', the name sounded familiar, the next two were marked 'St Regis'. She took all eight and replaced the documents in their original position. They obscured the space left by the missing tapes.

'Lock it up again,' she said breathlessly, 'and open the curtains.'

Bobbie did his part, she noticed he was sweating, Tricesta pushed the spools into her large handbag.

In the stuffy hall she looked up the stairs but there was nothing to be seen. The whole operation had gone almost too smoothly. They left the house and walked to the car.

Tricesta was shaking when she slammed the door.

'Drive off,' he said, 'this isn't the moment to flake out.'

She scarcely heard him but automatically reacted and drove out of The Grove.

'I wish all my work was so simple,' he said, 'do I get to hear those tapes?'

'No,' she snapped, 'but as it was so easy perhaps you'd like to drop the other two thousand quid!'

'Not bloody likely!' he said. 'I'll have it now.'

'It's at the flat,' replied Tricesta, 'it's only twenty minutes to ten,' she said, almost to herself. Her handbag remained wedged between the car door and her thigh.

Driving to the flat she glanced down every side turning expecting a squad car to be lying in wait. But they reached the King's Road without any disaster. Now that the job was finished she wanted to be rid of Bobbie; his use was over.

He followed Tricesta up to the empty apartment, she at once switched on the television and got the cash.

'There you are,' she said and handed it to him, 'thanks for doing it.'

'Call me in for the next one,' he replied, pocketing the bread.

'There won't be a next one,' she said firmly.

'Now I suggest we both do a little living,' he tried to kiss her. 'What! Not in the mood, you? I don't believe it! Come on, we'll start off with a few drinks at the pub. You'll soon thaw out.'

'No Bobbie, I can't, my parents are in London, they'll be here in a minute. Ring me tomorrow, we'll make it, but not tonight.'

'Never let it be said that I pushed myself,' he grinned, 'but remember, it's my body you're turning down! You might not get another chance.'

'I hope I do,' she lied prettily, kissing him at the open door 'you've got everything I dig . . .' But she did not finish the sentence.

After gently closing the door on him she rushed back to the television and turned up the volume.

' . . . and that's why I accuse Britain of being a racist society.' The antagonism of Edward X seemed magnified by the cameras and microphones. The camera panned over to Janie, who looked cool and replied: 'Speaking at a personal level,' she sounded good, not over-excited like the black spokesman, 'I think that's wrong. In a truly racist country like South Africa you'd never be allowed to make the sort of speeches for which you're famous. They would lock you up,' there was approving applause from the studio audience, 'you wouldn't be invited to air your violent views on television.'

'But you support South Africa,' he said, breaking in.

'Again I disagree,' replied Janie calmly, 'if you have a naughty child in your family you don't disown it. You try to help it. If that child refuses help at least you've tried. I believe every human being, every collection of people has some good in them. Even a self-appointed body like yours!' The audience laughed, but Edward felt that Janie, a girl whom he had considered sympathetic to the Third World had betrayed him. Give and take were dirty words to him.

'The establishment has brainwashed you,' he said thumping the table. 'Anyway we're not here to talk about South Africa but if that's what you want, I'll give it to you!' He stood up. 'Within the next decade,' he shouted, 'the white man will have been thrown out of "Black Man's Land". Africa will once again be black. All of it!'

Tricesta was surprised at Janie's calm and reasoned reply and especially the way she remained neatly sitting on the fence. Chocolate Biscuits would have no cause for complaint.

Tricesta switched off the television and played back the tapes marked with her name, they were genuine. When she had destroyed them she played part of the 'Brennock' tape.

'Obviously as a member of the Stock Exchange I'm in a position to plant the explosives. But I still insist that there be no loss of life. It must be done at night, with an accurate timing device.'

'Sure, but there must be serious damage, I want the city given a good shake-up.' Edward X's voice continued to explain what manner of explosion he wanted. Tricesta knew Julian Brennock slightly, he was a prominent stockbroker, married to the Hon Sarah Warsash, a staunch Roman Catholic. She switched off the machine and went to get her large tape recorder. Michael will be relieved when I give him back his tape, she thought, staggering back to the living room with the equipment, I'll re-record these four tapes and lock them away at Castle Mordaunt. They'll never be used and even if they were ever discovered they'd mean nothing. I'd like C.B. to hear them.

Listening to Flaxman's tape, she felt as though it concerned another young girl, not herself. Julian Brennock's was highly compromising and proved he was in Edward's grip and would be forced to plant the dynamite when he was ordered to do so. I'll give it to Michael, she thought, feeling pleased with her motives, he'll know how to approach the stockbroker and get him off the hook.

The next tape she recorded would need careful thought; it concerned Edward X and a member of the Police Force. He's been a busy fellow, she said to herself. The remaining ones were incomprehensible. Speech was in an African tongue, all she could make out were the words – 'South Africa', 'Zambia', 'Tanzania', 'Mozambique' and 'Angola'. Tricesta was puzzled with these tapes and decided an expert in African languages would have to translate them.

After re-recording the four tapes she removed the large spool from the elaborate machine. Tricesta put Flaxman's and Brennock's tapes into her handbag, and tied the others in a neat package which she sealed. It was ten minutes to eleven. She rang Michael to say she must see him at once. He said he was working on some briefs and would be pleased to see her whatever the hour.

'Good,' said Tricesta, 'now would you please ring Grandfather and tell him I'm on my way down but will be very late and would he have some sandwiches and milk left in my room.'

She left a short note to C.B. and drove to Westingshire. She arrived at Flaxman's house as the clock in the church tower struck one.

'Well,' Michael said expressively, when she had told him her story. 'I didn't expect to be holding this in my hand tonight, I can't tell you how relieved I feel.'

'The same goes for me,' she smiled. I'm sorry you haven't got the right equipment to play the Brennock tape. Take it up to London tomorrow, you must hear it before you do anything. He and Edward have obviously met before, this just confirms that Brennock will plant the explosive. It doesn't give a hint what hold Edwards has over him, it could possibly concern his wife.'

'Sarah!' exclaimed Michael. 'Don't be ridiculous, all she cares about is her jet-set image and the promotion of her husband's career. She'd never step out of line, certainly not in Edward's direction!'

'I don't know,' sighed Tricesta, 'stranger things have happened.'

'I thought highly of you before,' he smiled, 'but now, after risking your neck to bring me the tapes, I think you're the "greatest", as you would say! I'm really impressed.'

Tricesta blushed and her ego soared, she felt no guilt over re-recording the tapes; she knew she would never use them. But she couldn't totally relinquish the power they gave. The confidence she gained from owning such a weapon over-rode every other instinct. Like a nation with the atomic bomb, having it was enough.

Chapter 13

LORD PRESTIGNE HAD gone to bed when Flaxman rang to say his granddaughter was on her way, but he put on trousers and a dressing-gown to greet her when he heard her car arrive in the courtyard.

'Grandfather, you should not have got up, I'm sorry about all the disturbance,' she said, kissing him warmly, 'but I want to lock something important in your safe. Do you mind?'

'How could I mind?' he smiled, 'and I won't even ask what it is. I just hope you're not involved in any more trouble.' His observation was phrased as a question.

'Not now,' she said wearily, 'but I was. You'll never know how hard I've hustled to free myself.'

'Hustled?' he repeated the word, 'hustled?'

'Yes,' she nodded. 'I'm a hustler, because I know how to put things together. In the way you always have. It doesn't mean quite what it did. To us it means to force or to push positively. The opposite to drfting or lazing.'

'Then I'm glad you're a hustler,' he said, 'but I don't think I care for the word.'

'I know it sounds ghastly but we find it very expressive.' She closed her eyes, she was exhausted. 'By the way,' she snapped into awareness, 'what is the standing of Julian Brennock?'

'Very sound,' replied Lord Prestinge, 'he's a bit too flashy for me – too flamboyant, tries too hard. It's really Sarah that gets on my nerves, though,' he frowned. 'I admit she's bloody attractive but all this "professional" party-giving is aggravating.'

'She's supposed to be a paragon of virtue I believe,' said Tricesta.

'So she would have us think,' he replied, then smiled. 'I once went to one of their parties in London, what do you think I caught them doing?' Again he chuckled. 'They were smelling each other's breath, reassuring each other they were delightfully fresh! His sister told me she makes him examine her piles when they periodically appear! He hates doing it but she insists . . .'

They both laughed at this out-of-image behaviour. Tricesta said: 'I wonder if it's anything to do with being Roman Catholic?'

'Don't be ridiculous,' he laughed, wiping his eyes, 'but his sister assured me that their stock of the "pill" will outlast their necessity. That last encyclical from Rome was a shock but they ignored it. I don't know why I'm telling you all this but it's a pleasure to talk to a young person so frankly.'

'Talking about Roman Catholics,' she said, 'Father told me some doctors are saying that the rhythm method of contraception can be extremely dangerous for unborn children.'

'In what way?' he asked, puzzled.

'Well,' Tricesta hesitated for a second but decided to continue. 'He didn't use the medical jargon, which he said I'd never understand anyway, but what it boils down to is this; in countries basically Catholic, where they practise this method almost entirely, there is a higher percentage of malformed, backward and imbecilic children than in non-Catholic countries. This is apparently due to the male withholding his sperm until the safe period is reached. During this waiting period it becomes stale and is in poor condition when it reaches its objective. Not only that, but something may hold up the female ovary so that it becomes fertilised in the "safe period" and by this time the egg isn't up to much either. When the frustrated couple eventually make love, his sperm is almost dead and her egg is just about addled. A combination of these two conditions usually results in the child being malformed, imbecilic, or stillborn. Statistics bear this out and so does medical evidence.'

'I've never heard that before,' Lord Prestinge said, 'surely it must have been brought to the attention of the Pope?'

'Not necessarily,' she replied, 'but it's got to happen sometime of course. Imagine how it will disrupt their teaching. In backward R.C. countries many young men look old and lifeless and Father says it is due to lack of normal sex. Masturbation can help, but it is no substitute for the real thing. I hope I haven't shocked you,' she grinned.

'No, I'm just astonished at my innocence, medical opinions like this must come into the open soon – what happens then?'

'I'm sure the Catholic Church will deny it for as long as possible,' she shrugged, 'they want to retain their power. The more enlightened classes already ignore the ban on contraception, so their kids don't suffer too much. It's among the lower classes that the dreadful damage is done. It always astonishes me that intelligent people can be persuaded that the Pope is the only one qualified to have a hot line to the Almighty. It's a colossal con.'

'As you know,' said her grandfather, 'I don't hold with religion, but the majority of people need something to lean on, it's easier than assuming self-responsibility.'

'I agree,' she said, 'but no one person should claim he can speak on behalf of God. Now that I've righted the problems of man let's go to bed.' They both laughed, enjoying their remarkable new sense of communication.

Lord Prestinge opened his safe and made room for Tricesta's tapes. It was then very late but Tricesta was up early in the morning and was back in London by eleven o'clock.

'Helen's still in the kip,' was C.B.'s angry greeting when Tricesta walked into the showrooms. 'Go and kick her out of bed. It's getting crazy now!' His hands emphasised his annoyance. 'How's Grandpa? Never mind, Mother's preview was a riot and who do you think turned up?'

'Haven't a clue,' she said.

'Tarquin, our old hustler! He says he's arranging to exhibit

217

Mother's work at his gallery in New York. He's more grand than ever now that Massey White's almost in the White House. You'll be pleased to hear he's coming round tonight. And I've got a groovy idea; why not dump Helen on to him?'

'Wouldn't take,' she said, 'he's too much of a snob, he wouldn't go for a secretary, he'd rather make a play for Mother, she's got both a title and talent, not only artistic!' They laughed and Tricesta dashed up to the flat.

Helen moaned and turned over in bed when Tricesta drew the heavy curtains.

'Do you feel ill?' Tricesta asked with pseudo concern.

'I feel terrible,' she groaned, 'bring my handbag over, there's something in it.'

Tricesta did as she was asked. 'What do you want from it?'

'Open the inner compartment,' she instructed. Mystified Tricesta unzipped the soft black leather and removed a pigskin-covered case. Then she knew the answer; the neat case contained a gleaming hypodermic syringe.

'How long? she asked.

'Ten days,' Helen struggled on to one arm and stared at Tricesta. She looked ill, dilated pupils, pale skin, and deep grooves around her once sparkling eyes. 'I used to think it was a bad scene, but it isn't, I can work great on it, it's only 'til I've finished my book.'

Tricesta refrained from asking about her novel. She could see no needle marks on Helen's arm.

'Have you got anything?' she asked.

'That's the hang-up,' she admitted, in tears, 'my contact let me down. Can I melt those tablets down and inject them?'

'No,' replied Tricesta, still shattered at Helen's change of personality, 'but I did buy some hypodermic tablets last year. I've never opened the phial. If you want me to dig them out I will, but you'll need distilled water.'

'I've got that,' she replied eagerly, 'let me have some, please, I'll work better than ever. If you refuse I'll have to make some telephone calls, I'm not getting up 'til I've had a shot.' Tricesta agreed and went to her secret hiding place at the top of the house, she realised Helen was incapable of getting up until she'd had something.

In the bedroom Tricesta uncorked the small phial, marked 'Poison'. It contained one hundred tiny white tablets of Dia-morphine.

'Sterilise me a couple of spoons,' said Helen, staring at the stuff. Ten minutes later, with the efficiency of a regular fixer, Helen melted a tablet with distilled water in a tablespoon. She filled the hypodermic and ignored Tricesta. Junkies rarely fixed in front of non-junkies, but Helen was not inclined to be fussy. After all, she was using Tricesta's drug. Helen injected expertly into her backside. That's why her arms are clean, thought Tricesta. Helen sank back in the bed and smiled. 'Why don't you have some, you'll never regret it. Let me fix it for you. Shall I?'

Tricesta had noticed before, most addicts try to persuade those not addicted to have a shot. She had heard them boasting to fellow junkies about the number of people they had managed to 'turn-on'. In the way a missionary would discuss the number of converts he had made.

'Not just now,' said Tricesta. 'I've just had something else,' she lied, putting Helen at ease.

'I'll leave a couple with you,' said Tricesta, giving her two of the minute tablets, 'I'll hide the rest, ask me when you want more.'

Helen leapt out of bed, she bounded naked over to the dressing table and began to apply her make-up. It was becoming heavier and more vivid daily. Her eyes rivalled An-An, the panda bear. Suddenly Helen seemed normal, well controlled and looking happy, once again her usual cheerful self.

Tricesta hid the phial and returned to the flat. When the telephone rang she answered it quickly. Then she faltered, it was Edward X. 'Get over here now,' he snapped, 'I've got details of premises that would do fine for the Art Gallery.'

She gripped the receiver and said: 'I told you before, I'm not doing it, I'm too busy.'

He shouted: 'You've got no choice, get over here fast, and cool the shit talk!'

'I'm sick of your hysterical ravings,' she replied quietly, 'and I'm not seeing you again, so forget it! You cool it!'

'So that's where it's at!' he screamed, 'you and big brother paid my pad a visit last night when I was on television. When I've finished with him you'll be visiting him in hospital, not in his usual warm bed! Then I'll get back to you!' Edward slammed the receiver down.

Tricesta was frightened. That maniac thinks I got Brad to rob the safe. They'll kill each other, and Brad will discover that

219

I know baby brother. Christ! Things couldn't be worse!

She put the telephone down and wondered whether she should ring Brad to warn him that Edward was on his way to take him apart! But it was too complicated to explain on the telephone. I should have pretended to go along with Edward, she thought, by refusing to go he has guessed I was involved in the robbery. Why didn't I anticipate this?

Tricesta immediately took to her bed. Her usual reaction when she was afraid or confused.

She gave Helen an exaggerated version of Tarquin's history and she would not accept any telephone calls apart from Brad's.

Later that evening Tarquin Lloyd breezed jauntily into the flat, he carried an L.P. record. Helen made a play for him, he accepted this as his due and encouraged her. He looked prosperous wearing a Mr Fish shirt and a tightly-cut maroon coloured suit.

'Where's the escapee?' he asked C.B., referring to Tricesta.

'Too ill to leave her bed,' he grinned, 'she's watching the "Magic Roundabout" on the box. It's our favourite programme. Come into the bedroom, she's dying to see you!'

'Hello-hello,' laughed Tricesta, delighted to see him again. In spite of his faults he was extremely amusing provided one did not become involved with him. C.B. switched the television off as the 'Roundabout' characters faded from the screen.

'I've brought you a present,' said Tarquin, handing an album carrier to Tricesta, 'the grooviest band in the world led by your favourite drummer. It's called "Buddy and Soul". That's a gas of a title. Listen to it and dig the sound.' He placed the record on the deck. The aggressive but musical first number demanded all their attention.

'It's very good,' enthused Tricesta. 'Listen to this,' she said in delight, 'that's Greensleeves and it couldn't sound more modern. Turn it up, Tarquin, I'm crazy about it.'

They all listened attentively, excited that a 'big band' could make their sort of musical scene. Here was a brilliant combination of arrangement, great musicianship and modern leadership. A young awareness with the benefit of vast experience. That is the genius of Buddy Rich.

'I saw your mother, she's looking fantastic,' beamed Tarquin, lowering the volume and sitting down on Tricesta's bed, 'she looks so young – so groovy, they'll love her in New York...'

'Are you trying to make our mother?' asked C.B., laughing.

'Really! What a cheeky fellow he is,' grinned Tarquin. 'I just want to turn Manhattan on to her art, you know my scene by now! Your secretary seems very accommodating. Is there any action there?'

'She's just your speed,' said Tricesta, emphasising the last word; she winked at Tarquin who at once caught on and winked back, C.B. had not noticed. At that moment Helen burst in, 'I think you should take this telephone call, Tricesta, he sounds wild . . . . '

Without having to ask who was on the line she knew it was Brad. She leapt out of bed and dashed into the main room. C.B. was at once curious as to why she had not taken the call in bed.

'Darling, I've had a terrible bust-up with Edward, I've got to see you now,' Brad said breathlessly. 'He said he's known you for months, I nearly broke his jaw for that! He said a lot of other crazy stuff, do you know him?'

Tricesta took a deep breath. 'In a way,' she said, 'but it's not what you think – he's been blackmailing me!'

There was a brief silence, then Brad said: 'I'll kill him! This he doesn't talk his way out of! Come to my pad now and we'll straighten it out. I must know the facts.'

'I'll be over in half an hour,' she replied, 'I'm in bed at the moment. Don't do anything 'til I see you.' She returned to the bedroom and could see C.B. was fuming. 'We can guess who you sneaked off to speak to,' he said sarcastically, 'you won't get out of bed for Tarquin or me, but for a nigger you'll jump!' He looked furious, Tarquin's eyebrows shot up at the word 'nigger'. 'You're going the same way as Helen, I won't allow it! You've had your kicks, now quit.' He stood before her, she blushed vividly, but continued to dress. He continued to shout. 'You and your bloody superiority complex! He's black! That's it, with a spade there's no need to keep asserting your superiority, you are superior. With him you have no complex!'

'Don't be stupid!' she said feebly. 'That's rubbish. And it's just about the most racist remark I've ever heard, I always thought you had no colour prejudice. You're the worst of the lot! You'll be sorry you said those things, all I've been trying to do is to protect you.' She ignored Tarquin and went into the bathroom to finish her make-up. Her hands shook but she applied her eye make-up carefully. C.B. had hurt her, if they fell apart what was there? Of course Brad meant a lot to her but she felt totally committed to C.B. She loved everything about him. I know he doesn't hate spades, she thought. It's just that he's frightened that I'm too involved with one. If I mixed with a dozen he wouldn't be bothered. But being with the same one all the time worries him.

Brad looked frantic and his chin was cut. She fell into his arms, she felt safe at that moment. But she had to face life as it was, not the way she wished it was.

'What happened today?' she asked at last.

'It was horrible,' he said softly. 'Edward came to the office with six of his boys. He screamed at me to give him back the tapes, I said I didn't know what he was on about. He went mad, accused me of plotting with my white whore, meaning you, to smash his work. He told two of his boys to hold my secretary. Then I lost my temper and tackled them, but finally three of them held me on the floor. The others wrecked the office, smashed everything, he was searching for some tapes, stuff he said I had stolen last night. He swore and screamed but found nothing.' Brad paused for breath, then went on: 'Edward said he'd be back, that he'd ruin me and you. He said vile things about you, I tried to get to him but he was too well protected as usual. Whenever we have a fight he knows where to put himself, well out of the line of fire. And there's worse, out of my six drivers only two turned up this morning, the two English cats! The four West Indians had been threatened, warned not to work for me any more – or else! Edward's boys slashed the tyres on my cabs. My business came to a halt, and my secretary refuses to come back, she's frightened of them and I don't blame her. This is a real mess. But once you've told me the truth, all of it,' he added, 'I will know how to handle that cat. This time he's gone too far. I've overlooked a lot these last two years because he's my brother. Now we settle the score. He's dangerous now. Tell me the truth, what's been happening?'

'I've had a hideous time,' she said, looking full of injured innocence, 'in a nut-shell, Helen told Apos I made it with my brother, they got her story on tape, she said she had seen us. Edward tricked me into meeting him and played the tape to me. He demanded money or favours, I didn't fancy losing any bread so I agreed to do as he asked.'

'Oh God, the bastard,' said Brad, punching the table, 'but the tape could have been a fake, there must have been more than her lies . . . . '

Tricesta knew it was futile to pretend at this late stage, anyway the tapes no longer existed.

'The trouble was they weren't lies,' she watched his bewildered eyes, 'Helen planted a recording device in my bedroom. Your baby brother got firsthand evidence – please try and understand, C.B. needs me, he's highly nervous. I've had to keep all this from him, he'd never take the strain.'

'So you did . . . you had an affair with your brother?'

'Yes, it didn't hurt anyone. If you knew him you'd appreciate his temperament. Don't be angry.'

'I'm not,' he said, taking her hand, 'in my part of the world it often happens. I'm angry with Edward and that bitch Helen. What did he make you do?'

Tricesta gave him a weak version of the truth and elaborated on Edward's latest demand.

'I wish you'd trusted me enough before,' he said, 'I could have handled it, I know the cat too well. Darling, do you know where the tapes are now?'

'No,' she lied, 'Edward must have lots of enemies, even within the movement. I feel much better now that I've told you about it. But Helen is a real hang-up.'

'We'll settle it,' he said with conviction. 'Edward thinks we're in this together. Don't worry, I'll jump on him at the right moment, I'm wise to his tricks. Darling,' his voice softened, 'I love you, nothing must be allowed to spoil that, nothing. One day I'm taking you home with me, until then we'll just rave!'

Hoping to forget about the cloud hanging over them they did just that.

Before she drove home he told her what to do if Edward turned up at the flat.

'But take it from me he won't,' said Brad, 'he knows how to play this game. He hasn't finished with me, our real fight hasn't come yet.'

Tricesta returned to the King's Road feeling brighter, but kept a watchful eye open for Edward or any of his boys.

Nervous about C.B.'s mood she entered the drawing room with some trepidation, but Tarquin, Helen and C.B. were stoned, the room was hazy with thick, sweet smoke. Tricesta called C.B. outside.

'I'm sorry we had angry words,' she kissed him, 'come into

the bedroom, I'll explain some of it.'

Sulkily, but hoping for a sensible explanation he went with her. Tricesta told him about their affair having been taped. Now they were safe she felt he would be able to cope with what had happened. The version she gave him was toned down and slanted in such a way that he was totally reassured. He ended up by apologising with sincerity for having behaved unreasonably.

'I don't know how to make it up to you,' he said, 'I'm sorry I said all those things. You were right, what you did was purely for my protection. You're fantastic, I love you very much. I'll never get anywhere without you. But what do we do about Helen?'

'We've got to get rid of her,' said Tricesta simply, 'apart from the fact she's a compulsive liar she's now a junkie. It was entirely because of her lies that I came to be blackmailed. I understand she has been telling people I'm useless; that she's the real genius around here. I know she does this because she suffers from some sort of mental disorder. It's beyond her to tell the truth, even when there's no point in lying.'

'And there's always the possibility she might have a go at putting pressure on us herself, suppose she fancied becoming my wife. Christ!' said C.B. 'she's untrustworthy and unreliable, I feel nervous with her about. I only wish we could dump her into Tarquin's lap, he's a hustler, she's a ponce, but he'd never bother with her. So, put your perverse mind to work. How do we ease her out without a real hang-up?'

Tricesta looked thoughtful, checked that Tarquin and Helen were still smoking and listening to sounds. 'There's only one hope,' she said returning to the bright kitchen, 'get Apos to take her on. The drag is he doesn't give a damn about her. He's got all the chicks he can handle, but I might be able to persuade him she would be useful to the movement. Typing his reports, doing all the petty office jobs he hasn't time for. Unfortunately she'll want more,' she paused, then smiled. 'The thing that might pull him is if she could con him into believing she's going to have his baby!'

'Don't be stupid,' he said, 'if a chick told me that I'd ditch her as fast as I could. That really would finish me.'

'But you're not hung up on a so-called "Third World",' she said. 'Although he believes in Black Power he still stands for integration, especially on a personal level. If he can be per-

224

suaded he's got a kid on the way he might buy it. I've been told he's mad about children. He'd feel that having kids by a good-looking white bird would enhance his reputation among his own people. Apos doesn't go for Edward's non-integration line, few of them do if they're really honest.'

'I see your point,' he said, 'but it's a gamble . . . ' Tricesta quickly answered the ringing telephone, to her surprise it was Apostrophe Brown for Helen. She winked at C.B. and said: 'I'm sorry she's out at the moment, how's your scene?'

'Cool baby,' he drawled, 'but you've got a hang-up, Edward is fighting mad, so is Brad.'

'I know,' she said in a worried voice, 'I don't know what to do about it. What are you doing now?'

'This and that, baby,' he replied. 'Do you want to come and have a drink with me?'

Smiling she said, 'I'd love to and I'd like to ask your advice about the family feud! Where shall we meet?'

'I'm speaking from Janie's pad, she's out right now, come on over here, you'll feel more at home!'

Tricesta laughed and agreed. After hanging up she grinned at C.B. 'With a bit of luck I'll set the scene for Helen's exit. Keep her occupied, fix her up with Wonder Boy!'

When they returned to the noisy, smoke-filled drawing room Tarquin was saying: 'Yes, a couple of months from now I'll be freaking out in the White House!' Helen hung on to every word. He said: 'I'll be redecorating the White's personal suite and some of the other rooms too, maybe I'll even turn Lucy on! What a gas, the first groovy "First Lady"!'

'But he's got to win the election first,' said C.B.

'It's a dead cert, Biscuits,' he replied condently, 'can't fail, with that image, the good old Negro vote, the youth vote and the square oldies who fancy being in on the "progressive" kick – dead cert for sure. I'll invite you over for tea,' he said grandly.

'You are blocked – but really stoned!' laughed C.B.

Tricesta made an excuse for leaving them.

'You're always going out,' grumbled Tarquin. 'Are you still on the hustle?'

'What else,' she smiled, 'Once a hustler . . . !'

'Who was that on the blower?' demanded Helen.

'A fellow hustler,' replied Tricesta. 'I'll probably see you later at The Spot for dinner.'

Tricesta hurried over to Janie Craig's flat. Apos opened the door, smoking an enormous joint: 'Hi, come and get turned on,' he grinned, handing her the smoke, 'Janie's out, drumming up bail for a couple of kids.' Tricesta followed him down the hall into the main room. Records, books and posters were everywhere but it was a tidy disarray. Apos sat beside the telephone and retrieved the joint from her.

'I hear you're probably to become a daddy,' Tricesta said casually.

'A what?' he asked, taken off guard. 'Who said that?' he looked surprised but she sensed a reaction of pride.

'Oh, I shouldn't have said that,' she said quickly, 'I'm sorry, it should be strictly between Helen and you, forget it.'

'You mean she's – she's . . . ?'

'You'll have to talk to her,' muttered Tricesta, reaching for the cigarette again, 'but she's really happy, if you two go ahead the kid should be really something. Don't let her know we've met or discussed it, she'd not understand. Promise?'

'Sure,' he said, 'this is something else, you've knocked me out! Me a daddy!' Tricesta knew the idea appealed to him.

'Of course Helen's really hung up on helping you in your work,' said Tricesta, 'she's very sincere and this book she's writing could be a real shaker for Rhodesia. She's very capable, in fact she's wasted with us. Her dedication to your movement is mounting daily . . . .' She inhaled deeply.

'But yours isn't?' he said in a serious tone.

'You said that,' replied Tricesta. 'I agree you are facing big problems and much prejudice but I'm convinced you'll never make any great progress while you advocate violence, it has such a troublesome image!' she laughed. 'If Edward could be persuaded to publicly renounce militant methods you'd get a more sympathetic Press and much larger financial backing. Can't you get him to renounce violence? In public anyway,' she finished.

'I've never agreed with Edward about violence,' he said, 'everyone knows that. His dedication to our people can't be denied but I completely disagree with his bloodbath policy. After the success of the Notting Hill fire he has been even trickier to handle. If I could get him to make a speech reversing his violent doctrines I know we'd get ahead faster. If I did persuade him, he would be doing it with his tongue in his cheek, we all know that.' He looked despondent.

'What you need is a martyr,' she joked, 'to change the image. Edward X should make a dramatic "No More Violence" speech in public and be assassinated in the middle of it!'

Apos suddenly looked alert.

'What irony,' he said, 'pleading the case for peaceful protests and be shot while telling a pack of lies!'

'That would certainly get the movement sympathy,' she said, 'the past would soon be forgotten and then you'd really go ahead.'

'Not even for the good of the party could I condone murder,' he said with sincerity. 'I can't turn traitor on my conscience. I wish I could.'

'I see your dilemma,' she replied. 'Not even to save the movement could your conscience be persuaded to condone violence. Of course no one need know who had arranged the killing . . . .'

'But I would,' he said, sadly.

It was never far from Tricesta's mind that it was Apos who, whatever his excuse, had informed the American authorities she was carrying those lethal documents.

Janie arrived home and they dropped the subject.

'You must come to the Teach-In tomorrow at The Roundhouse,' Janie said to Tricesta.

'What's it about?'

'They've called it "Revolution and Us", it's a debate on revolutions, peaceful and otherwise. The Cuban, the Greek, the French, the Czech, the lot, and our position in it all.'

'Apos,' she turned to him, 'is Edward down to speak?'

'It's not settled,' he said thoughtfully, then suddenly he stood up. 'I've got to split.' To Tricesta he said: 'You've given me an idea, it's worth a try. Keep out of Edward's way,' he warned. 'I'll see you both, maybe at The Roundhouse tomorrow. It's a shame this isn't the weekly televised programme from there.'

'Goodbye, daddy,' called Tricesta, wondering what she had started.

'How did you feel about the television show?' she asked Janie after Apos had departed.

'It was better than I had expected,' she replied, lighting an Acapulco Gold joint, 'but Edward really must broaden his outlook if he's to continue the work. His image puts a lot of people off. I know two or three sympathetic cats who would give them bread but not while he preaches violence. Even so

227

I dig him, he's a beautiful talker when he wants to be. I hear you and Brad are having trouble with him, it's open war now, they say!'

'Yes,' sighed Tricesta, 'it's going to get worse before it gets better. Edward is fanatical and Brad is like an immovable mountain. Both are convinced they are right. If you haven't got anything more to do now, come over to the pad with me, Tarquin Lloyd is there. Do you remember him?'

'I'll never forget him! I'd like to eat with you but I can't stay up late, I've got to give evidence in court in the morning on behalf of those kids that got planted.'

'Let's go then,' Tricesta stood up, 'I'm a working bird too. C.B. will be pleased to see you. Don't mention in front of Helen that we saw Apos tonight.'

Although Tricesta was exhausted she entered the flat in high spirits. The air was still heavy with smoke. Tarquin and Helen were holding hands, C.B. had fallen asleep but stirred to life when he heard his sister and Janie. After noisy greetings, Tarquin flirted with Janie, much to Helen's annoyance.

'I'll ring The Spot and say we'll be over in half an hour,' said C.B., stretching his slender body like a sleepy cat. Helen got up and walked slowly to her bedroom. Tricesta immediately followed her and closed the door behind her.

'You're hitting it off well with Tarquin,' she said, watching Helen in the looking glass, 'how's the scene with Apos?'

'The same as usual,' replied Helen a little despondently, 'if it wasn't for that bastard Edward and his anti-white attitude things would be simple.' She squeezed eyedrops into her bloodshot eyes. 'We both know what we want but Apos plays it too cool.'

'I was told there's one subject on which he isn't cool,' Tricesta watched Helen's face come alive and continued: 'You'd pull him if he thought you were going to make him a daddy. He flips over kids, and kids by a white chick would really turn him on!'

'But I'm not pregnant,' said Helen thoughtfully.

'He can't prove you're not,' smiled Tricesta, 'pretend you are, say you feel sick every morning! Tell him how devoted you are to his work, how much you can help him in it and how you'd like your child to grow up with his beliefs. Flatter him, that will hook him. If Apos thinks you want his children his masculine ego won't be able to resist. All the whores he runs for bread would laugh at him for wanting a child, that's one scene they intend to avoid, especially a half-caste kid. That's how you should play it if you really dig him.'

'Wow!' Helen gasped, holding her unfertile womb. 'But suppose he insists that I give up my life here and live with him?'

'I'd be the last one to stand in your way,' said Tricesta with impressive sincerity, 'so would C.B., we both adore you but we know a bright girl like you has to make her own mark in the world sooner or later. You obviously feel strongly about Rhodesia's black population. Between you and Apos you could write a most controversial book. He's got a good mind but he needs the help of someone rather more practical to get it on paper. That's why I think you'd both make a great team. Your personal relationship could show how integration can be a success. But the first step is to convince him you want his kids.'

Helen's thoughts whirled, Tricesta had made her point; the answer was a baby, at least an imaginary one.

Tricesta left the now hopeful Helen and went to her own bedroom where she telephoned Brad.

'I just heard that when Edward and I meet it's a fight to the finish,' he said, obviously very upset. 'He's mad, he knows I can finish him, but he'll make it a dirty fight, using one of his pet knife throwers no doubt.'

'What do you mean?' she asked.

'He's got an expert knife thrower from home on his team, Sammy, he's a moron. Not a brain in his head but he'll kill anyone on Edward's orders, he really digs violence. His agression is in his hands, Edward's is in his mind.'

'Promise you'll keep out of his way?' she said. Tricesta was very frightened for him.

'You needn't worry on that score,' he laughed, 'I'll wait 'til I get Edward alone, then we settle this, man to man.' They talked for five minutes then said goodnight.

'Shall you and I spin a little?' Tricesta overheard Tarquin ask Helen in the busy restaurant. Junkies' jargon was limited but each understood the other.

'Why not,' she whispered, 'but will we have to chase around all night?'

'Baby,' he said loudly, 'I never have to chase around!' his voice dropped. 'Tonight we fly!'

In front of Helen, C.B. made a great fuss of Janie.

'Much as I love to rave with my favourite raver,' said C.B. holding Janie's hand on the table, 'I have to get up early, so do you. Can you bear to be without me this evening?' he asked in a mock sentimental voice.

'It will be difficult, my love,' replied Janie in the same vein, 'but I will bravely bear your absence from my bed!'

Helen made an elaborate pretence of not listening but heard every annoying word.

Tarquin pushed off with Helen after noisy farewells on the King's Road pavement, Janie roared away in her red Mini Cooper.

'I'm glad you came back with Janie,' sighed C.B., as they strolled back to their flat, 'it was such a drag. What were you up to?'

Tricesta told him briefly, he said very little.

'I wonder if those two will share a needle tonight?' she mused.

'I wouldn't know,' he replied, yawning, 'and I'm not interested enough to find out.'

At Edward X's house Apostrophe Brown had been pleading with his leader to publicly renounce militant methods. They were alone in the office and Apos had just about given up hope of getting anywhere, but he tried once again.

'Look man,' he said, exasperated, 'if you make a speech denouncing violence you become a hero. The Press will be far more sympathetic . . .'

'I don't need sympathy!'

'We all need it,' Apos snapped, 'and we need support from our M.P.'s, to say nothing about financial help. We won't get either of these unless you appear to reject bloodshed.' He hoped he was wearing Edward down and continued: 'Surely you'd rather be labelled a wise, far-sighted leader, than a rabble-rousing hooligan. Any little soapbox orator can stand up and talk violence but only a man with wisdom can explain to his followers why they must beat the system with the system's own weapons. The press will hail you as the new Luther King or at least the new Malcolm X. You only have to take this stand in public – you can still have your own private thoughts. Get in there and be a bit more cool. Give it a try, man.'

Edward X agreed that there were advantages in pretending to toe the line. 'But I am convinced we will have to take our rights by force,' he said, 'they'll never be given to us. The only thing that will make Whitey crack is for him to lose a bit of blood, that's the way it is, that's the way it's always been. Whatever I agree to say in public will never change that belief. Provided you understand that, I'm prepared to do what you say; I'll give it a try!'

Apos sank back in his chair and said: 'Man, you've made me the happiest cat in The Grove.' It was a start, he felt, and once this line was established perhaps he could make his weight count. He could drum up a lot of support for a vigorous non-violent campaign.

The following morning Michael Flaxman called at the King's Road shop to see Tricesta.

'Come upstairs for coffee,' she said, about to lead the way, but at that moment Helen returned from her night out, dishevelled and shaky. Tricesta gathered she and Tarquin had had 'a great freak-out' and that the night's excitement had been boosted with shots of 'speed' to such an extent that Helen could not recall what they had done or where they had been. 'But it was groovy!' she said. Tricesta could detect the first signs of withdrawal. Tarquin's generosity obviously had not extended to a parting 'shot' to keep her going during the day!

Fearing a scene Tricesta called Helen aside and gave her two diamorphine tablets. Helen quickly locked herself in the bedroom, filled her hypodermic and injected the drug into her backside. Within minutes she felt as though she had had a good night's sleep; she was ready for work and after freshening up her smudged make-up she joined the others in the drawing room.

Tricesta had always imagined that when junkies 'shot' dope they were propelled into fantastic mental and physical activity. This she now realised was not the case, once the body had become accustomed to the drug, an injection merely brought them to a level slightly above normal.

Helen offered to make coffee for Flaxman and Tricesta. When this was done she left them alone together.

'I'd love to kiss and hold you,' Michael began abruptly, 'but this is not the time or the place.' Why not? Tricesta wondered and smiled. 'I thought however you'd like to know I have delivered Brennock's tape to him.'

'Good,' she said, 'he must have been surprised.'

'He was, and grateful,' said Flaxman, stirring his coffee. 'I wouldn't tell him how it came into my possession of course. I asked him about his degree of involvement with Edward X but he refused to tell me. He said the tape got him off the hook to a certain extent. Finally, after a lot of hedging he admitted he was compelled to protect someone else.'

'He must have meant his wife, Sarah,' said Tricesta. 'Did he say any more?'

'Not really. He agreed the Stock Exchange plot was well organised. He still thinks they'll go ahead when they can, probably using someone else. I'm not sure that I believe him on that point, but he admitted he had been made to supply Edward with detailed plans of the building. Apparently Edward has several arms dumps spread around London. Black Power's militant plans will be considerably delayed now, thanks to you. I will have to warn the proper authorities, discreetly of course! I can't bring myself to believe Sarah is in some way involved with them.'

'It wouldn't have to be direct involvement,' said Tricesta, 'whatever it is, Edward pulls the strings. I must say he gets around, or his hustlers do!'

'By the way,' said Michael changing the subject, 'Enid is flying back tomorrow. She sent a telegram saying she wants to help me over my emotional crisis, my decision to leave the Plymouth Brethren that is.'

'Will you go back on your decision?' asked Tricesta, trying to appear interested.

'Of course not,' he replied positively, 'and I also intend to press Enid for a divorce. I realise we're totally incompatible, she'll never change her beliefs. I don't want to bore you, Tricesta, but you must be aware of my feelings towards you. When you've had a chance to think things over, would you consider marrying me? If and when I can get a divorce of course.'

She was not altogether surprised, it was the sort of 'correct' gesture he would make. Michael Flaxman was not the type of man to be happy with a fluid, easy-going relationship. He liked everything neatly in order, legally pigeon-holed.

'I can't consider marrying anyone,' she said gently. 'You know I'm promiscuous, so are most girls but they won't admit it. The majority say they will go to bed, even live with a man as long as marriage is ostensibly in the offing. That's just a nice piece of hypocrisy, they often get themselves engaged several

232

times a year. If I want someone and they want me that's it; no problems, provided I'm not likely to upset a third party. I try not to get involved with married men. No one will ever be able to accuse me of breaking up a marriage; that's not my scene.'

'I understand that,' he said, 'but I am finishing my marriage, you are not. It would appease my ego to say "to hell with you, if you won't marry me than I don't want you", but,' he smiled, 'I have no intention of cutting off my nose etcetera. I just want you to know that with you as my wife I'd be the happiest man in the world. I respect your honesty and half a cake, even a small slice of cake, is better than no cake at all!' He grinned ruefully. 'So I'd love to see you whenever you say. I wish I was twenty years younger....'

'It wouldn't make any difference,' Tricesta assured him.

'Maybe not, but oh, never mind. If you are serious about this novel I can give you a lot of confidential information. Stuff which couldn't get into print as fact, but facts which you could fictionalise, without damage to security or individuals. Does that appeal to you?'

'Very much,' she said, appreciating his potential. I'll hustle him for information, she thought, warming to him and his suggestion. 'That's a great idea. Maybe even a few disquieting facts could be brought to light as fiction. Will you give it careful thought?'

'Certainly, and I will be able to advise you on any difficult legal aspects. Ah! well, at least I have something to offer you other than marriage!' His eyes were slightly sad but he managed a little laugh as she kissed him enthusiastically. He knew they were friends, very close friends.

Shortly after Michael left, Brad telephoned her with bad news:

'My father died early today,' he said in a flat voice.

'I'm sorry.' She felt helpless, the old man had not been anything in her life but she was upset for Brad.

'This changes things,' he went on, 'I'll have to go home and sort out the estate. Father always wanted me to take it over. There's also a position open to me in the government out there. I've got to talk to you later, I'll ring you back.' He rang off. Tricesta sensed a conflict between desire and duty looming ahead, but as usual she drowned the thought with hard work. She concentrated on the story outline for her first novel. More and more she felt that she must achieve something by herself. The business did not now require her full attention. New challenges were presenting themselves to her ever-active mind. She wanted to conquer fresh fields and shine on her own.

Chapter 14

JANIE CRAIG TELEPHONED and persuaded Tricesta to accompany her to the Teach-In at The Roundhouse. They drove to the well remembered scene of their 'hippie' past. The gloomy dilapidated exterior had not changed. It reminded Tricesta of a rough-cast miniature Albert Hall. When they arrived, several people were climbing the wooden planks which served as steps up to the entrance.

Tricesta parked the car in a side street and crossed the busy road.

'I hope there are plenty of revolutionary types here tonight,' said Janie, carrying her notebook.

Torn, tired posters were peeling from the brickwork – 'Black Men – fight white racism – not Vietnamese!' or 'Fight Yankee Imperialism!' The French revolutionary posters were barely discernible, and those of other 'in' revolutions were quickly going the same depressing way. The 'now' 'Revolution and Us' posters were hardly dry.

'Is Edward speaking tonight?' Tricesta asked, buying her *International Times* and *Black Dwarf* from the enthusiastic 'underground' paper sellers.

'I rang him from the office,' said Janie, 'but he refused to give an answer. That, of course, means he is – one of his "impromptu" speeches knocking Whitey! The debate should amuse you.'

'Teach-In,' corrected Tricesta with a grin. 'Good God! They've started to redecorate the place. It'll never be the same again!'

They strolled through the new doors into the round auditorium.

'They've put in a false ceiling,' said Tricesta, 'built a platform and erected tiered seats. It looks more comfortable anyway.'

'It's a mistake,' said Janie, 'we used to enjoy being masochists, it made us feel more rebellious!'

Arc lights beamed down on to the platform and rows of hard seats. The overall impression was still one of bleakness. A number of people were already assembled. They smoked, drank coke from paper cups and greeted familiar faces. They were the usual mixture of pseudo intellectuals, anarchists, hotheads, curiosity cats, thrill seekers and a small responsible minority.

'Let's sit at the far end beside the platform,' said Janie, and attracting considerable attention they chose two seats in the second row.

An 'underground' pop group was testing the sound system and adjusting the microphones with the usual '1-2-3's' and the 'are you getting me's' muttered self-consciously.

'There are quite a few middle-aged "Mum" types here,' said Tricesta, 'why do they come?'

'I've never understood that,' replied Janie, lighting a cigarette, 'hoping to recapture their lost youth, to feel young and rebellious again, I suppose.'

'Is that a joint you are smoking?' asked Tricesta.

'No, herbs. And talking of grass I heard a funny thing today. The Black Power boys are refusing to sell any more hash to their white brothers! If they do the price will be as high as the stuff!'

'We can hardly complain to the Board of Trade,' laughed Tricesta.

Half an hour drifted by, the auditorium had filled up, a large number of foreign students had arrived and most of the speakers had assembled on the platform, pretending there was no audience present. At last after a further wait, a busy little man with large horn-rimmed spectacles strolled importantly to the microphone and assumed the chairmanship of the Teach-In.

'Good evening to you all,' he began, and immediately the microphone turned temperamental; no amount of adjusting would coax it back into action. Finally the frustrated chairman shouted: 'I'm sorry about this but we'll carry on without the mike, can everyone hear me?' A resounding 'yes' was returned and he went on: 'As you know we're going to discuss recent revolutions and where we as a nation stand.' Then he introduced the official speakers, all of whom had been present during one or more of the uprisings in various parts of the world. He finished by saying: 'And at half past ten we'll rave!' This was greeted with cool approval. Janie whispered: 'He's a real drag, wants to be Mr Big. I bet he won't let anyone else get a word in.'

'Let's get on!' shouted a voice from the back of the hall.

'That is precisely what we wish to do,' replied the chairman, 'but what I'd like to see is the abolition of this gap between us,' he gestured to the space in front of the platform. 'Until we get rid of this gulf there will still be a lack of communication between us. Let's try to reduce the separation, so will you all move up closer to the platform.' He beckoned the audience forward. No one moved. 'If you're so concerned about the division,' a voice behind Tricesta shouted, 'then you lot bloody well do something. You come down here with us!' A roar of approval arose, followed by enthusiastic clapping.

'They're coming,' said Tricesta, surprised, 'the weight of the masses. . . . ' Surely enough, the speakers glanced at each other, walked to the edge of the platform and jumped down on to the floor. They lifted their chairs down and walked into the centre of the auditorium.

'We've shown our good faith,' said the chairman, 'now you come forward.'

The entire gathering shuffled forward, and some of the younger ones left their seats and sat on the floor surrounding the speakers, and some of the speakers abandoned their chairs and sat with the proletariat. The microphone was produced and re-tested but it was still useless. Everyone re-affirmed they could hear what was said if the speakers did not mumble. Janie made rapid shorthand notes and Tricesta chewed Polo mints.

The four main speakers consisted of a huge man with a flaming red beard; an intense, wiry man with tinted spectacles; an enormous fellow with National Health spectacles; and a small jovial-looking man with nothing much to distinguish him.

'What we want to do tonight,' said the chairman, who was obviously in love with his own voice, 'is to let anyone speak who wishes to do so, provided it is relevant to the subject. There will be no prepared speeches, points will be made on which we can all express our feelings. We want everyone to participate. Now, our first speaker was in Cuba during the revolution and again last year. He will tell us what he saw and give us his evaluation of the present situation.'

Tricesta was not surprised when Red Beard moved forward. There were cries of 'Long Live Che's Ideas' and 'God Bless Fidel'. A very boring speech followed, the crowd became restless and the speaker ended his talk by saying: 'We must help our brothers of the Third World – it is our duty and we must support Cuba. Cuba is of great significance. Not only has she withstood tremendous pressure from Russia, she has also refused to capitulate to the United States! And never forget, comrades, it was the United States' C.I.A. men who assassinated Che!' It was only this last inaccurate statement that caused any interest or response.

'Time's up,' hissed the chairman, 'time's up.' Red Beard sat down to vigorous booing and a few weak cheers.

'If all the speakers are like that one we might as well push off now,' said Janie.

Then the chairman offered the floor to a noisy Latin American member of the audience. He was very big, wore scruffy clothes and looked and sounded like Speedy Gonzales, complete with a thick droopy moustache. 'Brothers and Sisters of the Revolution,' his heavy accent made Janie and Tricesta smile, 'wev'a all'a gotta fight Imperialist America! Cuba is'a international, we want'a worldwide support, Cuba is'a trying to abolish money! The telephone'a system is'a free. All'a students giv'a the State 45 days a year to work in the fields. . . .'

'I'll bet that's not voluntary!' shouted a voice.

'It is'a voluntary,' insisted the Latin American. He had nothing of great interest to say and was quickly booed down by the impatient audience.

238

Then followed a Pakistani speaker who talked briefly about the Chinese revolution and the Vietnam war. He received the same disrespectful treatment and soon gave up.

'National Health Spectacles' spoke about the Greek situation. The crowd were not enthusiastic about him either and he retired amid the rustling of underground news-sheets. The intense Mid-European with the tinted shades followed and gave a condensed account of the Czech revolt. He was clearly a Stalinist and promptly got engaged in a bitter argument with a Trotskyist. These two were quickly shouted down and the small jovial man took the floor. He dealt with the Irish problems then cut back to Cuba.

'I fail to understand how fellow comrades can hit out at Russia,' he said with sincerity. 'Russia pours many millions of roubles into this backward island of Cuba every year. They bring education to the illiterate and starving population.' Roars of disagreement arose, but he went on determinedly. 'How can anyone seriously knock Russia; she is the saviour of Cuba!'

'Shut up, you misguided bourgeois pig!' screamed a young man wearing a bright shirt and sitting on the edge of the platform. Laughter broke out.

'Oh, hush up, you're a drag,' called an American student to the colourfully dressed boy. 'What the speaker fails to mention is just why Russia invests millions of roubles in Cuba. They want to maintain their rocket launching pads there. Those that are directed against the heart of the United States!'

The speaker tried to reply but was told his time was up.

'Look,' whispered Janie, 'There's Edward, he's with Frenchy. I told you he would speak.' She appeared delighted and mentally sharpened her pencil.

'Apos is bringing up the rear,' said Tricesta. The trio of Black Power leaders strolled across the hall, passing behind the speakers. They looked confident and Edward X, dressed in his flamboyant African costume stopped beside the busy, pompous chairman. They were very conspicuous in the almost all white crowd. A ripple of expectancy ran through the gathering. The speaker of the moment, talking about the build-up of mercenaries on Rhodesia's border, was given almost no attention. To Tricesta's surprise the microphone was now working. She saw Sammy, the most violent of all the black militants, sitting some twenty feet back from the speakers. He called out: 'Bring on Edward X!' and continually heckled the speaker. Sammy was one of those men who enjoyed violence just for the sake of violence. It gave him pleasure to inflict pain even unto death. He was a natural for any group advocating violence, political pretensions were an ideal mask for his true nature.

Tricesta watched Edward and Frenchy consult with the chairman. He appeared to be irritated but nodded in some measure of agreement at the black progressive.

'Hi there, soul sisters!' Edward X greeted Tricesta and Janie sarcastically. 'Come to record the action? I want to see you when I've had my say,' he said to Tricesta, 'so don't rush off, you'd regret it!' She did not answer and wondered if he knew about the death of his father, if he did he gave no indication of it. Frenchy, as usual, chewed gum and grinned cheekily at the girls. His tight trousers emphasised his slender hips, his multicoloured shirt was a fine example of a West Indian's love for dazzling the eye. Around his neck hung a chain on which was a gold medallion. 'See you chicks later,' he called to them. Both men returned to the group of speakers ready for an oral assault on the crowd. The chairman took the microphone.

'I'm delighted to welcome Edward X to our Teach-In tonight,' he said with a hint of doubt in his voice, 'but before he talks to us Frenchy has a few words to say.' He offered the mike to the West Indian extrovert. He leapt over a couple of sitting youths and bowed in mock respect to the chairman; there were some titters at his display of insulting humour.

'Tell them where it's at!' screamed Sammy from the audience.

'Thank you, brother,' said Frenchy, standing with one hand on his hip, still chewing gum. 'I'll leave the telling to those who can talk,' he grinned, 'but what I will say is this: I used to go to the theatre for my kicks, not any more! I now come and listen to cats like those you've just heard.' He changed his stance, shook his head and muttered an 'Oh man' into the microphone and went on: 'All the speeches I caught tonight talked and talked revolution. But that's it! Nothing but shit talk. All that you young groovy people do, is to get your gear on and turn out once a week to talk revolution. When you cats are ready to prove your words you know where we are. Come and join us, we know where it's at, and you know where it's at! Let's stop fooling around and get on with the job.' Quite a number cheered him, loudest of all was Sammy. 'Instead of gassing all night you should be preparing yourselves. The police

240

are arming themselves with gas to throw at the voice of protest. You should go get fitted with a gas mask and prepare gas to chuck back at them. I promise you the fuzz are ready to charge their horses at any demonstration and crack any cat's head that gets in the way. Don't let them, fight them with us! We're on the same side. We're all fighting oppression by the system.' Cheers followed and he finished: 'So when you cats really want revolution instead of talk, come to us, because better than anyone here we know where it's at!'

Frenchy handed the mike to Edward X, he took it without a smile. Before he could speak the chairman grabbed it back.

'My friends,' a groan went up, so did a loud whine from the loudspeakers, making speech impossible, but the bore tried. 'My friends, we have just heard dangerous. . . . ' His plaintive voice was drowned by an ear-splitting whistle from all sides. Tricesta smiled when she saw what was happening. Frenchy stood beside the amplifier, his face a study in mystified innocence, while his right hand furtively twisted the knobs, playing havoc with the sound system.

Finally the chairman, unaware of the cause of the deafening interference, willingly returned the microphone to Edward X. He accepted it and stood up from where he had been sitting cross-legged on the floor. The electronic disturbance stopped and for the first time that evening a hush fell over the packed auditorium. Apostrophe Brown positioned himself beside the amplifier and sent Frenchy off to buy coca-cola.

Edward X looked small and for once not the menacing militant. Janie sat still, her pen poised.

'Peace and love to you all,' Edward began in a soft voice, 'it's great to see you, my brothers and sisters. You just heard Frenchy talk the sort of talk I taught him,' he paused, no one made a sound, 'but I came here tonight to tell you his advice will not solve our problem. Violence and bloodshed are not the weapons we should use!' Pandemonium broke out, could this really be Edward X talking? Tricesta turned round and caught the eye of Apos, he winked back.

'Let me explain,' shouted Edward above the noisy comments. 'Violence is the last resort, the final blow. I am now convinced we can assert ourselves sufficiently through other more subtle methods; the Press, television, the arts and other mediums. I'm sure you recall Sammy Davis's words when he spoke to us in this very building some time back; he said and I quote: "I know

now there is no problem that exists for black people in any part of the world that does not include another part of the world." We have seen the results of violence in America, what has it achieved? We all know the answer to that, it has brought black people into discredit. I know that Black Power in Britain can achieve its aims without bombs, gas or bullets! This has not been a sudden change of attitude for me. Weeks of deliberation and consultation lie behind my decision!' The crowd were astonished. 'I came here tonight to beg every one of you to support me, whatever cause you stand for. Violence can only lead to more violence, there would be no end to it. Any temporary benefit secured by bloodshed and destruction will not last. We must build on sound, vigorous but peaceful policies. Tonight I'm going to ask you to renounce any form of violent revolution – tonight. . . .'

'You fucking traitor,' screamed Sammy, 'the white man bought you – like he bought others. You traitor!' There was a flash of polished steel, Edward sank to his knees, a ten inch throwing knife embedded in his heart.

Sammy was instantly grabbed by four men who had been standing near him, his arm was still outstretched. Only the handle of the knife was visible, protruding from Edward's chest as he slumped slowly forward, dead.

Tricesta turned white and with everyone else jumped to her feet. Men surrounding Sammy, who was still shouting, started to attack the West Indian.

Apostrophe Brown leapt forward and examined Edward's body. Blood was beginning to seep through his robes. Girls screamed and youths panicked, uniformed police, who had been patrolling the gloomy corridors outside the inner hall ran inside to both protect and arrest Sammy.

It's my fault, it's my fault, Tricesta was telling herself. Apos took me seriously and set up the murder. He's got the party a martyr! She felt sick and guilty.

'The bastard!' Frenchy muttered to Janie, 'that bastard Sammy believed Edward!' Even Frenchy looked shattered. 'The whole thing was meant to be a gas!'

Apos knelt beside Edward's body and picked up the microphone. 'Please keep calm,' he said, 'there's nothing I can do except to honour Edward's last wishes.' He spoke deliberately. The bewildered crowd fell silent as Sammy was dragged out by the police, who had a hard job to keep revenge-bent fanatics

242

at bay. 'His last wishes were for us to reject violence,' Apos was getting through to most people, 'he died violently while pleading for peaceful protests. It's our duty to respect his beliefs, for, as he said, violence will only lead to more violence. It was a cruel twist of fate that he was killed at this great moment in his life.' Silence filled the hall. The plainclothes police made no move to interrupt Apos.

'I have always stood for non-violence and I still do. As the immediate successor of Edward X I shall continue our fight in the manner he outlined before he was murdered. If anyone here disagrees with that let him either kill me now or shut up, because I shall never change my beliefs.' Loud cheers followed these positive, sincere words. Apos placed his hand on Edward's body. 'He was my friend and my leader, I will not disappoint him, neither will I allow anyone else within our brotherhood to do so.' Tricesta was almost fainting, she noticed Apos was close to tears as he continued:

'Edward died a martyr but his death has convinced me even more, if that was possible, that we must not spill blood to gain our rightful ends.' He knelt down and kissed Edward on both cheeks. 'He is irreplaceable,' Apos murmured movingly.

'Thank goodness,' murmured Janie, scribbling feverishly. The ambulance siren could be heard outside.

'But I shall carry on until I find a better man to lead the fight,' finished Apos. 'Until then let us never forget why Edward X was assassinated.'

Apostrophe Brown handed the microphone to the stunned chairman, who continued to stare at the body of Edward lying at his feet. Suddenly he said: 'Let us pray,' and started to recite the Lord's Prayer. Most people moved away and left him to his pseudo chant.

'Not only does he want to be Ronald Reagan,' said Frenchy, 'he fancies himself as the Pope!'

The plainclothes police took over and one of them told the crowd not to leave the hall until they were given permission. The ambulance men came in carrying a stretcher. Edward's robes were soaked with blood, Sammy's aim had been so accurate death was immediate. Apos talked with an officer who made quick notes. Other police arrived with a doctor and photographer.

'I'd better sit down,' said Tricesta, 'I can't bear the sight of blood.' Janie pushed a chair under her and hurried away to talk with the people who had been standing beside Sammy when he threw the knife.

Apos watched as Edward's body was photographed and examined. The knife was removed by the police surgeon, the body was covered with a white sheet and carried from the brightly lit auditorium. When the ambulance men had disappeared Apos turned away and walked slowly over to Tricesta. She was shaking and jumped when Apos sat beside her.

'Please don't lie,' she whispered, did you . . . ?'

'Of course not,' he replied, looking at her, 'no one was more stupefied than me. I could never condone murder, let alone instigate it. All I did was to convince Edward why he should make that speech.' Apos nearly smiled. 'He cursed me but agreed, he knew it would pull in more bread and improve our image.'

'I think you'll find it has,' she said softly.

'As you said, we needed a martyr!' he replied without humour. 'Edward told Frenchy what to say first, so that it would emphasise his new public stand! None of us thought a psychopath like Sammy would blow his mind. The idiot fell for every false word Edward uttered. Sammy has killed before, three times back home, self-defence, it was said! He just flipped when he heard Edward's words, he saw him as a traitor to the cause. Sammy undoubtedly thought it was his duty to kill a treacherous leader!'

Most people in the auditorium had recovered from the shock and were quietly helping the police in their enquiries.

'See how cool the fuzz are playing it now?' observed Apos. 'We've got them over-sensitive about racialism, but we all know how prejudiced they are. I'll not rest until there's an independent body of enquiry concerning complaints against the law. Why should the police investigate the police? Your people have been pressing for this for a long time, I know, but it wasn't until the black man showed how terribly bent the system is that this issue was debated. Even so, all these matters are given very little publicity. That's why you've never read anything about the flyover supports being blown up.'

'What are you talking about?' she asked.

'A lot of things,' he replied, frowning, 'but specifically a certain flyover in the West London district; we made numerous applications to the council asking them to let us have a certain area beneath the flyover as a playground for the kids of the district, at first they refused us saying they wanted the space for a car-park!' His indignation was genuine. 'Then one of the supporting pillars of the flyover was blown up. We re-applied to the council, urging them to change their "final decision". They did, the kids got their play area.'

'Who blew the flyover?' she asked, watching the police who were still busy questioning eye-witnesses.

'That's not a cool question, baby,' he smiled, 'especially when you can guess the answer! The flyover in Edgware Road was also sabotaged, just a couple of pillars. That was hushed up too, but the fuzz stayed on disguised as workmen. The gas was they still wore their blue shirts and dark ties underneath their overalls.'

'But who hushed it up?'

'Oh baby, this isn't like you! The fuzz are scared that if this sort of thing gets publicity it'll trigger off a worse scene than in America. And it could be worse, the boys here are better organised, better put together and more determined. Distances defeat the U.S. riots, cities are too far apart. Here the establishment are squatting on a volcano, one incident could blow the lid.'

'But you can cool it?' she asked.

'Only for a while, unless things improve for coloured immigrants, especially police harassment, the riots here will make the American scene look like a quiet Sunday afternoon in Central Park. I'll never advocate violence unless violence comes to us.' That last statement startled Tricesta, had she misjudged the pacifist in the party?

'I don't want to take on the leadership of Black Power,' Apos continued, 'I'm a hustler. What we need at the head is a cat that is a good talker, a man respected by blacks and whites alike. A leader doesn't have the time or the opportunities to hustle. I'll keep going for a while, then I'll hand over to the best man available. Unfortunately the most suitable cat doesn't want to know; perhaps he'll change his mind now.'

'Do you mean Brad?' she asked. He nodded and stood up, a detective was approaching them.

'His father died today,' said Tricesta, 'did you know?'

'No, I didn't,' Apos replied and spoke to the officer, who asked Tricesta to identify herself and give her version of the incident.

This took five minutes and then she was given permission to leave. Janie was nowhere to be seen, her journalistic instincts had to be satisfied. Tricesta wanted to get away. Although she was now satisfied she had in no way been responsible for Edward's death she still felt a sense of guilt. It had shaken her badly, it could so easily have been due to her that the murder had been set up. It so happened that an unbalanced hothead had lost his self-control, no one had given any orders to kill.

Chocolate Biscuits listened to her story without interrupting. When she had finished the only comment he made was: 'It's just as I've always maintained; the immigration laws are far too lenient. If I had my way any immigrant that has entered Britain since 1948 would be deported.'

That night Tricesta knocked herself out with sleeping pills. C.B. was furious with her, she collapsed on the floor before leaving the drawing room and he had to undress her and carry her to her bed.

However, Tricesta was up the next morning by eight o'clock. The papers gave Edward's murder the front page treatment. And he had indeed acquired the status of a martyr. The Press narratives emphasised his rejection of violence. At 10.30 Helen returned from another spinning night with Tarquin, she was untidy, unsteady and unrepentant.

'He's gone to Bath,' she announced to the brother and sister, who made no reference to her ill-mannered behaviour. 'He's fixing up exhibition details with your mother.' Helen looked terrible, she was wearing a bright coloured dress and garish make-up. Tricesta knew that a junkie's sense of colour usually becomes distorted, she was worried.

Brad rang Tricesta and asked to see her at once. She agreed and drove over to his pad. He looked red-eyed and tired. 'I've been up all night,' he said, holding her tightly, 'I've made some tea for you!' He attempted to smile but couldn't make it.

'I was at The Round house last night,' she said.

'I know,' he sat on the divan, 'Apos told me, I've only just left him. Right now I'm not too well put together. Apos has asked me to take over the leadership.'

'I'm not surprised,' commented Tricesta, sipping her tea. 'What was your answer?'

Brad looked troubled, and uncertain. 'I haven't given one,' he replied, 'it's too important a decision to rush. First I must

246

go home, help my mother to sort out the estate. The government there wants an answer too. I have to choose whether I live and work at home or whether I keep the business on here and dedicate myself to a non-violent Black Power movement. Have you any suggestions?'

'I can't give you any guidance on an issue like that, I'm afraid. But I'm quite convinced that whoever the leader may be, there will always be a militant minority in the movement that will cause trouble.'

'The boys are getting more cool,' he replied, 'but if I stayed in Tobago, would you be happy to live there?'

Tricesta felt terribly trapped. She pulled nervously at her fringe.

'I can't wait to see your island,' she said, avoiding the obvious, 'but it might be too hot for me permanently. It's impossible to say. At the moment, what matters is where do you feel you should be?'

'I don't know,' he sighed, 'I just don't know. But after three months I will. The important thing for me is to be with you, wherever that is to be.'

They remained sitting in silence for a long time. Tricesta was aware of a difference between them, not of colour but of attitude. Brad wanted her to be dependent on him, to be a part of his world. He believed she was misguided, corrupted by a sick system, he attached no blame to her.

'When are you going home?' Tricesta asked.

'The day after tomorrow,' he replied, 'will you take me to the airport?'

'Of course,' she said and kissed him. Alone making love together they were in harmony, it was only when they were exposed to the outside world that the cracks appeared.

Tricesta returned to the King's Road and finalised the details for the new St Regis shop in Paris. Tim and Jim were to be in charge, after new staff had been trained. C.B. would soon need his own airplane.

Helen thought only of being with Apos. All he wanted was a hard working toy whom he could play with or use at will. They met early that evening at his pad. She looked great, having just had a 'shot'. Her dress was the shortest and brightly coloured. Her make-up was over-emphasised, especially her pink cheeks. Her black eye-line had grown progressively heavier as her hands had become more and more unsteady. To make up she had to

247

rest her elbows on the dressing table to steady her shaky arm. Her loss of weight was dramatic and her sense of responsibility diminished. She could no longer judge distances accurately and bumped her way expensively around the shop and flat. Her shrill giggles and loss of composure were irritating, but the most upsetting thing to Tricesta and her brother was her compulsive lying. She had become a secret eater. Refusing normal meals, then when the drugs were wearing off she would sneak into the kitchen and slyly eat huge sandwiches and biscuits. After a fix she became gay and solicitous again, but the gap was closing, time between shots was becoming less and less.

Apos ordered her into bed at once. Helen stripped immediately and did as he wanted. When Apos was satisfied, he looked at her: 'You on a trip!'

'No,' she protested, 'I haven't taken anything.'

He pulled the sheet off her and turned her over, her backside was dotted with needle marks.

'You just shoot straight,' he grinned, she kissed him and said she loved him.

'Can I come and live with you and work for you?' she asked. 'I'm not given a chance to use my brains with her,' she said, referring to Tricesta. 'It's a drag there, I want to do great things, really mean something.' Delusions of grandeur were another side-effect of the drugs. 'And her jealousy of me is a joke!' Apos grinned, but not for the reason she supposed. 'And there's something more important. I'm going to make you a daddy!'

'Yeah, no kidding?'

'No kidding,' she kissed him, 'I'm so excited, darling, but I don't want our child to be illegitimate. Do you?'

'Definitely not,' he said firmly, 'I'll come to the doctor with you tonight! I want to talk to him, find out what you are allowed to do. Our baby must have the best.'

Helen was stymied, she panicked. 'I'd rather go alone, I'm shy . . .'

'Oh, baby,' he shrieked with laughter, 'I dig that! I really dig that! Before you become my woman and have my kids you come off the junk,' he said, not smiling, 'come and live here, work with me but until you prove you're not fixing, you stay single!' He sounded very serious, she bit her lip. 'But I'm sure I'm pregnant,' she said, really worried.

248

'Then if you are you get rid of it,' he snapped, 'I'm not having my kid born a junkie. When you're clean you get the gold band.'

Helen was in a cleft stick. There was nothing she could say. She agreed to move in with him and work at the movement's headquarters. She vowed she would never fix again. But Apos knew that was a near impossibility. Anyway he had won a mistress, a cook and a secretary at very little cost.

'Remember baby,' he said, 'the moment you move in you belong to me. No messing about. I don't take that stuff from any chick.'

He had no intention of getting burdened with her. If she took a cure and really got put together he would arrange for one of his friends to get her hooked again.

Helen was worried how to tell Tricesta she was leaving. She need not have concerned herself. Tricesta had manoeuvred her departure all the way.

Chocolate Biscuits looked at his sister and said:

'Something has been worrying me. With my limited knowledge of book-keeping I find it difficult to understand how we have been able to repay Uncle Eric and at the same time set up such an elaborate establishment in Paris. Have we really made that much profit?'

Tricesta frowned. 'No,' she said, 'I'm afraid there is something I have not told you, I thought you would be upset and worried if I did, and your work would have suffered.'

'What is it?' he asked gently.

'Through Michael Flaxman I inherited the whole of his brother's estate, all one and a quarter millions of it.'

'Good God!' he said, 'Good God!' and repeated it several times. When he had recovered she told him the whole story.

'Will you lose interest in the business now? Are you bored?' She sat beside him and smiled. 'I'm not bored with the business – just my own position, and it's nothing to do with the money. The company is firmly established now, it doesn't need me so much.'

'But I do,' he replied anxiously, 'we planned our lives in order to remain together. You can't want to change that.'

'No,' she agreed, holding his hand. 'We'll always stay together, while we both wish it. But I do feel I must move on to fresh scenes. I have no intention of relinquishing my overruling interest in the business, certainly not the financial side. We can afford to buy the best brains and ability to help run the show. You will be able to concentrate more on new creations. But I want to write, I want to see if I can stand alone on my own merits. This is something I have to try.'

'I understand,' he said, 'but you won't leave the flat will you?'

'No, of course not,' she assured him, 'I need as many barriers around me as you do. It's only in writing I want to prove myself, the way you do with your designs. They come from you alone.'

'But I couldn't have done them without you setting me up. I never pretended otherwise.'

'I know,' Tricesta hugged him, 'but you're established now and I'm not. Not in the way that matters to me. I may not have many virtues but there are three ways in which I will never insult my morality. I will never be disloyal to anyone that I am committed to; I will never offend my conscience; and I won't knock the society I choose to live in – this may not be great but no one has shown me anything better. Those three things are important to me, but above all I want to write with honesty about the way I see our scene. In the last year I've learnt more of the way we are than in all the years that went before. I'd like to use this growing knowledge. It would be a shame to waste it. I think Janie can help me, we'll see. I can certainly use Michael Flaxman's special knowledge and experience. But I'm not convinced experience is the be all and end all, but as he said, you can't have youth and experience. I'm sorry I boobed with Helen ...'

'It was as much my fault,' he said ruefully.

'I didn't realise how destructive jealousy could be,' Tricesta said. 'And her copy-cat nature was something quite new to me. She's cunning but not clever, given an inch she takes a mile. Grandpa always says employees should never be treated as personal friends. I thought he was wrong. Maybe he's not! But I'll always help her if she needs it.'

'She is a junkie,' C.B. reminded her, 'just how much responsibility lies with you?'

'Very little,' she said, 'and what I did was to contradict her lies about us, well, she thought they were lies! She hates being second in command, and from the very start she tried to outdo me in everything.'

'What a mistake she made!' he laughed.

'I'm just beginning to see that one should choose one's enemies with even greater care than one's friends!' said Tricesta,

250

C.B. wanted to ask her about Brad but he restrained himself. He might be told something which he did not want to hear.

But he worried unnecessarily, Tricesta was not in love with Brad. Their affair had continued largely because she had enjoyed flaunting convention. The more she detected a shocked reaction from those who saw them together, the more defiant she became. She wanted to jolt prejudiced people, this was one way to do that. But as time went by Brad had become possessive and had talked of marriage, this had caused her to panic.

Brad was not the aggressive individual she had first thought him. Strangely enough Tricesta had found Edward X more interesting; he was an original. Brad had bought into white society, even though he maintained he was only playing a game. She did not believe this, he wanted to be a part of her world and show her off as his property. Because their relationship was a problem her imagination continued to be stimulated. Tricesta had never fallen in love with anyone but she felt a love towards her brother. She felt trapped by Brad, she postponed telling him the affair was over. I don't want to hurt him, she told herself. If only he could find someone else, it would make me very happy.

When Tricesta drove Brad to Heathrow Airport they hardly spoke. Both were close to tears.

'Don't come into the building,' he said quietly as she drew up at the entrance of No. 3 Terminal, 'I can't take much more.'

The sun shone, the travellers hustled about, the airplanes arrived and took off. But they were only aware of themselves. Most girls would have gone with him. Not Tricesta and Brad knew better than to ask her to do so.

'I hope one day we'll be flying out together,' he said, 'that hope keeps me going. You're the prize I'm striving for, you're what I want. Whatever I do now I think, would Tricesta like that, would she approve of what I'm doing – I'd better go in, I . . . ' his voice tailed away, he was crying, Tricesta said nothing, she dabbed at her damp eyes and was grateful for her dark spectacles. She squeezed his hand, he did not look at her but blew his nose noisily.

'Write to me,' she whispered, 'let me know how it is.'

'I'll telephone,' he replied, she noticed his brown nose was red. 'Never forget I love you. I'll be back in three months, then we'll go from there. By then I'll know where it's at. And us, I hope.'

Her eyes were hot and full of tears. Brad sensed this, jumped out of the car, took his case from the boot and said:

'See you, love.'

Still trying to control her emotions she drove away very fast and switched on the radio to loud pop music.

Tricesta's tears flowed as she accelerated up the M4 well above the speed limit. I'll go and see Michael, she said to herself, I'll write this book quickly, the way I feel it. Writing is what matters to me now, achieving a new ambition. There's nothing I can do about Brad. I can't change my attitude, it is Brad that is impractical, he'll see that in the next three months. I would like him to work with Apos, Black Power needs a steadying influence, otherwise the pot might boil over. I would hate to see that. That's one of the things I'll write about, I'll investigate the whole scene and use Michael's information and experience. I can't decide how to end things with Brad. Maybe my work will decide for me.

79 PARK AVENUE
by Harold Robbins

And now ... from the world-famous author of THE CARPETBAGGERS and THE ADVENTURERS comes the searing story of 79 PARK AVENUE. Harold Robbins lifts the lid on the call-girl racket and uncovers a world of corruption and brutality, of vice and violence and one girl – Marja Flood.

Marja was a wild-cat beauty determined to reach the top of her trade. A prostitute who gave her body to anyone, but her heart to only one man – Mike Keyes, who loved her, lost her and found her again when her address was 79 Park Avenue ...

NEW ENGLISH LIBRARY

THE BETSY
by Harold Robbins

The first major novel of the car industry.

Love, hate, sex, ambition – the ingredients of a fabulous novel from the world's most widely read author.

THE BETSY tells an unforgettable story of the lives and loves, the men and women, behind an automobile conglomerate and its make or break attempt to create a totally new car.

'Harold Robbins, perhaps the biggest bestseller of them all, has lost nothing of his touch in his new novel. It's full of power, sex, action, vintage Robbins' – **Sunday Mirror**

NEW ENGLISH LIBRARY

NEL BESTSELLERS

Crime

T013 332	CLOUDS OF WITNESS	*Dorothy L. Sayers* 40p
T016 307	THE UNPLEASANTNESS AT THE BELLONA CLUB	
		Dorothy L. Sayers 40p
W003 011	GAUDY NIGHT	*Dorothy L. Sayers* 40p
T010 457	THE NINE TAILORS	*Dorothy L. Sayers* 35p
T012 484	FIVE RED HERRINGS	*Dorothy L. Sayers* 40p
T015 556	MURDER MUST ADVERTISE	*Dorothy L. Sayers* 40p
T014 398	STRIDING FOLLY	*Dorothy L. Sayers* 30p

Fiction

T013 944	CRUSADER'S TOMB	*A. J. Cronin* 60p
T013 936	THE JUDAS TREE	*A. J. Cronin* 50p
T015 386	THE NORTHERN LIGHT	*A. J. Cronin* 50p
T016 544	THE CITADEL	*A. J. Cronin* 75p
T016 919	THE SPANISH GARDENER	*A. J. Cronin* 40p
T014 088	BISHOP IN CHECK	*Adam Hall* 30p
T015 467	PAWN IN JEOPARDY	*Adam Hall* 30p
T015 130	THE MONEY MAKER	*John J. McNamara Jr.* 50p
T014 932	YOU NICE BASTARD	*G. F. Newman* 50p
T009 769	THE HARRAD EXPERIMENT	*Robert H. Rimmer* 40p
T012 522	THURSDAY MY LOVE	*Robert H. Rimmer* 40p
T013 820	THE DREAM MERCHANTS	*Harold Robbins* 75p
T018 105	THE CARPETBAGGERS	*Harold Robbins* 95p
T016 560	WHERE LOVE HAS GONE	*Harold Robbins* 75p
T013 707	THE ADVENTURERS	*Harold Robbins* 80p
T006 743	THE INHERITORS	*Harold Robbins* 60p
T009 467	STILETTO	*Harold Robbins* 30p
T015 289	NEVER LEAVE ME	*Harold Robbins* 40p
T016 579	NEVER LOVE A STRANGER	*Harold Robbins* 75p
T011 798	A STONE FOR DANNY FISHER	*Harold Robbins* 60p
T015 874	79 PARK AVENUE	*Harold Robbins* 60p
T011 461	THE BETSY	*Harold Robbins* 75p
T010 201	RICH MAN, POOR MAN	*Irwin Shaw* 80p
T018 148	THE PLOT	*Irving Wallace* 90p
T009 718	THE THREE SIRENS	*Irving Wallace* 75p
T013 340	SUMMER OF THE RED WOLF	*Morris West* 50p

Historical

T013 731	KNIGHT WITH ARMOUR	*Alfred Duggan* 40p
T013 758	THE LADY FOR RANSOM	*Alfred Duggan* 40p
T015 297	COUNT BOHEMOND	*Alfred Duggan* 50p
T010 279	MASK OF APOLLO	*Mary Renault* 50p
T015 580	THE CHARIOTEER	*Mary Renault* 50p
T010 988	BRIDE OF LIBERTY	*Frank Yerby* 30p
T014 045	TREASURE OF PLEASANT VALLEY	*Frank Yerby* 35p
T015 602	GILLIAN	*Frank Yerby* 50p

Science Fiction

T014 576	THE INTERPRETER	*Brian Aldiss* 30p
T015 017	EQUATOR	*Brian Aldiss* 30p
T014 347	SPACE RANGER	*Isaac Asimov* 30p
T015 491	PIRATES OF THE ASTEROIDS	*Isaac Asimov* 30p
T016 951	THUVIA MAID OF MARS	*Edgar Rice Burroughs* 30p
T016 331	THE CHESSMEN OF MARS	*Edgar Rice Burroughs* 40p

T011 682	ESCAPE ON VENUS	Edgar Rice Burroughs	40p
T013 537	WIZARD OF VENUS	Edgar Rice Burroughs	30p
T009 696	GLORY ROAD	Robert Heinlein	40p
T010 856	THE DAY AFTER TOMORROW	Robert Heinlein	30p
T016 900	STRANGER IN A STRANGE LAND	Robert Heinlein	75p
T011 844	DUNE	Frank Herbert	75p
T012 298	DUNE MESSIAH	Frank Herbert	40p
T015 211	THE GREEN BRAIN	Frank Herbert	30p

War

T013 367	DEVIL'S GUARD	Robert Elford	50p
T013 324	THE GOOD SHEPHERD	C. S. Forester	35p
T011 755	TRAWLERS GO TO WAR	Lund & Ludlam	40p
T015 505	THE LAST VOYAGE OF GRAF SPEE	Michael Powell	30p
T015 661	JACKALS OF THE REICH	Ronald Seth	30p
T012 263	FLEET WITHOUT A FRIEND	John Vader	30p

Western

T016 994	No. 1 EDGE – THE LONER	George G. Gilman	30p
T016 986	No. 2 EDGE – TEN THOUSAND DOLLARS AMERICAN		
		George G. Gilman	30p
T017 613	No. 3 EDGE – APACHE DEATH	George G. Gilman	30p
T017 001	No. 4 EDGE – KILLER'S BREED	George G. Gilman	30p
T016 536	No. 5 EDGE – BLOOD ON SILVER	George G. Gilman	30p
T017 621	No. 6 EDGE – THE BLUE, THE GREY AND THE RED		
		George G. Gilman	30p
T014 479	No. 7 EDGE – CALIFORNIA KILLING	George G. Gilman	30p
T015 254	No. 8 EDGE – SEVEN OUT OF HELL	George G. Gilman	30p
T015 475	No. 9 EDGE – BLOODY SUMMER	George G. Gilman	30p
T015 769	No. 10 EDGE – VENGEANCE IS BLACK	George G. Gilman	30p

General

T011 763	SEX MANNERS FOR MEN	Robert Chartham	30p
W002 531	SEX MANNERS FOR ADVANCED LOVERS	Robert Chartham	25p
W002 835	SEX AND THE OVER FORTIES	Robert Chartham	30p
T010 732	THE SENSUOUS COUPLE	Dr. 'C'	25p

Mad

S004 708	VIVA MAD!		30p
S004 676	MAD'S DON MARTIN COMES ON STRONG		30p
S004 816	MAD'S DAVE BERG LOOKS AT SICK WORLD		30p
S005 078	MADVERTISING		30p
S004 987	MAD SNAPPY ANSWERS TO STUPID QUESTIONS		30p

NEL P.O. BOX 11, FALMOUTH, TR10 9EN, CORNWALL

Please send cheque or postal order. Allow 10p to cover postage and packing on one book plus 4p for each additional book.

Name ....

Address...

....

Title ....

(SEPTEMBER)